MW00935537

PRACTITIONER OF THE ARTS

BOOK 2, THE PHOSFIRE JOURNEYS

JAMES D. MACON

Cover Design by Liza Brown, Modern Art Media
Edited by Kathryn F. Galán, Wynnpix Productions
www.JDMacon.com

This is a work of fiction. Names, characters, places, brands, media, and incidents are either the product of the author's imagination or are used fictitiously. Any resemblance to similarly named places or to persons living or deceased is unintentional.

PRINT ISBN 978-1-9783-7695-3

For Lillian, Henry, and all who are family with love.

AUTHOR'S NOTE

Those of you who experienced life with Zeal and his fellow orphans, who were raised in the Temple of the Ladies of Life, through Book 1 of *The Phosfire Journeys,* will recall that he has spent his early life in the coastal city of Arlanda. He was taken as an Apprentice in the Trade by Master Slag, where he trained alongside his young friends Mehrle, Tulip, Liddea, Fronc, and Nester. Iris, a Steward, declared Zeal to be one of her Champions. It wasn't until Zeal was introduced to the Shadow Cats, Kit and her mother Essmee, however, that his unique and wondrous Phosfire ability was discovered. As *Practitioner of the Arts* opens, he is now on the journey to Havensharth, where he hopes to grow and expand his skills. Welcome to Book 2!

In this world, lengths are measured by hands; one hand equals four inches. Weight is measured in stones; one stone is fourteen pounds. A season is the equivalent of a year, a moon is a month, a sun is a day, and a mark is an hour.

PART ONE

PROLOGUE

BLINDED BY THE absence of light and restricted by hard, curved walls that delineated his world and prevented little more than minimal movement, he kept his form tightly curled, avoiding contact with the cold smooth surface around him. Attempts to free himself had failed; he could not break through.

The sack at his belly, which at one time contained an ample supply of food, was almost depleted. Once it was empty, the sack itself might provide a last bit of fuel for his body before the fire that gave him life burned too low, began to smolder, turned to embers, became hot ashes, and finally died.

His call for help remained unanswered.

Why?

He shifted, trying to find solace in the wet silence. He remained... alone.

CHAPTER ONE

CAPTAIN BAYLOR STOOD on the deck of the *White Swan* with Parish, his first mate, at his usual position on the captain's right. Baylor was pleased with the work of the *Swan's* crew. Her well-trimmed sails allowed the ship to fly, so to speak, before the wind. The surge of the ship's passage through the waves transferred through the decking and up his legs, letting him feel the vessel dance across the water. She reminded him of a frisky colt running through the tall grass of a meadow.

The weather was pleasant and looked to hold. As he studied the horizon, Baylor could see no evidence of a brewing storm. Land viewed astern lacked detail as it became a dark, rapidly receding edge. For a while yet, the sea birds would continue to follow them, flying overhead.

He returned his attention to conversing with Master Ice and Lady Mirada, the representatives of Havensharth who had commissioned the voyage. Peering over Lady Mirada's shoulder, Baylor noted the approach of the two apprentices: a boy and a girl. What was their relationship to Master Ice and Lady Mirada, he wondered. Documents allowing the children to leave Arlanda in their custody had been in order but hadn't been enlightening.

The girl, whose name escaped him for the moment, was dressed identical to the boy, in shirt and trousers. Their light gray clothes were clean, with stains that no amount of scrubbing could remove and normal wear and tear. The girl's dark brown hair was in a long braid that hung off her right shoulder down her chest. He suddenly remembered her name was Tulip.

The boy carried an animal Baylor couldn't recall having been aboard prior to the ship's leaving port. It was a large, tan-colored, mottled cat with dark markings. He hadn't been asked permission to transport an animal on his ship.

As he attended to his temper, he observed several of the crew pointing at the cat and two apprentices as they advanced toward him. There was something different about these children, he thought as they drew near.

Ice glanced over his left shoulder and his eyes widened at the girl, boy, and cat. There was a hint of surprise in his voice when he asked, "Zeal, how did Kit get here? Never mind. What's she doing on board?"

Zeal stopped and placed the cat on her paws. Once down, Kit lifted her head and tail high then padded regally away, disappearing down an opening into to the hold.

"Yes. Isn't it wonderful?" Zeal answered, his eyes following Kit till she vanished below deck. "We're going to be together."

Baylor interrupted the conversation. "You never said anything about bringing animals on board, Master Ice. Are there any other omissions you know of that should be brought to my attention? I, for one, would like to know how the animal got aboard the *Swan*."

"Captain Baylor, I am sure failing to inform you about Kit's presence was an unintentional omission on Ice's part," Mirada said.

Baylor turned to her, sensing her discernment of his displeasure. "I will not have animals on the *Swan* leaving their waste everywhere and spreading who knows what disease from port to port. Or to my crew."

"I promise you, Kit is no danger to anyone, sir. I will make sure she doesn't damage your ship." Zeal looked Captain Baylor directly in the eye as he continued to speak. "She will work her passage. Just wait and see if she doesn't."

"Work her passage? *Ha*! You will have to watch her every moment to make sure she's not eaten by a dock rat or one of the crew, who might like a bite or two of fresh cat." Captain Baylor smiled slightly at the distress on the boy's face before watching it turn quickly into determination. "Where is that animal anyway? Bring the beast here to me."

"Captain, I think you should look over there," Parish said, pointing.

Baylor and the rest of the group turned to see Kit walking directly toward him. In her jaws, she carried a large dock rat the size of his foot. It was not only one of the biggest he had seen but larger than anything the captain could ever imagine infesting the *Swan*. When Kit placed the rat on the deck next to his boot, he had to stop himself from stepping back and take a moment to compose himself. She then padded over to sit between the boy and girl.

Zeal announced, "Kit intends to bring you a rat every day we are on board, to earn her passage. She wants you to know nothing or no one is going to eat her."

What was going on? Baylor found himself intrigued. "She said that, did she? Well then, Kit can remain on the *Swan* as long as she does her job. If I see her slacking in her duties, she will have to answer to me. Is that understood?" He fixed his gaze on the boy.

"Yes, sir. It is understood. Will you please let the men who would consider eating her know they are to leave her alone? I would hate for one of them to get hurt or worse."

Baylor was taken back by the steely look on Zeal's face. He realized there was more to the boy than he had guessed. But what danger could the little cat pose? "The animal will be safe," he replied. "Don't you worry, boy." He glanced at the nearby crew and noted several of his men staring and making comments to one another about the cat and her prey.

"Pardon me, sir. Her name is Kit, and I am Zeal. If you will excuse us." He turned and walked away with Kit padding beside him.

"Captain, sir, please call me Tulip." She hesitated a moment, studying Baylor, before striding to catch up with Zeal and Kit.

Yes, the lad has spirit. Quite a bit of spirit, Baylor thought to himself.

"Please, Captain Baylor. I beg pardon for any offense Zeal might have caused."

Baylor turned to Lady Mirada. "No atonement is needed from you, Lady Mirada. It may be that it is I who should give an apology. I did tease the boy—I mean Zeal—a little. Most likely he and Kit will make this voyage entertaining. Now, if you'll excuse me, Parish and I need to see to the *Swan*."

* * *

Mirada waited for the captain and his first mate to leave then turned to Ice. "We need to talk. Who or what is *Kit*? I want to know what is going on."

Ice followed the apprentices and Kit's progress till they left the deck of the *Swan*. "Let us not talk here, with ears listening to our every word. Come with me."

Mirada allowed Ice to lead her to the raised deck on the bow of the ship. After he looked around, ensuring they were alone, she watched Ice begin to conjure. He turned in a full circle while gesturing with his left hand in front of him and then whispered a word she did not catch.

The air stilled around them. Sounds of the wind-driven sails and the *Swan* cutting through water quieted.

"There. That should provide a bit of privacy. Mirada, are you aware of the existence of Terrenes besides our own?" Ice asked.

"Yes. I was present on one occasion when Greyhook and Master Lindear, the current Chief Librarian of the Bardic enclave, were discussing the topic. Lindear stated there were reports in the library that documented a few of the known Terrenes. He also said the Practitioner's Archive held more complete information." Mirada paused so Ice could continue.

"Good. That saves me from having to explain their existence. Kit's mother, Essmee, is a Shadow Cat from the Terrene of Shadow. Essmee has claimed and bonded to Master Feneas, my former mentor in the Arts, whom I visited while we were in Arlanda."

Mirada wondered if there was something special about a

Shadow Cat. "So, what is Kit doing on board? And why did Zeal say he and she would be together now?"

"Kit has bonded with Zeal. It is rare for a bond to form before a Shadow Cat becomes an adult." Ice looked out to sea.

"Then how did this bonding come about? What will it mean?" Mirada glanced around to see if any of the crew was paying attention to them, but the two remained ignored for the moment.

Ice quietly stared at the horizon for a few moments before answering. "I don't know how the bond occurred, but I intend to contact Feneas and find out, once we've returned to Havensharth. It may have something to do with the fact that Kit is not pure Shadow Cat. Feneas informed me that Kit is half something else but did not know what comprised the other portion of Kit's heritage. And I am sorry, but I'm unable to describe to you what it means to bond to a Shadow Cat. Neither Feneas or Kit's mother have ever shared the particulars with me."

"Why does Zeal act like he understands what the animal— I am sorry! I sounded like Captain Baylor there for a moment. I mean does he understand what Kit is thinking?"

"That is easy to answer. You see, Zeal can understand what Kit is thinking if she wishes. Shadow Cats communicate through a type of mindspeak. They can exchange thoughts directly with one or more people when they so choose."

"How do they understand different languages?" Mirada asked, fascinated by the details of Zeal's Shadow Cat.

"It would appear the language of the mind is universal for them. They can even decipher a person's intentions and tell if that person is being honest or deceitful."

"I can see where having a Shadow Cat companion would be useful. How often does this bonding happen?"

"Currently I know only of two— Feneas with Essmee and, more recently, Zeal and Kit. Not many travelers to the Shadow terrene have reported even meeting a Shadow Cat—the creatures are encountered only when they want to be seen. They are masters of the hunt, and their intended prey most often are dead before becoming aware they're in danger. The Cats are very protective of their territory and their Pride."

Mirada began to share Ice's admiration for the powerful creatures. "I think Zeal has already proven he'll defend Kit. You said she is only a babe?"

"Yes, Zeal and Kit will safeguard each other, and it just so happens Kit is only a little over three moons in age. Feneas thinks she will grow larger than her mother." Ice grew silent again.

Mirada wondered if he was troubled by something so waited for him to think.

"Speaking of her mother, if Kit is here, it wouldn't surprise me if Essmee makes an appearance periodically during our voyage, to check on her cub. I have watched her raise a few of her other babes, and they usually stayed with her for care and instruction for a couple of seasons. Kit's education is obviously not yet completed, so I expect Essmee will remain very protective of her. She may even view Zeal as an adopted cub whom she'll need to teach. Do you have any further questions?"

"No, not now. No, I take that back. I do have one. I noticed you didn't want Zeal to say how Kit gained access to the *White Swan,* even after Captain Baylor asked directly. Don't you think it will present a problem if Baylor becomes aware of Essmee's presence on board the *Swan,* as well?"

He paused a moment before answering, "The captain won't even know when Essmee is here. Shadow Cats are able to create areas of shadow and darkness, and they have the ability to use shadows to travel from one place to another. That is part of what makes them such lethal hunters. They can attack from the shadow unseen." Ice placed a hand on Mirada's shoulder. "I trust you'll keep what I have shared with you to yourself. I don't want information regarding Shadow Cats to become common knowledge. Kit's mother and Master Feneas are of like mind."

"I will for now. But I shall discuss this with Greyhook, since we are bringing the three young ones to live and learn at Havensharth. He should be aware of any potential for problems. We'll need to decide with him where the three of them will live and who will watch over them. I assume you haven't considered their future care."

Mirada noted Ice's eyes tighten. "Or have you?"

"No, I must admit, I've not thought that bit through completely. Originally, I had planned for only one person's coming with us— Zeal. It seems I am to be his Master and he, my apprentice. Tulip's accompanying us was unexpected." Ice sighed. "I now have to consider Kit as part of the package. I don't know what to do about Tulip, let alone Zeal and Kit."

Ice seemed a touch overwhelmed. Mirada was surprised he hadn't tried to cross swords with her over her mentioning she planned to reveal his Kit secret to Greyhook. "I may be of some help as far as Tulip is concerned. We can discuss this further between us, but I think we should include Zeal and Tulip when we do. They should have some say in what decisions are made regarding them."

* * *

Zeal closed the door to the quarters he and Ice shared on board ship. *I guess these are Kit's quarters as well,* he thought, when Kit leapt onto the upper berth and settled down.

"What was that all about between you and Captain Baylor?" Tulip made herself comfortable on the bottom berth, removing her shoes as she curled her legs underneath her. "Are you trying to get us thrown off the ship?"

Zeal sat next to her and tried to understand his actions before explaining them. "I felt a little threatened by Captain Baylor and became defensive. I don't think he meant Kit or any of us any harm. It was as if the captain was testing me somehow. I thought it was best I walk away before I said or did something to make things worse."

Tulip placed her hand on his arm. "Just remember our teachings. We watch and learn. If there is any danger, we will face it together. We are family and look out for each other. Kit is now family as well."

"Thank you, Tulip. I feel better." Zeal stood, suddenly realizing he and Tulip had left behind everything they'd known. They were orphans whose upbringing at the Temple of Ladies of Life was at an end. Neither Lady Izlan, the Matriarch of the Temple, nor Iris, in the Temple mausoleum, would be around to look after them. Training with Master Slag and their former mentors in the Trade was over, too.

Most important, they had left behind those they considered their brothers and sisters: Liddea, who'd wanted to learn to conjure; Nester and Fronc, who'd helped make them stronger; and Mehrle, the one Zeal felt had truly led them.

He was thankful he didn't have to make this trip to Havensharth alone. Tulip volunteering to accompany him was a blessing. She knew him better than anyone. But what caused the smile on his face to burst forth from the sadness that attempted to grip him was the fact that he and Kit were together. Zeal was determined not to allow anything or anyone to come between them.

Although he was excited by his potential to become a Practitioner of the Arts, he was a little fearful of his Phosfire ability, which had made their leaving Arlanda necessary. He sincerely hoped Havensharth's enclaves of learning would teach him the tools he needed to survive.

CHAPTER TWO

THE *SWAN* HAD PASSED through a squall during the night. The canvas and rigging were wet from the rain. The wind carried a chill that cut through Zeal's clothing but could not penetrate his inner warmth.

He and Tulip had taken to heart the Trade Master's words that they use the ship to enhance their Trade training. This morning, they had chosen to practice their tumbling in the *Swan's* rigging. It was Zeal's turn to spot for Tulip. Her bare feet slapped the wooden spar and produced a sharp clap when she landed a twisting flip.

The ship chose that moment to dip into the trough of a wave. The abrupt change caused Tulip's balance to shift; her back foot slipped off the curved edge. Zeal reached out, grabbed her leg to steady her, and prevented her from falling to the deck.

Tulip, her features hard to see in the dim light of the coming dawn, spoke softly when she said, "Thanks, but I had it."

He gave her calf a gentle squeeze then let go of her leg. "I know you did. Let's break before we're noticed."

"Good idea. I want to try this wearing a blindfold."

"Only if the sea is calm. You'd think tumbling from high in the rigging of a moving ship would be enough of a challenge for you." Zeal glanced toward the deck.

"If I didn't know you better, I'd think you were a little frightened by my idea." Tulip laughed at her own challenge.

"So says the girl who used to be afraid of heights. We might want to wait a little longer and consider consulting Master Ice, for safety reasons." Zeal got to his feet and stood next to Tulip on the spar. "After you."

As he quietly followed her down the mast, Zeal reflected on how their life had changed since boarding the *White Swan*. The days were settling into a routine, but not all was according to his and Tulip's design. Master Ice and Lady Mirada had their own daily plans for them. Mornings usually found him and Tulip up before sunrise, working out on the spars or assisting the crew as they learned the rigging.

The skills of balance, climbing, rope usage, and acrobatics were challenged by the ship's sway, pitch, and yaw. Kit joined them infrequently, but when she did, her silent observation would sometimes end in play. Per Tulip's wish, the early hours were used to mask the use of a blindfold she and Zeal sometimes wore as they went about their doings, thus simulating the use of the Hood the Trade Master required them to wear, which forced them to enhance senses other than sight.

After the morning meal was weapons training with Lady Mirada. The apprentices continued to learn the use of sword, staff, bow, and knife. Afterwards, but prior to the midday meal, there was cleanup and laundry. Bathing in a bucket of fresh water conjured and heated by Ice was a luxury for each of them, since the alternative—freshly drawn water from the sea—discouraged any complaining on Zeal and Tulip's part. Following the midday meal, Zeal would retire to his quarters and meet with Master Ice. Once there, he received instruction in the use of the Arts, while Tulip endured additional martial instruction from Lady Mirada.

Each morn, when Captain Baylor made his appearance on deck to relieve the night officer on duty, he was approached by Kit, who delivered the day's official offering of dock rat. She waited for Captain Baylor to note her accomplishment before walking away and returning to her quarters to meet with her mother, Essmee, for her own lessons.

Essmee stepped into the cabin using a corner that mysteriously remained dark, arriving from the home she shared with Master

Feneas. She always looked ready to pounce as she made her presence known. She would then step away with Kit in tow but always returned her daughter prior to the start of Zeal's sessions with Master Ice. Sometimes, Essmee would stay on, quietly listening and observing, before returning home to Master Feneas.

The evening meal was eaten with Captain Baylor and Master Parish in the captain's cabin. It was not long before Captain Baylor complimented the fine additions to his crew he had in Tulip, Kit, and, Zeal. It was not lost on Captain Baylor that the next morning Kit delivered two dock rats instead of one at the *Swan's* steerage.

After the evening meal, the young ones were on their own. Zeal could be found high in the rigging on the yard, his back against the mast, next to Kit. It was at this time, when they were alone, that he would take out *The Book of Flames* given to him by Master Feneas and study its contents. Zeal knew Kit would inform him if another person approached, so he could put the book away.

The pages of *The Book of Flames* were written in a red-colored ink that glowed like hot coals in a fire. On one such evening, as he read, Zeal realized Kit was studying the book with him.

"Can you understand what is written on the pages of the book, Kit?" he enquired.

She extended a claw and traced one of the letters. *Do you mean the red scratches and markings on what you call pages?*

"Yes." Zeal traced a line with his finger, pointing to and saying each word out loud.

I hear your mind's voice when you look at scratches without speaking them.

"Ah, I understand. I bet I could teach you to read. Then you wouldn't need anyone to tell you what's on a page. Would you like to learn?" He looked at Kit's face.

Not if I have to hunt words alone.

"No, it won't mean that. But for when I'm not here to, as you put it, hunt words for you. Or, how would you like to be able to read to me?"

Others not know I listen. Let them read.

Zeal shook his head. "You are being a little lazy. What if the person isn't studying the information you want? You can't make someone else read for you, when you want to know something. Or can you?"

Kit thought a moment. *I have to ask mother.* But then she mindspoke, *Teach me.*

"First off, the scratching and markings are referred to as writing and drawing. Here, the writing is made up of words. Each word is made of letters. Drawings represent runes, symbols, and objects. This drawing, for example, represents the flames of a fire. This one is a tree covered in flames that are not meant to actually burn the tree. The writing describes how to conjure flames that are not harmful."

Then I will learn to read. But right now, I want to listen to you.

Zeal smiled. He gave Kit a kiss on the head and resumed studying *The Book of Flames,* now aware he was studying for the two of them. It never occurred to him to think that teaching Kit to read might be considered odd, impossible, or improper. It felt right.

* * *

Ice studied the sleeping Shadow Cat next to Zeal and imagined Kit was exhausted after spending time with her mother. He was wondering what it would be like to be bonded by a Shadow Cat when his thoughts were interrupted.

"Master Ice," Zeal said, "I know you said the ability to use the Arts is not limited to people. Does that mean anything has the potential to learn to conjure?"

Ice could tell by the way Zeal studied him that his apprentice was eager to hear his mentor's answer.

"I wouldn't put it quite that way. There are other creatures that have been known to conjure. Sentient plants exist that intentionally conjure. Insects, as well. For example, take the silk made by the Anrotean Spider. Each thread is naturally imbued with properties by the spider as she spins. Clouds don't conjure the rain that falls, but we've heard of storms that seem to be alive and seek to punish those who do harm to the land where they live."

"Are you saying the world is aware?" Zeal asked, eyes wide with wonder.

I must have set the boy's imagination rampaging, Ice thought before answering, "It is believed by many that such is the case. That is why the potential, the essence that allows the practice of the Arts is so widely spread to all things living and some that are not."

"Does Mother Essmee make use of the Arts?" Zeal asked quietly.

"I am not aware that she does. Shadow Cats have abilities that are a natural part of them. Abilities that make them what they are." Ice added, "In all the seasons I have known Essmee, I have never seen her conjure."

"If one always needs to use gestures or speak phrases to conjure, does that mean, if someone were to cut off my hands and gouge out my tongue, I wouldn't be able to use the Arts any longer?"

Ice looked long and hard at the boy. "That sounded very gruesome. I don't think I want to know where that thought came from." He leaned forward, making his fingers easily seen. "You already know words and gestures are called elements. Elements are mainly a tool used to help a Practitioner remember the structure needed to complete a conjure. Without this structure, the Practitioner can make mistakes that will cause the casting to fail."

He waited to see if Zeal had a question before continuing. "When a mistake is made, nothing usually happens. In rare cases, something detrimental can occur, causing an unintended result. You could summon something that would have you for a quick meal, for example. There are Practitioners who learn to conjure and have the discipline of mind not to need physical or verbal elements. This takes practice and adds to the difficulty of conjuring successfully. Those who can conjure in this fashion are at an advantage."

Zeal's face acquired a determined expression. "I intend to use the Arts without the use of elements. That way, even tied up and gagged, I would be okay."

"Zeal, where does this concern of capture come from? Is there something I should know?" Ice waited patiently for an answer.

"If you recall, Liddea and the other girls were kidnapped and held against their will till they were rescued. I don't want to be helpless and unable to do something for myself. Also, what if I don't want someone to know I was the one who conjured? It would be obvious, if I'm seen using the elements."

Ice had not expected this line of questions and was surprised by Zeal's point of view. "Wait, do you think the use of the Arts is secretive and should be practiced as one would use the skills learned as a Trade apprentice?"

"I have not observed a Practitioner who uses their skills openly. Master Feneas, Qwen, and yourself all seem to hide what it is you do. You only let people you trust with your secrets know about you."

Ice now understood Zeal's concern and the responsibility associated with accepting him as an apprentice. Inwardly, he smiled at the boy's innocence and honesty. His task was more than teaching Zeal the Arts. It would include the lad's learning not only to be responsible but how to also remain respectful and caring of others.

Ice thought of the security and love he always felt from Essmee and Master Feneas. Zeal needed the same from him. He moved to sit next to Zeal, placed his arm across the boy's shoulders, and held him close.

"We are not a secret society. It is true that it is up to each Practitioner to decide if they will use the Arts for good or bad. But you cannot use the Arts to complete every task or solve all of life's problems. I have met a few Practitioners capable of doing extraordinary things by utilizing the Arts. However, most of us are limited in what we can accomplish before we tire."

Zeal laid his head against Ice's shoulder. "What do you mean, tire?"

"Picture this. It is easier for you to use the muscles in your arm to wield a hammer than to conjure and use your will to pick it up and wield it. The heavier the hammer, the sooner your muscles grow weary from using the tool. Just as your arm eventually tires, so does conjuring fatigue the caster. Then you have to rest and recover before more work can be done.

"Because of this, the majority of Practitioners use their skills only when needed. Some will create objects that serve to store the energy required to conjure. Objects can be given the appearance of life or cloaked in illusion to hide their true nature from others. The Arts have many uses." Ice waited for Zeal to process the analogy.

"So I don't have to hide what I am learning? I just have to be discreet, like Master Feneas taught me?"

"When did Master Feneas do this?" Ice didn't remember that particular conversation.

"I went back to Master Feneas's cottage to say farewell to Kit. She and Mother Essmee weren't there, so I asked Master Feneas to let Kit know I'd returned and to please tell her I was sorry I wouldn't have a chance to say goodbye. Before I left, Master Feneas gave me this book." He reached into his pocket and removed a book that grew larger as he showed it to Ice.

Ice looked at the title, *The Book of Flames*. "I don't remember seeing this before. Is this the book you've been reading?"

"I didn't think folks were paying attention to me. I tried to be careful and not let anyone see what I had."

Feeling warmth radiate from the book, Ice slowly pulled away, leaving Zeal holding onto it. "I wouldn't allow others to hold this particular volume. Sometimes, when you hand an object to another person, it means you are giving it to them. Do you understand my meaning? I'll look over your shoulder and let you show me its contents."

"Oh, it wasn't my intention to give away the book!" Zeal exclaimed, surprised. "Master Feneas did kind of hint I shouldn't let others know I have it, but he also implied he didn't mean you. He made me promise not to use what I learned from reading it without having you or someone teaching me present, to guide me."

Ice nodded. "Good. Please remember that. We'll want to have you in a safe place where mistakes won't cause damage or harm anyone, as you master the contents of this book. What have you read about so far?"

Zeal answered excitedly, "I've learned how to create fire to light a candle or torch. Also, how to send the fire away, such as when putting out a candle. I recently read how to encase something or someone in fire without causing harm to them."

"I can see where that would be useful as a form of protection. Or possibly cause more harm, if a weapon were flaming when it was being used. Zeal, I hope you haven't yet tried to practice what you are reading about…," Ice posed gently.

"No, I am waiting, just like Master Feneas asked. I wish we could start soon, though. Do we have to wait till we get to Havensharth? I'm sure it would be safe to practice with a candle," Zeal suggested with gentle persuasion.

Ice smiled slightly. "Let me review the book's information with you and then let you know. Even though I think that lighting candles is probably not beyond us, I would still hate to set the *Swan* on fire with us on her."

"Ah, maybe we should wait," Zeal replied in a hushed voice, concern on his face.

"I am glad you understand there can be serious consequences to what we can do. Open the book and show me the section you reviewed."

Zeal leaned closer so they could study *The Book of Flames* together. Kit moved nearer and began to groom. "Master Ice, I have a problem and need your help."

Slightly confused, Ice looked at Zeal. "We've yet to start. How could you possibly already have a problem?"

"I want to teach Kit how to read. I have chalk but no slate. You see, I don't want anyone to know what I am doing. I mean, other than you, Lady Mirada, and Tulip."

"How do you know that Kit is capable of learning to read? Better still, does she even want to?" Ice was intrigued. He glanced over at Kit.

I wish to learn, so I will. Is there a problem for me to do so? Kit mindspoke to both Ice and Zeal, but directed her question to Ice.

Ice was completely taken unawares and took a few moments to organize his thoughts. "No slight intended, Kit. I'm just surprised to learn of your desire. I understand better now why Zeal wanted to know more about whom or what defines a Practitioner."

Excited, Zeal said, "I guess this means you have two apprentices, Master Ice. Kit won't have to pretend to sleep when she is listening and following along with us."

"It may be true. Yes, it may be true." Ice shook his head, amazed by the turn of events. "I will help you obtain a slate. The ship's cook has one. We might try to borrow it or, better still, wait till we dock at the city of Malaan, the *Swan's* scheduled last stop before she continues on to Havensharth. I am sure we can purchase materials to use to teach Kit there. We should keep knowledge of her reading lessons limited to our inner circle for now. I know that sounds secretive, but let's leave it up to Kit to decide when she wants someone to know she can read."

"How soon before we arrive there?"

"I will ask Captain Baylor. But for now, let's look in your book and establish if it is safe to allow you to light that candle."

As they searched for the lesson, Ice wondered what other surprises his apprentice had in store for him.

CHAPTER THREE

INTENT ON HER LESSON, Tulip was oblivious to the sweat dripping off her nose and chin which left dark dots on the wood planking. Mirada had drilled her steadily for the past two marks before calling a halt. Tulip's lungs heaved from her efforts.

She ignored the members of the crew who derived entertainment from watching her train with Mirada, who was barely perspiring herself. Tulip was aware her afternoon training was more intense than the morning sessions she shared with Zeal. She was left feeling incompetent, not quite able to meet Mirada's expectations.

"You have to work on regaining your balance after you miss a lunge. Even better, try not to lose your balance to begin with. Come to the cabin now. A massage will help prevent your muscles from tightening." Mirada threw Tulip a cloth.

Wiping her face and drying her hands, Tulip followed Mirada into their cabin and closed the door. Mirada lit the cabin lanterns to chase the chamber's darkness into the corners.

Tulip took off her tunic and breeches but remained in her small cloths. She lay down on the lower bunk and immediately winced in response to her sore muscles being kneaded. Intermittently, one area or another received a splash of minty smelling liniment that was cold when applied but soon turned hot under Mirada's probing fingers.

"This is a nice bruise. It should go well with these others," Mirada noted aloud.

"Please tell me again why I get to enjoy being beat up by you.

Why don't you pound on Zeal a little? He would greatly benefit, and I'm sure would enjoy a massage after, too." Tulip bit her lip as Mirada probed another tender spot.

"You are not like a man, who will think all it takes to defeat an opponent is brute force and big weapons. Learn to use your speed and brains in a fight and leverage your opponent's strengths against them. When they strike at you, you move away, no longer in position for the intended attack, and in the same moment strike back at them or another opponent. Like you, Zeal will use martial skills to defend himself, but he will also utilize the Arts. I have a feeling Kit will fight alongside him, as well. I predict the three of you will be deadly together."

"So, the only thing I'll be good for is as a bodyguard for Zeal or someone else?" Tulip didn't try to masque her frustration.

"No, Tulip. That is not what I meant. Roll over and look at me." Mirada took Tulip's hands in hers. "I have led a life fraught with fighting and, I admit, a bit of adventure. A good portion's been spent defending myself from others who wanted to cause me harm or kill me. I want you to be able to protect yourself until you have a chance to figure out what *Tulip* wants to accomplish in life."

A smile gentled Mirada's features. "In Greyhook, I have finally met someone who cares about me as much as I care about him. I no longer have to battle for everything I want. Even when I worked as a hired sword, I did so with people who looked out for me, and I looked out for them."

"You mean Lady Izlan and the others at the Temple?" Tulip quietly asked.

"Yes. I want you to be prepared just as I am. But know this— your skill in combat is just a tool to enable you to do things that can only be accomplished by other means. That is why we spend time exercising your brain, as well as your body. You are a talented fighter, but I want you to be the best there is. Not the best woman fighter. The best fighter. I would be proud to take up arms alongside you."

She gave Tulip's hands an extra squeeze and then stood and began to remove her own practice gear. "Now, let's both get cleaned up and eat a little something. Remember to drink extra water. I hear we will be docking in Malaan sometime in the next two marks."

* * *

It was late in the day. Sunset was still three marks away. Captain Baylor stood at the wheel of the *White Swan,* slowly guiding her into an open slip. Out of the corner of his eye, he saw his passengers approaching. "You have the wheel, Master Parish," Baylor said to his first officer beside him.

"Aye, Captain. I have the wheel." Parish exchanged places with the captain and continued to conduct the *White Swan's* docking.

Baylor looked over the party standing before him, which included the boy but not Kit. "We should be in position soon," he told them. "Once the manifest and ship's cargo are inspected, the port authority will allow you to disembark. Do you plan on being away from the *Swan* in the evenings? Or will you continue to sleep on board during our anchorage here?"

Mirada spoke for the party. "We have no plans to quarter in the city. How long will we be in port?"

"I plan to leave with the tide in two dawns. We have a small amount of cargo to shift on and off the ship and one passenger scheduled to come aboard. I expect to continue on and arrive at our final destination in half a moon. Now, please excuse me. I have to make sure the *Swan* is docked safely." He turned back to his first officer. "I have the wheel, Master Parish."

"Aye, Captain. You have the wheel."

* * *

Workers swarmed the dock like ants, shifting cargo between ships and warehouses. Gulls, roosting in rigging, on roofs, and flying above, called to each other. Periodically, one or more winged landward, attracted by a choice tidbit that had fallen to the ground.

Buyers haggled over the price of fresh catch being unloaded from a small fleet of fishing boats.

The ship was approached by three men whom Mirada identified by their determined walk as probable representatives of the Port Authority. Captain Baylor and his first mate met the men at the top of the ship's gangplank. She eased close enough to overhear their conversation yet remain unobtrusive, pretending to focus her attention on the activity ashore.

"Permission to come aboard. I am Dockmaster Walken, and these two are my assistants."

"Permission granted. Welcome aboard the *White Swan*, Dockmaster. I am Captain Baylor, and this is my first mate, Master Parish. Here is the ship's manifest." Baylor placed a large, leather-bound ledger into Walken's already waiting hands.

Walken didn't immediately open the ledger but instead asked Baylor, "What cargo does the *Swan* carry, Captain?"

"Mainly raw materials, agricultural products, tools, finished goods, and a few specialty items. Everything is documented in the manifest." He nodded toward the ledger.

"I am sure it is. What is the cargo's final destination?" Walken's eyes darted, taking in the activity of the ship's crew.

Mirada could see that the dockmaster, who was the shortest and roundest of the three gentlemen, seemed to enjoy the power of his position. He didn't *need* to know where the cargo was headed. She thought Baylor maintained a practiced air of indifference when he answered.

"The lading has been commissioned by representatives from Havensharth and will be delivered to the Enclaves there. Shall we get on with the inspection?" Baylor swept a hand toward the entrance to the hold.

As the five men headed to the hold, Mirada sensed a presence beside her. Turning her head, she discovered a smiling Ice standing beside her, with Zeal and Tulip next to him. Mirada moved her hand away from her knife hilt and glared at Ice. "You will end up at the business end of one of my blades, if you insist on sneaking up on me." She looked sharply at the children. "You two are just a bad as he is."

Ice's grin broadened. "It's not my fault you were too busy snooping to pay attention. Overhear anything useful?"

Mirada glanced around to make sure no one was listening in on them, but the crew was busy at their jobs, attending to the ship and making it secure at the pier. She took in a deep breath and frowned at the town's perfume. "I am always reminded why I don't live in large cities whenever I visit one. Ice, do you have a task to accomplish while we are in port?"

"Large cities do serve a purpose, but I agree. I prefer to reside elsewhere. To answer your question, Zeal and I have a mind to obtain a few supplies but shouldn't need more than a couple marks to find what we want. What of you and Tulip?"

"I have no need to see the sights of Malaan. But I don't want my desires to prevent Tulip from being able to experience the city. Would you mind if she accompanied you and Zeal?"

"I don't mind at all," Ice replied.

Mirada observed the smile Zeal and Tulip shared. She noted, even though they were quietly listening to her discussion with Ice, the two children were conducting a silent conversation between themselves by wiggling their fingers.

"I wonder if there is a bath house nearby," Mirada said. "It would be nice to have a good soak. In fact, why don't you enquire about one, Tulip, while you are out and about?" Looking pointedly at Zeal and Tulip, she added, "You could both benefit from a good soaking, as well."

"What an attractive idea," Ice said. "I'll see what's available."

"Where will Kit be while the three of you go into town?" Mirada asked Zeal.

"Kit plans to stay on board ship. She has something she wants to do. Kit does not like big cities, either. She says the city smells." He sniffed the air. "Kit is right—it does. Arlanda didn't stink like this."

"All cities smell, some more so than others," Ice said. "Mostly due to the garbage and waste created by their inhabitants. You were nose-blind and therefore unaware of Arlanda's distinct aroma." He pointed to the open ocean. "Once away from land, we all become accustomed to the fresh sea air."

Master Parish approached. "The inspection is complete. Passengers can now disembark and see what Malaan has to offer." He continued on his way without engaging in further conversation.

"I will leave you to your shopping," Mirada said, turning to Tulip. "Keep an eye on these two. Are you armed?"

Tulip glanced at Zeal. "We both are."

"Shall we go?" Ice asked, heading to the gangplank with the two young people in tow.

Mirada kept an eye on the three of them till they were out of sight. When she turned back toward her cabin, she observed the first officer approaching the captain hastily. She walked closer, to try to determine why Parish was gesturing excitedly toward the port side stern of the ship.

She followed the two of them to the ship's railing, looked down to where Parish pointed, and was surprised to see dock rats leaving the *Swan* by way of the stern line. Tracing the line to where it exited the ship, she saw Kit's head jutting from the opening. It seemed to all appearances that Kit was actively monitoring the rats as they left ship.

Baylor stood, staring, an astonished look on his face. "Tell me you are seeing the same thing I am, Lady Mirada. Kit is ridding the *Swan* of her dock rats. It seems they are all leaving."

Once ashore, the rats leapt off the rope and furtively scurried amongst the dock's gear and cargo seeking places to hide.

"I am just as amazed at what is happening as you both are. If this is truly the last of the vermin on the *Swan*, you'll not be presented with a morning tribute, once we resume our voyage." Mirada inwardly chuckled over the dumbfounded expression on Parish's face as she scanned the workers on the dock. The rats' exit had gone unnoticed. As the last rat left the *Swan*, Kit looked up and nodded to Captain Baylor then disappeared back inside the ship.

Captain Baylor gave Kit a brief salute in acknowledgement before turning away. "Master Parish, have the cook purchase a fresh scraud from one of the fishermen. I want it filleted, left raw, and cut into bite-size pieces. Kit deserves a reward, and nothing would be better than the delicate flavor of fresh scraud." He then asked Mirada, "Does Kit like fish, Lady Mirada?"

"Since I've never dined with her, I don't know if she has ever had the pleasure. But we could ask Zeal, when he returns from his excursion."

"Well, she is a cat, a remarkable one, and I've never known a cat that didn't like fish. Scraud is the best eating-fish I know of. If she doesn't favor it, then I will think of a different reward." Baylor turned to his first mate. "Master Parish, you have your orders. Notify the cook immediately."

If only you knew how remarkable Kit is, Mirada thought to herself.

"Aye, Captain." Parish left her and Baylor standing at the railing.

"I have never known of a cat eradicating a ship of her vermin," Captain Baylor muttered quietly to himself before he turned and walked away.

* * *

The next afternoon found Tulip sitting across from Mirada, chin-deep in the hot waters of the public baths. They were having a good soaking in a private tub after their afternoon workout. The water was slightly scented, and Tulip found the flowery fragrance pleasing, but, due to her Trade training, she would have normally avoided it. One could easily be detected or identified by odor.

There was an attached laundry, so they had brought along all their dirty clothing and bedding to be washed while they bathed. Zeal and Ice were in the men's side of the baths, attending to their own cleaning and laundry.

The night before, Zeal had showed her the primer and slate he intended to use to teach Kit how to read. At first, she'd wondered what he was thinking. But, after discussing the reasons with him and Kit, everything made perfect sense. Kit was not from here, so why couldn't she learn to read?

Tulip had a harder time accepting the idea that Kit could

possibly make use of the Arts. The seasons would tell if that was going to happen. Tulip stopped her musing when she realized Lady Mirada had asked her a question.

"Sorry, but would you repeat that please?" Tulip said shyly.

"I asked what you were thinking about so deeply."

"About Kit. I find the idea of what she and Zeal have planned unimaginable, yet impressive. When I close my eyes and listen to them talk, I never doubt Kit's abilities. I don't even picture a furry feline—I see a determined young girl, instead."

"We'll have to wait to discover if they'll be successful. I asked Ice what he thought, and he seemed confident they wouldn't fail." Mirada stretched then settled into a comfortable position in the water.

"I thought it very funny the way Captain Baylor made a big deal of Kit ridding the ship of her dock rats. The *Swan's* vermin, as he put it." Tulip grinned.

"Kit enjoyed her scraud. She'd apparently never had fish before. I am afraid the captain is going to spoil her. I hope she doesn't think she can get scraud any time she wants it." Mirada's face brightened. "Although Captain Baylor did keep a few extra fish on ice for her, to eat once we are under sail again."

Tulip laughed. "I think Kit has won the captain over."

"He's also impressed with you and Zeal, from what I hear. The crew thinks well of you both. Even Master Parish is fond of you, though he doesn't show it." Mirada looked at her fingers. "I've acquired wrinkles. I hate to leave this bath, but I think it is time to collect our things and the boys and head back to the *Swan*."

"Why can't ships have a bath like this? I know the captain and crew could use an occasional washing."

"The logistics of carrying enough water to satisfy our needs and that of the crew are already problematic. Plus, the bath water's volume would take away from space used for cargo, which would decrease the ships profit," Mirada explained.

"It wasn't meant as a serious question. I understand the limitations and was only imagining the luxury. It would be nice to have bigger cabins, as well." Tulip was warmed by the thought.

"One sun, when you have a ship of your own, built to your specifications, it shall be equipped with a bathing chamber. You will, of course, invite special people like me to enjoy the amenities, I hope."

"But of course. I wouldn't think of traveling without your splendid company." Tulip was joined by Mirada in laughter.

Mirada sighed as she rose out of the water. "We need to get going. Now, where did I put my hair brush?"

CHAPTER FOUR

THE LIGHT OF THE rising sun peeked through the clouds and reflected off the water's surface, leaving it painted pink. Zeal, Tulip, and Kit crowded together in the crow's nest after helping the crew release the sails. They watched the city grow ever smaller in the distance.

"I overheard three of crew discussing a new passenger who boarded the *Swan* late last eve," Zeal said as he moved Kit onto his shoulders so she could take in the view.

"I heard it was a lady passenger traveling alone," Tulip divulged. She is a merchant of some sort who is returning to Havensharth. Apparently, she had several large crates loaded on the *Swan* while we were at the baths yesterday."

"Wonder what kind of merchant. Do you think Lady Mirada and Master Ice know her?"

"We will probably find out at evening meal. I suspect she'll join us at the captain's table tonight," Tulip speculated.

Maybe there will be scraud for dinner, Kit wondered, establishing her priority.

"Zeal, you are going to have to take up fishing or teach Kit how." Tulip rubbed Kit's ears playfully. "I see Mirada waiting for us. We had better get down there."

Mother has come for me.

Zeal headed deckward. "Hope your lessons aren't as painful as ours, Kit. Give my regards to Mother Essmee."

* * *

The rest of the day proceeded as the others had before and ended in dinner with Captain Baylor and Master Parish. Zeal sat in his usual seat facing the door, with Ice on his left and Tulip on his right. He and Tulip followed their Trade training and Ice's habit, which was never to sit with your back to a door.

Kit had her own place of honor behind and to the left of Captain Baylor, on a sateen-covered cushion. She had been presented a fish-shaped dish colored and glazed to resemble a scraud. Just as Zeal leaned over to make a comment about it to Tulip, the cabin door opened.

Discussion ceased, and Zeal looked up to see a woman flow into the chamber. She sat in the empty seat between Parish and Mirada, directly across the table from Ice. Zeal studied the new arrival, using his Trade training. She was slightly taller than Mirada with definitely more curves. Long, dark-brown hair, graced with natural red highlights from the sun, flowed past her shoulders. The gown she wore was made of silk dyed a rich red, cut provocatively but tastefully in front. A single, clear crystal nestled between her breasts, hanging from a braided band of silver-colored hair. Her eyes, large and dark in color, were fixed on one person in the room: Ice.

Mirada, seated to the woman's left, also stared intently at Ice then, smiling broadly, leaned toward him. Ice stood suddenly. He had a look of alarm on his face and remained speechless.

"Ah, I see our last guest has arrived." Captain Baylor rose from his seat, alongside Master Parish. "I would like to introduce Lady—"

"Deena!" Ice exclaimed, breaking through his mute state.

"It would seem you know each other, Master Ice. Let's see if further introductions are needed. Lady Deena, are you aware of the identities of the other of the guests at the table tonight?"

"I know Master Ice and Lady Mirada. I, of course, have met Master Parish. But I am not familiar with the young Master and

Lady at the table, nor have I met your ship's cat. I do not even recognize the breed."

I am not the ship's cat, Kit complained to Zeal through their link.

Sensing Kit's affront, Zeal reassured her via the same fashion. *Of course not! The lady is unaware of how special you are.*

Captain Baylor continued his introductions. "I'm happy to say these three are both guests and crew of the *White Swan*. This is Master Zeal, Lady Tulip, and the lovely Kit, who is a close companion of Zeal's. You will have to ask him what breed Kit is."

Baylor turned to the steward. "Now that introductions have been made, you may serve the meal." He resumed his seat. "I would like to inform you I was made aware by Malaan's Dockmaster of the presence of marauders preying on ships sailing between Malaan and Havensharth. If we have an encounter, Master Parish will see to your protection, while the crew and I deal with the marauders."

Ice, continuing to stare keenly at Deena, said, "Let me reassure you, Captain, your guests here at dinner would be of greater assistance to you participating in the defense of the *Swan* than we would hiding in our cabins."

"Ice, does that include the two young ones and Kit?" Deena inquired, returning his direct stare.

Mirada answered, "Yes, it does."

Baylor studied each of their faces. "I have observed Lady Mirada and the children training. Zeal and Tulip are quite capable, but I have reservations regarding their fighting against grown men. Master Ice, from your suggestion I assume you are able to defend yourself. But what about Lady Deena? Is she also martially trained?"

Ice inclined his head to Deena, who gave him a slight nod. "Deena will not require that Master Parish defend her. I can assure you, I will have that particular duty well in hand."

"We can discuss this further then, if the need arises," Baylor said, ending the discussion.

As the crinkle of a smile crossed Deena's face, Zeal looked to Tulip, who silently mouthed, "Later." He redirected his attention to the behavior of the adults at the table.

Mirada continued to keep an eye on Ice, occasionally chuckling quietly to herself. Ice and Deena acted as if they were the only ones at the table for the rest of the meal, quietly staring at each other and sharing wordless moments of communication.

At the dinner's end, everyone thanked Captain Baylor for his hospitality. Deena and Ice excused themselves and left together. Zeal heard Mirada quietly say to Ice, "Engage your brain before you open your mouth and give voice," as he walked by her to the door.

Tulip stepped in front of Zeal as they exited the cabin and whispered, "Follow me."

He soon sat alongside her on one of the upper spars of the main sail with their backs against the mast. Kit was curled up in Zeal's lap. "I feel freer here in the rigging, away from the adults," he confessed. "Okay, give. Who is Lady Deena?"

"I had a long talk with Mirada while we cleaned up before dinner. Apparently, Ice was courting Deena back in Havensharth. They had an argument of some kind when she found out he'd agreed to go on the mission for the Enclave of Practitioners. Mirada isn't sure what caused the disagreement, but Ice left without fixing the problem. Mirada is sure it's his fault."

"Probably is."

Tulip continued, "Mirada has tried to get him to talk about what actually occurred, but Ice just becomes ill-tempered and walks away. He and Deena have not seen each other for the past seven moons, and Mirada said he has been crabby the whole period."

"I guess he did not know Deena was going to board the *Swan* in Malaan. Did Mirada?"

"No, she didn't. But Deena had one of the crew bring Mirada to her cabin earlier today, so Mirada knew she was on board and had used her business to be here at the same time as Ice. She helped plan Deena's entrance at dinner tonight."

"What kind of business is she in?"

"Deena is a Practitioner of the Arts and owns a shop that sells imbued items. Apparently, she is on an official buying trip," Tulip answered.

Zeal fingered a previously patched hole in the sail. "We seem to be meeting more and more Practitioners. I don't understand why we never ran into a Practitioner before we met Qwen."

"I bet we did and were unaware of the fact. As we have learned, they don't go around announcing who they are or bragging about what they can do." Tulip moved a blowing strand of hair behind her ear.

"Yeah, I get it. If you need to know, then you find out. If you don't need to know, then it is none of your business. I can live with that." As Zeal gazed into the night sky, a small light streaked toward the horizon.

"Now that I've told you what I learned from Mirada, you have to share with me any stuff you learn from Ice."

"Sounds like a plan. Maybe Kit can help out, as well. Right, Kit?"

You both are silly. Ask the elders for knowledge.

"Because adults won't give you a straight answer."

Tulip nodded in agreement.

"You think we will encounter the marauders?" he asked her.

"I sure hope so. I would love to board their ship and capture it," Tulip replied gleefully.

Kit cleaned a forepaw with her tongue. *Pirates have scraud?*

Tulip reached over and stroked Kit's back. "If they do, you can have it all."

As I should.

Zeal scratched Kit behind the ears. He never seemed to tire of touching her. "Well, Tulip, what are your plans for the rest of the evening?"

"I think I will stay up here and relax." She studied the horizon.

"Keep watch for ships, you mean," he teased.

"If I see marauders, you and everyone aboard will be happy I gave warning."

Zeal made no further fun of Tulip. "I'm going back to the cabin."

"To read your little book you mean."

Not taking any offense from her taunt, he said, "I guess we've never been able to keep secrets from each other." He placed a hand on her shoulder. "Let's make a pact. We will always trust one another to share and keep each other's secrets safe."

"Agreed." Tulip shifted on the spar to face Zeal. "But how do we make this pact? Since we want this to remain strictly between us, who can we ask?"

"I wish Iris was here to consult. She'd be able to give us an answer. Let's just make a pledge to each other."

Include me. We no hide parts of self from each other.

"Guess that means it is the three of us," Zeal said with a smile.

Tulip nodded agreement. "Sure looks that way."

Zeal reached for Tulip's hand and placed it on top of his left one then took Kit's paw and put it on top of Tulip's hand. With his right hand, he covered both before saying solemnly, "Tulip, Kit, will you join me in promising to share and protect our secrets, keep them hidden from others, and always aid one another, even when not asked?"

"I will." Tulip squeezed his hand under hers.

"I do swear." A feeling of warmth flowed through him.

We are Pride.

Kit's announcement was accompanied by what sounded like a cross between a bark and a sneeze.

"What was that? Do you smell that?" Tulip inhaled deeply as she looked around.

Zeal sniffed like Kit, delicately sampling the air, their nostrils flared. "I smell the fragrance of iris blooms."

Tulip nodded. "I recognize the scent now. How strange." There was no clear source of the aroma. She leaned toward Zeal. "Now, tell me about the book."

* * *

Zeal sat on the floor in the center of the cabin he shared with Ice, reading the *Book of Flames*. Kit slept curled next to him. Ice had yet to return for the evening.

The book had revealed a new section that described creatures composed of fire. The bulk of them lived in other Terrenes, with the majority residing in the Terrene of Fire.

The door opened. Ice entered and took a seat on his berth. "Zeal, how are you and Kit?"

Kit opened her eyes, yawned broadly, then stretched.

"We're fine. What about you?" Zeal had never before observed Ice acting… exuberant.

"I'm doing better, better than I have in a long while." He sported a large grin and seemed full of energy, one foot repeatedly tapping the floor.

Zeal asked cautiously "Does that mean you fixed the problem with Lady Deena?"

"What problem?" Ice appeared puzzled, and his foot stopped moving.

"You know, the one that caused her to become upset with you before you left Havensharth…"

"What do you know about that?" Ice's eyes narrowed.

"Nothing. That is why I decided to ask you about it. I heard the two of you had a fight. So, did you fix it?" he asked, putting the *Book of Flames* away.

"Let us say I am working hard on that and will let you know when I have. I want to warn you, though, if I do repair what I thought I shattered, then I will need to tell Deena about you and Kit." Ice looked contemplative for a few heartbeats before his lips curved into a slight smile.

"Why would she have to know?" The idea of revealing this information to Deena made him a little uncomfortable. Kit stirred in her sleep.

Ice leaned toward Zeal. "Trust me, it will be imperative Deena is informed of the particulars regarding a certain Phosfire and Shadow Cat, if I am to put things to right."

"I'll want to tell Tulip about any discussion regarding you and Lady Deena."

"It is fine for you to share what you learn with Tulip. I'm willing to bet the two of you have already begun to talk." Ice waved away Zeal's reply. "Now, are we going to work on lighting a candle tonight? Or continue to discuss my business? I think you have the control we have been seeking to establish. Come stand beside me and take my hand."

Zeal reached over and picked up Kit, placing her on his shoulders before he rose. Then he took Ice's right hand in his left. "I would like to attempt to conjure without the use of elements."

"Really? Well, I had better be prepared to prevent you from lighting something other than a candle. I would hate to have you set fire to the ship and leave everyone swimming with no place to go."

The candle sconces on the walls reflected light into the room. Ice pointed to one of them. "Put out the flame. I will count to ten. Then, relight it. Let me know when you are ready."

Zeal agonized a moment over the thought of setting the ship on fire, but he was determined to succeed and knew it was necessary that he conjure carefully. "I am ready."

For him, fire was alive, somehow part of him. He knew Kit could follow his actions through their bond, even if she wasn't in physical contact with him when she studied his conjure. He and Ice continued to hold hands, and Zeal could sense his mentor in the back of his mind, as if Ice were at a distance, ready to intervene if circumstances required.

Zeal snuffed the flame.

"One, two, three, four…" A light sheen of moisture appeared on his face as Ice started counting out loud. "…ten."

The effort Zeal needed to relight the candle was less than he'd used putting the fire out.

"Well done! And without using elements. Now, do it again, but I want you to affect two sconces simultaneously," Ice directed.

Zeal concentrated on a pair of sconces. He felt Kit focus on a third. They communicated without speaking. *Can you see how to sleep the flame? You do it like this.* Zeal walked her through the conjure he'd learned.

You not use conjure.

Are you certain? Zeal asked. He was confused by Kit's revelation.

You telling fire what you want fire to do. Kit showed him what she meant.

I hadn't realized. Zeal thought over what he'd learned.

Ice interrupted their discussion. "Having difficulty, Zeal?"

"No, I'm fine. Here we go." Then he said to Kit alone, *You first, then me.*

Kit's tail began to twitch. Zeal heard her make a soft vocalization. Having no hands, she had created her version of the elements for conjuring. The flame in the sconce she was concentrating on flickered, dimmed, and then ceased to burn. Zeal was momentarily caught off guard, watching her. He quickly focused and snuffed two other candles.

"Zeal, don't try to do too much at once," Ice admonished.

"The third sconce wasn't my doing," Zeal answered with a proud smile, glancing at Kit.

"Really? Now that *is* a pleasant surprise. One of you might want to warn me when next Kit decides to participate. How about you relight your candles after Kit does hers? Proceed."

There was a slight widening of Kit's eyes just prior to the candle's flame reappearing. *I want to do something bigger,* she announced to them both.

"Me, too!" Zeal was exuberant after easily lighting both of his sconces.

"Why don't we practice with the sconces a little longer before moving on to something bigger? I'm surprised and pleased with my two apprentices," Ice admitted. "As your mentor, I vow to attempt to do as well by you and Kit as Master Feneas did for me. Unlike Master Feneas, however, I am sure I'll make mistakes. Never forget, I'm always here for you. Please come to me anytime, for any reason."

"Thank you, Master Ice. Kit and I understand." Zeal decided not to mention Kit's discovery that manipulating flame didn't require him to use conjure.

Learning, like teaching, is not supposed to be easy.

Ice laughed. "Kit, you've been listening to Essmee. That is something she would say. I think it best we continue to keep your ability to conjure and your being a Shadow Cat limited to those who need to know. Okay, Zeal, let's see you try to manipulate the flame in all the sconces at once."

CHAPTER FIVE

TULIP SAT ON THE uppermost spar, with her back resting against the main mast. She could feel the movement of the ship as it coursed through the water. The ship's pitch and yaw were accompanied by vibrations communicated through the wood of the mast into her spine. It had been a quarter of a moon since the *White Swan* left Malaan.

She looked out and spied a shape on the horizon and then yelled to the crewmen in the crow's nest to gain his attention. "Ahoy! What is that in the distance?" She pointed astern.

The crewman caught sight of the target and proceeded to view it through his spyglass. After several heartbeats, he lowered the glass and said to her, "Tell the captain we've spotted a ship. I will let him know more in a mark."

Before scampering down the mast, Tulip located the captain at the wheel of the *Swan*. Once on deck, she hurried to him. "Excuse me, Captain Baylor. I wish to make a report."

"Yes, Tulip. Report," Baylor replied sternly, but a sparkle in his eyes softened his command.

"There is a ship on the horizon astern of the *Swan*. The watch in the crow's nest told me to tell you he would have further information in one mark." Tulip wondered if it was a marauders' vessel.

"Thank you. Carry on." Baylor turned away and approached Master Parish. They entered into a quiet discussion regarding the sighting that excluded her.

Tulip was due to meet Lady Mirada for their afternoon workout, which meant she would have to wait until afterwards to let Zeal know about the ship she'd seen.

Four marks later, she found herself in a meeting in the captain's cabin, sitting alongside Zeal and the adults. Captain Baylor had approached Mirada just prior to the end of the training session and informed her of the meeting. Tulip doubted the captain expected her and Zeal to be in attendance, too, but Mirada and Ice had insisted they be present. Essmee had not returned Kit to the vessel.

Baylor cleared his throat loudly. "I have been informed by the watch that the ship sighted earlier is gaining on the *Swan*. It appears to be under sail and oar, giving it the advantage in speed. I calculate it will be upon us shortly after full dark. I plan to use darkness to aid us in avoiding any encounter with them."

"Do you mean to infer that the ship is chasing us?" Ice asked, looking at the others around the cabin.

"I have had the *Swan's* course altered twice, and in each instance the ship changed its course to match ours. I have reason to suspect we are being pursued by the marauders we learned of while docked at Malaan."

"If that is the case, how do you intend to evade them?" Ice enquired.

"Since we'll only have a sliver of moon to light the night sky, I intend to have all light extinguished and hope to escape unseen," Baylor answered candidly.

Tulip saw Ice glance at Deena, as if for permission, before suggesting, "Perhaps there is something we could do to help improve our chances of escape."

"Any assistance is appreciated. What do you have in mind?" Captain Baylor asked.

"Lady Deena and I are Practitioners of the Arts, and we can possibly shroud the *Swan* from the other ship's sight while you make your move."

"You can shroud the whole vessel and crew?" The captain straightened in his chair and studied Ice and Deena carefully.

Tulip thought perhaps the captain hadn't been aware before now of the nature of his human cargo.

"It will be difficult, but I think it is possible. Lady Deena is more experienced in this form of conjure than I, and she thinks it can be done."

"I shall still have the crew prepared to repel boarders, in case we are unable to avoid contact. We'll have an early informal meal and make ready for tonight's confrontation." With that, Baylor concluded the meeting.

"We have our own planning to do and will discuss our part further with you when we get together later." Ice gave Baylor a slight bow. "Thank you for keeping us informed, Captain."

Zeal and Tulip accompanied Ice, Deena, and Mirada to Ice's cabin. Discussion did not restart until the door was closed. The small room was shadowy and although well kept, Tulip detected the slight odors of male and Shadow Cat.

Ice indicated for the ladies to take places of comfort before gesturing for Zeal to join him sitting on the floor. "Everyone here knows that Deena and I have what you might call a history together. You also know that Deena is a Practitioner. We both want to inform you of something we have decided. We are committed to become Life Mates."

Ice's face beamed as he looked at Deena, who held his gaze, smiling demurely in return.

"I see congratulations are in order," Mirada said, clearly pleased. "Have you decided on who will bear witness?"

Tulip clapped her hands in delight as Zeal asked timidly, "Does this mean you fixed it?"

Ice was still grinning broadly. "Yes. I fixed it."

"We thought it would be nice to have all of you bear witness." Deena said.

"This means we need to decide what to do about Zeal and Tulip," Ice continued. "I mean who will care for them and sponsor them in Havensharth."

"Oh, that is easy," Tulip interjected. "Tell them, Zeal."

"Tulip gets to live with Lady Mirada and Master Greyhook. Kit and I were going to live with Master Ice, but now we will live with both you and Lady Deena."

Deena quickly inspected the cabin from her seat before asking, "Where is your Kit, anyway? I haven't seen her since this morning. Does she have a place on board she likes to hide?"

Zeal turned to Master Ice. "Don't you think it is time to tell Lady Deena about Kit and me? She doesn't know, does she?"

"Thank you for asking, Zeal. No, Deena does not know, and I agree that she should. I was going to ask your permission first."

"What is it you both think I should know?" Deena demanded, giving man and boy a sharp look. "Out with it."

Ice sat a bit straighter. "Zeal and Kit both are Practitioners. Kit is a Shadow Cat and currently with her mother, who has not yet returned her to the ship. Her mother takes her away daily for instruction. You should also be aware that Zeal is a Phosfire."

Tulip worried Zeal might be rejected from joining the new life Lady Deena and Master Ice were planning. His face seemed open with need.

"Deena," Zeal continued, "do you still think Kit and I could live with you and Master Ice? If you don't want us to, we will understand."

Deena eased over to Zeal, knelt, and embraced him tightly. "Yes, dear. You and Kit are welcome to live with us. It will make me very happy for the four of us to be a family together." Her voice sounded husky with emotion. "I really want you both. When do you expect Kit to return?"

I am back. Mother told me to listen quietly. I am glad Zeal and I have a place in your Pride. Kit directed her thoughts to everyone in the cabin then jumped off the upper berth, where she had silently laid, padded to Zeal and Deena, and rubbed her body against them both.

Deena jerked her hand to her chest. "You can talk!"

I can do many things. Kit stared into Deena's face.

"You and Zeal will have to teach me more about Shadow Cats, I see. I was going to ask Ice to enlighten me, but I think I would rather learn from the two of you." She sat behind Zeal and pulled him to her until he was leaning against her. Kit sprang into his lap. "Are all Shadow Cats able to conjure?" Deena looked around the chamber. "And you said your mother has left?"

Mother says I am the first. She is not here. Do you wish her to return?

"That isn't necessary, but I would like to meet her someday. I'm sure she is very proud of you," Deena added.

"So, you are going to live with me and Greyhook. Is that right?" Mirada dropped to the floor and pulled Tulip close. "What if I had other ideas?" she gently teased.

"Well, since the other option was having the Mouse live with you, I figured you'd decide I am the better choice." Tulip wrapped her arms around Mirada's waist and laid her head on Mirada's chest. Mirada's tight hug was all the reassurance Tulip needed.

Zeal turned to Deena. "What is a 'shroud'?"

At his question, Tulip suddenly felt free of tension and enjoyed the new emotions of belonging.

"It is a way to make something disappear from view, and, if made well, it will prevent scent and sound from being revealed," Deena explained.

"Then we can make the *Swan* disappear and there will be no way the other ship's crew can see us?" Zeal asked with excitement.

Deena sat quietly for a moment. "There are ways to see through a shroud or even break it. But I would be surprised if anyone on the other ship has the ability."

"Kit and I can help," Zeal said, looking to Ice for support.

Yes, let us join the hunt.

Ice nodded his agreement. "That is one of the reasons I wanted Deena to become aware of your abilities. Practitioners can use a technique to jointly conjure, called Marhdah, which allows the many to do what one can't do alone. It would be best if we used Marhdah to create the shroud."

Mirada interrupted. "Zeal and Tulip have fighting skills, but is Zeal—?" Mirada glanced at Kit. "Sorry, can Zeal and Kit use the Arts without endangering themselves? Or us, for that matter?"

"Deena and I will be doing the actual work of the conjure. To place a shroud on the *Swan* capable of hiding her from everyone on the other ship would be tiring for both Deena and myself. Having Zeal and Kit join us in creating the conjure will make the endeavor easier and put less of a drain on each of the Practitioners involved in the work."

"But what is the risk to them?" Mirada asked Deena.

"Mirada, do you think I would allow Ice to endanger my future family? The young ones are in greater peril from the marauders than from exercising a skill they were born to use."

"I have already employed a form of Marhdah to enable me to monitor them during their training," Ice added.

"Ice, were you serious when you said Zeal is a Phosfire?" Deena asked, moving on from Mirada's concern. "Perhaps we could use his ability to our advantage, as well."

"Indeed, he is. And yes, that is a possibility. For example, if he could damage or completely burn the sails on the other ship, that would disable the vessel. The marauders' ship won't be able to overtake the *Swan* using oars alone."

Mirada said bluntly, "I think you're asking a lot of Zeal. How much training have you given him?"

"Some. I admit, Kit and Zeal have a lot to learn."

Zeal piped up. "Why is everyone so sure the people on the other boat mean us any harm?"

Tulip rolled her eyes. "You are so naïve. Never mind. Listen, Mouse, don't you think it's a good idea to get ready, in case there are marauders on the other ship?"

"Well, yes," Zeal muttered, obviously flustered. "But still, there may *not* be bad people on the other ship."

"Well, let's prepare for that eventuality, as Tulip suggests. If they need our aid, we will offer them help instead of a fight." Mirada brought their discussion to an end.

* * *

Zeal stood on deck of the forecastle between Ice and Deena with Kit on his shoulders. Deena wanted to practice using Marhdah together. Tulip and Mirada had retired to their chamber to gear up.

Zeal felt bolstered by the joining and support provided by Ice and Deena's strength. It was a feeling hard to explain. He likened the simple conjure they cast as a rope wrapped around a pulley with a weight tied to it. When conjuring alone, he was unable to lift the weight no matter how hard he tried. When linked through Marhdah, however, Ice and Deena were beside him, not at a distance, as Ice had been previously. They pulled together and easily lifted the weight. Kit was included in the connection but seemed to be mainly observing.

Ice faced Zeal. "See the lantern on the starboard side, at the ship's stern?"

Zeal moved his eyes, not his head, and made note of the light source then answered in a quiet voice, "Yes, Master Ice."

"Extinguish it."

Zeal reached out with his mind to the flame and asked it to sleep. The flame responded: it grew dimmer, flickered, and winked out. Smoke spiraled away from the glowing wick.

Deena, acting as a spotter, said softly, "It's done."

Ice responded by saying, "Relight it."

Zeal pictured the wick in his mind and concentrated on the small bit of fire he kept inside him. It began to pulse, accompanying the beat of his heart, before flaring. The lantern was relit, its flame reborn.

"Ice, I don't think Zeal is conjuring. If he is, he has a subtle touch and is not using elements. I detected minimal usage of energy on his part each time he manipulated the lantern's flame." Deena gazed into Kit's eyes. "Your presence in Marhdah, dear one, feels as if you are softly sweeping your cat tail gently across bare skin."

Kit lifted her head and returned Deena's stare, but remained silent.

"Zeal and I had a discussion regarding the use of elements. I'll tell you more about it later. But for now, his lack of their use will work to our benefit and prevent the crew from realizing Zeal is a

Practitioner. It is also possible that line-of-sight may determine the distance at which Zeal can affect fire. That is at least while using Marhdah." Ice surveyed the seamen who were attending to their assigned duties. "See anyone paying attention to what we're doing?"

"Not really." Zeal gestured with his chin. "Why are the men in the rigging wetting the sails down with buckets of sea water?"

"Makes it harder for the fabric to catch fire. Do you think you can get wet sail to burn?" Ice removed a linen square from his pocket and saturated the cloth with water from the damp deck. After squeezing out most of the moisture, he dropped the square and fixed it beneath the toe of his boot.

Zeal focused on a corner of the fabric. The area lightened in color as it dried, and then it began to discolor and turn brown. White smoke wisped from the surface just before the material burst into flame.

Ice quickly stomped the fire out with his foot. "Answers that question."

"Wasn't easy," Zeal admitted.

* * *

The setting sun's last rays painted the few clouds in the sky red. There was still enough light for Captain Baylor to have a clear view, through his spyglass, of the trailing vessel that was rapidly closing on his ship. He could see the crew of the other vessel preparing their weapons and gear. It was clear their intent was to board and capture his ship.

He had given the order for all hands to requisition fighting implements from the weapons locker. His men were armed with axes, short swords, and a few with crossbows. The fighting, if it came to it, would be up close and personal. He stationed the men with axes at the rails, each paired with another armed sailor wielding a shield to protect them both from missile fire. Their job was to cut the lines to the grapples used by the marauders to bring the vessels close for boarding. If unsuccessful, they were to kill the enemy.

All sources of illumination and flame on deck had been extinguished. The captain made his way to his passengers, who had gathered on deck at midship.

CHAPTER SIX

ZEAL STOOD QUIETLY with Kit on his shoulders and took note of Captain Baylor's approach. He turned back to watch the sun set. There was a sudden flash of blue light as the sun dropped below the horizon.

He'd discovered that sound traveled well over the water and could hear the voices and preparations of the men on the other vessel, as their ship maneuvered to approach the *Swan* on the port side. Kit grew still, her eyes closed, as if having fallen asleep on his shoulders. But she was actually awake, and they were sharing their thoughts with each other.

Your kind on the other ship are prey. We hunt them, not let prey hunt us. Why you worry for them?

I'm not worried about them. I am worried about me. I don't want to let anyone down.

You will do fine. I am here.

And I am here for you. Don't tell me you are not nervous. I feel your mind twitch, like your tail when you are studying a dock rat before striking. He touched her for comfort.

You should be more like Tulip. She is calm and ready to pounce.

I think she just hides doubts better. Anyway, Tulip thinks that fighting is a means to having a good time. Ask her if she has her workshirt on.

He glanced at Tulip, who was standing next to Mirada. Mirada was dressed in banded leather armor, with a buckler on her left arm, and festooned with weapons. She carried her helm under her right arm.

Tulip says yes, and I let her know you are wearing yours.

Good. We better listen. Captain Baylor is here. Zeal focused on the captain.

"Are you all ready? I anticipate we'll initiate the maneuver to move away in less than a mark. The marauders will be close enough to attack not long after." Baylor asked the two adult Practitioners, "Can you explain to me how you plan to proceed with the shrouding?"

To Zeal, the captain appeared to be worried, but, of course, he had the safety of everyone on board the *Swan* as his responsibility. And their fate was not entirely under his control.

"Ice and I will shroud the *Swan* from the other vessel, which should keep them from viewing your maneuver. Shortly thereafter, we hope to set the marauders' sails aflame, so that they lose the ability to follow us," Deena explained. "In this way, we can prevent any loss of life or damage to the *Swan* and her crew."

"Excellent, if you are successful. I do not doubt you, but I have seen plans collapse due to unforeseen twists of fate. I will have the crew ready to repel boarders, just in case."

Master Parish approached and whispered something to Captain Baylor before walking away.

"It would appear one such twist is occurring. The watch in the crow's nest reports the crew of the other ship has uncovered a ballista and is preparing it for use. Their weapon can shoot flaming balls of pitch to set fire to the *Swan* or disgorge stones that can damage man and vessel."

Concerned, Deena glanced at the marauders' vessel. "Unfortunately, we can be only a short distance from the ship, to succeed with the second part of our plan."

Zeal calculated how his need to be close to the other ship in order to conjure meant placing the *Swan* within range of the ballista.

"Then I will leave you to your task. Please let me know if I can offer any assistance." Captain Baylor retreated and positioned himself at the *Swan's* wheel.

The mark passed quickly. Darkness settled, a soft mantle on the shoulders of the world. Lights on the marauders' vessel allowed Zeal to have a clear view of the ship sliding into position on the *Swan's* port side.

When it was six or seven boat lengths away, an amplified voice was suddenly heard, loud and clear, emanating from the approaching vessel. *"Drop sail and prepare to be boarded! Any resistance and all aboard will be executed. You have a quarter of a mark to comply!"*

"How did they do that?" Zeal asked quickly.

"Probably an item made to amplify one's voice," Deena answered.

"You don't think there is a Practitioner on board?" Ice asked.

She shrugged her shoulders. "That would make things a little difficult. Let's inform the captain we are ready to begin." Deena reached over and grasped Ice's hand in hers, while Ice casually began to pet Kit on Zeal's shoulders. A physical and mental link was formed between the four of them, when Deena established Marhdah.

Tulip ran to the Captain, delivered Deena's message, and then ran back to the group. "Captain Baylor said to start."

Deena spoke in a quiet voice, gesturing with her free hand. "Apscon Foris Visu Soni Por Mundus. Axoclo Nostri… Hide from sight and sound the world abound. Blind our foe to where we go. Become unseen."

Zeal wasn't sure of the cause, but he saw colorful ribbons stream away from Deena's fingers as she conjured. A small part of him joined with her, the energy he contributed to the creation of the conjure.

His small inner core of fire remained untouched. He now realized it was part of, yet separate from, the source of energy that allowed him to be a Practitioner. For the first time, he was made aware of how empty the void inside of him seemed. The void was a vessel capable of storing a much greater volume and was waiting to be filled.

The ribbons streamed faster, reaching up and out. They wrapped themselves around the *White Swan*, leaving no part uncovered. The ship took on the appearance of a gift encased in pretty paper. Silence engulfed them.

Deena said to Tulip, "Tell the captain the shroud is completed. He can make his maneuver."

Tulip quickly ran to the captain, who nodded in acknowledgement and then turned the ship's wheel sharply. The *Swan* responded, heeling to port, and began to make her way past the stern of the marauders' vessel.

Zeal looked over at their pursuers' ship. Its deck was well lit. Most of its crew had ceased their activity and stood staring, pointing to where the *White Swan* had last been seen. A couple of them backed away from the railing with fear written on their faces.

As the ships drew close, one person was seen clearly gesturing in the *Swan's* direction.

"He can see us, that man." Deena pointed him out as she yelled, "He can see us!"

Zeal looked while Kit rose up on his shoulders. They saw a bald male, dressed in red robes, running to the starboard stern of the vessel, where he directed the crew to reposition the ballista.

As the bald male passed into the shadow cast by the main mast, he suddenly cried out in pain and dropped to his knees, his hands covering his face. Blood dripped from between his fingers and flowed down the front of his shirt.

The crew's focus changed to the howling man, who lay curled on the deck. It appeared no one else was able to detect the *Swan* as she silently slipped by. The shroud conjured by Deena had even eliminated evidence of the *Swan's* passage on the waters; there was no wake to detect. The crew, blind to the *Swan*, stopped their preparations to attack.

You can start your fires now, dear ones.

Zeal and Kit heard Essmee speak to them, although her physical presence was nowhere to be seen. Caught off guard, he wondered where she was and how long she had been near.

Big ones? Zeal heard Kit ask.

Let Zeal do what he does, little one. You just assist him. Essmee's tone was loving but firm.

Yes, Mother.

Yes, Mother Essmee, Zeal answered. When he reached for his inner core of fire, he felt energy pour into him from Kit, Ice, and Deena. Always before, he'd had to coax the flame to do his bidding. This time, instead, it leaped eagerly to his call. The feeling was natural, effortless; the use of fire his right.

He directed the energies to the mainsail of the marauders' vessel. As flames blossomed, the sail burned, completely engulfed. He felt the fire, hungry for more to eat, seek a new source of food. It found nourishment in the mast, and the pitch inside the heart of the wood caught fire all at once. He sensed the fiery mass inside the wood yearning to couple with the flames consuming the sail. The mast exploded. Shards of blazing wood flew outward in all directions. Startled and a bit frightened, Zeal flinched.

This was too much. His intent wasn't to cause the marauders' ship to burn, killing all aboard. Acting without thinking, he drew further on the energy provided to him through Marhdah. He captured the fire from each glowing bit—the blazing sail and every flame source on the ship—and coalesced them together into a large ball. Charred remains floated deckward, settling on the crew and surfaces of the crippled vessel.

Zeal caused the ball to shrink till it was the size of a sling stone and guided it to the *Swan*. Its final resting place was the wick of the lantern above the ship's wheel; it lit and then continued to burn, the flame was all that remained of the firestorm that had assaulted the marauders' vessel. The attacking ship was left in total darkness as the distance between it and the *White Swan* rapidly increased, Captain Baylor sailed his ship away.

The silence was broken by Tulip, who softy exclaimed. "Mouse! That even impressed me!"

Deena said quietly to Ice, "He is a Phosfire."

Ice kissed her on the forehead then answered, "And he is *our* Phosfire. Now you understand why he belongs in Havensharth."

"That was well done." Mirada looked around the *Swan*, where the crew was cheering the fate of the rival vessel. "Who was that man on the marauder's ship, the one who appeared to see through the shroud?"

"I don't know, but something caused injury to his eyes and

face." Ice glanced over at Kit. "I have my suspicions."

As the captain and his first mate approached, Zeal felt an absence when Deena and Ice relinquished the use of Marhdah. It was as if they had stepped out of the room they'd all shared and closed the door behind them. Zeal and Kit remained joined through their shared bond, of course.

Your mind is too open, young one.

Zeal wondered at Essmee addressing him, alone.

I will return later tonight and teach you how to conceal it. A hunter should never be seen, heard, or scented by another, unless that is the hunter's desire. You allow others too freely where they do not belong. You must learn to shroud your mind as you helped shroud this water house.

I was there, Mother. I was guarding, Kit said, defending him.

Yes, you were, little one. But he needs to learn to guard himself. And I want him to know how to protect you, as well. Together, you are both stronger.

Yes Mother.

What did I do wrong? Zeal asked both Kit and Essmee, confused.

I will explain later. I am proud of both of you, was Essmee's answer.

Zeal felt Essmee fade into the distance. He realized several crewmen were now standing around the party, thanking Ice, Deena, and Mirada for helping protect the *Swan.* Master Parish ordered everyone back to their stations, while the ribbons of energy Lady Deena had created dissipated. Finally, the last of the ribbons joined with the wind in a colorful steam and blew away in the night air.

The captain bowed. "I wish to thank you for your part in our defense. I admit I had doubts about the success of your plan. From what I observed, we'll not have to worry about the marauders' ship and crew for the rest of our voyage."

"Thank you, Captain," said Deena. "If you would excuse us, Ice and I need to recover from the expenditure of our energies."

"Yes, of course. Can I be of assistance in any way?" Captain Baylor asked, a hint of concern in his voice.

"No, we are fine. Rest is all we require. Thank you, Captain,"

Deena reassured him.

"No need for us to continue in darkness. Renew our lights and fires, Master Parish," Captain Baylor said to his first mate as they returned to the *Swan's* wheel.

"Shall we all retire to your cabin for discussion?" Deena asked Ice. "I have a few questions regarding what exactly happened aboard the other ship."

"I am guessing the rest of our journey to Havensharth won't be as much fun," Zeal whispered to Tulip.

She playfully elbowed him. "You had all the fun. I didn't have a chance to fight anyone."

CHAPTER SEVEN

LATE MORN FOUND ZEAL tired from his night's lesson with Essmee and morning workout with Mirada. As he sat next to Tulip, high in the *Swan's* rigging, he now understood what Essmee and Kit had tried to explain to him about protecting his mind and shrouding his thoughts from others. Essmee had promised to work with him more to strengthen his mind's defenses and promised to challenge him till she decided that he was capable. He hoped it wouldn't take long to satisfy her.

"Tell me more about last night." Tulip leaned closer to listen.

"Not much more to tell. I did sneak back and take the flame from the lantern over the ship's wheel. I wanted to keep it with the other flames I've collected." Zeal unsuccessfully tried to stifle a yawn.

"Such as the ball of flame you took from Ice and the one from the Temple, when the kitchen caught on fire? Have you any others?"

"Just the three." Tulip's way of always asking more than one question at a time almost made him smile. But he didn't—Tulip would demand to know why he was smiling and possibly think he was making fun of her.

"What do you do with them? Are they burning inside you right now?" Tulip retied one of the lines that had come loose from the sail.

"Not burning, but still living. It's hard to explain. You know, it feels really empty, the place where I keep them." He placed his hand on his lower belly to show Tulip the location he meant. "Right in here. And there is room for more, much more."

"How does it feel to have it go into you? Is it the same as having a drink?" She pantomimed sipping from a cup.

"I just grasp the fire, draw it into my skin, and let it spread throughout my body. It causes me to feel warm all over inside, much like when you blush and become hot on your skin. Then all the heat gathers together and settles in my middle."

Tulip placed a hand on his stomach for a moment. "Doesn't feel any different." She took her hand away. "Playing with fire must have taken a lot more out of you than you admitted last night. You seemed very tired and a little distracted during our workout with Mirada this morning."

"I'm not tired from our encounter with the marauders. I've acquired new lessons from Mother Essmee, and we started them last night," he confessed.

"What kind of lessons? Why Essmee?"

Zeal looked out over the horizon and the cloudless sky. He let the ship's motion help him sort his thoughts. "When I was linked in Marhdah last night, Essmee told me it would be easy for another to use the connection to attack or seize control of my mind. She has offered to teach me how to protect myself."

"You don't think Ice or Deena would do such a thing? Why didn't Ice teach you?" Tulip seemed suddenly concerned.

"No, I trust them. And I don't know why Ice didn't say anything. I haven't asked him yet." Zeal was certain there was no nefarious plot to worry about.

"Maybe it is just a problem you have. Problems do seem to seek you out," Tulip teased.

"Kit told me her mother has already trained her to protect her mind. I am glad she is teaching me, as well." He thought a moment. "What do you mean problems seek me out?"

Tulip grunted. "Maybe adventure would be a better word to use. Now, explain to me what it is you are learning."

"Essmee is teaching me to use my mind as a Shadow Cat would. I'm learning how to fight with my mind, as well. She said my mind should have claws and teeth and shadows to hide in. For now, I create a chamber inside my head that I allow people to visit. Then, the rest of my mind is hidden where they can't find it." Zeal thought it wouldn't be a bad idea to learn how to think as a Shadow Cat—it might help him to better understand and get along with Kit.

Tulip sat quietly thinking for several moments. "You should build a fortress inside your head, instead. You never know—you might need a building, such as the Temple, big enough to guard other minds and provide them a place to rest and heal."

"That's a good idea. Mother Essmee did say I needed to be able to protect Kit with my thoughts. Why not include more? Although I am not sure I could stand to have it get too crowded in here." He tapped his head with a finger.

"Good. I want my own room." Tulip grinned.

"You get a whole house," Zeal teased with a laugh.

* * *

Zeal awoke inside a dream. He was in the mausoleum of the Temple of the Ladies of Life, having a conversation with Iris. Her marble form glowed softly. She stood in front of him with the stone babe and kitten curled together, asleep at her feet. Gradually, he became aware of a pounding on the mausoleum's door. Master Obin, the spirit guardian of the door, was nowhere to be seen. The hammering, he realized, had been present for a while and was gradually getting louder.

The flames in their sconces suddenly grew to the size of torches, hissing as they filled the area with light and erased all shadows. The writing on the crypt seals, which bore the names of the guardian spirits, glowed with the reflected light.

Well done, little one, Iris said, using Essmee's voice. *Your protections hold strong even in your deepest sleep.*

I want to ask Master Ice why he never mentioned there could be danger in the use of Marhdah. But I am afraid, if I do, he may become angry with me, Zeal admitted.

Essmee answered with a rumble of light laughter. *Who do you think taught Ice? Rest. We are done for now.*

Night, Mother Essmee.

Goodbye, Mother, Kit added.

He was now aware that Kit had observed his lesson. As he drifted off into sleep, he pondered Essmee's revelation regarding having taught Ice.

* * *

A quarter-moon's passage found the *White Swan* tacking up the River Kuan, a broad, deep watercourse that flowed slowly to the sea. Captain Baylor navigated upstream during the day and set an anchor at night. There had been no further sightings of marauders.

Zeal's lessons with Essmee had advanced to the point where he was able to defend against her attacks. Although he was getting better at trying to think as a Shadow Cat, she easily evaded the mental traps he set to catch her. However, that morn, she had grudgingly admitted to him that his traps were getting better. Together, he and Kit learned to safeguard each other, as well as themselves.

A full moon shone in a cloudless night, reflecting off the mirrored waters of the Kuan. Bats flew along the shore, hunting insects. A fish jumped out of the water and caught a bug crawling on the surface, its body making a loud splash with its reentry.

There was cause for celebration this eve. Zeal stood on deck between Tulip and Mirada, Kit draped across his shoulders. The ship's crew had gathered around them, and in front of them all stood Captain Baylor, Master Ice, and Lady Deena.

Ice and Deena were holding hands, reciting the simple words of their joining as life mates. "From this moment on, our lives travel together as one. We promise to sustain, strengthen, champion, and love each other during our journey."

The captain asked, "Do all of you gathered here bear witness?"

Zeal shouted along with the observers, "We bear witness!"

Captain Baylor bowed. "May the stars guide you and the ever-changing moon be a reminder that the challenges you face can be overcome together."

Zeal blushed at the kiss Deena and Ice gave each other after receiving the captain's blessing. That evening, Ice moved into Deena's cabin, leaving Zeal and Kit alone in theirs.

At midday two suns later, the ship tied off at a dock on the south bank of the river. Zeal, who was standing at the rail next to Ice, counted the fifteen men who emptied out of a barracks next to three large warehouses and approached the ship. One of the warehouses had a stable attached.

"Welcome back, Captain Baylor and crew. We are happy the *Swan* had a safe journey," shouted the lead man as they neared the dropped gangplank. "Permission to come aboard!"

"Permission granted!" Master Parish yelled. He met the leader, who came on deck alone, and took him to the captain waiting at the ship's wheel.

"Master Ice, is this Havensharth?" Zeal asked. "I thought it would be bigger."

"Don't look so disappointed. We're haven't arrived at Havensharth. We've come to Mica's Landing, which is maintained by Havensharth." Ice watched the men milling patiently on the dock.

Zeal asked, "Who are all these men?"

"They are workers from Havensharth who are paid to meet incoming vessels, help unload incoming cargo, and load that which is outgoing. They transport the incoming freight to Havensharth. The majority of the cargo unloaded is put in the warehouses on shore." Ice indicated the three large buildings at a short distance from the dock. Several wagons were lined up in front of the farthest building. "The remainder will be placed on those wagons and transported along with us to Havensharth."

Zeal watched the leader return to the waiting figures on the dock. He didn't hear what was said, but the men filed on board and began to assist the ship's crew in unloading the hold. "Do they live here all the time?"

Ice shook his head. "They are here three moons and then replaced. Many are students who work here to help pay for their instruction."

"How long will it take to get to Havensharth from here?"

"If we were to leave at dawn, we would arrive at Havensharth in time for the evening meal." Ice turned from the rail. "Let's finish packing and meet up with the ladies. We need to thank Captain Baylor tonight at the evening meal for his care and safe transport."

* * *

To Zeal, supper was a somber affair. Although he was happy the voyage had ended, he was sad to soon be leaving the *White Swan* and her crew. He sat at the table and quietly picked at his meal. Not so Kit, who was contentedly licking her paws after consuming a large scraud for her final dinner aboard the ship.

He glanced at Tulip, who seemed subdued as well. He was about to lean over and ask her how she was when Captain Baylor stood and tapped his glass with a knife. The tinkling sound made by the glass rang out loudly, and the occupants of the captain's chamber quieted.

"I want to take the opportunity to thank you again for your assistance in the protection of the *Swan* during her brief encounter with marauders." After saluting Master Ice and Ladies Mirada and Deena, he continued. "You shall have free passage on the *Swan* in the future, as long as I am her captain." Baylor turned to his first mate. "Master Parish, what was the condition of the cargo upon its removal from the *Swan*."

"Captain, I wish to report that the condition of the cargo was exemplary. There was no spoilage noted or evidence of damage due to infestation. I have been informed by the *Swan's* cook and crew that rats or other vermin haven't been seen aboard ship since we stopped at Malaan."

"What do you estimate the difference in profit this represents for the ship and crew, Master Parish?"

"I believe it represents a fifteen percent increase in profit for the ship and crew," Parish continued in a sober tone, speaking in his capacity as first mate.

"Did you put forth my proposal to the men?" Captain Baylor maintained a stern visage as he weighed the first mate's responses.

"Yes, Captain. I did." Parish continued to stare straight ahead.

Zeal wondered where this conversation was going. Tulip shrugged when he looked her way.

"And what did the crew decide?" Baylor asked.

"It was decided that a share of the difference in profit should be given to all those who helped make this possible."

"All those, you say, Master Parish?" Baylor demanded.

Parish gave a brief nod but made no eye contact. "Yes, Captain. That is the answer I received and was asked to pass back to you from the men, sir."

Captain Baylor retrieved a small scroll from an inside pocket of his waistcoat. "I am aware that due to Kit ridding the *Swan* of her vermin, our final financial situation was improved. Therefore, the crew and I will present Kit with a share of the profits."

Baylor held up a hand, indicating he wanted continued silence.

"I would like to note that Tulip and Zeal, during the voyage, have worked side by side with the crew in the rigging. I have decided that Tulip and Zeal will also receive a share. This document is a letter transferring said shares for the three of them to accounts in the Havensharth branch of the Bank of Muldara." Baylor handed the scroll to Mirada. "Lady Mirada, I formally present this to you to hold for them, as you are a designated representative of Havensharth currently aboard the *White Swan*."

Zeal leaned over and asked Tulip, "What does this mean?"

Tulip answered with a wide smile, "It means we got paid!"

CHAPTER EIGHT

THE LEAVES OF TALLEN'S mother's ironwood tree fluttered in the breeze. The sunlight reflecting on their surfaces caused the leaves to appear to change colors—dark green to light green back to dark and again to light, in random patterns. Her tree grew next to the cabin, that backed into the hillside, built by Tallen's father.

Tallen leaned against the trunk, closed his eyes, and listened to his father playing the pipes. The music echoed through the meadow while his mother, who was weaving a basket from rushes, hummed in accompaniment.

Lulled by the music and the warm sun, Tallen drifted in and out of sleep. The pipe's song reached him as if from a distance. When it ceased, it was replaced by his parent's soft voices, but Tallen continued to fade, the meaning of his parent's discussion lost to him.

"Adder, men are watching us from the wood," Greenleaf said, keeping her eyes lowered as she continued to braid the rushes.

Her life mate, Adder, set his pipes down and picked up the wooden pitcher. He spoke a touch louder than necessary, saying "This is empty. I'm going to refill it. Why don't you take Tallen inside out of the sun? We don't want him to overheat." He leaned forward to kiss his wife and whispered, "I'm getting my bow. Where are they?"

Greenleaf put aside the basket. "To my right. There are five of them." She unhurriedly woke Tallen and helped him to his feet.

"What is it, ma?" His grumbled complaint was interrupted by an unfamiliar voice shouting, "*Hold*! Don't move!" Groggy, he looked up as a man, armed with a sword, stepped out of the trees. Dressed in brown leather pants and jerkin, he had unkempt hair and beard.

"Who...?" Tallen asked, but neither of his parents offered an answer.

Adder shoved Greenleaf toward the cabin. "Go!" He pulled his knife from the sheath on his belt.

Greenleaf grasped Tallen by the hand, as they ran to the cabin she huffed two words into Tallen's ear: "Be brave."

Tallen heard swooshing noises and thudding impacts, immediately followed by his father's cry. He looked past his mother and saw his father, impaled by arrows, fall groundward. "They shot Pa." His voice sounded weak in his ears. Four men wielding bows moved out of the trees to join the lone swordsman.

His mother looked over her shoulder and screamed, "*Adder!*" She pulled Tallen to a stop. "I want you to hide." She kissed his forehead. "Your father and I will always love you."

Tallen, totally engrossed in what was happening, remained rooted in place. His mother jerked the hatchet from the chopping block and ran to his father's side, where she took a stand, placing herself between him and the men moving toward them.

As Greenleaf swept her empty hand outward, the plants and grasses twined around the men's legs and feet. Two of the bowmen tripped and fell to their knees, their hands and arms grasped by the rippling greenery. They shouted in fear.

Tallen was aware that his mother had an affinity with all that grew from the soil, but in his twelve seasons, he'd never seen her command the vegetation. Although he'd been told to run, he couldn't take his eyes away from the scene in front of him.

"Shoot her!" The swordsman used his weapon to cut himself free of the strands holding him then ran forward and almost fell when a thick vine wrapped around a leg to stop him.

One of the bowmen responded to the order and fired. His hurried shot flew over Greenleaf's shoulder and struck her tree.

Greenleaf keened, "Come to my aid." Her skin began to take on the semblance of bark.

Tallen heard a strange rustling followed by the wrenching and cracking of wood. Three trees at the edge of the clearing uprooted and begin to creep toward his family's attackers.

The second bowman fired. The arrowhead entered the front of Greenleaf's neck as her skin was making its change and protruded through her spine. She collapsed next to Adder. The plants and trees ceased to move.

Unable to find words, Tallen ran toward his parents. Before he could reach them, his mother's ironwood tree bent over Greenleaf. Its branches reached down, picked up her and his father, and lifted them from the ground. Tallen slowed and walked to where his parents had once lain. He stood with silent tears running down his face and watched his mother and father disappear, pulled into the trunk.

Tallen reached down, picked up the hatchet, and turned to the approaching brigands. He lunged forward and swung at the swordsman with all his strength. The swordsman leaned away at the last moment and then hit Tallen on the side of the head with the flat of his blade, stunning him. Tallen dropped to his knees.

As he tried to get up, he heard the man tell his companions, "Cut down the tree."

Tallen received a second blow to the head and lost consciousness.

* * *

The sun slowly melted away the morning fog. The sound of the draft horse's shod hooves became more distinct, no longer muffled by the disappearing mist. Zeal had never been in a wooded area such as this before and was only able to see a short distance into the trees that bordered the road. It had taken two days to load the thirteen wagons that carried freight purchased for the Enclaves at Havensharth. The remainder of the *White Swan's* cargo had been stored in the warehouses at Mica's Landing.

Zeal sat up front with the driver in the foremost wagon. He was excited to be on the final leg of his journey. Tulip rode in the bed behind him, with Kit curled sleeping, her head in Tulip's lap.

Kit had grown on the voyage and was three times the size she had been when he first met her. Zeal estimated she now weighed close to two stone. From nose to base of her tail, she was six hands in length. Her tail was three hands long, itself. The bond they shared had deepened and evolved. He awakened each morning joyful because Kit had proclaimed him… *Mine!*

In the wagon trailing Zeal's, Mirada sat beside the driver of the second wagon. In the third wagon, Ice held the horse's reins. Sitting next to him, in animated conversation, her leg touching his, was Deena. When she leaned over and kissed Ice on the cheek, a rare smile appeared on his mentor's face.

Out of the corner of his eye, Zeal saw Kit stir. Her ears were twitching and her vibrissae moving. Something had disturbed her in her sleep. He used his Trade training and surveyed his surrounds while maintaining a disinterested appearance. Birdsong had ceased. The forest had become too quiet, as if holding its breath, waiting for something to happen.

The sharp crack of wood splitting and breaking disrupted the tranquil morn. The sound originated from ahead of the lead wagon. Zeal saw a red asdic tree fall across the road and block their passage.

The driver pulled back on the reins and applied his foot to the wagon's brake. Friction between the brake pad and wheel produced a loud screech, as the wagon shuddered to a stop. The twelve wagons behind them came to a sudden, clamorous halt.

Zeal shaded his eyes from the sun and stood to get a better look at the road ahead. Just as the driver leaned forward to wrap the reins on the brake pole, an arrow flew past him and struck Zeal under the left arm. The force of it thrust Zeal off his feet, propelling him from the wagon. He fell to the ground and into darkness.

Kit awakened with a loud howl, suddenly realizing that the minds she'd sensed while sleeping were *hunting* them. They represented a form of danger she hadn't recognized. Experiencing Zeal's pain, along with his abrupt absence from her mind, had shocked her awake. With her thoughts, she reached through shadow to the one she knew could help. **MOTHER!**

* * *

Feneas jerked his head up, his whole being focused on Essmee. Essmee rose to her feet then jumped, disappearing into the shadow in the room's corner. Call me if you need me, he said through thought.

He wondered what had occurred to make Kit cry for her mother through their mind link. Something must be terribly wrong for the young Shadow Cat to broadcast so loudly that he, too, heard her.

* * *

Essmee used the bit of shadow she kept attached to Kit to guide her to her cub's location. Travel through shadow was akin to passing through a door, leaving one chamber and entering the next. During her journey, Essmee's form flowed, changing shape and size as needed. She chose to arrive in a patch of shadow cast by a large tree, where she hid, scanning the thoughts of the minds nearby while scrutinizing the area.

Kit was under a wheeled hut, standing guard over Zeal, who lay on the ground, unmoving. Her cub was attempting to hide them by gathering patches of gloom around them. The girl, Tulip, knelt beside Kit, holding a metal claw. Essmee sensed that, although the girl was excited and ready to fight, she was concerned about Zeal.

Essmee separated the minds in disorder from those who had created it and frightened Kit. The convoy was in disarray: the drivers had stopped their wagons and were looking for the source of danger. She watched Ice approach the little ones under the wagon while, at the same moment, perceived a psyche that was targeting him with a branch-thrower.

She sought a patch of darkness alongside her prey and shifted her position. Then she extended her muzzle out of the shadow, bit swiftly through soft flesh, and crushed the spine of her quarry. Hot, salty blood flowed into her mouth. Its taste incited her to give her hunting cry, alerting nearby prey to their danger.

She heard an answering cry from Kit as the body of the archer fell out of the tree and lay crumpled on the ground.

Stay there, little one. This is not your hunt. Protect your Zeal, Essmee sent to her cub.

Yes, Mother, but I can't join with him! Kit sounded frantic.

Stop trying to beat your way into his mind. Let him know you are there, and he will reach for you as you reach for him, Essmee explained a bit tersely.

As she looked over at her cub, she knew, even though Kit could not see her, that the cub knew her location. She sent her babe supportive thoughts and noted by Ice's movements that he was casting a protective conjure to create an invisible barrier around him and the little ones. Then he reached a hand toward Zeal. Kit's eyes widened as her lips pulled back in a snarl, her fur stood along her back, and her tail twitched. She hissed at Ice.

Ice is trying to help, little one. Let him. Then Essmee located patches of shade and darkness next to her intended targets and created a mental path to each person who'd desired to harm her cubs and their companions.

Swiftly, she reached out of shadow and slashed her second target, her claws crushing his throat. Arterial blood sprayed. For the third victim, she placed the image of what he feared most into his thoughts and then purposefully made noises for him to hear. As he turned toward her, Essmee allowed him to see her visage—mouth wide-open, fangs bared. His scream of terror was cut short when her bite removed his face.

Her hunt continued. In a matter of moments, she ended the lives of five more assailants. She permitted each to cry out, and their horrified screams added to the confusion, affecting attacker and attacked alike. Stepping back into the dimness, she located her last kill: the one who led the pack she hunted.

The leader stood hiding in the wood, his sword drawn and his back to a tree. He'd heard each of his men cry out and then fall silent, one after another. A corpse lay at his feet, its head turned unnaturally, with its throat and lower jaw torn away. The convoy, which he could see through the trees, was in a state of upheaval. But his men's deaths were not attributable to the convoy's members. So to whom?

Essmee fed his mind thoughts of fear, which gave him a strong urge to run back to the safety of his camp. When he resisted the impulse, she swept her claws out of the shadow. He gasped from the searing pain across his back. His weapon fell to the ground as she intensified his fear, and he began to run away.

Essmee let the leader leave. One must always have a means to find the lair: this one would show her the way. She had taken away his long claw and marked him with her own. He would seek a secure haven, but it would not remain safe for long.

Remaining hidden, Essmee took a moment to send reassurance to Kit before following her prey.

* * *

Ice saw Kit visibly relax with every scream that echoed from the trees around them.

Mother is here. She is dealing with the bad ones, she informed him and Tulip.

"I know! Now, let me examine Zeal!" As he eased the boy toward him, Mirada and Deena arrived and knelt on either side. Tulip remained on guard, watching the trees with her weapon in hand.

"How bad is it?" Mirada asked, her sword also held at ready. Her voice was full of concern.

Ice extended the barrier he'd conjured to include her and Deena. "Having a look now. Kit wouldn't let me near him at first, but now she seems to be calming." He reached into his left sleeve, removed a short blade, and used it to cut an opening in Zeal's shirt where the arrow had penetrated.

Tulip quietly asked, "Where is the blood?" Zeal's appearance was frightening: he was pale and having difficulty breathing, his face scrunched tight with pain.

Ice felt the arrow come away in his hand. The shaft was broken yet still partially attached to the arrowhead. Under his shirt, Zeal was wearing a second garment.

"Is he wearing what I think he is?" Deena asked, a touch of surprise in her voice.

"He has on his workshirt, and I have on mine. We were told to wear them during our travel," Tulip said, peering out again at the woods where the arrow had come from.

Ice put his blade away and tugged at Zeal's workshirt, which was tucked tight in his pants. "I was unaware the two of you had on Anrotean Spider Silk!" As he helped Deena remove the pants, they discovered the garment extended to just above the boy's knees and tied around each leg. After loosening the ties, they were able to lift the workshirt and reveal Zeal's injury.

"Fortunately, the silk stopped the arrow from penetrating, but the force of the arrow has been spread out over this portion of his chest." Ice inspected an area of bruising about the size of his hand, gently probing it with his fingers. "As I suspected, Zeal has two broken ribs."

"I have *effusions* in my pack," Deena said, standing. "I'll go get them." She looked carefully around and then hurried away.

"I'll go with her," Mirada said to Ice. "You stay here."

"Are you free to tell me where you and Zeal acquired your workshirts?" Ice asked Tulip gently.

Tulip shook her head, remaining silent as she continued to stare into the trees.

Ice nodded, respecting her answer. "I want you both to continue wearing them. It saved Zeal's life. The fall from the wagon appears to have caused no additional harm to him."

"Why is it suddenly so quiet?" Tulip asked with a quivering voice. "And who is it that attacked us?" Although relieved by Zeal's prognosis, her body remained tense.

Mother is stalking the last bad one, Kit said in response.

Tulip passed this information on to Ice.

"She told me, as well. And I already knew—I've heard Essmee hunt before. She let one attacker live and is tracking him to his camp. He'll be dead soon enough. Shadow Cats do not allow a threat to survive."

The members of the convoy began to call to one another, seeking reassurance that all were well. The driver of Tulip's wagon jumped down next to them.

"The brigands have stopped their attack. Is the lad dead?" The driver, barely having entered adulthood, appeared shaken.

"He will live—the arrow only glanced him. It must have been deflected by a branch. Look, you can see it was broken before it hit him. The arrowhead is barely attacked to the shaft." Ice held the arrow up for the driver's inspection.

"Here's the *effusion*." Deena knelt next to Ice, opened the small vial, and handed it to him.

Ice lifted Zeal's head and shoulders with one arm. Deena tilted Zeal's head back while Ice used the bottle to part Zeal's lips and dribble a small portion of the liquid into his mouth. He waited for Zeal to swallow before slowly feeding him the rest of the vial's contents.

The *effusion's* effect was immediate. Zeal's breathing eased. The bruising and mottling faded. As they watched, the skin covering his broken ribs rippled as the bones underneath shifted and knitted into place. Color returned to Zeal's face, which relaxed, and his rest became peaceful.

* * *

Zeal stirred. Although the pain in his chest was gone, he still had a relentless pounding in his head. Then it dawned on him: Kit was frantically trying to communicate through his mental shield.

He opened his mind to her. *I am here Kit, why are you upset?*

You were struck by a branch, and I couldn't reach you.

His head stopped hurting with their joining. *The shielding that Mother Essmee taught me must have triggered. Why would a tree hurt me?*

Zeal felt confused.

No. Some of your kind attacked. Mother is taking care of them.

I don't remember any of it, but I'm better now.

Zeal sensed relief and love in Kit's thoughts. He sent her back his own.

You need to awaken. Open your eyes, and let everyone know you are well.

I didn't realize I wasn't awake. Zeal did as he was told and saw Ice staring intently at his face. Standing next to Ice were Deena and Mirada, who both eyed him with concern.

"Why is everyone staring at me?" Zeal's voice was raspy.

"You were struck by an arrow and injured," Deena answered. "Ice gave you an *effusion* to heal you. Are you experiencing pain?"

Zeal reached out and took her hand in his. He was not prepared for how distressed Deena appeared or how concerned she was about him. "I'm all right, just tired and hungry."

"That's not unexpected. After a healing, the body needs to rest and replenish itself." As Deena gently squeezed his hand, a tear ran down her cheek that she wiped away with her free palm.

"Why would someone shoot me?" He studied the adults' faces.

"I think the arrow was meant for the driver. Let's get you into the wagon." Ice helped Zeal clamber up.

Tulip retrieved the arrow and placed it in Zeal's free hand. He had yet to let go of Deena's. "You should keep it, Mouse. You never know when it might come in handy."

Ice instructed the driver, "It is safe to move about. The attack is over. Tell the other drivers to look in the trees on both sides of the road. You'll find the bodies of our attackers."

"I will accompany them, in case there are more attackers." Mirada reached over and patted Zeal's shoulder. "I am glad you weren't hurt badly. Get some rest." She then moved away.

There are no prey near, Mirada. Mother punished them. I warn if others come.

"Thank you, Kit. And thank Essmee for me." Mirada continued walking.

* * *

Mirada gathered the drivers together. After informing them the danger had passed, she divided them into groups of three to search in the areas from which the screams had been heard. Then she took her group in the direction from which Zeal's arrow had come. An archer's body was discovered on the ground by one of the members of her party. His spine had been crushed at the base of the skull.

As the others looked around with apprehension, the man who found the corpse asked, "What happened here?"

"He was punished," Mirada replied. "Take the body back to the wagons, and then continue the search for others. Collect his bow and those arrows."

She looked up into the tree at the spot where he had perched for his attack. He'd had the sun rising behind him, leaving him in shadow, and his clothes had been dyed to blend with the forest. His back had been to the tree, yet he'd been killed from behind. Alarmed by what this implied, Mirada made a mental note to ask Ice about her discovery later.

Eight bodies were recovered. Each individual's death had been grisly: fear, shock, alarm, and, lastly, panic were frozen on the faces of each man. At the location of the last corpse, which was discovered by Mirada herself, a single set of footprints led away from the body and an abandoned sword. She wondered if whoever made the tracks was aware he, too, would soon be dead.

CHAPTER NINE

SHIFTING FROM ONE SHADOW to the next, Essmee remained undetected by her quarry. Periodically, she enhanced the fear felt by her prey, which drove him faster to seek the safety of his lair. His thoughts were full of five other faces, members of his pack waiting back at the lair. Essmee kept their features in her mind, too, and marked them each for death.

Mother, Zeal has awakened, and we are together again. There was relief in Kit's tone.

I see him with you and will return when I am done. Essmee sent both cubs her love.

As the hunted came in sight of his destination, she extended her right forepaw and tripped him, bringing his flight to an end. She then pounced out of the shade, drove both front paws down on his back, and forced the air out of his lungs. She had no intention of giving him an opportunity to yell a warning to his men. The kill was finished with a crushing bite.

Waiting quietly, she checked to determine if anyone had noticed her attack. Fortunately, silence dominated the woods around her.

She sampled the thoughts of the occupants of the lair and located the five prey she'd marked for death. She designated several others as not yet targets; she would reconsider each of them, however, when her hunt was over.

Essmee chose not to alert the quarry to her presence. The thoughts of a not-prey caught her attention as she finished her last kill. She used a shadow to step closer and discovered a boy child sitting in the center of a cloth travel chamber, his hands and feet tied. He had his eyes closed, but he wasn't sleeping. He was listening.

She looked into him, appraised his mind, and saw a hunter with the potential to greatly benefit a Pride. As Essmee stepped out of the shadow behind him, she inhaled his scent and exhaled a puff of her breath onto the bare skin of his neck.

The boy momentarily froze then very slowly shifted his body and turned his head. His eyes widened at the sight of her bloody muzzle less than a hand's breath from his face.

She gave him a nod, followed by her smelling a familiar scent as a dark stain bloomed on the front of his pants. *One will soon come to free you.* She backed away and stepped into shadow.

* * *

Tulip had the sword she'd obtained from the Temple mausoleum slung so she could reach over her shoulder, grasp the pommel, and draw the weapon smoothly. She sat peering out of the wagon with a cocked crossbow in hand, supplied by Mirada.

Zeal lay next to her, his chest slowly rising and falling. He had been sleeping for the past mark, while Kit stood guard next to him. The Shadow Cat refused to leave his side, even though Ice had stated the danger to the caravan had been eliminated. Mirada had cautioned Tulip and Kit to remain alert, nonetheless.

Kit watched the wagon drivers bring the bodies of the brigands into camp and search them. Each individual's possessions were placed in a pile next to their corpse. It took two teams of horses to pull the tree blocking the road off to one side.

One called Deena comes, Kit notified Tulip.

As she followed Deena's approach to the wagon, Tulip hoped that she had information regarding Ice and Mirada, who were tracking the brigand who had fled during the attack.

Deena motioned toward Zeal. "How is he?" She spoke softly, so her words didn't travel.

"Sleeping. Kit no longer seems worried about him." Tulip lowered her voice, too, to keep their conversation private.

"Kit will be formidable when she is grown. I see that now. Ice shared more information about Shadow Cats with me, but until you see what they are capable of, one can't fully appreciate their ferocity."

"What did Master Ice tell the drivers? I mean what explanation did he give for how the brigands died?" Tulip glanced toward the men attending to their tasks, oblivious to her and Deena.

"He told them I conjured an invisible familiar, who defended us from our attackers." Deena chortled softly. "I asked him why he didn't claim *he* was the one who had done the conjuring. He said it would be more impressive if I was the one who'd saved us all. So, there has been no mention of Shadow Cats being involved." She tucked the blanket covering Zeal over his shoulders. "This is the first we've had a few moments together. How was it for you both to live at the Temple?"

"Life was good. We were a family of sorts at the Temple, and also family as Trade apprentices. Of course, learning Zeal had the chance to be a Practitioner changed everything." Tulip suddenly felt gloomy.

"You are not happy?"

"Not that. It is just I miss everyone I left behind. I am excited about going to Havensharth and living with Lady Mirada. Don't know if Master Greyhook will want me, but Lady Mirada has assured me I will be welcome. I guess I am a little scared about things. Maybe people won't like me in Havensharth."

Deena gathered Tulip in her arms, shifting the sword's scabbard to hold her. "Greyhook will love you, as Mirada does. If he doesn't, you will always have a home with Ice and me."

"Lady Mirada loves me?" Tulip could not keep the surprise of Deena's revelation from showing. She knew other adults in her life had cared for her, both at the Temple and then later as an apprentice in the Trade. But love was never mentioned, not even by Iris.

"Yes, she does. You couldn't tell? Hopefully, you will one day love her in return. Love is precious and should always be cherished.

Fight for it and never take it for granted." She kissed Tulip on the top of her head.

"Is that why you came for Master Ice? Was it because of the love you have for him?" Tulip felt sheepish, asking such direct questions. Her body tensed.

"Yes, it is why I came for Ice. I very well couldn't leave it up to him to decide if our love would live or die. Remember that, if you ever fall in love. If it is real, it is worth fighting for," Deena confided.

Tulip's tension diminished. "Aren't you worried about Master Ice and Lady Mirada out there alone, hunting down our attackers?"

"Yes, I guess I am a little worried, but don't let Ice know I told you so." Deena gave her a little squeeze.

Tulip leaned back, fully accepting the comfort offered. "Thank you for caring about us. But why do you? Care I mean?"

"I will leave that for you to figure out. Come talk to me again when you do," was Deena's response.

* * *

Mirada and Ice followed the footprints left by the fleeing assailant. There was only one set of tracks. Mirada silently led the way with bow in hand and arrow nocked at the ready. Half a mark later, Ice took the lead, saying, "Essmee is over this way."

They found Essmee eating the carcass of a boar she had downed in the brigands' camp. She had drawn the carcass into a large clump of bushes where she could eat unseen.

"Thank you, Essmee, for your help." Ice bowed to the Shadow Cat. "The brigands had a well-planned ambush. It would have succeeded if not for your intervention. I gather you have already dealt with everyone here in the camp?"

Mirada could see by Ice's posture and the way he asked his question that he considered Essmee a mentor.

Essmee's answer included Mirada. *No one threatens my cubs. There are not-prey in the lair for you to deal with.*

"Not-prey?" Mirada was puzzled by the reference. She received the image of a person restrained.

"I think she means prisoners," Ice explained.

"It was nice of Essmee to stay and guard the camp."

Ice snorted. "She only stayed to eat and recover the resources she used. Moving through shadow uses the body's fuel reserves, similar to any other form of extreme exertion. One kill through shadow would not bother Essmee much. But she has moved in and out of shadow multiple times to complete her kills, compounding the energy she'd used. Essmee will leave to check on her cubs after she is finished eating. She would have already returned to them if they were still in danger."

Essmee eyed them but continued to consume her meal.

"No other Shadow Cat babe is with us besides Kit though, correct?" Mirada puzzled.

"Essmee considers Zeal her other cub," Ice explained. "I was thought of as cub at one time, but she now considers me capable of mostly taking care of myself."

Mirada could not quite keep from smiling. "You were her cub? I find that image laughable."

"Not *her* cub. I belonged to Master Feneas. In her mind, I was his apprentice cub. She considered it her job to help Master Feneas teach me what I needed to know to become an adult. Let's investigate Essmee's not-prey."

There is a cub. Take him with you, Essmee said, not elaborating any further.

Mirada and Ice found the camp in a meadow a short distance from where they'd met Essmee. Before entering, they studied the site to assess any danger, out of habit. A fire pit smoldered in its center. A large tent sat to the right of the pit. Twelve smaller tents were scattered around the clearing. The cook's wagon was closest to the fire. It also likely carried the brigand's gear.

On the left, outside of the camp, fourteen horses were picketed. Five men lay, unmoving, in and around the encampment. The body of a sixth, the leader, was in the brush just outside of camp.

As they crept closer, Mirada slung her bow across her back. Even though Ice and Essmee had assured her there was no danger, she drew her long sword with her right hand and held her long knife in the left. She nodded approval when Ice conjured some kind of defense and unsheathed his own short sword before they quietly entered the camp.

The first three tents were empty, their former occupants' gear strewn haphazardly inside. Ice threw back the flap on the front of the fourth tent, allowing Mirada to step in with her weapons held defensively. She saw a boy inside, someone around the age of twelve seasons, with his hands and feet bound. The stench permeating the air suggested he had been tied there for a while.

"Are you hurt?" she asked quietly, trying to masque her disgust at how he had been treated.

"No. Who are you?" he asked fearfully.

"I am Mirada, and my companion is called Ice. We are here to free you. The men who did this to you are all dead. How many others are being held captive?" Setting her sword down out of the boy's reach, Mirada stepped closer and cut him free with her knife.

"My name is Tallen. Did you kill them?" His eyes searched their faces.

"No. We didn't," Ice said. "A member of our party did, using a conjured spirit."

Tallen looked around anxiously as he rubbed his hands and feet to ease the blood flowing back into them. "Is the spirit still here? I think I saw it…"

"It might be—"

"Ice!" Mirada interrupted. "Stop teasing the boy! The spirit is gone." We'll get you cleaned up, but first, where are the other captives being held?"

"They should be in the leader's tent, the large one."

Mirada allowed Tallen to precede her as they left the tent. When he saw the body lying next to the wagon, his face twisted with anger and he ran straight to the dead man. Yelling hysterically, Tallen repeatedly kicked the corpse ending any attempts by Ice and Mirada to be stealthy.

Ice quickly lifted the boy off his feet and pulled him away. Tallen continued to kick at the body of the man even as Ice dragged him backwards "Stop. Stop!" Ice shouted in alarm. "What do you think you are doing?"

"That was the one who killed my ma and pa. *I* wanted to kill him." Tallen sobbed, his head thrashing. "I should have been the one, not some spirit!" Tears flowed down his cheeks and fell to the dry ground.

Mirada stepped over to Tallen and slapped his face, hoping to bring the hysterical child back to his senses. "He is dead, boy. Better so, not by your hand. Now control yourself. You will honor your parents by the life you choose to lead from this point forward. We are sorry for your loss. Now come with us." After looking around for potential danger, she headed toward the leader's tent.

Ice sat Tallen on his feet but waited for the boy to collect himself before releasing him. Tallen took one last look at the dusty corpse before turning away. He wiped his nose with his sleeve then cautiously followed Mirada. Ice walked quietly behind him

In the central tent, they discovered four women tied together. They were all initially fearful but quickly became overjoyed by their newfound freedom. Mirada organized them to help strike camp so they could soon leave and join the convoy to Havensharth

The brigand's valuables were placed in a lockbox Mirada found in the large tent. Ice had discovered the key on the leader's corpse. The two of them intended for the wealth to be divided amongst the captives, providing them a grubstake.

With Tallen's help, Ice collected Essmee's dead and tied them on the backs of the horses. Mirada and Tallen drove the wagon while Ice rode one of the unburdened mounts. "Let's get out of here and back to the others," Ice ordered.

They followed the trail the brigands had used to bring the wagon to their camp. It led them to the road and they continued toward Havensharth. The horses, both those bearing the bodies and those unmounted, had their leads strung to the rear of wagon. The freed captives rode the remaining horses.

It was early evening when the convoy was sighted. It had traveled a short distance from the location of the attack and had then stopped in a clearing off the road to wait for Ice and Mirada's return.

As they approached the encampment, a hidden voice hailed them. It came from the trees to the right of the road. "Driver of the wagon, stop and identify yourself."

"Can't a person accompanied by freed captives travel the road to Havensharth without being accosted?" Ice replied.

Mirada saw the cautious look on Tallen's face and patted his leg. "These are our people," she assured him. "We are safe."

"It's Master Ice and Lady Mirada!" the speaker hollered toward the encampment. "They have returned!"

The road filled with welcome as word spread of their arrival.

Ice slid from his horse when he spotted Deena approaching with Zeal and Tulip in tow. He stepped smartly to her, lifted her up, and held her as he stared into her eyes. Then he slowly brought her close, and their lips met in a kiss. The two of them were lost in their embrace, as if the world existed for them alone. When they separated, Deena pulled Zeal to them and included him in the reunion hug.

Mirada caught sight of Tulip, who was smiling broadly. Tulip nearly collided with her when Mirada jumped from the wagon. They clutched each other tightly.

Ice looked Zeal over. "Are you feeling better? Where is Kit?"

"Yes, I'm back to normal. Kit left for a bit with Mother Essmee. They will return soon. Who are these people, and where did you get all the stuff? Are those more dead bodies?"

Deena gave Zeal a kiss on the head. "Don't mind him—he woke up a mark ago and has been busy filling the rather large hole in his belly. Now, who are these people?"

Mirada released her hold on Tulip and answered, "They were captives of the brigands. They can obtain help, when we reach Havensharth, and be given aid to return to their homes. Ice and I plan to sell the brigands' possessions to cover their upkeep and any costs of reuniting them with their families."

"There is one who doesn't have a home to go to." Mirada jerked her head toward the child. "The boy in the wagon has lost his parents. His name is Tallen. Perhaps you two young people could befriend him?"

Ice gave Zeal and Tulip a meaningful look. "That was not an order. I'm not sure why the brigands took him after they killed his parents."

"What you going to do with the dead men?" Zeal asked shyly.

"Zeal!" Tulip admonished. "You should be more concerned about poor Tallen."

"Well, I am concerned about him, but I'm concerned about the dead, too." He glanced knowingly at Tulip.

She rolled her eyes skyward. "You are so strange sometimes."

"I have been trying to decide what to do about the bodies," Ice replied. "I originally thought to take them to Havensharth. But perhaps it would be better to dispose of them here, before we continue on. There are enough workers to bury the bodies in a single mound, but that would take time. Maybe it would be best to burn them."

Zeal acquired a pensive look when Ice mentioned fire.

"We should be able to control a fire," Ice continued, "and not set the forest aflame. But that will mean we would have to stay here for the night. If we tried to press on to Havensharth, the horses would be exhausted before we got there."

"What about food?" Deena enquired. "What will everyone eat, if we stay? We were supposed to dine at home tonight."

"We have supplies to feed everyone courtesy of our dead friends." Ice pointed to the cook wagon.

"Can we go meet Tallen now?" Tulip turned toward Deena and mouthed, "Men."

CHAPTER TEN

TALLEN WAITED in the wagon, unsure about the people in this encampment. As he jealously watched Master Ice's and Lady Mirada's reunion with people they cared for and who obviously cared for them, he fought back tears. He wouldn't experience the love of his ma and pa ever again, and there was no other family out there for him. What was to come of him?

Although he was feeling morose, he remained curious and observant. He figured the boy and girl were close to his age in seasons and assumed, by their actions, that the boy must be Master Ice's son and the girl Lady Mirada's daughter. Tallen couldn't hear their conversation but did note the occasional glance sent his way. Eventually, the boy and girl approached him, along with Master Ice.

"Zeal, Tulip, let me introduce you to Tallen. Tallen, this is Zeal and Tulip. I want the three of you to help Deena find a place for those who were rescued and set them up in our camp. There are tents in this wagon and sleeping gear." He pointed out Deena to Tallen.

One of the drivers came up to them and said, "Master Ice, Lady Mirada sent me. She told us you have a job for us?"

"I need you to gather wood, so we can burn the bodies of the brigands. Also, guards should be posted at all times. Mirada is in charge of defenses, so talk to her."

The driver nodded. "We have axes. There should be enough dead fall and standing snags to build a pyre." He bent down, broke off a few blades of grass, tossed them into the air, and watched how they fell. "Wind is blowing to the east. I would place the pyre so the smoke and smell don't blow back at us."

"Sounds good. I'll go with you to help determine the best location and unload the bodies from the horses." Ice turned back to the young ones. "Tallen knows where everything is in the wagon. He helped load it. I'll send back a couple of workers to assist you." Then he walked away with the driver.

Tallen was left alone with Zeal and Tulip. He looked them over, waiting for them to speak first. Tulip had a real sword slung over her shoulder, and Tallen wondered if she knew how to use it.

There was nothing unusual about Zeal, who broke the silence. "We heard you were captured by the brigands."

Tallen shook his head. "Don't want to talk about that." He gestured to the inside of the wagon. "Let me show you where the stuff is." Not ready to share his grief, he decided to ask his own questions later.

The mood in the camp was subdued. Although the former captives were happy to be freed, as was Tallen, they were unsure of their future. A meal was prepared from the stores packed in the brigands' wagon. Everyone but those acting as guards gathered at the pyre.

* * *

Tulip held Mirada's hand, comforted to be with her. Zeal was on her left while the boy, Tallen, was sandwiched between them. Ice had an arm around Deena's waist on the other side of Zeal. One of the workers splashed oil on the pyre. Tulip didn't recognize its scent.

Ice spoke aloud to everyone gathered around. "These men meant us harm and died for their actions. Some might think it a courtesy to dispose of their remains in such a respectable fashion, instead of allowing scavengers the privilege. I would have sided with the scavengers, but there are those," he said, glancing toward Deena and Mirada, "who have helped me realize that a dead foe should be treated in the same manner as I would wish to be treated."

Moving closer to the pyre, he made a subtle gesture with his right hand. "Cenda," he said, creating a ball of fire that he threw onto the oil-soaked wood. The pyre whooshed into flames which rapidly spread amongst the bodies. Ice returned to Deena's side.

Tulip studied the faces of those nearest her. Tallen stood silent, stoically suffering as a single tear ran down his face. When she took his hand in hers and squeezed it gently, he didn't pull away and stood a little straighter.

Zeal stared intensely at the burning bodies. She knew he could see and talk with the non-living and wondered if he saw more than flames, when he gazed into the blaze.

Deena's and Mirada's features were remarkably similar; Tulip could not interpret anything from their composed visages.

Zeal turned his head away slightly, as though gauging surreptitiously if anyone was watching him. He glanced her way and gave her a wink before focusing again on the pyre.

The wood began to burn in earnest, becoming a fiery blaze that rose skyward in a column of bright light. In short order, the remains were consumed and the heat dissipated as the flames died, leaving nothing but smokeless ash.

Zeal said softly, "Master Ice, the fire is gone. The trees are safe." He then headed to the wagon they had ridden in earlier in the day.

"He does have a way with fire and that was a nice touch," Deena said, sounding a bit concerned. "Is Zeal okay? Where is he going in such a rush?"

Ice gave her a brief hug. "He is fine. Essmee has returned Kit. I think Zeal wanted to go to her. Let's give them a few moments together before we see about them."

Tulip beamed inwardly. She appreciated the amazed expressions of most folks after observing the burning of the bodies; she suspected Zeal's hand in causing the remarkable event. Initially, there was total silence, then quiet whispering followed by subdued discussion.

As everyone slowly dispersed and returned to the encampment, Tallen lingered behind. He knelt, holding a hand over the ashes of the former blaze.

Tulip quietly moved to him. "Are you all right? Can I help in any way?"

Tallen felt the ashes. "There's no heat. They're not supposed to be cold."

"That is what you get when you have Practitioners around. You'll get used to it. Are you ready to get something to eat? Why don't you stay with us? I mean me, Zeal, and Kit."

"Who is Kit? Another kid? And what do you mean by Practitioners?" Tallen continued to examine the remains of the fire.

Tulip saw his look of awe at the cool ashes and then his curiosity. "Well, Kit is… Never mind. You just have to meet her. It isn't hard to believe you don't know what a Practitioner is. I haven't known about them long, myself."

Tallen rose. "Well, tell me what you know."

"Practitioners use the Arts to conjure—that's the way I understand it. Master Ice created the fire on the pyre by using the Arts. In Havensharth, where we are headed, there is a place to learn to become a Practitioner, if you have the ability."

"I'm not sure I understand, but since I am headed to Havensharth, I guess I'll find out." He became quiet again and stared off into the darkness. The cold ashes dropped from his hand.

Tulip was sorry he had to fight to control his emotions. When his eyes welled, she felt there was no shame in his showing grief. Even though she didn't know him well, she hoped she, Zeal, and Kit could help Tallen heal his pain. "Come with me back to our wagon, and we'll talk with Zeal. He is learning to become a Practitioner."

Waving to Mirada, she called out, "I'm taking Tallen to the wagon. We will be with Zeal and Kit."

Mirada raised a hand in acknowledgement. "I'll check on you after assigning watches for the evening. Don't wander outside the encampment."

Tulip led Tallen back to camp without asking any further questions, leaving the boy to his thoughts during the short walk. As they passed tents scattered amongst the wagons where workers and former prisoners shyly mingled, cooking smells drifted through the air.

There was a lantern lit inside the wagon as they entered. Zeal was talking silently to Kit, who sat in his lap, staring up at his face. Tulip lifted herself up into the wagon before turning to help Tallen. "Tallen, meet Kit."

Tallen gave a yelp and flung himself backward. Tulip grabbed him by the wrist to prevent him from toppling out of the wagon.

"Tallen, what is wrong? What is it?" She searched all over the wagon for the source of Tallen's destress.

As he regained his balance, he pointed at Kit. "It killed them all. Why is it so little now? It was bigger…"

Tulip saw fear and confusion on Tallen's face.

He means Mother, Kit clarified.

"That wasn't Kit," Zeal said. "Tulip, help him to sit down before he jumps out of the wagon like a scared bobit."

Tallen sat as far from Kit as he could and still be in the wagon.

"What should we tell him?" Tulip asked.

"Can you keep a secret?" Zeal inquired.

"Yeah, I can," Tallen confirmed. "What does this have to do with what is sitting in your lap?"

"Is he speaking the truth?" Zeal asked Kit.

Yes, Kit said to Zeal alone.

"Tulip, I think we should provide Tallen with a little information." He leaned forward. "That was not Kit you saw, but her mother. Kit called to her to help us after I was shot by an arrow."

"You don't look like you were wounded," Tallen stated, doubtful. "Must not have been hurt that bad."

"Zeal was given an *effusion* to heal him. He was lucky," Tulip said, a bit defensive. "It happened when the brigands first attacked our convoy."

"What's an *effusion*?" Tallen was becoming calmer and beginning to show a little more interest in what they had to say.

"I am not an alchemist, so I can't give you the details, but it is a concentrated healing potion. Picture taking the contents of a large tankard that has been reduced to a single swallow, yet still has the full effect of a whole tankard when one drinks it."

"Okay, what about Kit and her mother?" Tallen pressed.

Zeal gestured toward Kit and Tulip. "We don't know you very well, so don't expect to be told everything." After studying Tallen for a moment, he continued. "If we decide we can trust you, then you will get more answers. Don't say anything about Kit's mother to anyone else. Master Ice, Lady Deena, and Lady Mirada know, but not the other members of the convoy."

"Why do you and Tulip act as if Kit can understand us so well?"

Because I can.

Kit inwardly laughed at Tallen, who became visibly upset after receiving her reply.

CHAPTER ELEVEN

LISTINA SCRUTINIZED the faces in the crowd that had gathered to welcome the convoy. The array of wagons and horses meandered its way through the trees that grew around the small lake in the central commons. Even though the trees were ancient and not to be harvested, she felt they were more of an annoyance, instead of a benefit. She would have had them removed long ago, if it were up to her.

Gawkers lined both sides of the road. Her nose informed her that a few of them could use a bath. Anyone who got too close received a stern look and, if that didn't work, terse words along with a sharp elbow. This kept an adequate area open around her, allowing her a clear view of the wagons as they passed through the market and came to a stop in front of the Repository. She figured folks ought to respect another's personal space, especially hers.

Listina didn't like other people much. She tolerated the ones she employed to fulfill her needs, but that didn't mean she had to like them. Of course, you had to make a select few feel special; her father had taught her that.

And then there were the Masters. So far, she'd managed to outwardly show them respect. She looked forward to earning the rank of Master. On that morn, she planned to let her so-called superiors know how she really felt about them.

As far as her fellow apprentices were concerned, she allowed them to help her but usually had a good excuse for being unable to offer them aid. After all, they were also beneath her.

She recognized Master Ice: he was assisting Lady Deena from the lead wagon. Listina wondered when the two had found the opportunity to reunite. She'd had a good laugh over their falling out. They were both so full of themselves.

But what was this? They had a boy with them who carried a large cat across his shoulders.

Listina disliked animals more than she did people. She allowed herself to fantasize for a few moments about a heartbroken boy crying over a dead cat. That would wipe the silly grin off his face.

Strange—after she had that thought, the cat turned its head in her direction. Listina shifted, positioning herself behind a tall senior apprentice wearing a red cloak to make it harder for the animal to spot her. She made a mental note to learn more about the pair later.

* * *

Tulip stood next to Mirada by their wagon. She was about to ask why they were waiting when Mirada's eyes narrowed. A man dressed in gray leathers with his left wrist ending in a polished hook was staring at Mirada from the crowd. He tipped a gray cap sporting a long feather, bowed, and then advanced toward them.

When he stood directly in front of Mirada, their eyes locked. Tulip felt sucked into the private pocket around them as they ignored the bustle and upheaval, so intent were they on each other.

"Hello, Grey." Mirada's voice was husky with emotion.

"Hello, Wolf. I've missed you. Let's go home. Ice can see to all of this." Greyhook waved his hand in the direction of the convoy.

"I have something to tell you first." Her brow rose.

"You do?" His face tightened.

Tulip thought from his posture he was perhaps preparing to defend himself, as though expecting Mirada to say something he would find painful.

"Put away such thoughts. My love for you has not changed during our time apart." Mirada took his hand in hers. "I want to introduce to you to the new member of our family. This is Tulip. I've invited her to live with us." She reached over and drew Tulip close.

Greyhook stared at Tulip for a moment before speaking. "Then I also welcome you. You must tell me all about yourself. I look forward to hearing the tale the two of you have to share." Turning to Mirada, he continued, "Now can we all go home?"

Tulip studied Greyhook's features. His face was open and honest, and his welcome was sincere. But she was not yet comfortable with this man who so easily accepted her. Mirada trusted him, so, for Mirada's sake, Tulip would give him the opportunity to prove himself.

"Yes, we can go home now." Mirada reached into the wagon for her crossbow. "Tulip, grab what you need. The rest will be delivered to us."

She quickly retrieved her pack and weapons from the wagon. Looking over her shoulder as they walked away, she waved to Zeal, who nodded, giving her the Trade sign for "We journey together." Then he pointed to Kit.

Tulip understood: Kit would be able to locate her in this new place. Even though they were physically separating, they would not be apart.

* * *

Zeal carried Kit draped around his neck. He loved the soft, warm feel of her fur on his bare skin. They studied the light-gray two-story dwelling that was to be their home in Havensharth. He'd been informed by Ice that the cottage was owned by Deena. It was not only her residence but also her place of business.

The grounds were well-kempt. He thought it strange the building had no windows on the lower level. A stone walkway led them to the entry where, surprisingly, the door had no lock. Zeal wondered if the people in Havensharth lacked the need to protect their possessions.

"Zeal, place your hand on the lintel." Deena reached over and took Kit from his shoulders.

Ice had to lift Zeal up to reach the spot Deena indicated.

She covered Zeal's hand with a palm, gestured with the other, and said, "Novi, leber adtis lecit… Accepted, unrestricted access granted." She nuzzled Kit. "Now let's do you."

Ice set Zeal on his feet and lifted Kit, who placed a forepaw on the lintel. Deena repeated the process with her palm covering Kit's paw.

Zeal thought the whole thing must look awfully silly to anyone watching. He glanced around but saw no one was paying them any mind. "What was that all about?"

"I had to let the Wards know that you live here now," Deena explained.

"You didn't do Master Ice. Are you going to allow him inside?" he asked playfully.

Deena smiled. "Ice has already been provided the privilege."

Must include Tulip, Kit mindspoke to Zeal, Ice, and Deena.

"Yes, please. If it wouldn't be too much trouble," Zeal appealed to both adults.

"I promise I'll add Tulip at the first opportunity," Deena reassured him. "Shall we go inside?"

Ice opened the door, but, before either of them could enter, he swept Deena off her feet and carried her across the threshold.

Deena squealed with delight and wrapped her arms around Ice's neck.

Zeal put Kit across his shoulders and together they entered the cottage. Once back on her feet, Deena gave Ice a kiss.

Ice beamed. "While you give Kit and Zeal a tour, I'll go back and make sure our things are delivered." He closed the door behind him when he left.

"As you can see, I've converted the front part of the building into a shop where I sell imbued items." Deena pointed to the large, empty glass counter and shelves. "Come this way."

She showed him a curtain-covered door behind the counter that opened to a short passage leading to a living space and kitchen. A stairway, on the far side of the living space provided access to the upper level.

Zeal was amazed to discover that the ground floor did indeed have windows that allowed one to look out, even though they hadn't been apparent when they walked up. They were somehow disguised on the other side. There was also a back door off the kitchen. He wondered what other security measures this unassuming cottage had. Upstairs were two sleep chambers, a bath, water closet, and a den with a small collection of books.

"You and Kit can have this room." Deena held the door open to the chamber furthest from the stairs.

He had never had a room of his own, having always shared one with Fronc and Nester at the Temple of the Ladies of Life. This chamber was furnished with a large sleeper that would more than accommodate two, a wardrobe, small worktable, and chair. There was a storage bench below the shuttered window in the wall on the right.

Someone comes, Kit informed them both.

There was a knock on the entry door below. Zeal hadn't expected the sound to carry so well up the stairs. Perhaps it was a feature of this place, he thought to himself as they returned to the front entry.

Deena opened the door. It was one of the wagon drivers.

The man tipped his hat to her. "Master Ice said to knock and ask where we were to put things."

Deena took a stopper off a shelf and used it to hold the door open. "You can place everything in this room, in front of the shelves." She stepped back to allow the man to see where she meant.

Through the open portal, Zeal saw Ice directing the unloading of their travel chests, along with the crates of supplies and components Deena had purchased during her travels. They made short work of the job, and all too soon the shop area was filled.

As the men were leaving, Deena cleared her throat and said, "Ice."

He sighed and grumbled something too softly for Zeal to hear. Ice thanked the men for their effort and gave several coins to each of them.

Deena put an arm around Ice's waist as the men climbed into the wagon and left. "They deserved a little something extra. If it wasn't for you, Mirada, and Kit's mother, one or more of them might not be with us. Remember, they are working to pay their apprentice fees."

Ice reluctantly nodded but gave Deena a broad smile when she kissed him on the check.

She then removed the stopper and closed the door. "Let me take my trunk into a more secure location." Deena knelt in front of the chest and tapped it in several places with her finger.

Zeal was unprepared for the container to float into the air and follow behind her when she stood and walked away. He softly spoke to Kit alone, "I wonder how Deena did that."

One should ask if he wants to learn.

"Let's go see where Deena is going to put the trunk." He and Kit hurried to catch up with Ice, who was following behind Deena, the container floating along between the two of them.

Deena placed a palm on the left wall of the short passage between the shop and living space. "Resindo... Reveal"

A portion of the wall disappeared, revealing a flight of lit stairs that headed downward. At the bottom of the steps was a large chamber. Deena turned to Zeal and Kit. "This is my work and storage room. You are only to come to this level if either Ice or I give you a reason to do so. Of course, you have permission to come down when I am working, if you need me. Do I have your word on this?"

"Yes, Lady Deena." Zeal was sure he could think of several reasons to visit her and find out what she did down here.

I will not hunt here, Mother Deena.

A large worktable strewn with tools Zeal couldn't readily identify occupied the center of the room. Floor-to-ceiling cabinets lined the walls, their doors closed and their contents hidden. A desk and chair were to the right of the worktable.

The trunk lowered to the ground next to the worktable. "I'll unpack and bring down the rest of the components I purchased tomorrow. Why don't we all get comfortable? It is good to be home. I can't wait to crawl into my own sleeper."

They left the workspace and headed to the kitchen. As the

opening in the wall faded and returned to a solid surface, Zeal felt his stomach grumble. The smoked fish and griddlecake he'd had for a morning meal were long gone.

"Kit is hungry. Where can I get her something to eat?" Zeal asked, interrupting the peace and quiet that had finally settled in the cottage. He did not mention he was hungry, as well.

"Right. Kit is hungry." It was obvious Ice wasn't fooled by Zeal's attempt to hide the fact that he was also ready to eat.

"What are we going to do about Kit?" Deena asked Ice.

"I think the best thing to do is hide her in plain sight." Ice sat in one of the chairs at the dining table in the kitchen. It was not as large as the kitchen in the Temple of the Ladies of Life but still big enough for two cooks to move around.

"What are you saying? Why do we need to hide her?" Zeal was a bit confused.

Deena took a seat and indicated for Zeal to sit, as well.

Concern replaced confusion. He climbed into the chair next to Deena, moved Kit to his lap, and tried unsuccessfully to get comfortable.

Deena reached over and patted his hand. "What I mean, Zeal, is how do we best introduce Kit to Havensharth. A Shadow Cat is rare and unknown. She will not remain a cuddly cat but will grow. We don't want the people living and working here to be afraid of her," Deena continued to explain. "Kit will become a capable predator the same as Essmee. We recently experienced an impressive example of her work. When you combine that with her ability to conjure, there may be some who might try to take advantage of her capabilities. They would not care if they harmed you or her, attempting to do so."

Zeal sat silent, thinking about what Deena had said. He sent to Kit, *I would rather leave than have something bad happen to you.*

Kit mindspoke back, **You are mine. We hunt together, either here or elsewhere.**

Ice interrupted their silent discussion. "Deena, let me try. Zeal, to some, knowledge is power, to be used for one's own gain. That is why the information regarding Shadow Cats, compiled by Master

Feneas, has been kept private." Turning to Deena, he added, "I think we should take Kit to the Apprentice Hall. She can have her introduction there."

"I understand why there is a risk in people knowing all about Kit and me, but why there?" Zeal inquired.

"Because apprentices from all the enclaves eat their meals and spend time in the hall together. Any information we share while in the hall will spread throughout Havensharth. I suggest we tell the truth but limit what we share. We'll just say we don't know what kind of cat Kit is and leave out that she can conjure. Kit can demonstrate her intelligence and get a feel for folk. Of course, Greyhook and Namrin will need to be told everything."

"Who is Namrin?" Zeal stroked Kit's back, which comforted them both. Kit snuggled close and continued to listen.

Deena explained, "Namrin is the Master of Instruction at the Enclave of the Practitioners of the Arts. He is also in charge of the Repository. A decision needs to be made regarding whether Kit studies to conjure openly or in secret. Either way, Namrin needs to be informed and kept apprised. I think Kit should decide who else knows about her."

I do not wish to be feared, but Mother taught me it is best to limit what others know about us, Kit said to them all.

"Namrin will also need to be informed that you are a Phosfire," Ice told Zeal. "I will arrange a meeting with him and Greyhook sometime tomorrow. That way, we won't have to repeat ourselves and can answer all questions once."

Deena nodded, thoughtful. "Maybe together we can think of a way to resolve this issue."

"Can we go eat now?" Zeal asked.

CHAPTER TWELVE

TALLEN SLUMPED OVER his trencher and nibbled at his food. The food was good, but his appetite wasn't, and he had to force himself to eat.

He sat alone at a table in the Apprentice Hall, a large, red-roofed structure situated between the Commons and the Enclave of Combat. One of the workers from the caravan had taken him to a building called the Guest House, where he'd been shown a room with a sleeper, wardrobe, and small desk. Then he had been brought to the Hall to eat. He'd chosen an unoccupied table where he could be by himself yet observe everything and everyone.

The well-lit Hall was full of people of all ages. Family units were dining together. A group dressed in leathers had drawn tables together to accommodate their numbers; some of the members of their party wore red cloaks. The majority of the folk, who chatted noisily with one another, wore common attire. This was good; the clothes Tallen wore didn't make him stand out.

Zeal entered the hall with Kit across his shoulders, carrying a fat cushion. He was accompanied by Lady Deena and Master Ice. Tallen admitted, even though it was Kit's mother who'd rescued him, Kit made him nervous. But still he felt relieved to see someone he knew.

Kit looked his direction and, after a few heartbeats, so did Zeal, who then tugged on Master Ice's sleeve and pointed to Tallen.

Ice nodded, and Zeal guided the four of them to Tallen's table, where he plopped down, leaving a vacant chair between his own and Tallen's.

"Hey, Tallen, how is the food?" He put the cushion on the empty seat for Kit, where she could easily reach the tabletop. Master Ice and Lady Deena sat across the table from them.

"It's good," Tallen answered through a large mouthful. Suddenly, he had an appetite. "Where are Tulip and Lady Mirada?"

"I doubt we will see them. Greyhook, I am sure, has prepared a dinner for them both. He loves to cook and would consider Mirada's return a special occasion." Ice leaned toward Deena. "Why don't you and Zeal serve yourselves while I go have a talk with the cook regarding something for Kit?" He stood and headed for the double doors on the far side of the room. Zeal followed Deena to the serving area.

Tallen was amazed by the wide variety of food on the tables. The main meat course was some sort of roast beast with sauces on the side and large bowls of greens sautéed in a light oil. There were small dishes of salt and spice, to add seasonings as desired. Roasted tubers, lightly dusted with herbs, were next to small bowls of butter.

Deena handed Zeal a trencher and indicated he should select any food he wanted as they walked along the tables. She made sure he chose a sampling of vegetables along with his breads and meats. Tallen smiled at that.

Ice met up with Zeal and Deena as they were returning to their seats. He carried a platter of bite-sized cuts of uncooked meats that he placed in front of Kit. Occupants of the Hall began to peer in their direction.

Kit acted as if she were unaware of the eyes on her. She just waited, along with Zeal and Lady Deena, until Master Ice returned with his own trencher of food before beginning to eat. She daintily ate her food piece by piece, using a claw on her right forepaw to select each morsel.

For a moment, Tallen wondered if Kit was as uncomfortable as he'd been, when first sitting alone at the table. He didn't imagine she'd want to be the center of attention any more than he had, which led him to discover he had concerns about her. When a piece of meat rolled off her platter onto the table, he reached over and returned it to its place, whispering, "I guess we're both going to have to get used to Havensharth. Don't let these folks bother you."

They will soon accept us hunters amongst them, Kit noted as she continued to eat. *We'll make Havensharth our lair.*

Tallen thought about Kit's answer and realized she had the right idea. Maybe he wasn't alone after all. As the meal progressed, the surrounding diners grew bored with the novelty of her presence.

After emptying his plate, Zeal said to Tallen, "This reminds me of how we ate our meals in the Temple where I used to live. So, where are you staying?"

"I am with the other former prisoners in a place called the Guest House." He looked to Master Ice for confirmation.

Ice nodded. "Zeal, we can take you by the location when we're finished here, so you'll know where to find Tallen."

I can find him, Kit mindspoke to everyone at the table.

Deena laughed softly. "I'm sure you could."

"We need to show you where we stay," Zeal added, pointing his fork at Tallen.

"I was told I could work here in the Hall until a decision is made on what to do with me and the others who were rescued." Tallen lowered his head. Talking openly about his unknown future was disconcerting.

Deena set her fork on her plate. "Tallen, don't worry. You will be included in the discussion. No one is going to make you do something you wish not to. Ice and I can assure you of that. If you have any difficulties, please come to us."

He felt better, hearing he still had a measure of control over his life, but he still wasn't happy. Tallen noticed Lady Deena studying him with eyes full of caring.

"What do you know about Havensharth?" Ice asked him.

"Don't know much. Pa traveled here to buy stuff once or twice. He told me folks could apprentice here, but not in what." He closed his eyes as a single tear rolled down his cheek and fell from his face. "My pa hunted and farmed a bit. Pa always said he just spent time conversing with Nature and was rewarded with her bounty. Ma..." He couldn't finish and fell silent.

"You don't need to tell us any more right now. But when you are up to it, we need to learn of your capture and how you survived living with the brigands." Turning to Ice, Deena continued, "If we are done eating, let's give the young folks a tour of Havensharth."

* * *

Tulip slid the dish away, unable to eat another bite of the savory meal. Master Greyhook was an accomplished cook, and the meal he'd prepared for her and Lady Mirada had been excellent. Earlier, they had conducted her through their house, but the Temple of the Ladies of Life was her home. Tulip did not yet know what this place was.

She'd tried to be happy, cheerful, and interested during the tour, but, inwardly, she missed Zeal and Kit. She wasn't happy being separated from them and wished the three of them were living together. Tulip hadn't anticipated how hard it would be, being apart from Zeal and Kit.

The manse was large and sprawling. Tulip was given a room and told it was hers to do with whatever she wished. Greyhook conducted the business of running Havensharth and the Bardic Enclave, where he and Mirada and, now, she also lived.

Tulip was shown a music room full of instruments, and she liked it the most. There was a large meeting room located across from Greyhook's study, which had walls covered floor to ceiling with shelves full of ledgers, books, scrolls, and maps neatly organized. A large wood desk, dark with age, interested her. Two uncomfortable-looking chairs were positioned in front of it, as if to pay it homage. The study was another room she wanted to spend time in and learn the secrets it held.

There were three guest rooms, including the one that now belonged to her, plus a large bedroom Mirada and Greyhook shared. The common room had a generous fireplace and comfortable seating for guests. The kitchen was almost as big as the one at the Temple, and she could tell it was fashioned for Greyhook more than for

Mirada. It appeared to be well stocked and well used, based on the quality of the dinner Greyhook prepared.

The manse was set among trees that grew between the Library and Amphitheater. Two outbuildings belonged to the property: the older and larger was a place for instrument construction and repair, while the newer was Mirada's retreat. Mirada promised Tulip a tour later.

Tulip's reverie was interrupted by a knock on the main door. Greyhook left the table to see who it was and returned shortly, accompanied by others.

"It appears we have guests who've arrived just in time for dessert." Greyhook guided Ice and Deena along with Zeal, Kit, and Tallen to seats at the table. Introductions were made before Greyhook retreated to the kitchen and returned with a small serving cart loaded with dishes, cups, and a selection of individual honey cakes. The cups were filled with mead for the adults and fresh berry juice for the children.

Tulip could barely contain her delight at seeing Zeal and Kit. She also grinned broadly at Tallen, who accompanied them. The visitors seemed to banish her gloom for the moment.

"Ice and I were showing the new arrivals around Havensharth. Zeal asked about Tulip, so your place was included in the tour," Deena explained between bites of her honey cake.

"Tulip, why don't you show Zeal, Kit, and Tallen around?" Greyhook suggested.

"That means the adults want to talk alone and would like us elsewhere," Tulip interpreted.

"Yeah, I even caught that one," Zeal said.

"We will leave you all to finish your cakes and retire to the common room." Greyhook winked at Mirada. "They are such intelligent children."

After waiting for the adults to leave, Tallen quietly asked Tulip, "What do you think they are going to discuss?"

"Us, of course. At some point, we'll be included, but for now, they are going to negotiate politely with each other."

"Why do you say that?" Tallen asked, puzzled.

"They are sitting in the open so they can see us. They can tell if we attempt to listen in and still keep tabs on us. If there was going to be shouting, they would retire to the study." Tulip looked to Zeal for confirmation.

"She has the right of it, Tallen. I bet Master Greyhook is being told everything about us." Zeal licked his fingers. "Well, I am full and ready to have a look around. How about the rest of you?"

Tallen looked under the table. "Where is Kit?"

"She is sitting in the other room, listening," Zeal answered nonchalantly.

Tallen nodded. "Now I understand. If something important is brought up by the adults, she can relay us the information."

"Let me show you my favorite room." Tulip stood. "Come this way." After passing through the kitchen and down a short hall, she opened a set of double doors.

* * *

Greyhook was able to listen to the tale spun by Ice, Deena and Mirada for almost two marks before rising to his feet and starting to pace. He found the habit burned off nervous energy and helped him focus. Being a bard, he could stay still, if needed, but he preferred to keep moving. They waited silently for him to comment after finishing their report.

He stopped his pacing. "I never expected to have the three of you return and drop such a complex dilemma at my door. Let's see if I heard everything correctly. Tulip and Zeal have both apprenticed with the Trade. Ice and his former mentor discovered Zeal was a Phosfire. Zeal has bonded with Kit, who is a Shadow Cat. Kit and Zeal are both learning to be Practitioners. On the road to Havensharth, the convoy was attacked by brigands and Kit's mother killed them all by herself. That alone is incredible, but it is mindboggling to think one of Kit's kind being able to conjure. Did I miss anything?" Greyhook took a seat next to Mirada and waited for an answer.

"Dear, you forgot the part about the attempted attack on our ship." Mirada was unable to hide the smile that crept onto her face.

Greyhook leaned forward and kissed Mirada on the cheek. "I just neglected to mention it. If I recall correctly, Kit is not the first unique entity to study here at Havensharth, though there has been none in recent memory. A review of the sagas may prove enlightening and provide us with the facts.

"I'll set up a meeting with Namrin. We can introduce him to Kit and Zeal and get his opinion on how to approach Kit's uniqueness. Best we assemble here, where I can guarantee privacy. I'll get back to you with the exact time." He looked down at Kit, who lay on the rug between Ice and Deena. "Kit, it has been made clear to me that you are capable of understanding the discussion we're having. You've remained silent. How do we communicate with each other?"

This is how. I speak to whom I choose, when I choose, Kit said to everyone the room. *I am not a danger unless your kind makes me so.*

Greyhook's eyes widened slightly at Kit's reply. As he was deciding how to react, he was distracted by sounds from outside the room. He rose from his seat, head cocked to one side, and stood with eyes closed, listening carefully.

"Does that address your concern regarding—"

Greyhook held up a hand, interrupting Ice. "I am sorry, but quiet a moment, please." He focused on the sounds. Someone was playing the pipes in the music room and doing a more than adequate job. And there was a girl's voice singing in accompaniment. "Do you all hear that?"

Not waiting for an answer, he softly walked away and stealthily extinguished the light in the hall outside the music room doors. Partially opening one side, he listened.

He was able to recognize the song with ease. It was about two lovers separated when the man went off to war. He was killed, his body lost on the battle field and never returned to be mourned over by his love. Greyhook knew the song's origins were a real battle between two kingdoms nine hundred seasons past.

Peering through the opening, Greyhook saw the boy, Tallen, playing the pipes as he intently watched Tulip. Tallen's fingers moved fluidly while Tulip's voice, though untrained, was beautiful. Zeal sat with his eyes closed, listening.

Greyhook fought the impulse to join them in their music. It was not until the song ended that he was able to force himself to close the door. When he turned away, he found everyone standing behind him, listening. They, too, appeared moved by the experience. He motioned them back to the common room.

Once there, he began to pace. "You never told me Tallen played the pipes or how well Tulip sings. Why did you hold that information back? Were you going to bring it up if I proved difficult?" He stared accusingly into each of their faces.

Mirada interrupted before Ice or Deena could speak. "Grey, we didn't know. Tulip never sang on the ship, at least where I could hear, and you know we just met Tallen. Now why would we keep information from you when it would be to our advantage?" Her eyes gleamed with mischief. She leaned toward Deena and whispered, "I think Grey has been hooked on the idea of having Kit and the children stay. His indignation is music to my ears."

CHAPTER THIRTEEN

ZEAL WOKE UP sneezing. Kit's whiskers were twitching in his nose, and Tallen's toe was poking him in one ear. Tulip was lost somewhere in the nest they had made of blankets and pillows on the floor of his room during the night. She and Tallen had accompanied Zeal and Kit to see their new home and ended up spending the night. Deena had agreed, saying that it was important for Greyhook and Mirada to have time to work out their differences and get reacquainted.

Upon rising, they took turns using the convenience and washed up. Zeal was impressed there was no outbuilding for the purpose of relieving one's self. You could do it inside the home; there was even a separate room to bathe in. He'd learned the water from the bath was stored and used to flush through the amenity. How convenient that was! Kit demonstrated even she could use the facilities. No need to clean up Kit's scat.

The morning meal was taken in the Hall. Zeal enjoyed the hot porridge he sprinkled with dried berries and laced with honey and cream. Kit had a dish of uncooked pieces of poultry.

At the end of the meal, Deena left to prepare her shop for reopening. Ice informed Tulip and Zeal he was taking them to a meeting but wouldn't say with whom. Tallen remained in the Hall, where he was scheduled to work.

Ice directed them to a warehouse in the Craft Enclave. Studying his surrounds upon entering, Zeal recognized that part of the cargo, delivered from the *White Swan* was being processed inside the building. When Ice knocked on the door of the overseer's workroom, a woman's voice yelled. "Enter!"

The portal was opened. A woman of forty seasons was inside, sitting behind a desk in a workroom best described as full of organized clutter. She was dressed in work clothes and her hair was placed in a tight bun.

"Close the door behind you," she said by way of greeting.

Ice did as he was instructed then made his introduction, speaking Trade tongue. "Zeal, Tulip, histe nes Adil... Zeal, Tulip, this is Lady Phyllis. She is head of the Trade here in Havensharth and the surrounding region. Lady Phyllis, I have brought them, per tradition, to meet you"

Phyllis spoke in tongue in return. "Thank you, Master Ice. I received a missive from Trade Master Slag informing me of your pending arrival. I heard you had an eventful journey. Zeal, have you recovered from your injury?"

"Yes, I have. Thank you for asking," Zeal answered in kind. He thought fondly of Master Slag who was the head of Trade in Arlanda. It was Master Slag who'd chosen him and Tulip to apprentice in the Trade.

"Tulip, I expect you and Zeal to find time to maintain your Trade studies. Master Ice will assist you in fitting this into your schedules. I welcome you and want you both to know I am here, if you need me. Trade Master Slag instructed me to remind you that the Trade is still your family."

"Thank you, Trade Master Phyllis," Tulip and Zeal answered in unison.

"There are Trade apprentices here in Havensharth?" Zeal inquired.

"Yes, there are. You will meet them all eventually. Do you have any questions for me?" Seeing that no questions were forthcoming, she added, "Remember, my door is always open to you. Now get out of here. I have work to do."

* * *

A message was waiting for them in the kitchen at the cottage, informing them when the meeting with Master Namrin was scheduled. It would be held at Greyhook and Mirada's manse in two marks. Kit and Zeal were invited for the discussion.

Zeal gazed around the kitchen and grumbled, "Is there a market nearby? We need to fill our cupboards."

"Let's go to my place now and have the midday meal together," Tulip suggested. "I'll find something to do with myself while the rest of you conduct your business with Master Namrin."

"Excellent suggestion. I'm always up for raiding Greyhook's larder." The corners of Ice's mouth lifted slightly. "Greyhook refuses to tell me the source of his hard-to-find ingredients. Tulip, perhaps you could find out for me?"

"With all due respect, Master Ice, you'll get no help from me gaining the intelligence you seek." She tried but failed to adopt a serious expression.

Will there be scraud?

"It's doubtful, Kit, but we'll see. I'm sure we can find something to your liking," Tulip told the Shadow Cat.

Ice and Zeal, with Kit padding beside them, followed Tulip to her home where they were greeted by Greyhook, who produced a meal to everyone's liking. Although there was no scraud, Kit enjoyed a platter of raw liver.

Near the end of the meal, Zeal heard a soft knocking. Greyhook rose and opened the door.

"Good to see you, Namrin. Please come in. We were just eating. Can I offer you food or drink?" He escorted Namrin into the kitchen.

Namrin was of average build, dressed in serviceable clothes, and clean-shaven, his dark hair streaked with gray. "Cool water will do for me."

"I'll get it," Tulip offered. She filled a cup with water from the chiller for him.

"Thank you, dear. And who might you be?" Namrin took a sip from the cup.

"Let me make introductions. This young lady is Tulip. She is Mirada's and my new ward. She is from Arlanda." Greyhook shifted to stand behind Zeal's chair. "I would also like you to meet Zeal and Kit." He indicated each with a gesture. "Tulip, Zeal, Kit, the gentleman before you is Master Namrin, the Master of Instruction of the Enclave of the Practitioners of the Arts and director of the Repository."

"Nice to meet you, Master Namrin. I think I'll leave now." Tulip finger messaged Zeal, "Good Luck," as she walked away.

"Well met, Master Namrin." Zeal locked eyes with him, and they assessed each other for several heartbeats. Zeal sent to Kit, *What do you think?*

One called Namrin wonders if cub is worth teaching.

Cub? But, there are two of us, not one.

Wait. We stalk now, make kill later.

Zeal sat quietly with Kit in his lap; they listened to the adults' discussion together. Ice informed Namrin that Zeal was a Phosfire and that Kit was capable of conjuring. Zeal used his Trade training to read the signals in Master Namrin's carriage, posture, and expressions during the conversations. The man didn't believe Kit could conjure.

"I think it's best we keep Zeal's status as a Phosfire between us," Namrin announced.

"What of Kit?" Greyhook wore a noncommittal expression.

Ice answered, "I don't want Kit's abilities disseminated. Her being an apprentice should be kept a secret, as well."

Namrin nodded. "Agreed. I'll formulate an explanation for her presence at the Repository and make it clear she is there with my approval."

Zeal noted that neither Ice nor Greyhook mentioned Kit's being a Shadow Cat. What was going on? Maybe they realized Namrin was skeptical, humoring them.

"Zeal, would you…" Namrin hesitated before saying, "…and Kit like to have a tour of the Practitioner's Enclave and the Repository?"

"Yes, we would Master Namrin." Zeal rose to his feet, as did the adults.

"I'll let you all go ahead. There is a problem I have to attend to, and you don't really need me along." Greyhook saw them out.

Zeal placed Kit across his shoulders and accompanied Ice and Namrin to the Enclave. When they were within visual distance of the Repository, Namrin began to describe its merits.

"The Repository functions similar to the Library that the Bards first established here. In the past, new skills and knowledge discovered by a Practitioner were not always passed on to another. The information became lost until rediscovered by someone else. The Repository insures what has been learned is stored here and made available for all Practitioners to share."

"I'd never heard of the Repository before Master Ice told me about it," Zeal pointed upward. "Why is there no roof?"

"There is a roof, but you are able to see through it." Namrin chuckled. "The building has a transparent dome made of a single, hardened crystal. It was created by means of conjure by a group of Practitioners linked in Marhdah. It took them a whole moon to grow the crystal and set it in place. A record of their undertaking is preserved in the Repository."

"What does the dome do?" Something about the dome felt strange to Zeal. He found, if he closed his eyes after staring at the crystal, light shimmered in a ghostly afterimage on the back of his lids.

"When you are a Master, you may come to learn the secrets associated with the dome. Until then, I must keep that information to myself." Namrin said no more.

Ice winked at Zeal. "I don't think Namrin expected you to inquire about the purpose of the Dome. Most people think it was made to let light in to the Repository and permit Practitioners in the past to show off their skill."

"What else is kept there?" Zeal was curious and anxious to explore.

"We have a collection of imbued objects, both naturally occurring and created. They are stored in the Archive, and Practitioners are allowed to study them. Much has been learned from them, and we've been able to reproduce several, but many of the objects are one of a kind," Namrin said with pride.

"Can we take a peek at them?" Zeal said to Kit, *Maybe it is for the better that no one else knows about you.*

Why?

Makes it easier for us to see that collection whenever we want.

It is best that you not hunt alone.

The entrance to the building led to a reception area. Namrin nodded at the guard who stood to the right of the double doors. A man at a desk stood as they arrived. "Greetings, Master Namrin, Master Ice. Do I need to sign in your guest?"

"That won't be necessary. This is Zeal, our newest Apprentice. I will see that he is registered before we leave. By the way, the feline is Kit. She is to have complete access to the building. Please make that clear to anyone who asks." Namrin turned to Zeal. "Shall we?"

Zeal walked between Ice and Namrin into a corridor to the right of the reception desk and then down a hall. They went a short distance past another set of double doors with words written above them: *Knowledge Gained, Never Lost.*

"On the other side of these doors is our library. Although not as large as the Bardic Library, it is just as important. To a Practitioner, our library is priceless." Ice held open one of the doors so Zeal could look inside.

He saw an open area with several tables and chairs. The library was occupied by a single individual silently perusing a document. Beyond the tables were floor-to-ceiling cases filled with books and scrolls. Maps, sketches, and paintings hung on the walls.

"Come this way. I will show you the location of the Archive. Only Masters and senior Apprentices are allowed inside," Namrin explained as they advanced up the corridor and down a flight of steps. "No one has leave to remove any of the materials stored in the Archive without my permission. The entrance is guarded and warded."

As they approached the Archive, a young woman on the verge of adulthood approached them. Namrin smiled widely when he saw her. "Listina, I would like to introduce Zeal to you. Zeal, this is Listina. She is a senior apprentice."

"I am very pleased to meet you, Zeal." Listina's smile did not reach her eyes.

Zeal saw through her casual appraisal. While living at the Temple of the Ladies of Life, he'd been around many older orphans who thought they were better than all the others. She clearly considered him dung under her shoe.

"Oh dear, is that an animal you have with you?" Listina focused her attention on Kit.

"I know what you are thinking, Listina," Namrin replied. "This is Kit. Although animals are not allowed in the Repository and the areas of study, I am making an exception for Kit. She and Zeal have a unique affinity. It would distress him terribly if they were parted. Since Zeal is joining us as an Apprentice, I have extended Apprentice privileges to Kit, even though we all know she isn't really here to learn."

Namrin seemed to gauge Listina's reaction to his explanation, which Zeal found quite creative.

"How interesting," Listina said, turning to Zeal. "It will be a pleasure to work with you. Feel free to seek me out, if you have a need."

Zeal figured what Listina really meant was she'd like to scrape him off her shoe.

She lies. She does not like us, Kit conveyed to him.

We will talk later. He was not surprised by Kit's revelation.

She hunts... us.

Zeal glanced toward Kit and saw her eyes change size as she studied Listina. Kit's mental thought carried surprise. He doubted she had ever had someone or something stalk her before, except when she had lessons with her mother.

"That is marvelous, Listina," Namrin said with a grin. "I hope everyone will be as open-minded as you are. I am happy you are willing to help out a fellow Apprentice. Thank you for coming over. Don't let us keep you from your business."

Listina gave them a merry wave as she departed.

Zeal sent to Kit, *We'll watch out for that one and avoid her whenever possible.* In return he received Kit's mental nod.

* * *

Zeal, after returning from the evening meal at the Hall, sat on the sleeper in their room with Kit, reviewing the day's events. Kit's novelty in Havensharth had yet to wear off given she had been the only animal in the Hall. They had just begun a discussion about Listina when there was a knock on their door.

Tulip is here.

Tulip entered without waiting for an answer. "Hey you, have you unpacked yet? Did you find anything?"

"Good to see you, Tulip. Unpacked? Unpacked what?" Zeal was unsure what Tulip was asking.

"Of course you haven't." From the floor, she picked up the pack Iris had given to Zeal, sat on the sleeper across from him and Kit, and then placed the pack in front of him.

Kit began to clean her paws, but Zeal knew she was paying close attention. He unfastened the flap, opened the pack's enclosure, and turned the pack upside down, dumping the contents on to the sleeper between him and Tulip. He couldn't keep from smiling when Kit took a sudden interest in the contents. While in Havensharth, he and Tulip had discovered that their packs held more than the size indicated. "Okay, what am I looking for?" he asked.

"Those." Tulip pointed.

Kit was separating three brown, roughly oval-shaped objects from the rest of the items on the bed. She used the pad of her right forepaw with her claws sheathed. Zeal picked them up. Held together, they were big enough to fill his hand. Kit returned to grooming herself.

"Okay, what are they, and how did you know I would have them?" A thought struck him. "Wait, I bet you found them in your pack, as well."

Tulip reached into a pocket and removed an identical brown ovoid, which she held up for Zeal to see. "They're called a rhizome. At the Temple, I once helped Lady Izlan plant a few outside of the kitchen. Guess what type of bloom this grows?"

Zeal could sense the excitement in Tulip's voice and suspected he knew the reason. "Why don't you just tell me?"

"Let me give you a clue. You remember, after boarding the *White Swan*, before we left Arlanda, we found something else in our packs we hadn't placed there?"

After thinking for a moment, Zeal exclaimed with enthusiasm, "You mean our amulets and Kit's ring, don't you? They are iris bulbs!"

"You guessed it, but they're rhizomes not bulbs. I found one last night while I was unpacking. I know I'd emptied the pack, but when I looked inside a mark ago, I found two more."

Zeal reached inside his shirt, removed the amulet Iris had given him, and began to study it. The symbol of Temple of the Ladies of life, a sun with an iris bloom at its center, was embossed on the surface. On the opposite surface was a feline in full pounce. He preferred to think it was an image of a fully-grown Kit.

Tulip wore her amulet hidden under her shirt, as he did. Although one surface was embossed with the symbol of the Temple, the other side of hers carried the image of a sword. Their amulets and box chains were both made of gold.

Kit had a ring she wore on her tail, a plain band engraved on the inside with an elaborate Z. When Zeal had slid the ring onto her tail, the ring had begun to glow. Midway down Kit's tail, it shrank to a perfect fit. Other remarkable properties of the ring were its ability to stay unseen; also, if you stroked Kit's tail, you couldn't feel the ring's presence.

He and Tulip had never told anyone about the items. They knew that Iris wanted them to wear them, but not why. He wondered for a moment if he should ask Deena about the talismans.

"I agree that the rhizomes are gifts from Iris, but what are we supposed to do with them?" He returned the amulet inside his shirt.

Tulip's eyes rolled upward and she shook her head. "We plant them. I placed two of them outside of my window right before I came over. This one I plan to put next to the entrance of the Bardic Library. I think they're Iris's way of showing us she is always with us."

Tulip seemed eager for him to agree with her, but he took a

moment to dwell on her revelation before answering. "Well, if that is true, I'll plant a couple of these outside my window and put the last one next to the Repository. That way, we'll see it growing whenever we pass by."

"If we get more, we should plant them in various places around Havensharth. But I think we should do it in secret. That way no one will know where the blooms came from." She scratched Kit under the chin. "I bet you can help us."

I would, Kit answered. Kit had never met Iris. In the past, Zeal had attempted to give her a clear mental image of Iris.

"Let's plant mine now." He was wound up and ready to go.

"Do you have a trawl to use? If not, I brought one. By the way, have you heard about Tallen?" Tulip asked in passing.

Didn't sound like bad news. "No. What about him?"

"Greyhook offered him an apprenticeship and found him a mentor who is an expert player of the pipes. The mentor's name is Master Gennis. Bards have to learn to play all instruments, but Tallen can specialize in the pipes, if he chooses. Greyhook told me the adults listened in on us the other night—we didn't even know it. That's how he discovered Tallen was able to play." She began to return the items Zeal had spilled back into his pack.

Zeal grinned. "That's fantastic. Good for Tallen. I wonder who originally taught him the pipes. Whoever it was did a great job. I think it's funny that the adults were spying on us while we eavesdropped on them."

Tulip sat quietly for several heartbeats before saying, "Tallen told Greyhook his father taught him. He said that he'd also learned to play the flute from his father. Greyhook told Tallen he would help him make an instrument of his own."

I like listening to Tallen play and Tulip sing, Kit interjected.

"What do you mean me *sing*? Were you hidden in the room with us?" Tulip asked.

I could hear you from where the elders were. Kit added, *You should sing for me more often.*

"Greyhook asked if I wouldn't mind taking voice lessons. I told him I'd think about it. Kit, if I take him up on the offer, you can come listen. Although it fits Tallen perfectly, I'm not interested in being an apprentice bard." Tulip's mood flattened. "I'm happy for Tallen. With all that life has taken from him, it is only right it provided him a place in Havensharth. I just wish he'd acquired a family the same as we have."

"I agree with you. And with Kit. You do sing pretty well." Zeal didn't understand why he was suddenly feeling shy. "Where did you learn that song? I don't recall you singing much while living at the Temple."

"Well, just because I never did it around you doesn't mean I wasn't. Most of my singing occurred when I was alone with Iris in the mausoleum. I learned that song and a lot of other old ones from her. I never felt uncomfortable with Iris." She lowered her eyes and looked away from Zeal.

He took her hand. "I wouldn't have made fun of you."

"I couldn't be sure of that. That's why I never sang when anyone else was nearby. But, for some reason, I didn't feel insecure the other night when I sang with you and Tallen." She squeezed his hand.

Kit rose then rubbed against Tulip. *We are Pride.*

"Thank you, Kit. Speaking of Iris, let's plant these rhizomes."

Zeal began to wonder if Iris had a reason for teaching Tulip the old songs. He'd totally forgotten about their earlier discussion regarding Listina.

* * *

That night, each rhizome they planted budded, forming three connected ends joined together. The next morning, six blossoms bloomed from each planting.

Over the course of the next half-moon, Zeal, Tulip, and Kit made an almost nightly sojourn to bury a rhizome that appeared in one or both of their packs. Irises grew and spread their fragrance and color throughout Havensharth. Two large beds flowered below the windows of two different sleep chambers: Zeal and Kit's room and Tulip's, as well.

CHAPTER FOURTEEN

DAWN FOUND TULIP eavesdropping on a conversation between Greyhook and Mirada. The two were deliberating on Tulip's immediate future. She hadn't intended to spy, but when she heard her name spoken as she walked past the mostly closed door to Greyhook's study, she'd listened for a moment and confirmed they hadn't called for her or been aware of her presence.

Mirada said, "…Tulip and I had a conversation, and she would like to apprentice at the Combat Enclave. Who is the new Head Trainer? I heard rumor that Master Penn has retired and been replaced."

Tulip smiled. She'd learned, from observing Mirada's and Greyhook's interactions, that Mirada thought it best to take the initiative when talking with him. Sometimes it was better not to give him time to think of his response. He was a trained debater, able to intentionally or unintentionally dominate any discussion, especially when he thought he was in the right regarding the matter in question.

"I know she has agreed to take voice lessons and doesn't want to apprentice as a bard," Greyhook replied patiently. "And you told me she has the talent to become a weapon's master—which is why you're encouraging her to pursue your area of expertise. You do know, had you wanted the job of Head Trainer, Penn would've been happy to pass the reins to you."

Tulip quickly peeked through the door. Greyhook was sitting at his desk with a smile on his face and appeared fully aware of the tactic Mirada was using against him. Mirada sat across the desk from him with her back to the door. Tulip was surprised Mirada had turned down the chance to become Head Trainer.

"This is not about me but about Tulip," Mirada snapped. "Now, who is the new Head Trainer?"

Tulip eased away from the opening. It wouldn't do to have either of them look toward the door and see her.

"His name is Cowlin. I've set up a meeting in two marks to have Tulip meet him and audition for a position. I made no mention of your involvement nor did I discuss with him her prior training, as I did not want to influence him in any fashion. He's promised to test her and make a decision based on her merit."

Tulip peeked in again and saw that Greyhook looked a little smug.

"*Hmmm*. You have set up a meeting, have you? Well, you'd be mistaken if you think I won't be there. I'll stay out of the way, but Tulip will have my support. I don't know anything about this Cowlin or know if I trust him. Tell me what you know about him." Mirada leaned on Greyhook's desk as if invading his field of battle, taking away the superior position.

"He is here with his life mate and child, a girl of six seasons. The life mate's name is Raysa, and the little one is Charese. There is something you should know about the daughter." Greyhook's face sobered.

"I'm listening." Mirada sat back in her chair.

"When Cowlin was on his last campaign, Raysa and Charese where attacked by an unidentified beast while picking berries in the wood bordering the land of Raysa's parents' stead. From the description, I suspect it was a bear. The beast was driven away by nearby foresters, who heard Raysa's and Charese's screams of terror. The foresters returned them to Raysa's parents, and the injuries suffered by Raysa and Charese were healed. They were lucky not to have died that day. Since then, Charese has refused to speak. She fears all animals and even flinches at small birds that fly near. She can be found clinging to one or the other of her parents and will not stay with anyone else."

"I imagine Cowlin is very protective of them both. So, I gather that is the reason he took the position of Head Trainer?" Mirada asked quietly. "So he could stay home with them?"

"You are correct in your assumption. May I suggest you let Tulip approach Cowlin while we observe from a distance?" Greyhook hinted.

"We?" She raised one eyebrow to accompany her question.

"Well, you both are important to me, and I also want to support Tulip."

At mention again of her name, Tulip quietly stepped way before she was discovered. As she entered her sleep room, she paused to contemplate on Mirada's and Greyhook's interaction. She found their discourse comforting; it made her happy to know that they truly cared about her.

* * *

Cowlin was making a mental critique of the match between two of his intermediate students when he was approached by the girl, Flower. *Or was it Rose? Wait, that wasn't correct, either,* he thought. Well, he'd forgotten the name Greyhook had given him, but it didn't matter. Cowlin didn't need to learn her name unless he agreed to take her on.

He watched her out of the corner of his eye. He liked that she stood out of the way, not interrupting, and waited to be acknowledged. She was assessing the two combatants, which was also good.

The girl was dressed in serviceable cloth trousers and shirt and wore well-worn boots on her feet. A pair of light, leather gloves were tucked on her belt next to a sheathed long knife. She had dressed to work and appeared ready to learn.

He had never trained a girl before. Hadn't even trained boys for long. This was his first position as an instructor. He was aware some women had become Master Class Mercenaries, but he'd never served with one. "Can I help you?" he asked the girl after the match concluded.

"My name is Tulip. I have an appointment with you."

Ah yes—Tulip. That was the name he'd sought. "I am Master Cowlin." After looking her over once more, he continued, "I understand you would like to apprentice with me. Do you have any prior experience?"

"Some, sir. I have studied the use of the majority of common weapons."

The girl seemed a little hesitant when giving him her answer. She'd need to show more confidence and demonstrate a skill for weapons, if he was going to take her on. "Well, let's see what you can do." He pretended to randomly choose a student, a boy twice Tulip's size. "Staffs. First touch wins. See if you can take her."

Cowlin scrutinized Tulip's actions. She moved to the racked staffs and examined them for size, weight, and balance until finally satisfied with one. After giving her selection a whirl, she rapped one end sharply on the ground to determine if it was sound and then stepped forward.

Cowlin looked over at the boy he had chosen. "That will be all. You would not fend well against her," he told him. Then he pointed to another boy. "You go."

As Tulip studied her opponent's approach, she gripped her staff in her left hand and stood with her right foot forward. She bowed in respect to her opponent and then waited for the command to begin.

Cowlin barked, "Engage!" *She is left-handed,* he thought. This was an uncommon finding.

At first, they circled each other. Tulip's opposition surged toward her and opened with a series of patterned attacks. Cowlin could tell she recognized the training forms the lad used. She struck his staff sharply with hers, deflecting it away, before stepping into the opening she'd created, and swept him off his feet with her stave. She brought the end of her staff down forcefully, rapping the dirt beside his head, then lightly touched him between the eyes.

"*Halt!*"

Tulip extended her hand and helped the boy stand. She again

bowed respectfully to him before turning to face Master Cowlin.

"Change to swords," he instructed, gesturing to another boy. "Let's see what she can do."

Tulip replaced the staff on the rack and proceeded to pick out a wooden practice short sword. Cowlin noted she maintained a view of her contender, who was also watching her out of the corner of his eye.

The girl's brows momentarily rose when her opponent equipped himself with a wooden shield with padded edge. Instead of a shield, she chose a wooden long knife for her off hand. *Interesting choice,* Cowlin thought. The long knife would compensate for her lighter weight. His best apprentice swordsman opposed Tulip. Cowlin waited for them to assume positions and bow to each other, then he gave the order to engage.

Tulip once again used a left-handed stance. The initial flurry of attack and counter was swift. Her opponent opened with a slash to her head that she deflected with her sword. She quickly brought her weapon across her body, but the intended blow was intercepted by the shield. The sharp crack made by the weapons colliding back and forth created a disharmonic cadence as they fended off each other's strikes.

* * *

Tulip considered her challenger. Not only was he not using prepared forms, but he was well trained and seemed confident of his skills. His face gave nothing away. When he suddenly took three steps back, she wondered what was going on. He shouldn't be tired already.

"Give me a moment." He set down his sword, slid the shield onto his right arm, grasped the sword in his left hand, and adopted an off-hand stance. "I'm ready."

Tulip switched weapons, moving her short sword to her right hand, and then switched her stance. She glanced briefly at Master Cowlin. The look on his face informed her he was surprised to see her change her technique. Mirada had forced Tulip to develop her martial skills ambidextrously. "You may proceed," she said.

Practicing patience, she studied her adversary. Neither of them was facile enough to gain an advantage over the other, as they traded blows. She was unable to find an opening in his defense but did perceive a trap he was setting for her. *Thank you, Mirada, for your teachings,* Tulip thought to herself.

The boy's last three attacks against her were preceded by a slight drop of his shield. He was too good a fighter to have a "tell" for her to discover so easily, so Tulip waited until the opening was presented again. Then, feinting, she acted as if she were going to take advantage of the opportunity. Her challenger quickly stepped in, sword swinging, but only hit air. She had already moved.

Her sword smacked the outside edge of his elbow striking the nerves controlling his forearm. She continued past him and used her long knife to divert his return strike. Finally, she spun to face him. His shield hung useless at his side, his arm numbed by her blow.

As she moved to attack, she heard Master Cowlin yell, "*Halt!*"

She stopped, held her weapons defensively, kept her eyes on her foe, bowed, and backed away. Another lesson from Mirada: always make sure a match was truly over.

"That is enough. I will let you know my decision. If I do decide to accept you, you will need to be fitted in proper leathers." Cowlin looked at the student swordsman. "Have the trainer look at your arm."

He turned his back to her as she thanked him. Then, not sure what to do, she took the practice weapons and returned them to their rack. As she did so, she was approached by her second opponent, who was still rubbing the feeling back into his right arm.

"Hi. I'm Addis. For a moment there, I thought you were going to take the bait I put out for you. Nice move. I look forward to having you with us."

"My name is Tulip. Master Cowlin hasn't accepted me yet. You heard him say he would let me know. I'm not even sure he liked me."

"He will. Accept you I mean. He'll have to, if you keep defeating every contender you are challenged with, as you were about to do me. Where do you stay?" Addis asked in a friendly fashion. "In the barracks?"

She was surprised. He didn't seem the least bit bothered by having been bested by a girl. "No, I live with Master Greyhook and Lady Mirada."

"Oh, you're the one who hangs out with the boy with the cat." He leaned close and lowered his voice. "Word of advice. Don't have your friend bring his pet around Master Cowlin."

"Why is that? Master Cowlin does not like cats?"

Addis looked around as if to make sure no one was listening. "His daughter doesn't do well around animals. He also doesn't have anything to do with our training with horses, in case she comes to visit with her mother."

She saw Ice and Mirada heading her way. "I'll try to remember that. See you around." She wasn't sure what to think about Addis's news regarding Kit but would talk to Zeal about it later.

"Well, I am sure I'll see you soon." Addis smiled and walked away.

Tulip waved goodbye. She decided that she enjoyed talking with this likable male.

"That was nicely done," Mirada said, gathering Tulip in her arms. "What did Cowlin say? Did he accept you as an apprentice?"

"Not yet. He said he would let me know once he has made up his mind. Master Cowlin still may tell me no," she said anxiously.

"I don't think there is any way that will happen," Greyhook said, reassuring her. "Mirada has the right of it—you fought very well. If Cowlin doesn't take you on, it will be his loss."

CHAPTER FIFTEEN

ZEAL WAS IN the cottage kitchen, having his morning meal with Kit, when Ice entered. The past three suns had advanced quickly for him, and he was a little tired from his late-night planting excursions with Tulip and Kit.

"Good. I'm glad the two of you are up early. You're coming with me to the Casting Quad," Ice announced.

Zeal felt Kit's sudden interest match his. "Master Ice, why are we going to the Quad?"

"We are meeting Namrin. He plans to determine if you are capable of conjuring and confirm that you're a Phosfire in the safety of the locale." Ice raised a hand. "Before you ask, the Quad was built to protect Havensharth from the conjures cast by Practitioners. It is also possible to tune the safeguards to prevent anyone from viewing or hearing what occurs inside, maintaining the occupants' privacy."

"I don't think Master Namrin believes what you and Master Greyhook told him regarding Kit being able to conjure."

Ice sat opposite him at the table. "That was my impression, as well. But I'm sure Kit will cause Namrin to lose his doubts. Won't you, Kit?"

I will pounce and kill them. Kit curled her lips, opened her mouth, and bared her teeth.

"That look was pretty scary." Ice was quiet for several heartbeats. "It might come in useful sometime."

Zeal stifled a laugh. "Sorry, Master Ice, but that was Kit's grin.

She's been practicing."

Your kind speaks with smiles. I learned from you.

Ice stood. "Kit, I hope you don't pick up any of my kind's bad habits, too. Shall we go?"

Zeal walked alongside Ice while Kit padded between them. They spanned the distance between their cottage and the Casting Quad in silence, each lost in their own thoughts. Zeal was worried about Tulip. She hadn't heard from Master Cowlin regarding her audition. On the other hand, he was excited for Tallen. The bard-in-training deserved a bit of good, after all he'd lost. Ice's voice interrupted his ruminations. "Excuse me, Master Ice. I didn't hear what you said."

"Pay attention! You and Kit both need to know how to control the shields. But only senior Apprentices are allowed to use the area without a mentor present."

They were approaching a rune-carved archway. The runes reminded him of the ancient symbols carved in the walls and main gate of the Temple of the Ladies of Life in Arlanda. He scanned the writing but was unable to decipher its meaning. "What do the runes say, Master Ice?"

"If you seek balance, then enter." Ice allowed Zeal a few moments to process the answer then asked, "Tell me what you think it means."

After contemplating the question for several heartbeats, Zeal said, "I think balance equates control."

Ice gave Zeal's shoulder a squeeze. "Very good. The Quad enables a Practitioner to acquire discipline, discover his or her limits, learn restraint, and gain mastery of their ability. Come."

When they crossed through the opening, Zeal tensed. He expected the arch to react to him when he walked under it and was a little disappointed when nothing occurred.

The Casting Quad's boundaries were marked by columns three times the height of the average male. Each one was made from ivory stone and rune-carved, similar to the arch. Zeal counted four columns on either side of the arch. The space between columns he estimated was twice a column's height.

There was another archway opposite the one they'd entered. By his count, there were ten columns between them. The interior of the Quad was a large rectangle, the ground naked, hard-packed soil without plant growth of any kind. Not even a weed dared to set its roots into the surface. Zeal felt the area needed an iris bulb badly.

Master Namrin was waiting for them in the center of the Quad. *Watch what happens here closely, please,* Zeal asked Kit.

Always, she messaged, reassuring him.

"Zeal, Ice, glad you're finally here," Namrin said in greeting. "First things first, let's teach you how to use this area safely. Here are the physical elements needed to conjure the appropriate casting." He used slow movements of one then both hands. After repeating the motions, he suggested Zeal try.

As Zeal attempted to mimic the Master's gestures, Ice moved close and helped correct his mistakes. When Zeal surreptitiously glanced in Kit's direction, he saw her creating a complimentary set of movements using her tail, ears, and vibrissae. Master Namrin, who'd been ignoring her since they'd arrived, was oblivious to her actions.

"I think you have the physical element down." Namrin looked as pleased with himself as with his student. "As you know, a Practitioner's intent is key to producing a conjure. To activate the Quad's protections, use the phrase 'Vertus.' You deactivate them using 'Vertas.' I'll teach you the advanced form of conjure, which prevents anyone or anything from entering or leaving the confines of the protected zone, during a future session."

"Will that also prevent anyone from viewing what is happening inside here?" Zeal saw people going about their business when he looked between the columns.

"Using the form 'Vertus Um' does that. Let me demonstrate the ward's activation, and then you have you try." As Namrin used slow gestures, saying "Vertus," a shimmering, semi-transparent field appeared between the columns. When he used a similar set of gestures and said, "Vertas," the shimmering faded. Namrin changed the physical element then said, "Vertus Um." The field formed, darkened, and lost its transparency, preventing anyone from seeing in or out of the Quad. "Now you give it a go."

Zeal took a moment and relaxed the tension in his body he'd

hardly noticed before. He walked himself through the progression of the conjure, using his mind alone. At the point he realized he could complete the casting without using elements, he stopped.

"Don't feel badly if you aren't successful right away," Namrin said, his tone encouraging.

Zeal assumed Namrin had mistaken his silence and delay as a sign he lacked confidence. He glanced over at Master Ice, who gave a nod. Zeal fell back on his Trade training to help him concentrate. Without hesitation, he combined the physical and verbal elements then completed the conjure, exclaiming, "Vertus!"

When the ward activated with a quiet hum Zeal hadn't previously noted, he saw that the runes carved into the columns were faintly glowing a green color. When he repeated the process using "Vertus Um," the hum rose slightly higher in pitch, the color of the runes turned from green to blue, and the field blackened.

Namrin looked pleased at Zeal's accomplishment. "Wonderful! Well done. I didn't expect you to succeed on your first try."

"Excuse me, what about Kit? Doesn't she get a chance?" Zeal asked.

"Ah, yes. Kit." Namrin turned to Ice. "Why do you both insist Kit is capable of practicing the Arts? I have yet to see a creature conjure."

Ice crossed his arms in front of his chest. "Namrin, whatever gave you the idea we weren't serious? I figured you for an open-minded individual."

"I thought Zeal was fixated on the animal and everyone was trying to humor him," Namrin replied somewhat defensively.

Zeal attempted to follow Ice's example and contain the frustration he felt toward Master Namrin. "Excuse me, Master Namrin, but why don't you talk to Kit."

You gave good lesson, Kit said, including Namrin. *I conjure this way.*

Namrin's eyes widened in distress at hearing Kit's thoughts. He backed a couple steps away and stared at her intently.

Zeal dropped to one knee next to Kit to protect her, in case Namrin considered her a threat.

Kit's tail and ears moved in a determined fashion. She vocalized softly with a deep rumble. The Quad's ward dropped. Then she produced a sound different from the first and conjured once more. When she finished, the protections were again in place.

"Breathe," Ice suggested to Namrin, who stood, unmoving, as he stared at the Shadow Cat.

You will consider me when you teach, Kit admonished Namrin.

"I owe all of you an apology. Especially you, Kit. I am guessing Zeal is truly a Phosfire then?"

"Why don't you ask Zeal?" Ice winked. "But first, I think you should lock us in, so no one else wanders into the Quad and gets hurt."

Zeal studied Master Namrin closely, noting the elements used to bar entrance.

Namrin gathered himself and conjured. A dome appeared over them made of blue energy that also filled the spaces between the columns and sealed the openings of the arches.

Did you hear the verbal element? Zeal quickly asked Kit through their link.

Vertus Um Tolus, was Kit's answer.

CHAPTER SIXTEEN

LISTINA PRETENDED to examine the bolts of sateen displayed by the weaver at her stall. The merchant's location provided Listina a direct view of the Casting Quad. She'd overheard Master Namrin say he was testing the boy, Zeal, there today, so she had timed her presence in the market to coincide with the Master's arrival.

Initially, she saw Master Namrin enter the Quad alone but didn't have long to wait before Master Ice arrived with Zeal and the animal. She was still frustrated not to have been able to identify the cat's species. It wasn't long after the group entered that the wards were activated and her view of the inside of the Quad was cut off. Her curiosity was roused even further when the safeguards were enabled and the dome materialized over the space. Why would Namrin need to lock down the area just to test a new Apprentice? They were hiding something, and she wanted to know what.

Setting the cloth down, Listina recognized Raysa, the wife of the Head Trainer, who was examining a bolt of homespun at the end of the table from Listina. Her damaged daughter was by her side. An idea formed in Listina's head as she studied the girl.

"What a lovely daughter you have." She reached for a white ribbon and held it out to the mother. "You must allow me to gift her with one of these marvelous ribbons for her hair. Let me introduce myself. My name is Listina, and I do so love little children."

Raysa jerked with surprise when Listina approached her but quickly gathered herself. "I am Raysa, and this is Charese. Thank you, but I can't accept such a costly gift. I am sure you need your coin to pay for your studies. You are an Apprentice, I assume?"

"Yes. For Master Namrin at the Repository." Listina knelt down and held the ribbon out to the little girl. "Would you like to hold the ribbon?" The child gave the response she'd expected.

The young one grabbed her mother's leg, scrunched her eyes closed, and then buried her face against her mother's thigh.

Listina stood and said with mock concern, "How sweet she is so shy. I hope I did not frighten her."

Raysa rubbed the back of Charese's head. "She doesn't take well to people she does not know. You will have to excuse her."

"Perhaps she would like a new doll or, I know, a stuffed animal? I saw someone selling them in the market today. Every child loves a cute little plaything."

"I don't think a gift will be necessary. Charese had a bad experience that has left her with no desire to play with a real animal or stuffed toy." Raysa's brows furrowed, and she began to stare at Listina suspiciously.

"I am dreadfully sorry. I did not know. Please forgive me. But then, it must be hard for your daughter to eat in the Hall with a creature there. I'm not even sure what kind of beast it is. Possibly some kind of cat, if you don't mind me saying so. By the size of its paws, I doubt that it's fully grown." Listina warmed to her role and continued, "Its presence must cause you concern about its effect on your daughter. Someone should do something about that creature. If it were up to me, I wouldn't allow it to sit at a table and eat raw meat as if it belongs." She thought the comment regarding the paws was a nice touch.

Forcefully, Raysa said, "I had a discussion with my life mate just this dawn regarding the feline. Charese has not had a decent evening meal since the beast's arrival." She held up a hand. "I'm sorry. I shouldn't discuss our problems with a stranger."

Listina saw that the woman's suspicion had been supplanted by anger while Charese trembled in response.

Listina noted the child's upset. "It would be tragic if the creature were to attack someone." She looked down at the girl for her mother's benefit, as if studying her for the first time. "Oh my, I think our talk is upsetting your little one."

Raysa glanced down and saw Charese silently crying. Not only was Charese's face wet, but so was the front of her pants. "Excuse us." Fighting back tears, she picked her daughter up and left.

Listina threw the ribbon on the table, satisfied with the result. She looked forward to observing the outcome of the seed she'd planted.

* * *

As she rounded the corner of the outbuilding, Tulip heard someone calling her name. Mirada had informed her that this building was dedicated to the repair and construction of instruments and other music-related gear. She saw Tallen standing in the open door, furiously gesturing for her to enter.

"Howdy there. How have you been?" He held the door for Tulip.

"I'm fine." When Tallen looked as if he didn't believe her, she sighed. "Well, maybe not fine. When I hear the result of my audition with Master Cowlin, I'll then know how I feel."

"I hope you hear something soon. Lady Mirada told me that you fought well. Master Cowlin will accept you, don't you worry none."

Tulip appreciated Tallen's support and hoped he was right. "Guess the waiting is making me nervous. I don't know why it is taking him so long to give me an answer. But enough about me. How are you doing? Still excited about learning to be a bard?"

"I am doing well. Master Gennis has me picking materials to construct my own set of pipes."

Tulip looked around. It was just the two of them present in the shop. The place smelled of wood, glue, and other scents, mostly pleasant. She saw instruments in various stages of completion on the many workbenches.

"Master Gennis has pipes crafted from different types of wood and a few made out of various metals. He even has a set created in stone. You won't believe how the tone changes depending on the material used to construct it. I've been trying to decide on what I want to use." He looked at Tulip shyly. "Maybe you can help?"

"Sure. Don't know what I can do, though." Tulip hoped that assisting Tallen would distract her from her own worries.

"Well, I have an idea. Promise not to laugh?"

"I'll promise to try. Will that do?" She grinned.

"I want to use wood for my first set of pipes. What I need you to do is sing at the samples as I hold them. I'll be able to compare the resonance caused by the effect of your voice on the different woods."

"Are you serious?" she asked, surprised.

"Yes, I'm serious. Why don't you sing the song we performed together the other night in Master Greyhook's music room? Where did you learn it, anyway? I never knew there were words to the music my pa taught me. But I recognized the melody right away."

Tulip thought about the many times she and Iris had spent harmonizing together. "A friend taught it to me. She told me the song was meant to keep alive the memory of the sacrifice made by Mendorian soldiers after they died in defense of their kingdom. When I first heard it, I cried, it was so sad."

Tallen fingered a wood sample. "Do you know the name of the saga?"

After thinking for a moment, the name came to her. "It was called the Battle of Lost Sons. There are several parts to the narrative. We should perform the whole thing sometime," she suggested, pleased to help a future bard.

"I would like that. Once I've made my new pipes, let's do so. I've narrowed my choice of wood down to four samples. They are right over here on the table." He directed her to another part of the chamber.

Tulip followed him and looked over the different options. "What kind of wood is each of these?"

"They are all hard woods, for their durability. The one on the far left is white oaken." He continued, moving to his right, "This is blue holly, lesser ironwood, and the last piece is red asdic."

Tulip started to sing. She wasn't sure she put a lot of trust in the way Tallen was choosing his material but was happy they were the only ones in the outbuilding.

Tallen held each individual sample in front of her moving lips and positioned his ear close to the wood. Tulip's eyes closed and she became lost in the song. As she held the last note of the refrain, she became aware of an accompanying tone. When she opened her eyes, she stared in wonder at a piece of wood that had not been one of Tallen's four choices.

"Did you hear that?" he asked her softly. "This sample responded to your song. It was sitting on the table next to us. I saw it moving—vibrating in response to your voice. When I picked it up, I could hear the tone it made."

"I did hear it. What kind of wood is that?" She studied its fine, caramel-colored grain.

"It is morra. At least that's what I think it is. Morra trees are rare, and the wood very valuable. After how it reacted to your voice, I will use this wood, if Master Gennis grants his approval."

Tulip placed a hand on Tallen's arm. "I can talk to Greyhook for you, if you want. I thought you were playing around—I didn't expect anything to happen. How did you know this would work?"

"It was something my pa once told me. He said Ma sang to the wood he used to make his pipes." After Tallen answered, he became introspective.

Tulip perceived his discomfort as he grew quiet and lost in thought. "Sorry. I didn't mean to make you sad." She quickly hugged him. "I need to go."

Tallen shouted his thanks, and she left the building with mixed feelings. Maybe voice training wouldn't be a bad thing after all.

* * *

Ice reviewed his earlier conversations with Zeal regarding the *Book of Flames*. One involved encasing someone or something in fire while not allowing the person or object to be harmed by the blaze.

He took off his coat and spread it on the ground. "Zeal, I would like you to encase my coat in fire without allowing any damage to occur." He stepped out of the way.

Zeal thought for a moment before beginning the conjure. He used a small, circular gesture accompanied by the verbal element, "Indific." Then he walked over, lifted the flaming coat up, and draped it across his shoulders.

"If you want, Master Ice, you could wear your coat. It won't hurt." Zeal shrugged out of the garment and held it toward Ice.

Ice glanced toward Namrin, who was silently watching, and then took his coat, quickly slid his arms into the sleeves, and allowed it to settle comfortably on his shoulders. Not only was there no heat, but the light produced by the fiery garment was contained; it didn't shine into his eyes and obscure his vision. The properties of the burning garment didn't affect the wearer, just as the *Book of Flames* had documented.

"Would you like to try this on, Namrin?" Ice asked.

"Ah, no thank you," he finally answered.

"Can I try one more thing, since I can't cause any damage to the Quad?" Zeal looked initially to Ice then, after a few heartbeats, to Namrin for permission.

"Yes, but you have to return my coat to its original state first." Ice did not try to disguise the pride in his voice. Zeal was doing well.

Zeal held out his right hand and repeated, "Indific." The flames left the garment, reshaped into a small globe, and settled into his cupped hand. Quietly, he said, "Insific" and flung the ball away from the party. It spun through the air to the far end of the Quad, where it pulsed and then exploded, spreading fire in all directions.

The shock wave it produced pummeled them with fine grains of dirt, stinging their exposed skin. Because Zeal had placed the orb at a distance, however, the energy it released had greatly dissipated before reaching them.

"Glad I didn't try that on the *Swan*." Zeal's eyes gleamed with excitement. "But I always wanted to."

Ice grasped him in a warm hug. "I am glad you didn't, either. You need any more proof, Namrin? I hope you don't have any further doubts regarding Kit and Zeal."

CHAPTER SEVENTEEN

TULIP ENTERED THE Apprentice Hall ahead of Mirada and Greyhook. They'd accompanied Zeal, Kit, Ice, and Deena to join Tallen for the evening meal. He waved to get their attention when they walked in. Fortunately, he'd arrived earlier and claimed a table large enough to accommodate their numbers. To Tulip's surprise, the Hall was unusually full, and she couldn't figure out why. After obtaining their food, they joined Tallen at his table.

"Hello, everyone. Thank you for coming." Tallen rose to his feet and was greeted in return.

He smiled when Tulip eased into the chair next to him and shyly looked away. Zeal sat on Tulip's other side with Kit on a cushion beside him. The adults made themselves comfortable and began to gossip.

"I had an interesting discussion with one of the alchemists in their shop while Kit and the boys were playing in the Quad." She gestured toward Ice and Zeal.

"Really?" Greyhook asked. "What was so interesting?"

"The owner, Meva, was excited about the plants that have recently appeared around Havensharth. Specifically, the bounty of blooms flowering at your place and ours."

"Yes, I know the blossoms you speak of, and I am also curious about the plants. I gave an order to research the species in the archives this morn. What did Meva have to say about them?"

Tulip gave Zeal a knowing look. He nodded subtly.

"Well, Meva is under the assumption that there is something unique about the flowers and has attempted to harvest a few, to test her idea. For some reason, each sample has turned to dust soon after being cut. She has yet to discover a way to preserve the blossoms."

Mirada gestured for the party to come closer and then spoke just loud enough for them to hear. "I'm familiar with the plant. It is a species of iris. I first saw the flower when I was a junior officer in Izzy's Raiders. It appeared in the tent of my former commander, who is now the Matriarch of the Temple of the Ladies of Life. Ice, the same irises were in bloom at the Temple when we were in Arlanda. Don't you remember seeing them?"

Ice thought for a moment. "I might have. But I was distracted by the task of convincing Lady Izlan that Zeal needed to come to Havensharth. And then there was the kitchen fire we had to contend with."

Tulip elbowed Zeal and whispered, "Stop looking so smug. Someone will notice." When she looked across the hall, she saw Master Cowlin and his family had arrived and were seated at a table.

He and his wife appeared to be in a heated discussion with each other while their daughter sat hunched in a chair between them, staring wide-eyed around the dining room.

"I'm wondering whether I should ask Master Cowlin what his decision is regarding my apprenticeship," Tulip said to her companions. "I am tired of the waiting."

"She is never one to wait," Zeal told Tallen between bites.

"You are one to talk. You're much worse than I am," Tulip quipped, giving Zeal a strategic eye-roll. He ignored it.

"I doubt that's a good idea, Tulip." Tallen pointed with his knife. "Master Cowlin doesn't appear happy over there. Wonder who his little one is gawking at? She is so pale, she appears spirit-scared."

She looks at me. I scare her, Kit confided to the three young companions. Kit stopped eating and locked eyes with the little girl.

"What is Kit doing? Why is she staring at that little girl?" Tulip whispered to Zeal. He tilted his head toward Kit with his eyes closed.

As he and Kit continued to stay motionless, Charese suddenly screamed, swooned, and fainted. Her father lunged from his seat and was able to grab her before she fell to the floor. Then he swept the table clear with one arm and gently laid his daughter on the tabletop.

The room stilled, with all eyes and ears focused on the little girl and her parents.

Raysa jabbed Cowlin in the chest with her finger. "We shouldn't have come here tonight. I told you what happened at the market today."

Cowlin hung his head as his wife ranted.

"Look at her! *Look at her*! Look what you've done to your daughter. *Now* will you do something?" She pointed at Kit. "Why is it staring at our daughter?"

A chill crept through Tulip as the expression on Master Cowlin's face when his eyes focused on Kit changed from confusion to rage in a few heartbeats.

"Do something? I'll do something!" He snatched the long sword he'd leaned against the wall. The blade rang when it was drawn, and its sheath hit the floor with a thud. Then Cowlin, weapon in hand, staggered like a drunken man toward Kit.

* * *

Kit peered out of a mental shadow inside Charese's mind. The girl child was open, her thoughts unprotected, and the little one was in danger. Kit was puzzled by her observations. She reached for Zeal and pulled him into the blackness beside her.

Zeal quietly evaluated his surroundings. *Kit, why are we no longer in the Hall?*

I need you to explain. She indicated the activity outside the cave.

Where have you brought us? He stared out into the well-lit area.

Inside the one called Charese. She is howling for help. Why haven't the elders helped their cub?

We are in her inner spirit self?

Yes, the same place Mother taught you and me to protect.

You are learning a lot from Mother Essmee. I gather our bodies remain in the Hall?

They are. Learning Mother's teachings can be hard. Mother tells me it is because I am not fully like her.

You mean because you are not all Shadow Cat, it is harder to do Shadow Cat stuff?

Kit wasn't ready to discuss her limitations so ignored Zeal's question. She padded to the edge of the darkness to better encounter Charese's thoughts. Zeal followed and knelt beside her.

Their view was from above, as if looking out of a cave, the opening located partway down the side of a cliff. Below them, Charese cowered in a small courtyard surrounded by a palisade. The posts making the palisade walls were her parents, not wood. Her mother stood, her feet planted, shoulder to shoulder with her father. Alternating mothers and fathers encircled the courtyard until they came to a gate that was composed of mother posts only.

Animals of all kinds were gathered outside the palisade. To Kit, a number of the figures represented creatures she recognized from real life, but others had been created by Charese's imagination. Kit saw hairy birds with teeth instead of beaks and long talons. Flying dock rats had feet as big as their bodies, their claws wet with red. One beast with the head of a serpent ate any other creature when it came near. With each bite, it grew larger till it was big enough to peer over the palisade.

Charese's protective barrier was under continuous attack. The gate was slowly being eaten away. The beasts that could fly were swatted out of the air by the father posts when they neared the parent walls. No matter how high creatures flew, the arms reached up, beat them back, and prevented them from flying over the barricade.

What means this?

Instead of answering her question, Zeal asked, *Kit, will our being here cause Charese harm?*

Not certain. Do you refuse her aid?

I would never do such a thing.

One reason I chose you.

Charese and her mother were attacked by some kind of animal when she was younger, Zeal explained. *Here's what I think. Charese retreated inside her head to this place to be safe. She feels dependent on her parents to protect her. But I don't think she believes they can do it forever.*

After chewing over Zeal's explanation, Kit came to a conclusion. **All I see is prey. Let's kill them.**

It might not benefit Charese if we do the slaying for her. I believe she needs to dispatch what she fears by herself.

Help her kill then?

That might work. But I am not sure she'll let us. Can we talk to her?

Yes.

Take us down there next to her then. You should try not to appear ferocious.

In less than a blink, they were standing next to Charese. Kit was the size and appearance of the new babe she'd been when she and Zeal first met. She lay on her belly and gazed intently at Charese.

Zeal squatted, clearing his throat to alert the girl to their presence, and softly said, "Charese, I am Zeal and this is Kit. Will you talk to us?" He reached out, intending to run his fingers through Charese's hair, but realized she might not want to be touched, so he pulled back.

"Go way." Charese's lids scrunched tighter.

"We can do that. But first, can you let us help you?" he asked gently.

Charese opened her eyes and looked at him. "How you get here?"

"Kit brought us. See she is here, too."

Charese saw Kit for the first time. "No! No! NO!" Quickly, she scooted away, curled into a ball, and covered her head with her arms. "*No eat me!*"

I no hurt Charese.

"Kit won't harm you. Look at her. You don't want to make her cry, do you?"

"Me make her cry?" Charese peered at Kit through the gap between her arms. Tears showed on her face.

"Yes, you can hurt her. You don't like to feel sad. Well, neither does Kit," he explained.

What is this sad and cry? I don't cry, Kit mindspoke to Zeal.

Pretend for me. Think of how it would feel to never eat scraud again. Crawl over here and let me hold you.

Charese cautiously sat up and watched Kit move slowly to Zeal, her head hung and tail between her legs.

Zeal tenderly gathered Kit up and stroked her fur. "It's all right. You know I love you. Charese didn't intend to be mean. She won't hurt you again."

Kit was able to sense Charese's unease change to curiosity. *I will allow her to touch.*

"Kit loves to have someone pet her. You try."

Charese crept forward, gradually reaching out her shaking hand till her fingers encountered soft fur. Zeal felt Kit tremble beneath Charese's fingers then the girl laughed, surprising Zeal with her intensity.

"Would you like to hold her? She would like that." Zeal waited for Charese to sit in front of them before easing Kit into her lap. He was warmed by her awed expressed when Kit snuggled against her arm.

A mark or two passed while they talked and got to know one another. Zeal listened to Charese describe in her own words the attack she and her mother had suffered. During their discussion, the severity of the assault on the palisade diminished but then intensified again after Charese finished her tale.

Get rid of prey now? Kit asked Charese.

Charese looked at Zeal. "What's prey?"

He pointed to the beast attacking the parent wall.

"They want get me." Charese snuggled closer to Zeal and held Kit protectively.

After a moment's hesitation, Zeal placed an arm around the girl's shoulders. "Kit told me the beasts are actually more afraid of you than you are of them. I bet they will leave, if you really want to be rid of them."

"Scared of me?" Charese asked, surprised.

Zeal shared with Kit, *Charese has been frightened for a long time. She finds it hard to believe something can be afraid of her.*

"Hunters kill prey. You are a hunter." Zeal tucked a lock of hair from Charese's face behind her ear.

"You kill them," Charese demanded demurely.

Zeal felt they were close to breaking through the hopeless, fearful, shell Charese had encased herself in and didn't want to make a mistake. "Kit and I could do that for you, but prey will then run from us, not you. Now, if *you* did it and we just helped a little, it would be you they are afraid of."

"I too little," Charese whimpered.

"Look how small Kit is. She's not afraid." Zeal scratched Kit under the chin, impressed by how she'd made herself appear not the least bit intimidating.

Charese shuddered. "Her got teeth and claws. I got none."

"How about I give you a weapon of your own?" Zeal reached inside his left sleeve and removed his blade from it sheath then held the pommel toward her. "I call this my Fang. It was given to me to help protect me. It is special and has never let me down. You can use it, but it's not yours to keep. I expect you to return the Fang to me when you're done with it."

She shook her head. "Don't know how."

"Sure you do. You've watched your father teach others how to fight with weapons your whole life. Just try. You'll see." He gestured with the blade for Charese to take it.

"You help me?" She peered into Zeal's eyes.

I protect Charese. No prey will touch you. Kit's rough tongue quickly caressed Charese's face, removing the salt left behind from her tears.

Charese giggled then took the Fang from Zeal. It fit comfortably in her hand, as if she had handled the weapon before. She pointed to an iris bloom on the blade. "I know flower."

Kit kept a watch on the weapon. She wasn't sure if she was ready to trust Charese holding something that could possibly injure her when the girl was so close by.

Zeal told Kit, *Charese means the blossom pattern etched in the Fang's blade. They're identical to the irises growing around Havensharth.*

"You are small. How you chase prey away?" Charese asked Kit.

"You can ride Kit. She won't let you fall and will fight right along with you. The prey won't have a chance against the two of you."

Charese looked away. "Like horse? I scared of horse."

You're not afraid of me. I can carry you.

Charese grinned. "You silly. How?"

Put me down. Watch. I grow for you.

Charese stared, mouth open and eyes wide, as Kit grew to the size of a small pony. Zeal placed her on Kit's back before Charese could become frightened about the idea then led them around the courtyard till Charese was comfortable with riding.

"You promise I no fall off?" Charese asked anxiously.

"As long as you wish to stay on, nothing can knock you off," Zeal assured her. "You are the master— I mean mistress of this place."

She gave him a puzzled look. "What now?"

"You open the gate and show the prey you aren't scared anymore. Kill them and chase them away. I will be right with you. By the way, don't forget to yell your war cry."

"War cry?" Charese asked with a questioning look on her face.

"Your shout will scare them and they will know how tough you are," Zeal explained.

I will show you how, Kit assured her.

* * *

Conversation ceased at their table as the drama played out across the room. Tulip felt everyone in the hall draw a shared breath and then hold it. The chamber closed in on her, as if she were in a tunnel.

The walls and tables seemed to channel Cowlin toward them, his naked sword in hand. The look in his eyes frightened her. For the first time in her life, Tulip realized Death was walking toward her. She freed her Fang from its sheath but kept it hidden under the table.

She elbowed Zeal sharply. "Mouse, pay attention! Master

Cowlin is headed over here. I think Kit is in trouble." She didn't understand why he and Kit continued to sit, unmoving, with their eyes closed. "What wrong with you?" she hissed in his ear. When he didn't respond, she stood. Remaining on their side of the table, she eased between him and Kit, with the Fang behind her back.

Mirada grabbed Greyhook's arm. "Grey, we have a problem. Look at Tulip. I'm not sure what is wrong with Cowlin, but I think we need to intervene." She reached under the table and pulled a long knife from her boot.

Greyhook rose, moved to the front of the table, and interposed himself between the approaching arms master and his companions.

"Pleasant evening, Cowlin. Can I help you?" he said, employing *Voice*.

Ignoring Greyhook, Tulip bit her lip and remained focused on Cowlin.

The weapon's master hesitated and looked Greyhook's direction. For a moment, it seemed Cowlin was coming back to himself. His lips parted, but, instead of speaking, a guttural noise escaped his mouth. He jerked his eyes away from Greyhook and slowly shuffled Kit's direction.

Greyhook scowled. Adding *Compulsion* to *Voice,* he shouted, "*Cowlin!*"

Cowlin visibly flinched and turned toward Greyhook. The only visible evidence of his internal struggle against Greyhook's compulsion was the twitching on the right side of his face.

Mirada softly said, "Ice?" She slid Zeal's chair back from the table and positioned herself on Tulip's left.

"Deena and I are on it," Ice answered discreetly.

Tulip had trained with Mirada long enough to know that her mentor, if action dictated, intended to fight alongside her. They would use their weapons to shield each other.

Ice and Deena had risen to their feet and were both subtly preparing conjures. Tallen appeared surprisingly calm, crouched behind his chair, a heavy mug in hand. Zeal and Kit, however, remained preoccupied and unaware.

"Try to disarm, not kill, if you can," Mirada whispered to Tulip.

* * *

A Shadow Cat is most often a silent hunter. Their prey is rarely aware it is about to die. Shadow Cats do use their cry to call to a mate, warn others away from their territory, or intentionally cause fear. Kit used her scream in a different fashion, to celebrate the joy of living. She rumbled a roar that let the whole world know, *"Fear me, because I EXIST!"*

Charese, who was astride Kit, felt the yell vibrate through her body. Compelled to respond to the challenge, she cried out her name, *"CHARESE!"*

The mothers of the palisade's gate marched in unison to create an opening in the wall. Charese held tightly to Kit with her legs as the Shadow Cat propelled them out of the sanctuary. The creatures that had been created by Charese's imagination charged them from every direction, attacking with claw, fang, tooth, and spine, intent on tearing her and Kit apart.

"Above you!" Zeal yelled, pointing over Charese's head.

She looked up to see a large flying lizard diving toward them with its talons extended. Too afraid to close her eyes, she stared at the horror as she spilled the words, "I too little."

Yes, you are little. But together, we are huge! Kit sent. Leaping into the air, she twisted. Her forepaws reached out and tore through the diving beast, which exploded, turning into a cloud of darkness. Kit continued her rotation, directing her paws downward, and pounced, ripping, tearing, and biting the myriad beasts assaulting them. A cloud of darkness bellowed up from beneath her.

Charese's arms were pulled from her body by the force of Kit's spinning movement. While inverted, the Fang she gripped tightly arced groundward. The blade cut through three of the mental spawn that leaped into the air to attack them, turning them into clouds of fragrant golden petals.

The flowery scent broke through Charese's cowardice. Tentatively, she began to swing the weapon, slashing and piercing her fears. With a shout, she attacked with purpose, cutting left, right, up, and down, destroying one nightmare after another till there were no more left to attack. Fallen petals fell into the fertile soil of her mind and grew roots, creating a field of flowers with blossoms identical to the ones etched on the weapon.

"We did it! *I did it!*" Charese yelled to Zeal. Kit padded over to him, and Charese returned his blade. "Thank you."

She looked past him at the area that had protected her for so long. The palisade was gone. In its place was a mound bordered by small saplings. A path led through the trees to a fountain at the center of the mound; it sprayed water into the air, and light created a rainbow in the mist.

"Yes, you did." Zeal returned the blade to its sheath, lifted Charese from Kit's back, and stood the exuberant girl on her feet. "You should rejoin your parents. They're worried about you."

"How?" Charese asked, uncertain.

You are not prey. Open your eyes. Look upon your hunting grounds.

"Kit and I will be there when you do," Zeal assured her. He sent to Kit, *How do we get back?*

I will take us.

Zeal knelt and hugged Charese tightly. "Ready?"

"Wait!" Charese turned from him and commanded Kit, "Get small."

Kit shrunk to small-cat form then Charese sat, gathered her into her lap, kissed Kit on the nose, and buried her face in Kit's fur. "I don't want to lose you."

You will see me. Kit gave her body a shake. Her whiskers tickled Charese's nose and caused her to giggle.

After setting Kit on her paws, Charese said to herself, "I am ready." She awakened with a loud bellow.

* * *

"Cowlin, put your weapon down. Let me help you," Greyhook said, trying to reason with the distressed man before him.

Pointing at Kit with his sword, Cowlin said, "I've tried, but nothing helps my daughter. That animal is making Charese worse. You heard Raysa. I have to do something."

Tulip felt movement against her right arm. Glancing down, she saw Zeal leaning forward to look around her. Kit no longer stared at the little girl; she was focused on the father.

Greyhook took a step forward. "You don't want to accidently hurt someone or do something you'd later regret. I promise we'll remove Kit from the Hall."

Cowlin's reply was interrupted by a guttural shout from behind him, closely followed by Raysa's scream. He spun, weapon held at the ready, prepared to defend his wife and child.

Charese was standing on the table with her hands on her hips. "Papa!" she said sharply. "You *no* hurt Kit!" Stomping her foot for emphasis, she slid from the table and marched to her father. "Kit help me!"

Raysa stood, voice lost, eyes wide, palms covering her mouth.

Cowlin's sword dropped from his hand, its point driven into the plank floor by its own weight. Everyone in the hall heard its *thunk.*

"Charese, you spoke?" Cowlin slowly knelt and gathered his daughter in his arms.

Eyes still flashing with anger, she squirmed. "Papa, let go. Put me down. You no be mad at Kit!"

Holding Charese firmly but lovingly, Cowlin rose to his feet and waved Raysa over. "It's fine, love. I won't do anything to Kit."

Charese turned to her mother. "Mama, make Papa put me down."

Raysa reached with trembling fingers and stroked Charese's hair and face. "My baby is back. Cowlin, we have our baby back."

Greyhook pulled the abandoned blade out of the floor and tossed it back to Mirada, who snatched it out of the air by its pommel. He said to the family, "Perhaps it would be best if we went somewhere else?"

Charese reached out and gently wiped the tears from her mother's face. "I'm no baby. I a big girl. Want eat meal with Kit."

"We can pull up another table," Greyhook offered. "You are welcome to join us, if you wish."

Cowlin hung his head. "I don't think I can. I almost..." He couldn't continue. He moved the struggling Charese to his right arm and gathered his wife with his left. "Greyhook, can we talk later? Let me take my family home."

"Of course." He patted Cowlin on the shoulder. "I'll ask the cook to have food delivered to you after you have a chance to get settled."

As they walked away, Cowlin suddenly stopped and looked back. "Tulip, your lessons start tomorrow. Wear your leathers." Then he faced forward and escorted his family out of the hall.

Charese stopped her struggling but looked over her father's shoulder and waved as she yelled, "Bye, Kit! Bye, Zeal. I find you tomorrow."

Tulip peered around the table. Mirada had placed Master Cowlin's sword behind her chair with its point again buried in the floor's planking. Zeal and Kit both looked at Tulip unperturbed. She could sense Tallen had questions.

The Hall remained subdued as the occupants of the other tables slowly began to return to their meals. Many stared toward Kit, unsure if the evening's drama had ended.

After Zeal scooted his chair forward, Tulip leaned in and whispered, "What just happened? Why weren't you and Kit paying attention?"

He glanced at Tulip's Fang and felt under his sleeve for the blade in its sheath. "It appears Master Cowlin has agreed to apprentice you," he whispered back, quickly adding, "I will tell you what happened when we can be alone together."

"Yes, you will," Tulip said, putting her weapon away.

After their quiet discussion, Tallen stated, "Don't even think of leaving me out. I want to hear this."

Zeal glanced at Tulip, who nodded agreement. "You're one of us, Tallen."

Greyhook rejoined the rest at the table and said quietly, "I, for one, think we need to discuss what just happened, but not here, with so many eyes and ears observing. Since both of our places are warded, either one is a better location for a talk."

"Let's go to your place," Ice said. "The drink is better." Looking at Zeal, he added. "You and Kit are included, so don't disappear when we leave."

Mirada smiled at Tulip. "You did well, and congratulations. I am proud of you." Standing, she said to everyone at the table, "I feel we've provided enough entertainment for the Hall tonight. Grab what you want. We'll eat at our place." She covered her food with a cloth, removed Cowlin's sword from the flooring, and proceeded to the door.

* * *

Listina threw her goblet against the wall in frustration after receiving her informant's report on the incident in the Hall. As the sticky liquid inched toward the floor, a new plan began to form in her head. She decided to take direct action to address the Zeal problem.

CHAPTER EIGHTEEN

A MEET WAS CONDUCTED in the common room where Tulip lived with Mirada and Greyhook. The deliberation lasted long into the night. Deena insisted that everyone finish eating and help with the cleanup before allowing further discussion. Then all eyes turned to Zeal.

He was unsure what to say or where to start, but Kit rescued him. She gave an account of the part they had played in helping Charese fight free of her internal prison.

Tulip scooted closer to Zeal. "You mean Charese was hiding inside herself? How can that be?"

Tallen remained seated at a neutral distance, in front of the unlit hearth. Zeal didn't blame him.

Greyhook took a sip of his drink. "A more important question I have is do Kit's abilities pose a risk to the residents of Havensharth? Ice, since you are the resident expert on Shadow Cats, what should I consider?"

I am threat to prey and all that seek to menace me or mine, Kit mindspoke to everyone.

"Thank you, Kit," Ice said before turning to Greyhook. "Kit is just like everyone else here and will protect herself, if endangered. As we saw tonight, Havensharth has proven to be a hazard to her, not the other way around. And, I must point out, through no fault of her own."

Zeal, uncomfortable with the direction of the discussion, raised his hand. "Excuse me, Master Greyhook, but do you want Kit to leave? If she's not allowed to stay, then I won't, either."

Greyhook rose, walked past Zeal, knelt in front of Kit, and looked into her eyes. "You will grow. As you grow, some will fear you, because you represent something they do not understand. Newcomers to Havensharth may see something that frightens them, and it is your reaction to them that concerns me."

"What if she doesn't grow?" Zeal felt the feather-light touch of Mother Essmee on his mental shields. Did she mean to take Kit away? he worried.

"What do you mean not grow?" Greyhook continued to stare into Kit's eyes.

"I think Zeal has a good idea." Deena took Ice's hand in hers. "Didn't you once tell me that Shadow Cats change size and shape as they move through shadow?"

"That is what Master Feneas speculated in the treatise he showed me. But they are only able to do this as they travel. He also stated this is a strain on their system and may contribute to why they become fatigued." Ice squeezed Deena's hand.

Deena's face brightened. "Ice, I suggest we imbue an item that will allow her to maintain her current size and only change to her true form when she desires? I have something in mind and will need your help with the conjures. And we shouldn't involve a Practitioner not already present—Kit wouldn't want others privy to the secret of what she wore."

"Deena, have you forgotten that Zeal and Kit are Practitioners?" Mirada gently chided. "They can provide assistance."

"You're correct. I did, and they can. Thank you for reminding me."

Zeal asked, "Will it be safe for her?"

"I would never make something for Kit that would harm her. She is as precious to me as you are," Deena reassured Zeal.

He felt a surge of warmth course through him, like he'd absorbed a quantity of flame. He was still getting used to the idea of having someone care for him the way Deena did. Then a sudden thought struck him. "What about her weight? Wouldn't a horse the size of a dog still be a dog that weighed as much as a horse?"

Deena stared off into the distance for several heartbeats. "We can compensate for her weight. I see I have to put more thought into this. Let me think about this further."

"Grey, her being small in size will not make Kit less of a danger." Mirada poured herself more drink from the crock of mead. "Anyone need a refill?"

"I am aware of that. Small, female, and lethal—that describes you and Kit, both. But people judge what they see. If they only see the small and female part, they never think of the lethal." His eyes no longer locked to Kit's, he returned to his seat and drained his drink.

Zeal wondered if anyone else appreciated Greyhook's change in mien.

Tulip asked, "What am I to do? I mean, do I show up for training in the morn and pretend nothing happened in the Hall?"

"Let me take this, Grey," Mirada said, turning to address the young ones. "Ice, Deena, Grey, and I will have a discussion with Havensharth's Arm's Master in the morn. Tulip, you will present yourself as your mentor has requested. I have a set of leathers for you to wear, and you'll act as if nothing happened in the Hall last eve."

Mirada pointed to each Apprentice, including the furry one. "No one here will engage in idle discussion or gossip with their fellows. But everyone will listen and learn what is said. Any information acquired should be discussed with me, to see if it warrants action. Anyone have questions?"

Zeal said, "What she means, Tulip, is—"

"Zeal, I got this." Tulip sauntered over to Mirada and laid her head on her shoulder. "The adults are going to handle any problems Master Cowlin still has regarding us. We need to let them do it and not interfere. They will explain later what the outcome is. The kids should not do anything to add to the disruption, just act as information-gatherers. We are their other eyes and ears. People say things around us they would not say to them. We should report anything we learn, because we need to let them judge what is or is not important."

"See, Grey. Told you I had this." Mirada gave Tulip a kiss on the top of the head.

Deena rose from her chair. "Ice and I will start on the item for Kit. We'll let you know when we have something. Zeal, are you ready to go?" She seemed amused by the exchange.

"If it is all right with the adults," Zeal replied, indicating Tulip, Tallen, and Kit, "us kids would like to have a meeting of our own, either here or at our place."

As everyone began to go their way, Tallen sighed and said to himself, "What part about having fought inside Charese was not important? I wanted to hear more."

* * *

Essmee had sensed Kit's anxiety. Even though she'd always maintained an open awareness of her cub, since the attack in the woods, she'd become more sensitive to Kit's moods. Feneas jokingly described her as being twitchy. Curiosity caused her to step and see what was causing Kit's distress.

She'd detected no danger to her cubs, Zeal included, only concern for them by the adults. She decided she needed to have a discussion with the one called Greyhook. Having made her point to him, she gave her cubs her love and returned home to Feneas.

* * *

Tulip was alert but tired from staying up all night. The prior evening's proceedings had ended with Zeal's kids' meeting, which had lasted to almost dawn. The story of Charese's fight for freedom had been retold, and Tallen had had a chance to have all his questions answered. Afterwards, they took the opportunity to catch up on the changes occurring in each of their lives.

When she entered her sleep chamber, Tulip discovered a set of gray leathers set out on her sleeper. She wondered if there was any significance to the choice of color. There were matching boots, gloves, and even a helm. Her sword and long knife were encased in new, gray scabbards. She thought of dyeing the sheath of her Fang so everything matched. But, since she kept her Fang as her hideout weapon, no one would ever see it to notice the sheath's color was not the same as the rest of her kit.

While she was excitedly exploring her gear, she sensed someone watching her from behind and looked over her shoulder. Mirada was standing in the doorway.

"Do you like the color?" Mirada had an unusually vulnerable look on her face.

An unsure Mirada was a new sight for Tulip. "It's all amazing. I never expected anything this nice. Yes, I love the color, but why gray? It doesn't have anything to do with Greyhook, does it?"

"No, nothing like that. The leathers were mine. I used to pretend and call myself the Gray Ghost when I wore them. That was way before Greyhook came into my life. I wanted you to have them. Being a woman, you stand out, so why not take pride in the advantage—and occasional disadvantage—of being a woman."

Happy, Mirada visibly relaxed as she continued. "The leather is made from an Argguile hide. It's tougher, more durable than even some metals and will remain flexible and comfortable to wear."

Tulip appreciated the pliant nature of the armor. "I've never heard of an Argguile."

"I think there is a drawing of one in the library. They are rarely encountered, thankfully. The one this leather was made from took twenty experienced fighters to bring down. Even so, it took ten fighters to the grave with it."

"It still looks new. You must not have worn it much." Tulip tried on a glove, marveling at how well it fit.

Mirada smiled. "Actually, every day for five seasons, until I outgrew it."

"Thank you for giving it to me." Tulip's voice was husky with emotion.

"Give it to you!" Mirada laughed. "Consider it on loan. I doubt you'll ever wear it out, but I hope you'll one day loan it to someone you care for and want to protect, just as I have with you."

"I love you, Mirada." Tulip's eyes welled but she willed the tears away.

Mirada caught her up in an unexpected embrace. "And I love you. Believe it or not, I think you've even somehow won Greyhook over. So don't be surprised if he desires to join us in our love fest. Now, take a bath and have a good breakfast before you go. Greyhook and I are going to accompany Ice and Deena to a meet with Cowlin in a mark. I'll see you after you return from your lesson. Be careful today. Fatigue can cause you to make mistakes."

"I will. I promise." After one last tight squeeze, they released each other. Tulip's eyes followed Mirada out of the room, and she began to undress. She was going to get smelly so decided not to wash, but a hot bath would be welcome after her lesson.

She was about to remove her workshirt but then decided to wear it under her new leathers. If Zeal had not been wearing his workshirt the day they traveled the road to Havensharth, the arrow would have killed him. Being able to equip extra protection in her chosen profession was not unwise. Tulip decided to make wearing it a habit.

She tucked the medallion given to her by Iris inside the shirt. While pulling on the gray leather pants, her stomach rumbled. Tulip finished dressing then carried the weapons and helm to the kitchen.

Sliced breakfast meats, cheeses, and bread were laid out on the table, along with boiled eggs and a sealed carafe. Tulip filled a cup with steaming tea, blew on the liquid, and then took a cautious sip. The tea, brewed strong, was lightly sweetened with honey. Tulip made sure not to overeat. After putting away the remainder of the meal and cleaning up, she headed to the training arena.

No one seemed to pay attention to her when she entered. Addis was directing the other Apprentices in calisthenics. They stretched and warmed up in preparation for the day's training. When he finally noticed Tulip watching, he directed the others to continue and walked over to her.

"Told you Master Cowlin would take you on. Welcome back." He welcomed her with a bright smile.

"Where is he?" she asked, looking around the arena so she could report to him, personally.

"He'll be here. He came to the barracks at dawn, woke me up, and told me to start warming up folks. Said he was going to be late due to some meeting he had to attend. He did say to be on the lookout for you, that you were coming today. I like your leathers, but don't you think the color is a bit unusual?"

"Thank you." Tulip glanced at a sleeve. "Gray is not the hue I would have naturally picked out myself, but I must say it is growing on me."

"Were you at the Hall last night for all the action?"

"Action? Not sure what you mean?"

"You know, with Master Cowlin and his family? Do you know anything?" Addis attempted to stay nonchalant.

Tulip used her Trade training to get a read on Addis. It was apparent to her he was overly curious but attempting to hide the fact from her. "I wasn't really paying that much attention. I don't have much to say about it."

Addis studied her for a moment. "That's too bad. I heard it had something to do with your friend's cat. Guess I got it wrong." He pointed to the other Apprentices. "Let's move over and get you warmed up. I always hated having to break in new leathers. They always rubbed me raw in certain places till they became supple."

"I am sure I will be fine. Thanks for looking out for me," Tulip replied pleasantly.

"I'm here to help. I think we are going to be good friends." Addis seemed happy.

In a little under a mark, Master Cowlin entered and took over the session. Tulip smiled when she saw that Charese, full of chatter and questions, had accompanied him. She wore a bright yellow flower in her hair over her right ear, a blossom cut from one of the bulbs she and Zeal had planted. *Interesting,* she thought. Charese's iris bloom hadn't turned to dust like the ones the alchemist, Lady Meva, had attempted to harvest.

CHAPTER NINETEEN

KIT PADDED INTO Deena's kitchen at Zeal's heels. Both were hungry for something to eat after a training session with one called Namrin. Kit was satisfied that Namrin was taking her apprenticeship seriously. He'd called her a fine Apprentice, as he should.

Zeal began to gather ingredients for a midday meal. "I wonder how Charese is faring."

She is well. I looked earlier.

"Thanks for letting me know." Zeal chose a knife from the block. "Let's see what we can find in the larder."

The market and hall should provide scraud.

"How about we go into the woods and see if you can catch a bobit or a couple of diddle ducks? Master Greyhook can show us how to cook them, though I'm sure you'd prefer to eat yours raw." He found a platter of uncooked meats in the cold case and cubed a portion, placing the cut pieces on a trencher for Kit. The remainder he returned to the cold case.

I would feed you.

After fixing a meal of bread, cheeses, and fruit for himself, they sat at the table, Kit on a cushioned seat. Deena called up from her workspace as they were tucking into their food, and Kit wondered about the meeting the elders had had with one called Cowlin.

"When you two finish eating, come down. By the way, a message was delivered from Lady Phyllis. Zeal, you are to attend her tomorrow. She plans to claim the same day every quarter moon for you to continue your Trade study. Ice will inform Namrin that you have tasks on those days."

"Be there shortly," Zeal answered back. "I forgot Tulip and I have to keep up our Trade training." He chuckled at Kit's empty dish. "You sure wolfed your food down."

Imagining he saw her as a canine, she said, *I should bite you. Hounds are inferior.*

"Didn't mean anything. Sorry." He rose from the table, took the dirty dishes to the sink, and quickly washed them. After putting them away, he followed Kit to Deena.

When they entered her workspace, Deana was manipulating a fine-linked chain that spun in the air in front of her. Kit was mesmerized by the piece. The metals of the chain were of differing types and various dark colors. As the piece twisted midair, its unpolished facets danced away from the light as if to avoid it.

Deena looked away from the piece. "Kit, would you come over, please? I have something to show you. This will be for you. I first thought of a bracelet that could fit above one of your paws, but it would catch on things. A collar wouldn't be appropriate, for you are not someone's pet. So I settled on a chain for you to wear around your waist. One that will cling to you, blend with your natural coloring, and not draw attention to itself." She smiled briefly at Zeal, who was observing intently.

You are correct, I will not wear a collar. Kit walked in a circle under the chain with her vibrissae extended. *It hums. Is it finished?*

"No, this is just the base medium, which I will imbue with additional properties. I wanted to incorporate your desires in its design, since it is for you. Let's see how it fits." She took the chain out of the air. Her thin cloth gloves were patterned in symbols and runes written in gold and silver thread. Kneeling, she stretched the chain till it was big enough for Kit to step through.

Kit entered the metal circle in front of her, turned her head, and watched Deena release the chain around her middle. The circle grew smaller till Kit felt it settle at her belly. The humming stopped as the metal's colors blended with her natural coloration. She felt a tickling sensation as the chain snuggled in close to her skin.

Kit stepped into a nearby shadow, only to appear moments later out of another across the room. She felt no inhibition or resistance in her travel and was even surprised to discover she liked the idea of having things to wear. She all but strutted back to Deena.

It will do. She leapt onto the table.

"Zeal, I'd like your opinion." Deena pulled him over.

He leaned in and probed Kit's fur with his fingers. "The chain has camouflaged itself. I can't see or feel it." His eyes were bright with curiosity.

Deena felt around Kit's waist, lifted the links away from her body, and pulled them once again into a large circle. Kit stepped out. Deena repositioned the chain, which resumed its hum and twisting movement in the air in front of her.

"How were you able to find that?" Zeal started to reach toward the chain but drew back.

"Can't hide from these." Deena held up her hands. "Although it did try to avoid my grasp."

"I should have known you wore those for a reason. May I?" Deena nodded, so Zeal shyly touched the cloth hand covers. "I thought the symbols and runes would feel alive or something."

Kit eased herself forward and stroked the warm, silky fabric with one paw before walking away.

"Zeal, I have something I wish you to take to Tallen." Deena showed him an old, dark-brown chest made of worn wood that was sitting on the end of the worktable. When she lifted the lid, there were rusted metal tools inside with deteriorated leather-wrapped handles.

"What are they?"

"They are woodworking tools. I understand he is planning to carve a set of pipes out of wood from a morra tree. Tell Tallen I think he should use these to make the pipes. He can return the tools to me when he's done with them."

Zeal studied the corroded assortment, picking a random tool to examine. In his hand, its leather softened and thickened, making it comfortable to grasp; the tool's metal altered in appearance, its dull edge sharpening. The tool, although not new, was well maintained.

When he returned it to the chest, its degenerated appearance reappeared.

"Are they imbued?" he asked, startled and surprised.

"That they are." Deena smiled. "I was waiting for you to see through the glamour the maker placed on the set. Both you and Kit need to practice looking at the world to see it as it truly is. Always take time to view what is real."

"Yes, Lady Deena, I will try."

Perhaps you should just say Deena, Kit mindspoke to him. She watched Zeal and Deena closely, sensing they wanted the same thing and were waiting for the other to act.

Zeal took a deep breath and exhaled. "I would like to know if you would allow me to address you in an informal manner. May I call you Deena?"

She gathered Zeal's hands in hers. "I would like that."

"What about Master Ice? Would it be proper for me to ask him? He still refers to Master Feneas as master."

"You have the right of it. Ice continues to refer to Feneas as master, even though Feneas has been more of a father to him than a mentor. We'll give Ice the opportunity to react to our change and see what he does. When you give Tallen the tools, he may need help to truly see them. Once he does, he always will."

"How do I do that?" Zeal asked.

Deena closed the lid of the chest and twisted a piece of wire in the hasp. "The best way is for the two of you to hold one of the tools together, with your hands touching."

Kit offered Zeal an observation as he lifted the chest. *Your kind has strange ways. You make life thorny.*

"I guess we do," was his reply.

* * *

Zeal and Kit found Tallen in the workshop behind Tulip's place. Tallen was alone when they entered.

"Hey, Tallen. Got a surprise for you." Zeal held up the chest, which was lighter than he'd expected.

Tallen waved them to the back of the shop. Workbenches, some more cluttered than others, lined both sides of a central walkway. Instruments of all types and in various stages of construction and repair awaited completion.

Zeal set the chest on an unobstructed area of Tallen's workspace. Tallen's bench was more organized and in less disarray then the rest of the shop.

"Hello there, Kit. Nice to have you and Zeal visit." Tallen put away the rasp he was using.

Kit leapt up and sat next to the chest. *Have you finished your song sticks?*

"Not yet." He picked up a knot-free piece of red wood and showed it to her. "I'm using red asdic to learn the process, so I don't waste material. Then I'll take the knowledge I gain and apply it to this." He held a caramel, tight-grained sample for her to see. "This is from a morra tree."

Zeal took a length of morra to examine. "Very nice. I like the color and pattern of the wood. I hope the pipes you construct will sound as good as they will look."

"You and me both." Tallen ran a hand over the chest's lid. "This has been well cared for. How did you know I needed something to store things in?"

"I am sure you can make use of the chest, but you will find what's inside it even more useful. Deena asked me to bring it to you. By the way, it and its contents are on loan."

"So 'tis no longer Lady Deena for you. Are you disrespecting the fine lady who has presented me such a magnificent gift?" Tallen pretended to be offended.

"I have permission, and you know it." Zeal's face brightened but then sobered when he thought of Tallen's loss.

"Don't be sad for me." Tallen placed his hands on the bench and leaned forward. "I am happy for you and Tulip. When we first met, I thought you were the son of Master Ice and Tulip the daughter of Lady Mirada. Only later did I find out you were orphans who'd found someone to care for you. It made me realize I, too, might have a family again."

"Tallen, I know I speak for Tulip and me, both. We are your family now. What say you, Kit?"

He is not furry enough to be family. But I will make him Pride.

"I think you should take that as close to an agreement as you are going to get." Zeal laughed along with Tallen.

"Tis a fine offer, Kit, and I accept. So, what is in the chest? If it is made of ironwood, as I suspect, it should be heavy, which would mean either you have gotten stronger or there is something special about it. Am I right?"

"We need to open the lid together, so the chest will know you. Deena said it will then attune to you. You'll also be able to move the chest wherever you want. Otherwise, it *is* real heavy. And yes, I am that much stronger."

Zeal watched Tallen's face closely as they opened the chest together. Instead of appearing disappointed to see old rusted tools, he looked pleased, as if being reunited with a long-lost friend.

Tallen picked up a curved drawknife and ran his hand along the blade. "It only needs a little loving and care to be put to right. I'll start putting them to right after the evening meal. It shouldn't take me long to have them all ready for use. You must thank Lady Deena for me. No, I will thank her myself."

Zeal respected Tallen's reaction and realized he'd just learned a lesson from his friend. He took Tallen's hand and grasped the knife handle. "Look again," he said with encouragement.

Tallen's mouth opened: the drawknife blade was no longer rusted. Its metal now had the fine patina that a well-used tool acquired over time. Its edge was sharp and no longer chipped and pitted.

"Deena told me to tell you to use them to construct your new pipes. You can return them when you are done. Tallen, always remember. You have us. You are not alone."

"You are right. I'm not." His eyes were bright with wonder.

Tallen took each tool out of the chest and examined it carefully before taking out another.

"How did you know the chest was made of ironwood?" Zeal

asked.

Tallen closed his eyes, lost in memory. Whatever he was thinking must have been quite dear: a single tear ran down his right cheek.

"My mother often took me into the forest when I was young. She told me about the trees, plants, and wildlife. How we and they are the skin of nature's body, how we share life with each other. I learned what was safe to eat, to use for illness or for injury. Mother taught me to care for the forest and be respectful. There was a tree she called 'her' tree. It grew next to our house, which was built into a hillside. Mother said Father met her sitting under her tree, an ironwood tree. Father said he knew they were meant to be together at that first meeting. He always said nature provided for him and would provide for the family, as well." Tallen grew quiet as he lovingly began to replace the tools in the chest.

Zeal stood quietly next to him, offering his support. He couldn't find appropriate words, so he remained silent.

Kit placed a paw on Tallen's arm. *I will feed you, and you in turn will protect the Pride.*

* * *

He sat and thought about his reply before answering Listina's question. "No, it was just those two evenings. Zeal and the animal left their residence, went directly to the Quad, entered, and spent several marks there. I couldn't see what he was doing because the barriers were raised."

Listina sat at her desk, across from her visitor. They were in the sitting area that adjoined her sleeping chamber. She'd let him in through her window and closed the shutters before unhooding a lantern. "You are sure Zeal was there alone? No one else was with him?"

"Only him and the animal." He shifted position in the uncomfortable chair.

"You can go. Continue to keep an eye on him, and report back to me." She reached for the lantern and darkened it.

"You said I only needed to spy on him for a short period. I did what you wanted."

"You owe me and will follow Zeal as long as I tell you to. Why the sudden change in heart?"

"Zeal's a good kid. I don't see why he caught your attention." He wasn't going to tell Listina the real reason was he'd recently learned that Zeal was a member of the Trade. As an apprentice to the Trade himself, he was aware that Trade did not betray each other. Perhaps he should approach Zeal and confess or bring this matter to Lady Phyllis.

"Don't concern yourself with my business. Do what you are told for another quarter moon, and I'll forget what I know about certain transgressions. Now, go. I've other means to discover what Zeal is doing in the Quad."

CHAPTER TWENTY

THE CLOUD COVER made the night a touch darker than usual, keeping the light of the moon and stars from gracing the land. Zeal, with intent, extinguished the candles in his room, absorbing the fiery motes into his being. He peered out through the partially open shutters and searched for anyone present below, above, or in the trees. The bed of blooms below his window had not been trodden. No illumination revealed the presence of a traveler using the light to show their way.

No one is here. Kit lay across his shoulders. She'd previously detected a male observing the cottage who'd not been much good at stalking them.

Zeal, once aware of the presence, had been able to locate the person watching them, hidden in a tree. On the last two occasions when they'd ventured to the Casting Quad, he and Kit had been followed. Zeal had considered approaching the person but believed it was one of the young Apprentices of the Trade who was practicing his or her night work.

Taking advantage of natural handholds on the exterior wall of the cottage, Zeal climbed out the window and down the wall, dropping silently to the ground. As he squatted amongst the plants, reducing his profile, he waited and listened for sounds from the house. He desired to make sure their exit was unnoticed. It felt good to practice the skills he'd learned in the Trade.

In Arlanda, he would travel the upper road, moving roof to roof, but the buildings in Havensharth were too far apart. The trees weren't good to use, either, as they did not grow close enough to one another to move branch-to-branch unseen.

Satisfied that he and Kit were unobserved, he stealthily carried her to the Casting Quad. Once there, he meant to try a conjure he had recently read in the *Book of Flames*: crystal fire. Now *that* was intriguing.

* * *

The sun had lowered to treetop level when Qwen blew into the wood outside of Havensharth with his five Zephyr companions. He'd assumed the aspect of a Zephyr to travel to Havensharth from Arlanda. The creatures of air were capable of moving at speeds that varied from a gentle breeze to a raging tempest.

Even though he was a Practitioner of the Arts and a Tzefire—one aligned with the element of air—he was hungry. Landing next to a small pool and broad-branched tree, he changed back to what his friends referred to as his "land-bound" self.

Studying his reflection in the water's surface, he adjusted his hat then removed a blue tarp from his travel satchel to place on the ground and prevent his clothing from becoming soiled. Appearance was important. He enjoyed having others think of him as a superficial dandy: it led them to overlook the true person disguised under the façade.

The branches of the tree gently bobbed and swayed as his companions played tag in the boughs. They would let him know if anyone came near. He dined on aged blue cheeses, fresh corn muffins, crisp battered fish filets, and toasted greens he had prepared in his kitchen before leaving Arlanda. His berries and cream for dessert were washed down with a fine, complementary pale ale.

As he repacked his satchel, he thought back on his instructions from the Trade Master of Arlanda. Slag had simply informed Qwen to wait in the Casting Quad and prevent Zeal from killing his adversary. Qwen was not to otherwise interfere; he would know when the moment to act had arrived. Qwen wished Slag had been more forthcoming and less cryptic. Whatever the outcome, it would be a pleasure to be reacquainted with Zeal and Tulip.

Perhaps, while in Havensharth, he should look in on Greyhook and make use of his excellent kitchen, Qwen thought to himself. He had last visited the Enclaves eight seasons ago, to do research, and had made friends with the head of the Bardic Enclave. Who knew bards collected recipes in their library?

Changing back into airy form, Qwen rejoined his associates, and together they flew into Havensharth. Darkness approached as they took up residence inside the Casting Quad. Qwen floated in the air, near the top of a pillar, across from the Quad's entrance.

Joining with his companions, he said, "You remember Zeal and Tulip. Please locate them for me. Let me know when he is coming." Two of the Zephyrs separated and flew off.

Qwen had become acquainted with Zeal, Tulip, and the other Trade Apprentices prior to one of them, Liddea, being abducted. With the Apprentices' help, Liddea had been found and rescued. Then, while Qwen was away dealing with one of Liddea's escaped abductors, it was discovered that Zeal had the potential to become a Practitioner. Slag had informed Qwen that Zeal was also a Phosfire—a Practitioner with an alignment with fire—incredible as that seemed. Qwen planned to have a discussion with Zeal regarding his Phosfire ability during this visit to Havensharth.

Three marks passed before a hooded figure entered the Casting Quad and crossed to the opposite side. Tempest, one of Qwen's friends, flew down to the figure and, after a brief inspection, rejoined with Qwen. This new land-bound was a female Practitioner; Tempest was able to identify persons capable of conjure.

Carefully venturing close to the female, Qwen conducted his own examination. He found it difficult to locate her, as the cloak she wore allowed her to blend with her surroundings, making her almost impossible to see when she stayed still. If he hadn't tracked her as she came into the Quad and observed her final position, he might have missed her altogether, although her scent did give her away.

Her fragrance on the breeze assaulted Qwen's heightened sense of smell. It was apparent this land-bound preferred to wear an inferior perfume. Even a humble Trade Apprentice was taught the nose is a tool; having no odor was preferable, if someone wished to hide unseen.

Flowing in and out of his companions, Qwen returned to his observation spot. "Keep a watch on her please."

A half mark later, he saw movement at the Quad's entrance. He didn't need help from his companion, who followed alongside the newcomer, to recognize Zeal, silhouetted by the moon's light. Zeal had grown since leaving Arlanda and was tonight accompanied by a rather large feline that he carried draped across his shoulders. This gave the boy the appearance of being hunched over with a deformed back. The cat was at least twice the size of any Qwen had ever seen and seemed to be surveying the area.

Zeal stopped in the Quad's center and called out. "I know you're here, so you might as well make yourself seen."

Qwen thought for a moment. Did Zeal know about the female? Or the Zephyrs? As he pondered this dilemma, the female caster broke her camouflage and approached Zeal. Qwen decided to listen awhile to their conversation and not alert them to his presence.

"What are you doing here? Are you lost, Apprentice?" the female said with condescension.

"I was just passing through. It is easier to walk through the Quad instead of around it," Zeal answered defensively.

Qwen thought Zeal should have been more creative with his excuse.

"You know you are not to enter the Quad without a mentor. I bet you're up to mischief, aren't you? Let's take a good look at you"

Qwen recognized the conjures being used by Zeal's accuser. First, she created a light to illuminate the area. This casting was followed by conjures to activate the Casting Quad's protections, shrouding and warding it. The verbal component spoken for each conjure was carried to him by his companions, whose movements stirred the air inside the Quad.

Qwen saw Zeal look around and then whisper, "A breeze. Why is there a breeze—the Quad is locked down."

"Do you remember who I am?" the female asked.

"Your name is Listina. You're a senior Apprentice. I don't know what you want with me, so just please tell me." Zeal held his hands where Listina could see them.

Zeal kept his eyes downcast and appeared humble. Qwen wondered why he was not demonstrating the backbone he'd known the boy to have.

"You are correct. I am Listina. You know you are not supposed to use the Quad alone. From now on, I own you. If you don't want the Masters to learn about your little night visits in here, you will do whatever I want. Do you understand what I mean?"

The more Qwen listened, the more he decided this Listina needed mastery. He intended to have words with her mentor and with Namrin, the Master of Instruction.

Qwen noticed Zeal's demeanor change. He straightened and looked Listina directly in the eyes. "I don't think so. Now, if you know what is good for you, drop the wards. Kit and I will take our leave. You can tell the Masters whatever you want. I don't care."

This was the Zeal he remembered. Oh, the female twit is vexed now, Qwen thought to himself.

Listina's face clouded with rage, her nostrils flared, and her lips peeled away from her straight teeth. Qwen cringed when Listina whispered the word, "RiGor," and was unprepared to counter the casting. Listina had used a malefic form of Necromancy.

Qwen saw Zeal and the feline suddenly engulfed in a black cloud of smoke that rapidly thickened, compressing around them and hiding them from sight. Suddenly, beams of light pierced the cloud and pushed back the darkness, which began to thin. Qwen could see a band of luminescence emanate from near the base of the cat's tail along with a second source at Zeal's chest. As the haze began to dissipate, the aroma of iris blooms permeated the air.

"What did you conjure?" Zeal angrily demanded of Listina.

Qwen took solid form. Two of his companions gathered underneath him and held him aloft, but, given Slag's mandate to not interfere, he did not stop Zeal. Instinctively, the boy had known he and his feline had avoided a substantial peril. How would Zeal respond to the attack?

All at once, Qwen recognized the danger. He quickly asked one of his companions to carry his words, along with physical force. Then he yelled.

* * *

Deena was notified by the cottage wards that Tulip and Tallen were at the door moments before they knocked. She welcomed them in, saying, "If you are looking for Zeal, he is not here. I thought he was with you." The wards had informed her when he'd left out the window with Kit less than a mark ago. Deena had neglected to enlighten him of a certain aspect of her protections that allowed her to keep track of everyone entering or leaving the cottage.

Tallen looked at Tulip and hesitated before answering. "No, he's not with us."

Tulip shrugged. "It's not his evening to work with Lady Phyllis. For some unknown reason, I have a nagging feeling about him."

Deena thought for a moment. "He has nothing scheduled that I'm aware of. I'll have to train him to keep me informed of his plans, as I've done with Ice. Does Mirada know your whereabouts?"

"Yes, she knows I am here and that Tallen is with me," Tulip replied.

"Lady Deena, many thanks for the woodworking tools," Tallen said shyly. "They have made a huge difference in the quality of work I produce, but I can't repay you for their use."

One of Deena's eyebrows rose. "Yes, you can. By playing your new pipes for me, once you've finished them."

Tallen smiled broadly. "That *is* something I can do."

Suddenly, the scent of irises filled the room. Deena saw Tulip turn pale. "Tulip, what is wrong?"

"I don't know, but something is not right, and Zeal is involved. You can thank Lady Deena another time, Tallen. We need to find

Zeal." She turned sharply toward the door.

"Wait! I'll trust you're somehow aware Zeal may be in a predicament. Can either of you think where he might go this time of night?" She studied their faces, starting to feel uneasy herself.

"Possibly the Hall for a snack—he always talks about how hungry Kit is. But we all know it is really Zeal who's hungry. I don't know where he puts it all." Tallen quickly added, "I doubt Zeal would find trouble there."

"True, but he hates to eat alone. I think he would have looked for one or both of us to join him." Tulip stopped and turned back to Deena. "Being new to Havensharth, I don't know if Zeal has a place he'd seek out to be alone. Perhaps there is someplace in the Repository similar to our mausoleum back at the Temple? Are you aware that Zeal can talk with the dead? He often kept company with the guardian spirits in the Temple mausoleum."

Deena wasn't aware of that particular talent of Zeal's. "There is a crypt in the lowest level of the Repository, but it's doubtful Zeal has discovered its existence. Even so, I can't think of any danger for him there, if he has." She turned the red crystal of her ring from Ice toward the palm of her right hand. Deena rubbed the gem with her left thumb and felt her ring match harmonies with the one Ice wore.

Yes, love? she heard Ice ask in her thoughts.

Meet us at the Repository. Tulip thinks Zeal may be in trouble and might be in the crypt. Tallen is with us.

Ice's response was quickly returned. *I am already at the Repository. I'll look around and ask if anyone has seen him.* The communication ended within a few heartbeats.

"Come," she said. "We are meeting Ice at the Repository."

Tallen hurriedly followed. "Why is Zeal so fascinated with spirits?" He received no answer.

Deena set a brisk pace, so it did not take long to cross into the Practitioner's Enclave and reach the Repository. As they approached, she noticed the Casting Quad in the distance was shrouded in darkness, indicating it was in use. When the wind suddenly intensified, she felt it gently push her in the back, as if guiding her toward the Quad.

They were met by Ice and Namrin on the steps of the Repository, where Ice took Deena's hand in his. "I was in a meeting with Namrin when we linked. With his aid, we were able to ascertain that Zeal is not in the building and has not entered this evening."

Namrin, next to Ice, cleared his throat. "May I ask why you think Zeal is in peril?"

All eyes turned to Tulip, who was trying to maintain her balance as she, too, was repeatedly pushed from behind.

Namrin reached into a pocket and removed a pair of gazers and he placed on the bridge of his nose. When he looked at Tulip through them, his eyes widened in recognition. "Tulip, how long have you had a Zephyr attempting to gain your attention? It appears the wind creature is striving to aim you in a particular direction."

"Excuse me, what did you say was trying to get my attention?"

Just then, the wind gusted hard enough to force Tulip to take a step forward. Deena looked through a monocle placed on her left eye, and Ice said, "Viseus," along with making a quick gesture so he could view the unseen.

Tallen asked, "What's a Zephyr?" just as Deena said, "Ah, I see."

The three Master Practitioners saw the Zephyr coiled around Tulip's chest. Serpentine in shape, its supple undulating body had no appendages, but its head had large, oval eyes and a maw that appeared and disappeared from view. The creature gently pulled Tulip away from the party.

Deena knew, if the Zephyr wanted to, it could lift Tulip into the air and carry her wherever it wished.

Tulip looked back over her shoulder. "I think Zeal is over there." She began to walk fast in the direction of the Casting Quad.

"It appears we're needed in the Casting Quad," Deena said, hurrying to catch up with Tulip. "Are you coming, gentlemen?"

* * *

"ZEAL, STOP!"

The words blasted loudly in Listina's ears along with a gust of wind that blew Zeal away from her. He landed forcefully on his back, and she heard his lungs empty with a grunt. He lay, momentarily stunned but somehow still cradling that damn cat in his arms.

Everything had been perfect. No one knew the three of them were in the Quad. She'd intended to report finding their bodies by accident... A new Apprentice, doing who knows what in the Quad, alone... how horrible.... Now, her plan was ruined.

"You both should be dead," she whispered. She had expected to experience both Zeal's and Kit's deaths, but the killing fog she'd conjured had been nullified by a strange, bright light that had left her victims still living.

Zeal stared upward. "Master Qwen, what are you doing up there?"

Listina followed his gaze. Above them floated a figure dressed in sky blue from head to toe, likely the source of the interruption. She closed her eyes to keep the grit and swirling wind from blinding her.

Suddenly, all was still. Listina's arms were being held to her sides by some unseen force and her hands, fingers open, were pressed against her thighs. She opened her eyes and looked up to see this Qwen person, who had to be a Master Practitioner. But who was he, she wondered, and what did the boy mean to him?

That there was a witness to what she'd done made her fearful. Worse was when the Quad's protective barrier and shroud dropped, and Masters Namrin, Ice, and Lady Deena entered, accompanied by Zeal's two playmates.

Namrin bellowed, "*What* is going on here?" He looked up. "Is that you Qwen? *Explain!*"

Listina decided to try to spin the events in as positive a light for herself as she could. But she was shocked to discover, not only was she held in place, but she couldn't say a word. She could breathe, but every time she opened her mouth, an airy pressure pushed her words down her throat. She was being held prisoner in her own body!

"I am here to prevent one of your students from killing the

other." Qwen's gaze was focused on Listina.

She cringed. Nothing she could do would change things now.

"What do you mean? Your answer please, sir." Namrin was confused and furious. His eyes danced from Listina to Zeal and back to Listina. "Surely you don't mean you stopped Listina from attacking Zeal?"

"No. I didn't come to Havensharth to impede her, although Listina did assault him. I am here to restrain Zeal." Qwen floated to the ground, took Zeal's hand, and helped him to his feet.

"Master Qwen, wait! Let me explain," Zeal began, but he was interrupted by Qwen.

"You'll be allowed to have your say, but for now, hold your tongue and listen. Zeal was attacked by Listina. She used a lethal form of Necromancy against him and his pet. Somehow, he repulsed it. I kept him from conjuring in retaliation, as his conjure would surely have killed her."

Listina wondered what Qwen was talking about. Zeal had yelled like the scared little boy he was and never begun any form of conjure. What was going on here? Why did Namrin and the others look like they believed Qwen? She tried to remain focused until she could learn what they knew.

"Listina, you will retire to your quarters until you are sent for. I intend to review the evidence and Qwen's accusation. Do you understand?" Namrin stood waiting for her answer. When she didn't respond to him, he asked, "Qwen, do you have Listina held in some fashion?"

"Yes. One moment." Qwen turned to face her. "Let the land-bound go."

Listina felt her bonds release and her throat empty. Since her word would carry less weight than a Master's, this was not the place or time to plead her case. She bowed to Namrin. "I go to my rooms."

With one last openly hateful look at Zeal, she headed to the Quad's entrance. No one saw her smile as she walked away.

CHAPTER TWENTY-ONE

NAMRIN SUGGESTED that further discussion occur in his study in the Repository. Once there, he sat behind his desk and had comfortable chairs brought for everyone else. Qwen, Deena, and Ice were in attendance, as were Zeal, Tallen, Tulip, and, of course, Kit. Refreshments were provided on Qwen's request.

After everyone was settled, Namrin listened to Qwen's testimony. Qwen started his recitation with his arrival to Havensharth. He reviewed Listina's actions upon entering the Casting Quad and the interaction between her, Zeal, and Kit, after the latter two had made their appearance. Qwen then described, in detail, the result of the conjure used by Listina. He ended with how he had interrupted Zeal.

"How did you know this event was going to occur?" Namrin asked.

Qwen looked to Ice. "Is Namrin aware of Zeal's former area of study?"

"Yes. I informed him that Zeal was an Apprentice with the Trade before his abilities were discovered, that he is a Phosfire, and that Kit can conjure," Ice replied.

"Who is Kit?" Qwen asked.

I am. Why did you not let Zeal finish the hunt? Although her question was for Qwen, she mindspoke to everyone in the chamber. *I am not a pet or a kitten,* she added.

Qwen sat straighter in his chair and focused on Kit's features.

Namrin chuckled to himself. He enjoyed seeing someone else confounded by discovering Kit's uniqueness. He gave Qwen a few heartbeats to digest the news. "So, how did you know?"

"Yes… Sorry." Qwen looked away from Kit. "I was approached by the Head of the Trade in Arlanda and given explicit instructions to be in the Quad this evening with the coming of darkness. You already know my purpose for being here."

"Why did you not stop Listina's attack on Zeal? Or, for that matter, inform me of the event and let me decide on how to deal with the matter?" Namrin felt somewhat offended.

"Specifically, I had one task to attend to, as stated. It did not include your notification beforehand," Qwen replied, unintimidated.

While Qwen meant him no disrespect, the fact that Namrin was the Master of Instruction of the Enclave of the Practitioners of the Arts and Director of the Repository in Havensharth seemed not to have influenced Qwen whatsoever. After thanking him for his assistance, he asked Zeal, "Why were you in the Quad tonight? Did you know Listina was going to be there?"

Zeal held Namrin's gaze. "I had researched new information regarding flame and discovered the existence of crystal fire. I wanted to test this discovery in a safe environment. I knew the Casting Quad was not scheduled for use tonight. But no, I did not know Listina would be there waiting for me."

Namrin studied him for any deception as Zeal continued. He found himself disturbed by Listina's intent to control Zeal for her own unknown purpose. Who else had she influenced in such a way? he wondered. This was something he needed to look into. When Zeal arrived at the part where he realized the lethal intent behind her attack, Namrin interrupted. "How did you survive?"

"I don't know for sure, but I have an idea. Please give me a moment." He gestured to Deena and approached her, and they had a quiet discussion. He pulled a medallion from inside his shirt and showed it to her. Deena conjured a casting Namrin recognized as one used to decipher the properties of an imbued object.

"The medallion he wears provided protection from the conjure Listina used against them," Deena confirmed.

Namrin asked to inspect the object himself. "This is very old. I don't recognize the make. How did you come by it?"

"It was given to me by someone special, before I left Arlanda."

Namrin waited for Zeal to elaborate, but when no further information was forthcoming, he pushed on. "Zeal, you weren't going to kill Listina, as Qwen suggests, were you?" Although the boy had a lot of talent and was a Phosfire, Namrin believed him to be still too young to have lethal thoughts.

As if the chamber were living, it grew silent, waiting for Zeal's answer. The air's warmth was sucked away and the temperature dropped. Namrin could not detect anything amiss when he looked around the workspace or discover the source of his unease, but he saw the whites in Zeal's eyes momentarily glow the color of melting metal in the heat of a forge.

"I wasn't going to hurt her for trying to harm me. But for trying to kill Kit, she would have burned, if Master Qwen hadn't been there. To be honest, she still may. I haven't decided yet." Zeal's voice was steely.

If I had not yielded the hunt to Zeal, she would have been my prey for trying to harm what is mine, Kit added.

Appreciative of Qwen's intervention, Namrin said, "Zeal, I would like you and Kit to promise me not to seek vengeance on Listina. Let me handle her. Will you both agree to this?" He looked from Kit to Zeal and back, not yet certain they would comply with his request.

Zeal and Kit looked into each other's eyes and held an internal discussion. After a brief period, they both turned to Namrin.

"Kit and I agree to wait for now. That is all we will promise. We don't trust Listina and will protect each other from her. Listina will not be given the opportunity to harm either of us or anyone we care for." Zeal pointed to Tulip, Tallen, Ice, and Deena when he finished speaking, making it clear to whom he was referring.

Namrin turned to Deena. "Take the Apprentices home. Qwen and Ice will remain and witness Listina's testimony with me. Once I decide on her future, Ice will inform you of the outcome. Zeal, I have yet to determine the consequence for your inappropriate use of the

Casting Quad."

Deena shook her head. "Even though I am not fond of Listina, I will not have her interrogated by a group of males, however well meaning, without female representation."

"I wouldn't argue the point, Namrin," Ice said, taking Deena's hand in his, "if I were you. Plus, I agree Deena should remain. I can accompany the young ones."

"There's no need for you to go." Deena eyed each of the Apprentices. "The four of you head directly to the cottage. You are not to leave until I return home. Kit, I trust you to take charge and ensure my orders are carried out."

I will nip them if needed, Mother Deena.

"You are not to discuss what occurred in the Quad or Listina's part with anyone currently not present in this chamber." After receiving an affirming chorus from Zeal and the rest, Namrin rose to his feet and escorted the Apprentices from the workroom.

Through the open door, he directed a runner to summon Listina. Namrin felt angry, not only at Listina but also at himself, for not seeing how Listina had manipulated him.

* * *

The next morn, Zeal awakened with Kit curled beside him. She had taken over the pillow. Their minds and bodies were connected, and Zeal felt secure, knowing they were together. Kit augmented him and made him a better person, but he wondered what she received from him in return.

Blankets and pillows were mounded in the room's open area with him and Kit in the center. Tulip and Tallen had stayed over but had already left the group sleeping-nest they'd made in his room after Deena had informed him it wouldn't be proper for everyone to crowd into a sleeper.

The sun was already riding high in the sky. He and Kit had been allowed to sleep in. "Well, Kit, Tulip and Tallen must have gone to their training. I wonder what Master Namrin's punishment is going to be… Whatever he decides won't matter, though, because I'm happy you weren't hurt last eve." He rubbed his face on her fur.

I am glad you continue to hunt, she replied with reassurance.

After attending to his toilet and grooming, Zeal set his room to rights. If not for Kit informing him that Deena was in her workspace, he would have thought they were alone in the cottage. He made a meal of the toasted bread and boiled diddle duck eggs that Deena had set out for him. Kit had her usual chunks of raw beast. After cleaning up their dishes, he decided to face Deena.

He found her right where Kit said. Deena had her back to them as they entered her workroom. She was peering through her monocle, studying Kit's chain and a red crystal encased in a white metal bezel that she'd added to its construction.

That is for me! Kit's thought practically rumbled in his mind.

Yes, and I agree. You will make it look just as stunning as it does you.

"Did you find something to eat?" Deena asked without looking away from her work.

"Yes, we did. Thank you. What purpose will the crystal serve?"

"I think you meant to ask if I am upset with you. The answer is no. Actually, I am equally proud and disappointed in you."

Zeal felt mixed emotions: surprise, frustration, embarrassment, and humility all warred inside him. And… guilt.

Deena continued, "I am proud of who you are and how you value those you care for. I am pleased at how you handled yourself last night, and I'm satisfied you had justification to respond as you intended. What I'm not happy with is your not trusting me to help you. No, don't apologize. Nothing you say will suffice or satisfy me. Now, how about we come to an arrangement? If, in the future, you include me when you feel the need to use the Casting Quad for your… studies, then you and Kit, if she wishes, will be taught what I know of imbuing."

"I wanted to go someplace safe," Zeal tried to explain. "I didn't want anyone to get hurt."

Deena interrupted him. "So, you would risk Kit, instead?" She turned to look at Zeal for the first time.

"No! She was not in danger."

"Then I won't be, either."

Deena is like Mother. We should listen to her. Mother would not be this gentle, Kit mindspoke to them both.

It hurt to know he'd let Deena down. "You are both right. I will honor this... understanding." He didn't know how, but he wanted to make it up to her.

Deena's brow rose. "One more thing. No more leaving through your window without informing me of where you are going and when you are coming back. I don't care if you enter and exit that way. If Ice can keep me informed of his business, so can you. Understood?"

You should agree before her claws show.

Zeal could see how hard it was for Deena not to laugh. "I promise." It was different, having someone looking out for you in life, after seeing to himself all these seasons, as he had. He now realized it didn't have to be that way any longer.

No, it does not, Kit added to Zeal, alone.

Deena placed her monocle over one eye. "You asked about the crystal. It is capable of storing a conjure—up to three, actually. I thought about what you said regarding Listina. I think the casting she used was pre-conjured and stored in an object she had in her possession. If so, she would only need to use a verbal element to release it."

"Speaking of Listina, what was decided last night about her? Do you know?" Zeal asked.

"Nothing. I talked with Ice, who told me, when Namrin sent for her, it was discovered she was no longer in Havensharth. She left, taking with her several items she had been allowed to study from the Repository. Namrin as her Mentor felt responsible for not having recognized the faults in her character." Deena removed her monocle. "Word was dispatched to her father regarding the matter. If she comes back and returns the objects, Namrin will decide if she's to be allowed to complete her studies here."

The hunt, it is on? Kit asked both Zeal and Deena.

"The hunt is still mine. Next time we meet, she will need to answer one way or another for what she tried to do. If Master

Namrin is unable to find her, I doubt we can. I just hope she stays away and doesn't come back."

Zeal thought about how Qwen had located the linen square he'd given to their friend Liddea, which helped find her after she was abducted. It might be possible for Master Namrin to do the same with one of the items taken from the Repository.

"You need to let Namrin handle this. You both need not worry about Listina. She will be dealt with." Deena patted the top of the worktable. "Kit, hop up. I am finished with your chain. Zeal, would you like the honor of placing it on her?"

Zeal's head bobbed up and down excitedly. He took the chain and held it open for Kit to step into. It was a beautifully crafted, working art form, like all of Deena's pieces. The links absorbed the light instead of reflecting it. Its subdued colors were a mixture of dark, metallic hues. The chain rapidly sized itself and disappeared from sight, blending with Kit's fur.

It feels right, but I still see it, Kit said, twisting to view the chain better. It fit snug to her middle, just above her hips, with the crystal just below her umbilicus.

"That is because you're the one wearing it. You alone are able to view it, unless you will it to appear to someone else. Of course, there may be a conjure or other ways to allow someone to become aware of its presence, much like the ring on your tail, which I can see through my monocle." Deena made a final adjustment, shifting the links so they weren't twisted.

Zeal was speechless. It seemed like Deena knew all his secrets. "Iris gave Kit her ring. It protected her from Listina's conjure, same as the medallion I received from Iris did for me."

"I would like to hear more of your Lady Iris sometime. Kit, maybe one sun you will let me examine your ring. But for now, it seems I have a visitor in the shop upstairs. Come, let's go see who it is."

It is one called Qwen, and I will show my ring to you.

* * *

Qwen walked around the shop, inspecting the merchandise for sale. Most of the items were either imbued, ready to be imbued, or were raw materials used in the process.

He was accompanied by two of his companions. The others were enjoying the skies above Havensharth. He had asked them last eve to search for Listina, and while they had her scent, they informed him she was no longer in Havensharth or anywhere nearby. He suspected she had conjured a means of transport and was now some distance away.

He was admiring a lovely blue crystal, its bezel fastened on a headband, when the proprietor stepped out from behind the curtain across the counter. She was accompanied by Zeal and Kit.

"Good day, Master Qwen. Do you bring us word of Listina?" Deena asked.

"Qwen. Please. May I address you by Deena? I am sure we'll become confidants, since we both have Zeal's best in mind." He studied Kit, who was clearly nobody's house pet, as he'd first surmised. He wondered what Zeal had gotten attached to.

"Yes, please by all means. Zeal thinks highly of you, and by your intervention, you have already demonstrated that you care for him."

"Sorry. I don't have news related to Listina. However, I want to ask if I could talk with Zeal. May we borrow your kitchen? You are welcome to join us, of course." Qwen made a shallow bow to her.

"My kitchen? I am not sure I understand your request."

"Well, you see, I do my best thinking while cooking. I also find that good food carries the conversation. I wish to become reacquainted with my young friend here. If I recall correctly, he likes to eat. I hope that hasn't changed." He glanced in Zeal's direction.

"Not if it is something you've fixed, Master Qwen," he happily answered.

Pleased with Zeal's smile, Qwen tapped his satchel. "I have the makings of a fine bread pudding and a sweet, spiced mead sauce to accompany it. Just call me Qwen. No Master is necessary. We are going to get to know each other way too well to allow that between us. And you must let me get to know Kit, as well. That is, if it is okay with you, Kit."

Do you have scraud in your bag?

"No, but I could have some for you for the evening meal, if that would suit you."

That will do.

"May we use the kitchen, please? I will help clean up," Zeal asked eagerly.

Deena gestured for Qwen to come around the counter. "By all means, put my kitchen to use. I hope you are as talented at food preparing as Zeal hints."

Qwen nodded his head. "We shall see. Thank you, Deena. Zeal, you will help me make the pudding. Cooking is similar to conjuring. Both require one to relax and focus the mind on the task at hand. You, young man, need to learn how to cook."

Qwen was directed to the kitchen, where he removed a pan, large bowl, wooden spoon, and several ingredients from his satchel.

"Oh, before I forget," Qwen said mostly to himself. From a pocket inside his jacket, he retrieved a charcoal stick and paper. After briefly scribbling a message, he folded it along with several coins and placed them in a cloth bag.

He opened a window, held the bag out, and let go of it. The bag remained suspended in the air, held by one of his companions. "The two of you, please take this to Thacky. Return with the contents of the bag after Thacky finishes making the exchange. Yes, before night comes would be nice. Don't wear yourselves out. Thank you." The bag was whisked away.

"I've never seen anyone talk to a sack before. Has it been imbued?" Zeal stared through the window, looking up at the sky.

After quietly conjuring, Qwen touched Zeal and Kit on their forehead with a finger. He could tell by their expressions that they could see his companions. Kit, indeed, had quite the look: her ears stood straight, her nostrils flared, her eyes widened and their color darkened, her vibrissae extended, and her tail twitched slightly.

"Who— What are they?" Zeal pointed to the mostly translucent, iridescent forms he saw flowing around the room. He turned to Deena. "Can you see them?"

"Not at this moment, but I knew they were here. They are

Zephyrs, creatures of air." She put her monocle to her eye.

"That is not the name they call themselves." Qwen did not elaborating further. "I did a service for their kind and have had the pleasure of their company ever since. As a Tzefire, it would be easy to abuse their gift. I've chosen never to do that."

"I've read about creatures of fire. Do you think I will meet any of them?" Zeal asked.

Qwen was caught by Zeal's enthusiasm. "I think, one day, you will. I implore you to address them with respect. Treat them as you would wish to be treated. Help them when you can, without expecting anything in return. Champion them as you would one of our own kind. As a Phosfire, that is your duty."

"That is a lot to place on him, Qwen," Deena cautioned. She stepped to Zeal and draped an arm across his shoulders protectively. Kit crept closer, as well.

"I appreciate your concern, but I have to be certain Zeal understands the responsibility he has to all creatures of the elements. Dealing with beings of fire, however, will become his forte." Qwen passed a bowl and leather-covered box to Zeal. "Open these and put them in the bowl."

Zeal inspected the outside of the box before opening it. The box was padded inside and contained fifteen diddle duck eggs.

"Take three yolks and place them in this cup," Qwen instructed. "They will be used in the sauce. The rest go into the custard."

Can I lick the shells? Kit asked.

"By all means. My companions will help with cleanup as we go along. When you are done with the shells, just place them to the side. Once you finish with the eggs, I have a flask of cream to add and several spices. Deena, would you please ready the oven for us?"

"Only if I get to have a taste of this—what did you call it?" Deena took a tinder twig and lit the fire in the oven.

"I call it bread pudding. I came by the recipe at the Bardic Library when I was here last. It has been a favorite of mine ever since."

Zeal put the empty shells on a dish that he set on the floor for Kit. "Where is the bread?"

Qwen withdrew several hard crusts of bread from his satchel. "I use the ends and old parts that folks normally feed the birds. Dried out, the bread soaks up the custard and softens. The dried fruit, nuts, and spices we add make a delicious dessert. The sweetness of the sauce will complement the pudding. Now, stop playing with those eggs and get to cracking!"

Ice came home to a dinner of scraud and shellfish cooked in a butter broth, both flown in fresh. They were accompanied by sautéed fresh greens and, of course, bread pudding for dessert. Zeal, on Qwen's insistence, sent an invitation to Tallen, Tulip, Greyhook, and Mirada to join them. Kit had scraud just the way she liked it, served raw in her dish from the *White Swan*.

* * *

Listina sat next to the warm fire prepared for her by one of the servants, enjoying her tea. Everyone in Green Keep had worked hard this past moon to anticipate her needs. It was a remote location that belonged to her mother's side of the family. No one would think to look for her here.

Word from Havensharth was slow to reach her. She had been banished from the Enclave; the Repository was now off limits to her. Namrin, the old ninny, had passed his judgment in her absence.

Her father promised to find someone to complete her training. He hadn't given her any indication of his feelings regarding the circumstances behind her departure from Havensharth. She was, however, pleased with his continued support. She was family. Family was all that mattered.

Zeal would pay. No one had ever crossed her and not suffered for it. She needed to prepare carefully and gather more intelligence about him. It didn't matter how long it took. She'd learned from their encounter that she needed to develop patience.

Turning the page, she resumed reading the *Treatise on Necromantic Arts* by T. A. Feneas, which she'd stolen off Namrin's desk. She wondered if the old bore had even missed it yet.

PART TWO

CHAPTER TWENTY-TWO

ZEAL LAY ON the top of the Repository's crystal dome with Kit on his chest. He had learned that the material of the dome absorbed the energy released by all living things in the area. Namrin had told him the energy was used to fuel the protections built into the building and to preserve the Repository's contents. He placed a palm on a facet. Its surface had a slight warmth that did not seem to be due to residual heat absorbed during the day.

The sun had set four marks ago. There was not a cloud in the sky, and the moon was yet to rise. Zeal admired the twinkling stars. The pathways below were empty except for an occasional stroller, and people tended not to look up. As long as he lay still, no one would notice them.

You need to get a gift for Tulip and Tallen.

"I know. So much has changed in the last five seasons for all of us. They'll earn their journeyman designation at the end of the moon. I can't decide on what to get them. Have you selected your gifts?"

Why don't you tend to your own hunt?

Kit was telling him she had taken care of her choices already, so he should do the same. "I'll finish imbuing the bow for Tallen. He has become quite the archer since Mirada told him he needed to learn to defend himself." Tulip's gift, however, was harder for Zeal to decide on. Like him, she never needed much.

Anything from the heart to another member of the Pride is

cherished.

"When did you become a wise Shadow Cat?" Zeal scratched Kit under the chin.

A loud thunderclap shook the trees and buildings. A flaming ball passed overhead, loudly roaring as it fell to the earth. It struck the ground short of the horizon. A bright flash in the distant trees momentarily lit the sky, followed several heartbeats later by the boom of an explosion.

Startled, Kit extended her claws. Only Zeal's workshirt, worn under his cloths, prevented her from accidently drawing blood. *A star has fallen!*

Zeal thought Kit may have the right of it. Unknowingly, he'd closed his eyes against the bright glare. As the afterimage of the light faded from the back of his lids, he reopened them and saw trees burning in the distance. It suddenly occurred to him there might be traces of star metal at the site. He also wanted to sample the fire and keep some for himself.

"Kit, would you please tell Deena I am going to search the woods where the star struck. Contact Tallen and Tulip. I would like the three of you to meet me there." He rolled onto his side, placed Kit on her paws, and then rose to his feet.

I will do.

Zeal utilized a portion of his inner fire to cast a conjure he'd learned from *The Book of Flames*. "Alai Cenda." Crude wings of flame grew from his back.

More functional than esthetic, they began to flap, and he was lifted into the air. Each beat carried him higher and faster toward his destination in the distance. This wasn't the same mode of flight that Qwen utilized, but Zeal enjoyed the occasional use of the wings.

* * *

It was hungry. Unable to remember why it had traveled here, it inhaled deeply, sampling the breeze. The scent of prey was detected, so the hunter headed in the direction of the smell's origin.

The hunter's eyes were weak compared to other creatures. It used stealth, quietly moving on its six legs as it slowly stalked its prey. Instinctively, it remained downwind of the musky odor.

As the scent strengthened, it discovered droppings on the ground that were moist and still steaming. When it remained still, the hunter's gray hide gave it the appearance of a large stone resting against the hillside. It was close enough to see its quarry browsing on the succulent leaves of a low bush. It sat immobile, letting the creature come closer.

Finally, it sprang forward, fore claw reaching, and snapped the hind leg of the animal as it frantically attempted to escape. The speed and strength used to make the kill and pull the victim toward its open maw belied the size of the attacker. Its jaws clamped down, crushing the animal's spine and ending a life.

As it ripped open the soft belly and began to feed, a loud, bright, hot thing crashed from the sky, throwing it away from its prey. Everything became dark for the hunter.

* * *

It didn't take Zeal long to travel the distance from the Repository to the locus of the fallen star. The forest in the immediate area was aflame, the conflagration gorging on brush and trees.

Zeal became concerned. If the fire continued to spread, it might reach Havensharth, killing the woodland creatures and destroying their homes as it burned its way.

While he glided on ascending currents of air, generated by the heat below, he caused the flames to rise up to meet him. The firestorm rose from the ground into the sky in streams and joined with the flaming wings at his back. Multiple rainbows of crimson light flowed toward him in the darkness. Working steadily, Zeal concentrated the fire and stored it in the vast empty space inside him.

He was thankful that his bond with Kit allowed him to see as well in darkness as he did in light. Tallen and Tulip had no such advantage. Zeal left a few, camp-size fires blazing, to provide illumination for them once they arrived. One burned beside a large boulder next to the crater formed by the fallen star. Smoke drifting from the hole prevented him from viewing the bottom. A small glint of light reflected from the boulder, it appeared a piece of metal may have lodged itself there.

Zeal drifted over the crater and used an updraft of air to clear the smoke from the cavity. Something glowed hot at its center. Once he was certain the forest fire was contained, he alighted on top of the boulder, which he estimated stood at least his height from the surface. The charred remains of a dead animal lay nearby.

Kneeling, he placed one hand on the stone to balance himself and then leaned forward and peered at the dimly glowing object in the pit's center. The rock was still warm to the touch. Zeal absorbed his wings, returning the fire to his core, and took a moment to rest. He didn't know how long it had taken him to gain control of the fire, but hopefully Kit, Tallen, and Tulip would arrive soon.

Engrossed in his study, it took a moment for him to notice the shudder under his hand. He was surprised to discover an open eye in the surface next to his fingers. The eye, covered by a transparent, nictitating membrane, shifted and then widened, as if to focus on him.

* * *

Tallen's horse followed behind Tulip's. Her mount, guided by Kit, took them deeper into the wood. Light from the crystal Deena gave her before they left lit their way, forming the boundaries of their world. There was a smoky haze; the wood felt threatening. She thought she perceived movement out of the corner of her eye, but when she jerked her head to get a better look, there was nothing there. The further they rode, the thicker the haze became.

She and Tallen had brought a third horse for Zeal to use for his return to Havensharth, even though he had conjured his way out. Tallen had become an accomplished rider. Tulip had overheard

Masters Greyhook and Gennis talking about him a couple moons previous; clearly they thought highly of Tallen's bardic skills, which pleased her. She also didn't think it hurt that Tallen was a good person and easy on the eyes. Several of Havensharth's other young women had made a few jealous comments, in fact, because of her close association with him.

Even though she'd matured in the past five seasons at Havensharth—filled out, as Mirada put it—Tallen had remained only a close friend. She now stood taller than Mirada and, unfortunately, had outgrown her favorite gray leathers.

Zeal, on the other hand, had yet to get his growth.

Kit sat in front of Tulip, her eyes closed to the brightness of the crystal. The horses accepted Kit as if she were one of them, because she'd played with them when they were colts, to make sure they were familiar with her presence.

The forest's trees seemed unusually quiet. The smoke was beginning to thin ahead, and Tulip could see the light of several small fires as they rounded a copse of thickly grown red asdic and entered a clear, scorched space. The bare area was slightly larger than the Casting Quad. At its center was a small crater. Tulip saw Zeal kneeling on a large boulder on the near edge of the pit. As she was about to yell a greeting, the stone moved.

A large paw struck at Zeal, who was already in motion, leaping away. Tallen gasped when the claws brushed Zeal's right leg and spun him awkwardly in the air. Zeal deftly turned the spin into a tumble but still hit hard, his head bouncing off the ground. He lay there, dazed and unmoving.

The gray creature lumbered onto six thick appendages, each equipped with long, black claws. Its body was round, like the stone it had resembled, and twice the size of a stocky war stallion.

A piercing scream sent a chill through Tulip. It was the hunting cry of an enraged animal. A large cat appeared from out of the darkness, preparing to pounce on the back of the beast. Tulip had rarely seen Kit in her full-grown Shadow Cat form, since she always maintained a small, unassuming size around Havensharth.

Kit was one and a half times her mother's size, standing an

impressive twelve hands to the shoulder, thirty hands long including tail, and now weighing thirty stone. When she landed on Zeal's attacker, she clawed it with her front paws, raking with her hind ones and attempted to sink her fangs into its neck.

Tulip and Tallen jumped off their mounts. The horses were wide-eyed with fright and ran off.

Tallen readied his bow and nocked an arrow. "Tulip, no!" he shouted as she advanced toward the beast with sword in hand.

For something as big as it was, the creature was quick. It banged against a large tree, knocking Kit off its back. The beast raised onto its hindmost legs and then struck Kit with its four other limbs.

Kit disappeared into the creature's shadow then reappeared next to Zeal, who had yet to move.

"Hey, you! Try *me!*" Tulip shouted. She had approached the creature unnoticed and wanted to gain its attention.

The brute turned, and as it bellowed at the new threat, it revealed a substantial mouthful of pointed teeth, with two large canines dripping a green substance. It charged Tulip, who stood defiant in its path.

Tallen drew the bow's string to his cheek and timed the arrow's release, concentrating on the up-and-down motion of the beast's head as it ran at Tulip. His missile flew true, striking the creature's right eye, but his jubilation turned to disbelief when the arrow bounced off. The creature merely flinched but was distracted enough to fail in its attack on Tulip.

Although the beast's fangs didn't sink into its intended target, Tulips sword pierced the open maw and was shattered by the creature's teeth when it bit down on the blade. Struck by the beast's shoulder, Tulip was knocked off balance. She twisted acrobatically in the air and landed on her feet.

The animal stopped its charge and spun to survey its opponents. It sniffed the air before focusing on Zeal, who was attempting to stand, favoring his right leg.

Kit stepped into a shadow. Tulip was watching the beast when she saw a claw reach out of the shadows and rake the creature's belly.

Kit returned to Zeal's side. Her claws had no effect other than to scrape dirt from the animal's tough hide.

Tallen fired two more arrows, each of which broke when they impacted his target.

Kit's nose and ears began to twitch. She was conjuring. A blue nimbus formed on her muzzle and claws.

Tallen dropped his useless bow and extracted his pipes from a case on his right hip. The morra wood shown warmly in the firelight as he began to play. The melody formed itself, the notes given birth from need. The animal hesitated, appearing perplexed by the music.

Tulip gained strength from Tallen's song. She drew her long knife with her left hand and her Fang in her right. "Make it roar again. I need to get by those teeth!" she yelled. Both hers and Zeal's Fangs were imbued; maybe the Fang could wound this creature.

Tulip maneuvered close enough to strike the beast. She heard Tallen fumble a riff of notes as his song turned discordant. He was visibly distressed—was his concern for her?

The creature immediately focused on Tulip. Lashing out with a middle paw, it slapped the Fang from her hand. The weapon spun through the air and its blade embedded in the trunk of a large tree.

At the sound of bones breaking, Tallen stopped playing. "*Tulip!*"

She welcomed the pain and used it to help her focus on her adversary. Luckily, she'd not been struck by the creature's claws but by its hardened flesh.

Kit pounced out of the darkness, attacking from the rear. Her paws and muzzle glowed with the blue nimbus. Her weapons gained purchase and finally penetrated the creature's hide. The beast roared in pain, twisting away from Tulip and toward its new attacker, who was no longer there.

Tallen resumed his play, and the music strengthened their will.

Tulip heard Zeal call out her name. She dropped her long knife and reached up with her good left hand to grasp his Fang out of the air. "Hey, you!" she shouted. "*I'm still here!*"

As the beast turned back and began to move toward Tulip, Kit attacked. The creature shrieked.

With a quick snap of her wrist, Tulip sent Zeal's Fang into the animal's open maw. Zeal conjured as the blade left her hand, giving the weapon the impetus it needed to pass through the roof of the creature's mouth, pierce the bone, and enter its brain. The beast collapsed to the ground, unmoving.

Kit gave a final cry from atop her vanquished foe, as if she alone had defeated the creature.

Tallen stopped playing and hurried to Tulip. "How is your hand?

"Now that the fight is over, it hurts." She cradled her swollen, bruised extremity against her chest.

Zeal hopped to the creature on his uninjured leg, grimacing with each step. "Tulip, help is on the way. Kit sent a message to Deena. Tallen, would you retrieve Tulip's Fang from the tree over there?"

"Sure." Tallen found the Fang deeply imbedded, with only a quarter of the hilt protruding from the bark. He gripped it as best he could and pulled, but the blade was held fast no matter how hard he tried. Frustrated, he leaned his head against the trunk. Suddenly, an image of his mother arose, unbidden, in his mind—a memory of him watching her in the wood.

The bark of the tree was hard yet comfortable. He placed his right palm on the trunk, held the hilt with his left hand, and then spoke to the tree. "I am sorry you were injured by the metal. We did not mean harm to you. I have need of the blade, if you would kindly return it. I offer you the blood of the one who injured you in return." Five heartbeats passed before Tallen felt the hilt move in his hand. The tree extruded the blade for him. His whispered "Thanks" was given to the tree and sent to his mother.

Sap oozed from the wound left in the trunk. The weapon and Tallen's hand were coated by the sticky substance reminiscent of blood. He held the blade away from his body and returned to his waiting friends. "Here it is." He handed Zeal the weapon hilt first.

"Much appreciated." Zeal conjured, "Opifur Manibus," and the carcass rose from the ground into the air as if lifted by unseen hands. As it rotated onto its side and lowered, Zeal dropped painfully to one knee.

Let Tallen do, Kit mindspoke to them all. She was guarding

Tulip, who sat hunched, watching.

Zeal nodded. "I should have thought of that. Here, Tallen, take this back. Before you ask, only an imbued weapon will penetrate this hide. Cut open the belly for me and remove the liver. Kit needs to eat and replenish her energy. This creature is the closest source of food.

Tulip shouted, "Try to do as little damage to the hide as you can please, Tallen!"

As he set to work, Tallen grumbled, "Would help to have more light."

Zeal conjured, "Laevin," and a globe materialized above them that brightly lit the area.

Tulip's blade easily pierced the skin. Tallen directed the tip and edge so as not to cut into the intestines and organs. It took a bit of effort to hold the flaps open so he could see what he was doing and avoid the spilling guts. He removed the liver in three pieces and took them to Kit while Zeal hobbled behind.

You are a worthy member of our Pride. Your food is welcome. Kit helped Zeal ease to the ground next to Tulip before beginning to eat.

Tallen bowed. "It is a pleasure to feed you, my lady." He returned to the carcass, opened the chest, removed the heart from the cavity, taking care not to spill the blood from its great vessels, and carried it to the tree.

"Where are you going with that?" Tulip asked. "What are you doing?"

"I made a vow, and I need to make good on it. I will explain later." He squatted in front of the roots that extend into the ground from the tree's trunk. Holding the heart directly over them, he sliced the heart's chambers and spilled blood over the earth.

Leaves above him, left unburned from the fire, rustled in their branches. Tallen noted that there was no wind present to move them. He watched the wound made by the Fang close, the bark in the area scarring to form into a burl. After patting the trunk, he used a cloth square normally reserved for cleaning his pipes to wipe the blood and sap from Tulip's Fang. Task complete, he picked up the heart and returned to his companions.

"Are you all right?" Zeal asked as Tallen gave Kit the heart. "You appear a little lost."

"I'm fine, but I have a lot to think about. Might have something I want to share later." He handed Tulip her Fang. "Cleaned it the best I could."

"Thanks. I'll give it a little attention later." Tulip slid the weapon into the sheath under her sleeve, taking care not to move her injured hand.

Tallen pointed to the dead beast. "Either of you know what that thing is?"

"Yes," she answered. "I do. It is an Argguile. I hope it hasn't got a mate out here."

Tallen shuddered and looked around cautiously. "Me, either."

* * *

Zeal used his Trade training to set aside the pain in his leg, but it still hurt worse than when he'd been shot in the chest by an arrow. Despite the ache, he had to investigate the glowing object in the crater. *Help me up*, he sent to Kit.

She knelt, waited for him to grab hold of her fur, and then lifted him till he was balanced on one foot. *I'll come.* Kit crab-walked alongside Zeal to the edge of the depression.

"What are you two doing?" Tallen asked.

"Going to take a look." Zeal scooted into the crater.

"Describe what you see," Tulip said from where she sat. "I'm not moving."

"There is a partially buried lump of metal." Zeal felt the air with the skin of his palm. "Too hot to touch for someone other than me. We'll have to wait and let it cool down, if we're going to move it by mundane means." He carefully climbed out, taking care to avoid putting weight on his right leg. A thought came to him. "Tulip, I am sorry about your hand and the sword. Was that the blade you obtained from the Temple?"

"Yes, it was. Don't worry about it. My hand will heal." She

pointed to Zeal's the leg. "Tell me about the harm that creature did to you."

"My leg is broken, but it will get better with attention. Kit has been researching ways to restore health with conjure. Would you like her to try to help you?"

Tulip eyed him askance. "I think I'll wait. I don't see you asking her to fix your leg."

"Well, she is new at it. She hasn't had any injuries on which to practice." He rested next to the head of the Argguile.

I'm too tired to fix your bodies, Kit informed them all. *But will lick your wounds, if you come closer.*

"Kit, I'm sure you would do a fine job," Tulip said gently, "but I would like to see you gain a little expertise first."

"Tallen, would you please help me. I want to retrieve my Fang. We'll need a strong piece of wood to put in this thing's mouth, to hold the jaws open."

Tallen gathered several serviceable branches. Working together, they pried the jaws apart and inserted a couple of the lengths of wood to keep them from closing. Kit and Tulip observed their every move.

Taking care to avoid the sharp teeth, Zeal felt into the opening. The edges of bone around the hole created by the blade in the floor of the braincase snagged the sleeve of his shirt, almost tugging it off his arm. He was up to his elbow in warm, gelatinous gore before his questing fingers felt the knife's hilt.

Shifting closer, he reached in as far as he safely could. The pain in his leg flared. Even with his training, it was hard for him to focus. He closed his eyes, put the pain aside, and conjured, "Intraven Tenu Gomet." The blade slid into his hand, and Zeal carefully extricated himself.

It took more strength than Zeal anticipated to overcome the suction around his arm. He jerked the blade free. The creature's muscles spasmed in death, and its jaw contracted, snapping the branches as it closed. The teeth crunched tightly on the Fang's blade, which did not shatter as had Tulip's sword, but they barely missed his fingers. Zeal realized he had almost lost his hand or worse.

Tallen shuddered. "That was close."

Zeal's response was interrupted by a yell.

"Will you two stop playing with that creature before someone gets hurt? We can't allow you to play outside without someone getting injured." Greyhook stepped out of the trees followed by Mirada, Ice, and Deena. "We had to leave the horses further back. They balked at the scents around here. Mirada, is that what I think it is?"

"We became worried when your horses returned to Havensharth without you," Ice said. "Our concern worsened when Kit contacted Deena."

Mirada rushed forward, taking a moment to study the carcass before kneeling next to Tulip. Greyhook dropped behind Tulip and leaned her against him. "Tulip, you're injured." Mirada gently probed Tulip's hand with her fingers. "Deena, would you give me an *effusion* please?"

Tulip moaned. "We killed an Argguile."

Deena handed Mirada the *effusion*. "Are you hurt as well, Zeal? Or did you just decide to wear a blood-and-slime sleeve today?"

"He said his leg is broken," Tallen said.

Ice examined Zeal's injury, confirming to Deena, "Both bones, but they haven't punctured the skin." He glanced over at the Argguile. "Tallen, you need any assistance with that blade?"

The Fang was freed and returned to Zeal, who cleaned the knife and his hand with a cloth from Ice. The adults had a mixture of admiration and concern on their faces. As he put the weapon away, he admitted to himself he was relieved they were there.

Kit padded back over to Zeal and changed into what Tulip referred to as her "hiding size." *Good. You have your claw.*

Moments after drinking the *effusion*, Tulip cried out, every visible muscle of her body trembling. The bones of her hand shifted under the skin as they returned to their proper positions, and she buried her face in Mirada's chest as she screamed.

Deena knelt and gave Zeal a tight hug before opening the *effusion* and offering it to him. Glancing over at Tulip, who was resting with her head on Mirada's shoulder, Zeal swallowed the contents of the vial fast.

This is going to really hurt, he thought, just before the bones in his leg started to move into place.

CHAPTER TWENTY-THREE

ZEAL AWAKENED STILL exhausted, but more from his healing than from the evening's activity. The rapid healing the *effusion* provided used his body's reserves to accomplish its work.

He had gone to sleep pondering the rough shard of star metal he had retrieved from the shoulder of the Argguile before they'd returned to Havensharth. The piece had a polished surface and was large enough to make into a knife. There were flakes of dried blood on it but no sign of corrosion. An oblong, irregular-shaped ball bigger than his head had been discovered cooling in the center of the pit. To his surprise, the metal was light: he had been able to hold the larger piece all by himself.

I see you are finally awake. You have slept away the early hunt.

Zeal looked around for Kit, only to discover he was alone. Through their bond, he attempted to decipher her location. She was in the kitchen, eating from the flavor of her thoughts. Thinking of food caused his stomach to rumble. He needed to refuel, himself

I am hungry enough to eat scraud raw, he sent back.

If you wish, I would go get one for you.

Where? Wait — no. How would you get a scraud?

As your kind says, I have my ways.

Zeal felt Kit's rumble of laughter flow. *Have you talked to Tallen or Tulip yet?*

I have visited both. Tulip, unlike you, has been about. She has claimed the skin of our kill, so she can wear it. Tallen has taken the

eye covers, claws, and one of the long teeth. Charese has claimed the other long tooth. I have all the choice bits to eat. Argguile meat tastes sweet. Zeal again felt Kit smile in his thoughts.

What part have you all selected for me? Zeal pretended to include a touch of indignation in his thoughts, although he was perfectly happy for Tallen and Tulip to use the beast however they wished. It did not surprise him that Charese had included herself, but he did hope Tulip had harvested the poison glands for Lady Phyllis.

That she did. You can share in my feast. What I have is yours. It was decided you get the star that fell, since that is what you were after.

I am hungry enough to take you up on your offer but will wait, for now, to try Argguile. If it is possible to craft weapons from our find, then I want to replace the sword Tulip lost. It will be my journeyman gift to her.

And what for Tallen?

An imbued bow will still be my gift for him. Such a bow would have helped in our fight last eve.

Mother Deena says to come eat. She has prepared food for you.

Let her know I am on my way. Zeal quickly dressed, and after freshening up and making his sleeper, he headed to the kitchen. A hiding size Kit sat on her pillow, grooming as Deena put food on a platter. The abundance of delicious smells made his mouth water.

"Good morning," Deena greeted, adding a warm embrace. She seemed to hold him longer than usual. "So, do you want to let me know what possessed you all to tackle an Argguile by yourselves?"

"It gave us no choice in the matter. Tell her, Kit. We didn't start that fight."

But we made the kill, Kit announced to both Zeal and Deena.

"We did indeed." Zeal snorted as Kit attempted a grin, which would look downright scary to someone who didn't know what she was doing.

"There has never been an Argguile sighted in the valley before or even the nearby areas. I wonder what it was doing around here." Deena placed Zeal's meal before him. "If it had made its way into Havensharth, a lot of people would have suffered. It could have caused a lot of deaths. We are blessed with luck that the two of you were only injured."

"Tulip told us they were rare and had territories they guarded from others," Zeal said with his mouth full of food. "They don't even tolerate another of their kind, unless they are mating." He didn't mention Tulip's comment that the Argguile had seemed to focus on him as its primary target.

Yes, it wanted you, Kit mindspoke to him.

Zeal wondered who would send such a thing for him and how they'd controlled it.

Deena smelled a cloth-wrapped joint of smoked meat before placing it in the cooler. "Kit, this is the last of the boar."

I will hunt. How soon?

"Why don't you fetch the boar tomorrow? I'll ready the smokehouse."

It shall be done, Mother Deena.

"I appreciate your contributions to our larder." Deena gave Kit a kiss on the top of her head. "Zeal, do you have plans for what Kit calls your fallen star? I have tried working with small pieces of the metal in the past. Unsuccessfully, I might add."

Zeal buttered a biscuit still warm from its baking. "Why is that? I wanted to use part of it to replace Tulip's shattered blade."

"Well, my understanding is that very few have had much of the material to work with. It seems impossible to heat the substance enough to manipulate it, let alone melt. Otherwise, it is too hard to reshape." She placed a second biscuit in front of Zeal. "Lore has it that as the star falls, it is heated by the sky's forge and tempered in the land's embrace. It acquires the property of light weight from the air, and of strength and durability from the ground. The amount you found would be worth untold wealth, if you could utilize it for other than a parchment-weight on your work desk."

As Zeal listened intently, a possible way to make use of the star metal came to him.

* * *

Brost pounded the glowing rod around the horn of the anvil and shaped it into a horseshoe. He was barrel-chested with broad shoulders and a thick neck. The corded muscles of his arms bunched with each blow of the hammer. Shorter than the average man, he stood just over fifteen hands in height with a clean-shaven face and head. Hair was something that caught on fire, so he kept it off. He wore work clothes and a leather apron to protect him from the hot bits that invariably flew off his work.

The lad and his pet stood, watching, as he finished the shoe and quenched it in the water to cool. Brost had seen them around and about Havensharth. He'd heard that the boy was studying to become one of the conjuring folk. The cat moved about as it liked, and no one seemed to be bothered by the idea.

After making the young one wait a reasonable period, he decided to see what business the boy had with him. Perhaps the lad had been sent by his mentor to place an order.

"Well, out with it. What do you want?" Brost hung the finished shoe on a peg.

"My name is Zeal. I seek your expertise to craft a weapon."

"I see. And how do you plan to pay for my service?" Brost knew that most boys this age had no coin. Although Zeal's clothes were of good quality, the lad didn't appear prosperous, and Brost didn't work for free.

Zeal took a shard of metal from a cloth wrapping and gave it to Master Brost. "Once we decide on a price, I can pay your fee, sir."

Brost admired the feel of the metal. He tried to picture the form that the metal desired to take. "I'll accept the commission, if you can afford me, but this little bit won't make much of a weapon. Do you have more?"

"Yes. I want you to make a bastard sword."

Good, he thought. Straight to business. "Who is it for? It would be best to measure the person and fit the blade to their hand." The fighters Brost had worked with were a finicky bunch and quite particular about the quality of the tools of their trade.

"It is for a member of my family. Based on your reputation, I'd hoped the fitting wasn't going to be an issue. I have the hilt of their former weapon. Would that help?"

"Yes, it will." Brost continued to study the sample. "What is this made of? I don't recognize it."

"It is star metal," Zeal replied.

So *that* is what it is. "Are you one of the three Apprentices who defeated that Argguile?" Brost looked the lad over with a critical eye.

"Yes, Master Brost," he said shyly.

Brost appreciated Zeal's not boasting about the accomplishment. It demonstrated good character. Disappointed, he handed the shard back. "I am sorry, but I can't work this. Why did you bring it to me?"

"You were recommended to me by Lady Phyllis."

"I was, was I? I'll have to thank her for sending you to me then. But it doesn't change the fact that I can't develop the temperature needed to work your metal." Brost wondered what Lady Phyllis's interest was in this young man.

"What if I told you I have discovered a way to utilize conjure to help your forge reach the needed temperature? Would you be willing to try?" Zeal fingered the star metal.

"I would. But if doing so damages my forge, you will cover the cost to replace it." By the lad's shrewd look, Brost wasn't sure he was being completely honest.

"I agree. But, since I will work alongside you to make the weapon, I expect a discount on the price I have to pay."

Brost appreciated a good bout of haggling and felt back in his element. "What? You want to be compensated for me teaching you? I am paid to teach others. How about I discount the price of your lessons?"

"I imagine gaining the reputation of being the only craftsman capable of mastering star metal isn't worth much…." Zeal turned toward the door. "Perhaps I should approach another who'd appreciate the recognition."

Brost stopped the boy from walking away. "Hold a moment. You do have a point. How about this? I will take your commission and utilize your assistance. You are welcome to acquire any knowledge you can during the process."

Zeal turned around. "And how much is this going to cost me?"

Brost figured he could create several small items from Zeal's piece and sell them at a profit. "The material you have currently in hand."

Zeal glanced toward his animal. "If we are successful, it is yours in payment. If not, then I retain possession. I will ask Lady Phyllis to draw up an agreement." The boy stood straighter. "That is, if my word alone is insufficient."

Brost studied Zeal with a keen eye, taken with his careful manner of conducting this bit of business. It pleased him that one so young took commitment seriously. "Your word is good, and so is mine." He held out his hand and took Zeal's. They shook, sealing their bargain "Let's begin with this sample. If we can bring it to temperature, we'll make your sword."

"Agreed. Thank you, Master Brost. We'll be back." Zeal took a last look around before he headed to the door.

Brost wondered if there would be a risk in attempting to work the metal. He had respect for the materials he worked but had come to know them. He trusted them to have consistent character as they bonded in the heat of his forge. What properties did the star metal have? And what problems would it present for him?

* * *

Tallen sat across from Tulip in Greyhook's kitchen kingdom, nibbling a small hole in the skin of a ripe stone fruit before sucking out the sweet juice and liquefied flesh.

"You are enjoying that a little too much." Tulip sat, exercising her injured hand by squeezing a ball of clay. The hand was still a little stiff from the healing but would be fine in a few morns.

"*Mmm-hmm,*" he replied, careful to keep the fruit from bursting and have the juice run down the front of his shirt. He had stopped by to see her after first checking on Zeal and finding him absent from his home.

There was a knock on the exterior kitchen door. Tulip rose and opened it.

The senior Red Cloak named Addis stood in the entry, holding something behind his back. "May I come in? I hope I am not disturbing you." He peered around Tulip to see if the kitchen was occupied.

"Not at all. Please, come in. Addis, you and Tallen should know each other." Tulip held the door open and waited for Addis to enter.

He stepped past her into the kitchen. "I won't stay long. I brought you this."

Addis drew a sheathed short sword from behind him. Tallen wondered why *he* hadn't thought of giving Tulip a weapon to replace the one destroyed by the Argguile?

"I heard about your blade and thought you needed a replacement. I have several weapons and will never be able to use them all. You would be doing me a big favor, if you took this off my hands and put it to use." He bowed, offering the sword to Tulip with both hands.

Tulip bared the blade. "This is too fine. I can't accept it." She gripped the pommel, which had a cloudy crystal embedded on its end.

Even though he wasn't training to become a weapon's master, Tallen could tell the sword was of high quality. Its weight and balance would fit Tulip well, and she seemed to truly admire the weapon Addis had so casually gifted. Tallen wondered why something about this troubled him.

"Okay, then, why don't you consider the weapon as being on loan and use it till you get another? I chose this because of your preference to fight with both hands armed. A two-hand sword would not work well for you. Now I'm going to leave before you try to give it back." Addis hurried out the door. "Hope to see you at training as soon as you are fit to return."

Tallen's unease remained long after Addis had left. He was sure it had nothing to do with another male giving Tulip a gift. No, not at all.

* * *

The sun's rays warmed Kit as she lay perched on the sill of the open window, watching Zeal harvest iris blossoms below her. Light reflected off his scissors as he snipped the blooms and placed them in a large bowl.

Picking flowers for Mother Deena?

No. I'm going to soak the petals in brandy to create an extract. I plan to pour half of it on the fuel of the forge, to give the impression of heightened flames and heat, while I pretend to conjure. In reality, I'll use my inner fire to heat the sky metal.

What of other half?

Zeal glanced up to her window. *I'll mix it with rainwater I've collected that has drained off the crystal dome of the Repository. I'll use that mixture to temper the sword.*

Are you sure this is going to work?

It should. I already have the concentrated essence of the fire from where the star fell. If I focus the heat on the metal, the sample should soften enough for Master Brost to work it. From what we saw earlier, I don't think the metal needs to melt. Zeal entered the cottage and headed to the kitchen to continue his preparations.

Why the flowers?

I intend to imbue the blade and want it to receive something from Iris. Our Fangs have iris blossoms engraved on the blade. If I use them in the tempering solution, possibly something from Iris will transfer in the process. What do you think?

I believe you should ask one called Iris. I will take you.

Zeal was surprised by her offer. *I hadn't considered that. You are as intelligent as you are beautiful. I am glad you chose me.*

She sent her own pleasure to him. **I did choose well. We could get scraud and visit mother.**

Let's plan a trip soon and take Tulip with us. Can you manage that? If not, we could use Marhdah and conjure us all to Arlanda.

I can manage. Kit continued to keep Zeal company from her sunny spot in the window while he finished his work.

* * *

Brost had an ache in his back from cleaning and refueling the forge. He'd removed the clinker that had accumulated during the day's work. No matter the quality of material he worked, there was clinker formed from impurities in the fuel. If not removed, it would block the air draught and stick to the metal as it heated.

He thought it best to attempt the working of the star metal during the coolness of the evening. That should compensate for the heat generated to reach the unusually hot temperatures.

He looked up when he heard Zeal enter pulling a small wagon. His cat rode on a barrel next to a small cask.

"Good! You are the timely sort. What you got in the wagon?"

Zeal pointed first to the barrel and lastly to the cask. "It is liquid in which to temper the metal and an elixir to increase the temperature of the forge."

"I mixed a higher ratio of coke to coal, so get ready for a strenuous workout on the bellows to light it and keep it burning." Brost smiled, ready to encourage little Zeal to step up to the challenge.

Zeal continued, "If we sprinkle a portion of the elixir on the fuel, the heat should release the liquid's properties and increase the efficiency of the forge."

Brost stepped back, concerned Zeal was trying to sell him something he didn't want or need. "You don't say, young sir. Well, the moment has come to get your irons hot, as we say in the smithy."

Zeal handed him the star metal then carefully poured half of the cask's contents evenly across the fuel in the forge.

Brost detected a flowery fragrance mixed with alcohol. "How long do we have to wait on your alchemy to work?"

"We can start any time you wish."

Brost didn't like the smug look on the lad's face. "Don't you need to wiggle-jiggle and speak in tongues first? You know, do that conjuration thing to get things started? I've seen you folk work before, you know."

I don't think he is fooled. This one would make a good hunter.

I am trying here. If you have a helpful suggestion I am all ears.

Perhaps honesty would have been better. This one can be trusted.

Zeal took on a studied look, as though caught being untruthful and grasping for a good story to tell. Something was on the lad's mind.

Zeal took a deep breath and let it out. "Master Brost, I would like to be honest with you."

"I think we should be honest with each other. Out with it, lad. What has your bellows flow restricted?"

"I am going to trust you with a confidence." Zeal kept eye contact with Brost.

"Would this have anything to do with our business, young man?"

"Yes, it does."

"Then we are in agreement. Now, tell me what you have to say. The mark grows long."

"Well, I haven't any conjure or elixir to help with the heating process," Zeal admitted. "I am sorry. I made it all up."

"I see." He tried to hand the metal back to Zeal. "This won't be needed then."

"No, it will. You see, sir, I have a kindred spirit with fire." Zeal turned to the forge.

Brost saw no jiggle-wiggle and heard no mumble. The lad simply reached out, and every source of fire in the smithy leapt to his hand and coalesced into a ball. The ball then separated into finger-sized segments that returned back to their previous locations. A lone section remained in his hand and was flung into the forge.

Brost moved away, expecting to hear and see a whoosh of flame caused by the alcohol poured onto the contents. What happened instead caused him to smile. He saw his name burning brightly in the coals.

Kit jumped up and sat on a nearby bench, eyes focused on Zeal, who placed the shard, barehanded, in the center of the forge. As Brost stood watching, the blaze intensified. The forge's contents ignited all at once, the coke included, no need for the bellows. Also, no clinker was forming; it, too, was consumed.

"You need to make it hotter, lad. Mind the forge now." Young as he was, the sprig was truly a Practitioner, a Master demonstrating his craft to another. Brost wore his gloves, apron, and the leather hood he rarely used, expecting the higher temperatures needed to work the metal. But, so far, there was much less heat in this working than he'd expected.

Using a pair of tongs, he turned the metallic shard, which had changed in color to a dull red. "Not hot enough. The color has to be right. It needs to be an orange-yellow, like the way the sun looks to you." He picked up his hot set, prepared to portion the sample, which had become medium-red in color. He was shocked to see the coal and coke had been consumed.

The boy didn't need a forge. He was one.

Brost could tell Zeal was starting to tire. White-knuckled, Zeal tightly held onto the handle of the bellows in order to stay standing. His pale face was damp with sweat. Whatever forces were being welded, Brost knew, were soon to be consumed. The shard's color had lighted to a bright red.

"Don't burn yourself out, lad. It is not worth it," Brost warned.

Zeal's arms trembled from the strain. He looked like a man burdened by more iron than he could comfortably carry.

"I can't make it any hotter," he suddenly admitted, his voice expressing his defeat.

Brost grabbed the shard with his tongs and placed it on the anvil. Choosing the portion of the metal he wanted to separate, he positioned his hot set and struck it with his hammer. The hot set left a small crease in the star metal before deforming.

They were close, but he still couldn't work the material. He also realized he did not have tools that could withstand the temperature without melting.

"Stop what you're doing!" Brost commanded. He plunged the shard into the water barrel beside him. The water immediately began to boil.

Zeal stood wavering on his feet. Brost lifted and laid him on the nearby bench next to Kit, who immediately settled at Zeal's head and began to rub her face against his.

"Stop what you're doing," he repeated, more gently this time.

"I thought it would work. It should have worked," Zeal whispered, exhausted.

"You gave it a good effort. It was close. That means we have a chance. Perhaps there is something in the Bard's or your kind's libraries that will help us. You just need to look." Brost sensed Zeal had ceased his efforts and was listening. He no longer heard the water boiling in the barrel.

Later, when he was alone and cleaning the smithy, Brost pondered the deformed hot set and tongs he had used, which had begun to melt from the heat. There was a shallow imprint in the anvil made by the star metal's brief contact with its surface. The water in the barrel had mostly boiled away, only a few buckets' worth left after removing the shard.

He marveled at the evidence. Zeal had somehow controlled the heat produced during the process. Brost would have been more astounded if he had known about Kit's participation that night.

CHAPTER TWENTY-FOUR

MORE REST AND SLEEP than awake and aware. Persistent hunger. Cold reached deep inside him. When the chill reached his heart, its beating would stop.

A thought not his own brushed against his consciousness.

Who are you?

Who was he? He hadn't thought of himself as an entity for so long. *Help*, he whispered in response.

I Kit. What is your name?

Firemyst. His identity rose from inside him. He was Firemyst, and he was dying.

I come.

* * *

Zeal was busy. He had too much to do, he thought to himself, and not enough marks to do it in. How had this happened? He envied Kit. She didn't have to juggle apprenticing with two different Masters, helping Deena in the shop, learning as much as he could from the *Book of Flames*, and also acquire the right journeyman gifts for Tulip and Tallen.

Kit studied what she wanted, when she wanted, and with whom. The only Masters at the Respository who knew she was a Practitioner were Masters Ice, Qwen, and Namrin. So the rest of the

Apprentices and Masters at the Repository tended to overlook her when she pretended to sleep in their presence. All the while, she was absorbing their lessons.

The rest of the time, she played with the children around Havensharth and had girl visits with Charese and Tulip. He couldn't imagine what they did during girl visits.

Maybe he was just feeling sorry for himself. Only a quarter-moon had passed since he'd failed in the working with Master Brost. Zeal still hadn't figured out a way to successfully forge the star metal, and research he'd conducted in the Repository hadn't provided any useful information. Perhaps he'd have better luck looking in the Bardic Library, he thought, or discussing his problem with Master Greyhook.

To top it off, he couldn't get over the conversation he'd had with Kit a few marks ago. She'd told him to grow up and stop acting like a child. When did *she* become an adult? Well, technically, it was two seasons ago, when Mother Essmee told them she no longer considered Kit a cub and also pointed out that he wasn't whelped yet.

Mother Essmee still checked in on them from time to time, always saying she'd stopped by to see how her two-legged cub was doing, and she and Kit occasionally stepped away together. Kit had been correct the night she'd told him that he needed to be honest with Master Brost.

Suddenly, Kit mindspoke to him. *I need you.*

Do you want me to go to you? Or are you coming to get me? He could sense Kit wasn't in any danger but decided to prepare a conjure to help shield them from physical harm anyway.

I come for you.

Zeal grabbed his pack and slid under the sleeper, which sat on a platform five hands above the floor. It was skirted, to keep light from shining underneath it, and was kept clear of clutter to provide a shadowed place for Kit and Mother Essmee to travel to and from this den. He felt Kit make physical contact before she stepped them to a new locale.

Zeal held still as he listened and looked around, moving only his eyes. Even though they were in complete darkness, he was able to see as if there were light, due to his bond with Kit.

They were in the middle of the wide central aisle of an expansive chamber. Lanes split off to the sides, and these branches led to tables topped with odd-shaped items. There were shelves draped with cloths that hid secrets from view. Chests and wardrobes were chained and locked closed. A tapestry on one wall hurt his eyes when he looked at it.

He was surprised to realize that Kit had taken him inside the Archive of the Practitioner's Repository. *I thought this place was impossible to enter once locked up.* Zeal didn't want to talk out loud and possibly trigger an alarm.

It is, for your kind.

I'm impressed. You've been holding out on me. He should have considered the possibility before now. *Not that I'm not curious why you've been visiting the Archive after hours, but how can I help you?*

Someone else has a need, not I.

Okay, last time we did something like this together, we were inside Charese. Please don't tell me this place is alive and we have to rescue it. Zeal shuddered at the thought.

One called Firemyst is calling for aid. It is trapped.

What do you mean, it? he asked, curious.

I have never tasted similar thoughts, so I can't tell what makes them.

What can you tell?

It is immature, an infant. And it is dying.

You're right. We have to do something. You once told me that, when we are together, your ability to detect forms of life becomes more sensitive. Is that why you need me, because you could hear but not locate Firemyst?

You are correct. Now join me in looking and listening.

With Kit's help, he was able to see the living things in the Archive. Small rodents cowered behind a barrel to his right, fearful of Kit's presence. A spider on the ceiling was searching for a meal. Something was imprisoned in an imbued container across the way. The touch of its mind felt wrong—demented and hungry.

That one seeks freedom to kill and destroy. It is not Firemyst.

Ignore.

Zeal shivered. He was thankful Mother Essmee had taught him how to protect his mind from invasion.

All at once, they found it: an image unlike any of the others; it resonated with his inner core. A fire waning, fading, and perishing as the resources it needed to live were taken away; it sputtered in its effort to continue to burn.

Zeal felt the being's essence reach out to him for warmth, for help, transmitting through the flames inside him.

He felt as if he'd awakened from sleep. Kit, hiding size, stood beside him. He'd walked, guided by the fragile entity, to a spot in front of a ceiling-to-floor tapestry on the wall. There was a large, metal-banded wood crate in front of the wall covering. Firemyst's thoughts were coming from behind the crate.

Help me move this container, Zeal said as he contemplated the best conjure to use to move the heavy item, Kit grew to hunting size. She used a forepaw to pull the container from the wall. It scraped loudly as it slid. Then Kit returned to hiding size.

That works. Zeal waited to determine if the noise had activated an alarm.

I listen, as well.

Reassured, he peered behind the crate but didn't see anything. Then Zeal pulled away the folds of the tapestry and discovered a dull, reddish-gray ovoid twice the size of a person's head.

"This it?" Zeal asked Kit, seeking confirmation.

Yes.

Suddenly, he realized what they were looking at: the ovoid contained Firemyst. It was an egg.

Zeal recalled seeing a similar sketch in his *Book of Flames* seasons ago. It was in the section on creatures of fire. As he excitedly dragged the wall hanging away from the egg, the hanging broke from its anchor and fell on top of him. Its weight dropped him to his knees and forced his head down.

Kit grew beside him and removed the weight from his back. He erupted in dust-born sneezes, and so did Kit. He was concerned they'd made too much noise, but she did not seem alarmed.

He picked up the ovoid. It seemed to weigh a couple of stones. Its surface was irregular and pebbly, and it was cool to the touch, like a metal object. As he returned to his feet, he noticed the glowing red outline of a door drawn on the uncovered flat wall.

He secured the egg in the crook of his right arm and touched the nearest red line. A door, with keyhole included, materialized, replacing the drawing. *What do you think is on the other side of the door?* He felt strongly he was meant to open this portal.

Kit looked from Zeal to the wall. **What door?** she asked, returning to hiding size.

When we first met at Master Feneas' place, there was a portal that Mother Essmee said was not for me. It was similar to this one. For some reason, I believe I was meant to find and open this. Hold a moment.

He carefully set Firemyst's egg down and picked up Kit. He placed one of her forepaws on the wall's surface and concentrated on what he saw in front of him.

Now do you see it? he asked her.

The door did become apparent to Kit, with Zeal's help. **I think this door is for you, but Firemyst must come first.**

You are right. I don't think Firemyst can wait. Let's take this back to our place and see what we can do. I can examine the door later.

We must leave now. Someone is entering the Archive.

Help me push this back against the wall.

Kit changed size, pushed the crate to its original position, and helped Zeal arrange the wall hanging to give it the appearance of having fallen from the wall on its own. After giving Zeal a moment to retrieve Firemyst, Kit stepped them home.

* * *

Tulip smiled at Kit and Zeal as they exited out from under the sleeper. "Where have you two been?" She noticed the large, reddish-gray stone Zeal held in his arms. "What've you got?"

"You could have warned me," he admonished Kit. "I almost dropped Firemyst."

Tulip deduced "Firemyst" must be the ovoid-looking stone.

"What's so important about this rock? Why have you named it?" She moved to make room on the sleeper for Zeal and Kit to join her.

"This is not a rock. It's an egg." Zeal gently set it down before pulling his *Book of Flames* from an inner pocket of his vest. After he set it down, it enlarged to its full size and opened on its own accord to a page showing the drawing of an object identical to the ovoid. Also, hatching from it was an avian creature composed of flame. The red writing beneath the drawing flickered.

Excited, Zeal read, "I was right! It *is* an egg, and Firemyst is something called a Firebird. The book says it has to be hatched in the warmth of the world's flowing fire. It also says birth from the egg is a Firebird's first one. I am not sure what any of that means."

"I bet Greyhook would know," suggested Tulip. "We could ask him. You still haven't told me where you found this." Curious, she ran her hand over the egg. It felt cool, but the heat from her palm absorbed into the surface, which felt weird.

"Kit was in the Repository and heard its cry for help but couldn't find its location. She asked me to help her, and together we were able to track down and retrieve the egg."

One called Firemyst is dying.

Kit's announcement alarmed Tulip. "Dying? Why is it dying? We can help it, right? Keep reading—your book must know what needs to be done."

Zeal continued, "The book says here if the egg isn't placed in the fiery embrace of the world before it depletes its own energies, the entity inside will cease to exist."

"We can't let that happen. You're the Phosfire," Tulip reminded Zeal. "Do your thing and warm it."

Tulip knew about Zeal's recent failure to work the star metal but not what he was trying to make for her with the substance. He rarely doubted himself, but at the moment, he did.

He picked up the egg and his hands began to glow. Blazing tongues flowed out and licked the egg's surface, and the area nearest his hands began to shine liked the polished surface of a newly oiled blade.

More... More!

Tulip looked around. The voice had been very faint and its consistency of thought was... different... Foreign. Like the sound of damp wood burning in a brazier. "It must have been Firemyst who spoke."

Yes, Kit confirmed.

Zeal looked startled. "That's the first time I've heard it speak. You're right. This did help. We need to find out where to go to enable it to hatch."

"You can't walk around holding it especially with it looking like that. I'll go get Greyhook and bring him back."

"Wait a moment. Let me try something." Zeal paged through the *Book of Flames.*

Tulip knew Zeal conjured his castings without using gestures and verbal triggers, but he had a tell, like many of her fighting opponents. Mirada had worked hard to rid Tulip of her own tells; sometime soon, she needed to help him purge his own.

Faint musical notes splashed her body, like she was standing naked in a beginning rain, her body hit by a drop now and then. After only a few heartbeats, the music stopped. It was new for her to be linked with Kit or Zeal when they conjured.

Firemyst's egg was encased in a flaming crystal. Zeal held it toward her and nodded. "Take it."

"It is lovely." The ovoid was heavier than she'd expected and felt as if it were encased in glass that radiated with the rich luminescence of flames in a hearth. "It is not hot," she said with surprise. "In fact, it is drawing the warmth from my hands. Just as before, when I touched it."

"Let me hold that with you." Zeal shifted closer to her.

Tulip held still as Zeal covered her hands with his. Even though his hands were rough like hers, they were not as calloused, and his touch was gentle, comfortable. She felt his warmth flow into her and from her into the egg.

"I hadn't noticed that happen before. Somehow Firemyst is pulling ambient heat to it. It might not be safe for you to hold this for a sustained period." He tapped the coating. "This is crystal fire. It should maintain a constant warmth and keep all its hotness inside, for Firemyst. I'll need to re-conjure it periodically. If I place the egg in the pack from Iris, it will stay insulated and protected."

"I knew you would think of something. Now, let's go see Greyhook. Kit, will you tell Tallen to meet us there? We'll probably need his talents, and he would never forgive us if we didn't include him."

Tallen knows and will meet us. Mother Deena has been told we are leaving and where we are going.

* * *

Extra chairs were brought into Greyhook's workroom to accommodate everyone, including him, Mirada, and the four Apprentices.

As Greyhook examined Zeal's egg-like object, he considered their request. Mirada only shrugged when he showed her the stone and didn't offer an opinion. "Fiery embrace, you say? That sounds a lot like the Blood of Sartus."

"What is the Blood of Sartus?" Zeal asked.

Greyhook pointed to Tallen, indicating that he should answer the question.

The bard Apprentice stood, eyes closed, for several heartbeats, composing his response. Then he opened his eyes. "Lore describes an entity named Sartus, who fought alongside others to defend our world, which was then mostly covered in water. At that time, only two small landmasses existed, what we now call Dorraan and Lloraan. Sartus was mortally wounded in the final battle that saved our sphere. Cradled by the forces of nature, the blood that flowed from his wounds formed a new land mass, Oraan. It is believed that rivers of the blood still flow beneath the land. And it is also written that there are a few sacred places where one can gain access to the blood."

Greyhook opened a chest near his desk and removed a rolled parchment. As Tallen recited the history, he opened the roll on his desk and weighed the corners down with small objects.

"Thank you, Tallen. That was well rendered. This is a map of Oraan. Everyone gather closely." He placed a finger on the map's center. "Show location Havensharth." A small spot appeared that radiated a green glow; Havensharth was written above it in fine blue script. "Show nearest location of Blood of Sartus." A second spot, radiating red, appeared in a mountain range in the southernmost portion of Oraan.

We could use a map like that, Zeal told Kit.

I always know where I am.

Greyhook smiled. "Knowledge has been added to the charts I have in this chest over the seasons, showing the locations of many places. A few of these places are couched in myth and legend. Others have been confirmed as real. The location shown for the 'Blood of Sartus' is one I have yet to explore. It may or may not truly exist."

"We have to go there and prove its existence," Zeal said urgently. "Firemyst does not have much time." He glanced at Tulip, who used finger talk to tell him to be patient.

Greyhook had never known Zeal to exaggerate, but he had doubts about the large rock. "Zeal, you said earlier you only recently acquired this egg. What evidence do you have to substantiate your claim? We have no idea how long this has been around or even how long the entity you call Firemyst has to live. After the Ceremonies of Advancement are conducted by the Enclaves, I'll mount an expedition to this locality and see if it is real."

"Grey has a point." Mirada picked up the egg to inspect it.

"If I had more proof, I'd give it to you." Zeal stared at the map. "According to the chart, that spot is quite a ways from here. How long would it take to get there?"

"I would estimate two to three moons by horseback, if there are no obstacles to overcome." Greyhook could tell his answer did not sit well with the young one or his other, non-furry companions.

Kit mindspoke to everyone in attendance, *The one called Firemyst needs to be born sooner.*

Greyhook realized Kit and Zeal were both certain of their opinion regarding the egg. "Let me talk with Ice and Deena. Ice is currently organizing the Practitioners' Progression Ceremony. I'm sorry, but it may be difficult for him to get away. Tallen, start preparations so we can leave after the advancements are complete. Don't forget, you and Tulip have your own ceremonies to prepare for." Then he rolled up the map and returned it to the chest, making sure to lock it.

* * *

Zeal awakened feeling more tired than before crawling into his sleeper last eve. Kit lay, sharing the pillow and staring him in the face. "How is Firemyst?"

One called Firemyst still hunts. Don't forget to redo crystal conjure.

"I won't." Zeal reflected on his discussion with Ice and Deena after his return home the previous night. It had almost been an exact rehash of the one with Greyhook and Mirada.

Ice had even suggested Zeal return Firemyst to the Repository and let older, wiser Practitioners take care of the problem. Fortunately, that suggestion was dropped when Deena reminded Ice that those same sage, insightful minds hadn't recognized that the rock was really an egg, so they'd likely have no idea what to do with it. If it wasn't for Kit's intervention, with Zeal's help, no one would be the... WISER!

The idea that they might take Firemyst away scared Zeal. He wondered, however, why no one had questioned Kit's being in the Archive to begin with. He surely hadn't brought it up in front of Master Ice. "Kit, why were you in the Archive the other night?" he asked. "You never told me"

Kit began to groom herself. *You never asked.*

"Up until now, we've been busy trying to help Firemyst, so the right moment hasn't come up." Zeal scratched her behind the ears.

I was curious.

"Don't go all Shadow Cat mysterious on me." He paid special attention to her favorite spot. "Give."

I spend time there to learn more of the Practitioners of your kind.

Zeal lifted Kit's chin so they could see each other's eyes. "I'm listening."

Kit stared back at him. *It is important to know what is hunted by other predators. I will not let another Practitioner consider us prey, as did one called Listina.*

Zeal nodded, understanding. "I regret not having finished our dealing with Listina, but she hasn't been a threat to us for seasons. I think we are done with her. You let me know if you develop a concern regarding anyone else."

Do you give up your right to the kill? If so, she is my prey to take. Kit licked her muzzle in anticipation.

"No, I still claim the right. If we see her again and she is still a threat to us, I will put her down."

What of Firemyst? When are we leaving? Kit rolled onto her paws and did a long, lanky cat stretch.

"I guess you do know me well. I made a promise to Qwen to aid any creature of the elements when I could. I don't plan on allowing Firemyst to die."

I will help you keep your promise. It is wise that you do so.

"Let Tulip and Tallen know we leave before dawn two eves from today. Have them prepare, if they decide to come with us. They should bring whatever they think we'll need that horses can carry. That includes food. We should be able to supplement what we carry with what we can hunt along the way. Let me get dressed and freshened up, then we go get something to eat."

* * *

Deena heard rumblings from the kitchen. The young ones were fixing their first meal of the day.

"Zeal, come down with Kit when you are done eating, please," she shouted from her workspace.

"Yes, Deena."

Ice was at the Repository, finishing the testing of those who would advance. There would be two new Masters soon; both were good people. After the incident with Listina, all Apprentices had been reevaluated. Those who lacked morals or were just out for themselves and unable to change their ways were asked to leave. Fortunately, only one other person was discovered who fit the "Listina" criteria.

Deena was cataloging rods when Kit and Zeal entered.

"How can we help you?" Zeal asked, still chewing on a piece of meat in hand.

She smiled inwardly at his bright, courteous face.

"In the future, I may want you to act as my scribe and record each rod's description and effect for me. These in particular are multi-use and can be recharged. Listen closely—the duration of effect for each use lasts twelve marks. The blue one with the silver bands and whirling symbol conjures quickening on the target creature cast. Whereas the green one with the brown bands and symbol of a leaf budding from a seed casts the conjure causing transfiguration." She handed Zeal the items to study.

Kit jumped onto the worktable and gave them her own appraisal.

Zeal returned the rods to Deena. "I need to tell you something."

She had hoped working together would give Zeal the opportunity to discuss his plans. Maybe this was the moment. "Yes, dear one? I am listening."

He grew more solemn. "If you recall, I made two promises, one to you, and one to Qwen. To Qwen I pledged to aid creatures like Firemyst. But to you, I gave my word to trust you with my intentions and seek your counsel. I can't help Firemyst without leaving Havensharth. Deena, Kit, and I need to go. We have to find a place to allow the egg to hatch or Firemyst won't survive."

Deena knew Zeal tried hard to live up to the ideals that those who cared about him had instilled in him. She meant him to have the tools he needed to enable him to make the right decisions. "Why do you call Firemyst an it?"

Zeal was quiet for several heartbeats before saying, "Because I don't know if Firemyst is a boy or girl—wait. I mean male or female."

"I understand and am pleased you trust me enough to confide in me. Try to be careful," Deena replied, as a directive and not a question. "Will Tulip and Tallen be accompanying you?"

"I think they will. Why don't you come?" he shyly asked.

Deena took his hands in hers but had to quash the hope in his eyes. "I would love to, but I can't. I have to stay neutral and not get between Apprentices and Mentors."

Zeal became still. "Why aren't you trying to stop me, *uh*, us?"

"I couldn't lock you away even if I wanted to. Not only would I be up against Tulip and your Trade skills, but Kit has shown a remarkable ability to go places herself, if you haven't noticed yet. You could have left already and not told me. The fact that you haven't shows you are thinking, planning, and not running off in a haphazard fashion."

"I guess I shouldn't discuss leaving with Master Ice…" Zeal grinned slightly.

"No, I don't think that would be a good idea. I doubt he would be as open-minded as I am. An Apprentice should avoid betraying his Master's trust." She heard Kit huff in agreement.

She pointed to a rune-carved bow made of red asdic. It had a white crystal in its grip below the arrow rest, and it lay beside a quiver. "Tallen's bow is completed. I imbued the three black arrows in the quiver. Tell him not to use more than two of them at a time. If one or more of the arrows is left in the quiver overnight, then any that have been fired will replenish. Don't worry—I just finished what you started. It is still the bow you wished him to have."

She gathered Zeal in her arms and held him tightly for several heartbeats. Zeal hugged her in return before she released him and did the same with Kit.

"Go now and work on your preparations. Don't forget to take along *effusions*, just in case.

She didn't allow them to see her concern and worry as they left. She hoped she was not making a mistake in electing not to prevent them from leaving.

CHAPTER TWENTY-FIVE

ANYONE WALKING BY would have thought the three young people—two males and a female—sitting at the edge of the lake were lounging after an afternoon meal. The female appeared to be sleeping with a cat curled next to her. The males sat silently beside her, quietly contemplating the waters.

They were actually having an in-depth conversation using what Zeal now referred to as "battle mind." Kit linked their thoughts together.

Wish we'd thought of this when we were fighting the Argguile. We'll definitely have an advantage in combat and stealth, Tulip sent to the others.

Pride members have to learn to hunt together.

I want to thank you for coming. Even though I'd hoped you would, I wasn't certain. Zeal picked out a flat stone and skipped it along the water's surface.

You would have been knee-deep in horse doo-doo, if you and Kit had left without me.

I agree with you Tulip, but could have done without that image. Tallen skipped a stone of his own. *You do know our Mentors are going to be furious with us. I was looking forward to acquiring Journeyman status.*

Don't worry, Tallen. Going from Apprentice to Journeyman is only a change in reputation. You determine how capable you are, not some label. Zeal selected another rock. *Practitioners don't use the designation. We go from Apprentice to Master with nothing in between. Your and Tulip's ability speaks for itself. Are we all set for tonight?*

Yes, Tallen, Kit, and Tulip confirmed.

Zeal could sense through battle mind that they were indeed ready and eager to leave. *Tallen, Tulip and I have a meeting with Lady Phyllis in a couple marks. After the meet, everyone should try and get some rest. We'll gather in the stables three marks before dawn. Kit and I have been trying to communicate with Firemyst and let him know what we are doing, but he is not answering.*

How did you decide on his sex? Tallen asked. *I thought we were going to have to turn Firemyst upside down and blow away the fluff to tell the sex, same as you would a diddle duck chick.*

Zeal laughed out loud at the image. *It's the way his thoughts feel to me and Kit. I'm not certain he comprehended everything we discussed, but at least he knows he is not alone and that we are trying to help him.*

One called Firemyst understands.

Tulip opened her eyes and sat up. *Do you know why Lady Phyllis wants to meet with us tonight? We aren't scheduled for training. You haven't done anything to get us in trouble with the Trade Master, have you, Zeal?*

Zeal was still amazed that Lady Phyllis, so small in size yet big in presence, reigned as head of the Trade in Havensharth. *No, I haven't, and I don't know. A message was delivered to me this morning, same as you. Guess we go find out.*

Tallen gathered the remains of their meal and placed them in the basket. *You two go on ahead to your meeting. I'll take care of cleaning up.*

Thanks, Tallen. Zeal stood, stretched his arms up straight in the air, and rose on his toes. Then he reached down and gave Tulip a hand onto her feet. As Kit led the way, Zeal addressed her directly. *We need to let Deena know we are leaving tonight. I don't think we should wait and tell her after we've gone. Would you see if she is available?*

Will do.

Zeal soon sensed Deena's presence. *Yes, dear one, is it time?*

Soon. We leave a few marks prior to dawn. He wished Deena would change her mind and go with them.

Are you sure this is what you need to do? Deena asked them.

Zeal could feel her concern for him and Kit and appreciated that she wasn't judging or questioning his decision. *This is the only option left. I have to do this for Firemyst.*

Thank you for keeping me informed. Ice and I love you both. Remember that. She sent them a mental hug.

I love you, too. Zeal told himself not to cry when Kit sent her love to Deena.

We are Pride.

* * *

Lady Phyllis sat comfortably behind her desk while she dressed down the two Apprentices before her. The cat sat on the floor between them grooming herself. Phyllis was still tracking down rumors regarding the animal but had not yet discovered anything useful.

Lines creased Phyllis's forehead. Sternly, she continued, "Zeal, Tulip, I'm disappointed in both of you. I had to learn from this individual that you are leaving on some kind of journey against your Mentor's wishes." She nodded to a woman sitting next to her desk. "Not only did you neglect to inform me of your intentions, but you didn't even consider asking for my help. You should have come to me. What do you have to say for yourselves? No, don't speak. I don't want to hear your excuses. This will never happen again. Do you both understand?"

"Yes, Trade Master," the two young ones answered simultaneously.

As Phyllis studied her delinquents, she noticed the subtle glance between them and the cat.

"This emissary from Trade Master Slag arrived last eve with information regarding your undertaking." She glanced at the figure who sat on her left. The woman was dressed in black, form-fitting cloth, a snug hood, and mask. She had a brace of throwing knives across her chest with blacked-metal blades and harness.

"I've confirmed the source and reliability of the information. Slag's missive stated you will need this person and her skills on your venture. She is going with you. There will be no discussion." Phyllis watched Zeal close his mouth before making a comment. "She will meet you at the stables, so don't even think about leaving without her. I will have the specialized gear requested by Trade Master Slag delivered there as well."

After giving her charges a final, icy stare, Phyllis dismissed them. "Now get out of here. I have work to do."

* * *

"I honestly didn't think to ask Lady Phyllis for help." Zeal was huddled with Tulip on a small knoll overlooking the lake with Kit in his lap.

"The idea never occurred to me, either," Tulip replied.

"I can't help wondering who that person was with Lady Phyllis." Zeal was frustrated. "We only recently decided on our course of action and haven't confided in anyone."

Tulip answered after several heartbeats. "We never did learn how Master Slag knew to send Qwen to help you, seasons ago. The Trade Master's sources were always good about stuff happening in Arlanda, but he seems to know about things in Havensharth, as well. It is strange, though. It's almost as if he were here and a part of everything. Now he's sent a stranger to aid us."

Zeal nodded in agreement. "Kit, can you tell us anything about the person in Lady Phyllis's office? Who is she?"

She had guarded thoughts. She only thought of scraud. I am hungry now.

"That's strange... Why that particular fish?" Zeal wondered. "Tulip, do you think we're doing the right thing? Firemyst needs help now not later—he's barely hanging on to life, I think. But what if our plan ends up causing more harm than good for the Firebird?"

"Yes, he does. Trust your instincts. I know you are worried about Tallen and me getting into trouble over this. Didn't you learn anything from Lady Phyllis tonight? You can't do this alone. Master Slag would not have sent Mystery Woman, if you could, and he obviously felt her presence is needed. One thing I noted about her. She is dressed all in Spider Silk, like our workshirts, and resembles a member of Master Turk's Set."

Zeal thought back to Liddea's kidnapping. The Set was the enforcement arm of the Trade in Arlanda. Master Turk was the Set's commander and answered to one person, Master Slag.

"Let's keep a close watch on her. Kit, you continue to listen and see if you hear anything other than scraud. She has to take care of girl stuff sometime, so you and Tulip try to catch a glimpse of her uncovered face."

Zeal felt he was losing control of matters and they hadn't even left Havensharth yet.

* * *

An overcast sky prevented the stars from illuminating the area. A damp mist brought a chill to the air, but Zeal's inner warmth kept it at bay. He sat, unseen, in a tree that allowed him to view all approaches to the stable and attached paddock. He noted Tallen's arrival. Kit had let him know Tulip and the Mystery Woman were already inside, as was Charese. He intended to find out why Charese was present once he joined them.

Kit padded a circuit around the stables. If it hadn't been for their bond, Zeal wouldn't have been able to follow her progress: the absence of light hid her from detection. Between Kit's senses and his own, Zeal was certain no one other than they were nearby.

When he'd returned earlier that evening to his room, he'd found a cloth-wrapped bundle on his sleeper. He recognized the two rods and the ring he'd removed from their wrapping; he must thank Deena for her largess upon his return. Next to bundle was a blank piece of parchment along with a quill and ink block. He'd immediately comprehended the purpose of the parchment and chided himself for not thinking of it before hand. He sat down and composed a message that he'd left on his sleeper.

Master Ice and Deena,

I am sorry I had to leave without your blessing. I know you have doubts, but I have none. Firemyst would not survive a delay. Tulip and Tallen have joined Kit and me. We will be careful and will keep in touch. I have borrowed a ring of communication and I am sure Deena can find its mate. I will endeavor to contact each evening to inform you of our progress. We'll not long be in range to get in touch in other ways, if you know what I mean.

Love to you both

Zeal

He'd dressed in cold weather clothes, asked Kit to tell Tallen and Tulip to do the same, and grabbed a cloak. Next, he'd refreshed the crystal fire heating Firemyst prior to leaving the cottage and placed the egg back in the pack from Iris.

The continuous warmth had revived the chick somewhat. The firebird had once again attempted to communicate, although his thoughts were not any stronger or clearer. Zeal was still unable to hear Firemyst without Kit's assistance, but he had the impression that the chick was increasingly less active inside the egg.

Firemyst didn't use words like he or Kit did. A new means of communication was evolving. The Firebird's thoughts still sounded to Zeal like burning wood: they sizzled, hissed, snapped, sputtered, and popped as they spat sparks of understanding.

Zeal climbed down the tree. Once safely on the ground, he

readjusted his pack and gear. Growing up at the Temple of the Ladies of Life, he had learned to call the gear his kit. But that had become too confusing once he met Kit, so gear it was.

Nervous, he kept to the shadows, staying hidden as much as possible from view in the predawn night. He stopped to listen and look one last time before entering the stable after Kit told him all was clear.

She met him, and together they opened the side entrance and slipped inside. He closed the door behind before they joined Tulip, Tallen, Mystery Woman, and Charese. Everyone hushed as Zeal approached.

The stable was well lit by flameless lanterns to prevent an accidental fire from starting. Having Practitioners of the Arts around provided certain advantages. The animals were in their stalls except for four warhorses, which stood behind the group of people

"Glad to see you all made it here safe," Zeal said quietly. "I didn't expect to see you here, Charese."

"Just so you know, the Flower Lady told me in my dreams that I needed to be here tonight to help you. She said I couldn't go along." She was quiet a moment as the horse next to her nuzzled her hair. "I made sure the horses were rested today and not taken out for training. They've been fed, watered, and have new shoes."

Zeal detected disappointment in Charese's voice. "What Flower Lady?" Tulip shrugged her shoulders, unaware of the reference, herself.

She means this, Kit replied sending them all a likeness.

The image of an iris bloom appeared inside Zeal's head.

"Oh! She means Iris!" Tulip exclaimed.

"That is a lovely name. Lady Iris is so nice." Charese smiled, walked to the nearest horse, and patted the saddle. "This is a flight saddle. She showed me how to equip them on the horses," she added, nodding toward Master Slag's emissary.

The Trade Master and Iris had again anticipated Zeal's need. He asked, "Are you sure we're all capable of riding warhorses? I thought they were trained to respond to one owner?"

Charese replied, "You are right. That is the way they are trained, but these four colts were raised together and have been listening to Kit their whole lives." Charese stroked one horse's neck. "This is Hunter, and he has always been the leader of the group. Zeal, you will ride him. Hunter followed Kit as would a puppy, when he was younger. The others follow him. If Kit tells them to carry you, they will. Of course, the black male over there already belongs to Tulip.

I told them, when they were cubs, I would not eat them, so they listen, Kit mindspoke to Zeal. Her thought was woven with meanings, including the idea that the horses would not think to do otherwise.

So, this must be one of the things that happened when the girls got together, Zeal thought, he'd not been aware that combat Apprentices would have horses. "I didn't know you had a horse, Tulip. What did you name him?"

Tulip rubbed her horse's nose. "He is called Templar. I named him after the Temple, to help remind me of the family we left behind. I figured he would take me back to Arlanda one day to visit everyone. Even though I love our life here, there is always a part of me there, as well."

"We'll return together. I promise." Zeal asked Kit to convey a private thought to Tulip alone. *We can ask Kit and Mother Essmee to take us to Arlanda. That is once we recover from the consequences we earn from this endeavor. I agree, we are overdue for a visit.*

Charese continued her introductions. "The last two are twins, Strider and Striker. Strider loves to run and will run his heart out for you. Striker, well, he is fond of kicking his opponents. I think the lady over there looks as if she can handle him. We can seat Tallen on Strider."

"I have a passing acquaintance with Strider already," Tallen said. "We'll do fine."

Master Slag's emissary nodded her agreement but continued to maintain her silence.

"What's your father going to think about us taking Hunter? I thought he was grooming him to replace his current mount?" Tulip stroked Templar's nose.

Zeal pondered Tulip's question and waited for Charese's reply.

The hole he was digging kept getting deeper and increasingly full of debts he would have to pay back. But helping Firemyst was worth it.

"Oh, you know him. He's going to lose his temper and then take his anger out on his Apprentices, because he wouldn't dare yell at Mom or me. Luckily, Tulip won't be here," Charese added.

"True. But when I return, he will take it all out on me, because I will be one of the horse thieves." Tulip gave an exasperated sigh.

"I'm the one borrowing horses," Zeal said clearly. "You can't get in trouble for riding your own mount. I'm the one responsible and due all the blame for whatever we do to aid Firemyst."

Charese picked up Kit from beside her, and they rubbed their faces together. "You better take good care of my girl. She may have chosen you, but I've claimed her. She'll get tired of you one sun and come around to my way of thinking. I guess you better take care of yourself, as well, since right now you seem to be part of the 'Kit' package. That kind of means I have chosen you, too."

Taken back, Zeal did not know how to respond to Charese, and Kit didn't offer any help. The subdued laughter of his companions accompanied Kit's scary-happy grin.

Charese set Kit on her paws before checking on Hunter's tack. His saddle had an extended area of padding with a leather roll in front of it.

"She truly has you well wrapped, Mouse," Mystery Woman said, laughing as she finally broke her silence.

Zeal whipped his head to stare at Slag's emissary. He hadn't heard this voice or laughter since leaving Arlanda. "Mehrle? Is that you?" He rushed over to wrap his arms tightly around her, and she hugged him intensely in return. He did not know why Mehrle had been sent by Master Slag but was happy to have her here nonetheless.

"It took you long enough," Mehrle said jokingly.

Zeal glanced over at Tulip who had a wide, knowing smile, herself. He told Tallen, "Tulip, Mehrle, and I were Trade apprentices together when Tulip and I lived in Arlanda. You might say Mehrle was the leader of our little group."

"Nice to meet you. So, why do we need to dress so warmly?"

Tallen asked. "I'm cooking in this clothing."

Back to the task at hand, Zeal said, "Let's get out of here first. Then we can talk things over where we won't be discovered." He gave Mehrle one last squeeze and walked away feeling less down on himself.

Under Charese and Mehrle's direction they loaded and balanced their gear on the horses. Zeal placed Kit on the front saddle pad and mounted Hunter. He had done a little bit of riding but wasn't as comfortable in the saddle as Tulip and Tallen. Even Mehrle seemed at home on a horse.

Relax. Let body learn from Hunter, Kit mindspoke to Zeal.

Is it safe for us to leave? he asked her.

After a few heartbeats, she replied, *Clear. Let's hunt.*

Charese opened one of the stable doors and waved silently to each of them as they moved past. Charese continued to bear witness to their departure till they were lost in the darkness and had ridden away from the safety of Havensharth into the unknown.

CHAPTER TWENTY-SIX

AT SUNRISE, MEHRLE looked out of the trees lining the edge of a ridge that sloped into a small valley. A stream meandered below. Her horse had smelled the water earlier and was eager for a drink. Striker had proved responsive and good-natured.

Zeal pointed to the stream. "We should take the horses down and, after watering them, bring them back here." He startled when Hunter started forward on his own.

"It appears Hunter's mind is set on the liquid refreshment." Tallen gave his mount leave to follow.

"He and I are still working on developing an understanding on which of us is the superior being," Zeal replied.

Hunter turned to look at Kit, who huffed a laugh.

Mehrle wondered why Zeal wanted to return to the top of the ridge after the horses had drunk their fill. She was no longer familiar with her former companions from the Temple of the Ladies of Life. They had changed from being scrawny orphans who, along with Liddea, Fronc, and Nester, had been apprenticed to the Trade together. The six had been inseparable. They ran the streets, sewers, and rooftops, claiming the city of Arlanda as their own. But who were Zeal and Tulip now? Mehrle wondered, assessing them with an awareness derived from her training in the Trade.

Tulip had grown taller than Mehrle and was dressed in serviceable dark brown leathers with color-matched gloves. The short sword she wore had a cloudy, gray crystal on the pommel, very different from the one Tulip had taken with her from the mausoleum, when she and Zeal left Arlanda. There was no sign of Tulip's Fang, but Mehrle figured it was hidden. Tulip had developed an aura about her that said, "This person is dangerous," which impressed Mehrle.

Zeal, on the other hand, hadn't changed much—he still appeared too trusting and small for his age. But Mehrle knew, even though he wore no obvious weapons, he should not be overlooked or taken for a mark. She figured his Fang was somewhere on his person.

She had not yet ascertained why Zeal was attached to a cat—he'd never been one to fancy animals in the past. But Kit was unusual: her ears had tufts, and her eyes were large and egg-shaped with black and white markings around them. Her light gray and tan coat was short and looked soft to touch. Mehrle swore the cat had actually laughed at Zeal.

She was not sure what to make of their thin, strongly built young friend, Tallen, the soon-to-be journeyman bard. He carried himself with an air of mystery. Along with his weapons, he also traveled with a large leather case worn on his belt. She wondered what it contained and felt a little jealous that he was so close to her former companions.

When she arrived at the stream, Tulip dismounted and led Templar to the water, staying close by to monitor how much he ingested. "Don't let them drink too much, or they will get cramps," she suggested to the others. "They can have more before we leave. And we should feed and water ourselves, too, now that we have a moment."

After watering Striker, Mehrle guided him to a grassy area and removed the bit from his mouth, to allow him to graze. She dropped the reins, indicating to him he was to stay. "I think the morning meal is already prepared." She removed a black satchel strapped to Striker's saddle and handed it to Zeal. "Qwen told me to give this to Zeal once we were away from Havensharth. Tulip mentioning food reminded me."

Zeal took it, noting, "Except for the color, this is identical to the blue travel satchel Qwen had when he was here last. It is how he transports his food and drink." He reached inside and removed a cloth-wrapped bundle that gave off the aroma of fresh-baked honey scones. "They're still warm!"

Mehrle gathered with the others while Zeal spread a large blue cloth on the ground for them to sit on. Next to the scones, he set out whipped lavender butter and a pitcher of hot beryl tea along with white cups. Her mouth began to water even before he drew out the last small bowl.

"I believe this is scraud," Zeal said to Kit. He put the bowl of raw fish in front of her.

Kit sampled the flesh. *It is scraud. I shall make one called Qwen Pride.*

"What's your plan, Zeal?" Mehrle took a bite of scone liberally slathered with lavender butter.

"What all do you know regarding our journey, Mehrle?" he answered while chewing.

She took a sip of tea. "Master Slag called me into his office two moons ago and told me he was sending me to aid you and Tulip with a venture. I was informed it would involve an element of danger, and he expected me to give a good accounting of myself. He said you would inform me of my duties and that the kit and tack needed would be delivered to me. Qwen saw to my transportation."

Zeal stopped eating and looked from Tulip to Tallen to Kit. "Do you have any idea as to how the Trade Master acquired his intelligence? I wasn't even aware I would need to go on this odyssey two moons ago."

"I don't know how Master Slag was able to foretell your future. But here I am and there you sit, apparently destined to fulfill a mission of some kind. So, what is it?"

Zeal stood and untied his pack from Hunter's saddle. Mehrle recognized it as one of the packs Iris had given each of them; she and Tulip still had theirs secured on their own mounts.

Zeal removed a large, oval-shaped object encased in crystal that resembled flames. The crystal pulsed with colors of light, just as a dancing fire did while burning. The luminescence moved eerily around the ovoid, which, from its size, should not have fit in the pack. She knew from experience, though, that their packs had no trouble accommodating what Zeal held and more.

"This egg contains Firemyst. If his egg isn't hatched soon, he will die. We are taking him to place him in the Blood of Sartus. Those wiser and older than us agreed to mount an expedition to attend to Firemyst, but at a future date. If we wait for them, it will be too late for him." Zeal sat and placed the egg next to him.

"How far away is the Blood of Sartus? And what is it? Do you even know how to get there?"

"The Blood of Sartus flows under the land we live on." He looked to Tulip. "As far as where we can access a source of the blood, Tulip can help with that answer."

She retrieved her own pack and removed a scroll, which she unrolled, using small stones to weigh down the corners.

Mehrle saw that the scroll was actually a map. In the southernmost part of the continent, labeled *Oraan*, was a glowing red dot with the *Blood of Sartus* written under it. A similar green dot labeled *Havensharth* was also on the map.

"Isn't that the map from Master Greyhook's chest?" Tallen asked. "He keeps that chest locked. How did you get it?"

"Yes, it is, and yes, he does. You forget who you are addressing." Tulip wiggled the fingers of her right hand at him. "Grey should have a better lock, if he expects to keep us from borrowing his map."

Mehrle thought it nice Tulip was keeping up on her Trade skills. "That's a long distance away by horse, Zeal," she said, not sure she was going to be happy with his answer.

"With this map, we can always tell where we are and make sure we are traveling the correct direction. You're right. It is a long way to our destination. Therefore, we won't journey by horseback. We'll fly there by hippogriff, which will allow us to get there more directly and avoid the obstacles associated with land travel."

"Hippogriff!" Mehrle realized, as she loudly repeated the name, that Tallen and Tulip had echoed her response. Everyone was surprised, full of questions. "Now I understand why Master Slag sent the flight saddles. Where do you plan to find hippogriffs?" She didn't actually know what hippogriffs were.

Zeal waved his right hand in the direction of the horses. "There stand our hippogriffs." He reached into his pack and removed a green rod, holding it for everyone to see. "Using this will transform our warhorses into them."

Mehrle had a difficult time accepting what she was hearing. She'd had limited experience with what Practitioners of the Arts were capable of doing. But Tulip and Tallen seemed to believe Zeal could pull this off. She couldn't hold her questions back. "Zeal, have you ever seen a hippogriff?"

"No, I haven't," he replied patiently.

"So, your stick will turn a horse into one?" she pressed.

"It's called a rod, and a Practitioner can use this particular kind to change a living creature into another with which they are intimately familiar." Zeal remained quiet for several heartbeats. "We could all even be changed into hippogriffs. *Hmmm*, I hadn't thought of that until just now. But then we couldn't pack our gear on one another."

Tallen interrupted. "Excuse me, I did hear you say *intimately* familiar?"

"Yes, you did."

"But you said you've never encountered a hippogriff. Then how do you plan on using your rod?" Mehrle asked, somewhat taunting Zeal to prove himself. Then she laughed. "I am sorry, Zeal. I didn't mean to sound like that. Please explain how you plan to do this."

"That's all right, Mehrle. I'm incapable of transforming them. We have another Practitioner with us who can do so."

Mehrle looked over at Tallen.

"'Tis not me he is referring to," Tallen replied.

"Tulip, is it you?" Mehrle asked, though she hadn't imagined the fighter capable of conjuring.

"No, not me. Zeal is referring to someone else here with us." She said nothing more in explanation.

Becoming frustrated, Mehrle looked around for another person hidden from her, but there was only the four of them and the cat. She studied, Kit, whose eyes were watching her intently. They couldn't mean…?

Well, it took you long enough. I am not just some little cat! At that moment, Kit chose to grow to her hunting size.

Mehrle examined the creature, whose shoulders were as high as Zeal's armpit and whose maw could easily encompass the boy's head. Hunter and the other horses looked up from their meal of grass, their nostrils widening briefly as they took in Kit's scent before resuming their eating, finding nothing amiss.

The others watched Mehrle closely.

"You might want to put that away." Zeal, with a concerned look on his face, gestured to Mehrle's left hand.

She was holding one of her throwing knives and hadn't realized she had drawn it. Her hand trembled slightly as she reseated the blade in its sheath. "What is Kit?" she asked in a whisper.

You will keep what you learn regarding me to yourself and share with no one else, unless I tell you, Kit mindspoke to Mehrle alone. *Thinking of scraud will not help you.*

Mehrle understood she had been given a command and not a request. She expected to learn more about and from Kit eventually but decided to take cues from Tallen and Tulip. "I will hold your trust. I was told by Qwen to practice the exercise at our first meeting with Lady Phyllis. Does he know about you?"

One called Qwen knows. You may talk to him about me. Kit included everyone when she answered, *Mother is Shadow Cat. I conjure. Zeal is mine.* Then Kit returned to hiding size.

"That mostly sums it up, Mehrle," Zeal said. "We can fill in more details along the way. And you," he addressed to Kit, "are mine, as well."

Tulip sat next to Kit and scratched her behind the ears, redirecting everyone back to the important question at hand. "Kit, why does Zeal think you can turn Templar into a hippogriff?"

I hunted hippogriff with Mother. They have good flavor, but Argguile is sweeter.

"That is familiar enough I'm thinking." Tallen moved a large rock aside then sat comfortably in the depression left behind.

"Let's unpack and unsaddle the horses." Zeal rose to his feet, walked to Hunter, and began to unload him. "I don't think we want anything on them during their change. Not sure what would happen to them or our stuff during the transformation, if they were still geared."

As the others attended to their mounts, Zeal waited for Tulip to help him with the horse's bit and bridle. "When did you learn how to ride, Mehrle?"

She explained, "After you both left Arlanda, I continued my Apprenticeship with the Trade. A little over a season ago, Master Turk asked if I was interested in training to be an Enforcer and join his Set. I realized I did. I learned that Enforcers have to be able to ride—not just horses, but other creatures as well."

"Have you ridden other creatures?" Tallen placed Strider's tack beside his own gear.

"No, I haven't. But Masters Turk and Slag made sure I was taught the principles before I was sent here. Now I think I know why I had to learn. So I could help Zeal." Mehrle winked at her friend.

"We are glad to have you with us, even if we don't know all the reasons for you joining us." Zeal grinned.

"I agree," Tulip added.

Zeal walked Hunter to an open area. "Let's have the horses stand over here, then Kit can conjure."

CHAPTER TWENTY-SEVEN

IT WAS A HUNTING SIZE Kit who exited the shadow, carrying a large feather in her mouth. She'd briefly stepped away to refresh her awareness of the beast she planned to conjure. She had returned to the location of a hunt her mother had taken her on when she was younger.

Hippogriffs were aggressive flying creatures. They had the features of a horse and giant raptor. When using the rod, the feather's fresh scent and texture would help her to focus her intent.

She surveyed the camp on her arrival, touched the thoughts of her companions, and discovered all was well. The horses stood with their tack and rider's gear laid out next to them.

Do you need to feed? Zeal asked her.

Had a snack before returning. She sent him an image of the partridge she'd killed. **I am ready.**

She sat on her haunches facing the horses and placed her forepaw on the feather. Zeal held out the rod, and Kit took its handle in her mouth, taking care not to damage it with her teeth. A tingling from the rod's surface traveled through her tongue and flowed to the paw holding the feather. Starting with Hunter, she released and directed the conjure contained in the rod.

Through their link, Zeal joined with her in Marhdah. His strength would ease her working of the conjuring. She felt him follow along as she used the rod's properties on Templar, Strider, and, lastly, Striker.

Kit's young companions watched her sit with her ears laid flat to the skull, hissing and growling, while her tail flexed straight out behind her, its tip twitching. A stream of drool ran from the corner of her mouth.

Each horse was encased in an opaque-green sphere that hovered slightly above the ground. The animal's shadowy form could be seen inside, morphing as it changed shape.

When Kit sat the rod down next to the feather, Zeal moved in front of her, placed his forehead on hers, and scratched behind her ears just the way she liked. Physically and mentally, he gave her his love. *That was amazing, Kit.*

One by one, the spheres darkened before settling aground once more. The shells, now blacked, fractured into pieces that rained to the earth. The remnants formed a gray mist around the talons of the beasts they had once enveloped and then gradually dispersed. Each mount had retained its coloring: Hunter's black, Templar's gray; Strider and Striker both were still bays. Feathers had replaced their manes and tails in a darker hue that accented their beauty.

Kit touched Hunter, nose to beak. Yes, he smelled right. His odor was of hippogriff with a very slight after-whiff of horse. She communicated their need to him and the others.

A piercing screech knifed the air. The call, trumpeted by Hunter in acknowledgement, sounded nothing like a stallion's cry. He was joined in chorus by the other hippogriffs, who had gathered around her, their wings held out above as if to shelter her. Their eyes searched the sky and surroundings, looking for anyone or anything that dared to challenge them. The tail feathers rose and their manes crested.

They are hippogriff, Kit informed her companions.

"Kit means she is done, and it is time for us to saddle and equip them," Zeal added.

Kit knew he was eager to leave.

Tallen stared at the mounts with joy and awe. "'Tis a wonder. Tonight, I will start a journal, even if it is just for us to have."

Kit returned to her hiding size and found a warm patch of sunshine to relax in. Now that she'd done the hard part, she decided to get in a little cleaning, while the others did some actual work. The rest of her Pride quickly loaded their mounts while managing to avoid getting into each other's way.

Strider said his carrier is too close to his wings and has more weight on one side. Kit indicated Strider's right flank with her forepaw then continued to give corrections from cues received from the former horses.

Once all the baggage was placed, she sprang up on to Hunter's riding harness and settled just behind the rounded cushion on the front of his flight saddle. Zeal mounted and sat behind her. Mehrle gave individual instructions on how to use the ties and straps to hold the rider safely in flight.

They walked the former horses back to the rise overlooking the valley. Zeal was of the opinion that the height might ease the hippogriffs in their first flight. Mehrle then checked that everyone was correctly tied. Kit allowed Mehrle to place a harness on her, certain the restraint would not prevent her from stepping into shadow.

"What now?" Mehrle mounted Striker and fastened herself in place.

"I think Kit and I will test out how this works, and then, if all is well, the rest of you can join us. That is unless you want to go first?" Zeal suggested.

"No, that's okay. I don't mind following the leader. Remember, I never said I'd ridden a mount that flies. I've just had ground training. You can go first." Mehrle gave Zeal an abbreviated bow.

Zeal sent, *Kit, will you tell Hunter I am ready?*

Kit sunk the claws of her forepaws into the pad. Hunter's muscles bunched tightly beneath her, and his talons left furrows in the soil as he used them to gather purchase. He went from standing still to a full run in just a few steps. His wings swept from his sides, capturing the air as he leapt upward, and he left the ground. Ascending skyward, his legs no longer needed the slope beneath him. Hunter's joyful scream was a challenge soon met by his fellow hippogriffs, who followed his lead and flew below and behind him.

When Kit turned her head, she saw Hunter followed in flight by

Templar, Strider, and Striker, flying in a V formation. The twins placed themselves behind and on opposite sides of Hunter, with Striker on the left. Templar took a position behind Striker. Kit inwardly laughed whenever the other hippogriffs' riders cried out in distress. One sat with arms flailing, while another lay along the neck of their hippogriff, holding tightly with arms and legs, and the third leaned so far over the side that, if not for being tied to the saddle, they would have already been unseated.

Her surprised companions had clearly not expected their mounts to suddenly leap and follow Hunter. They quickly learned they were not in control.

The former horses were excited to take to the air and follow their new natural instincts. They were all instantly lost in the pleasure called flight. She pictured in their minds the desired destination. As one, they turned and began their travels.

* * *

Tallen realized he'd been granted an unexpected wish: to see the land from above as a bird and fly as one on high. He was happy and thrilled by this encounter.

The ground was far below him. The river flowing under them was a silver ribbon sometimes met by bright threads that joined its weaving. The only sounds accompanying the flight were the creaking of the tack, the soft rustle of the air as it moved off the feather tips of the hippogriff's wings, and the wind, which carried all he heard away. The trees below were a melody of colors, the different varieties intermixed and forming no distinct pattern. Sometimes, single species appeared to band together to form a grove.

The experience had given birth to a song, which he hummed to himself and would chronicle in his journal, once they made camp tonight. He saw birds at wing, although none reached the height their hippogriffs attained.

The mounts took turns, in a random fashion, deciding who

would lead their small flock. He supposed this enabled them to somehow work together to make their flying easier.

Behind Tallen, Kit had gathered shadows around her, so her figure was not easily seen as she rode in front of Zeal. Tulip smiled often, enjoying the experience as much as he. Mehrle, still masked, sat bent into the crisp chill wind. Tallen appreciated Zeal's directive to wear warm clothes, although Zeal never seemed to feel the cold as the rest of them did.

The riding straps enabled him to relax, secured, and familiarize himself with the difference in movement between ground and air travel. He had become attuned to the dip and sway, the beat of the wings, but not yet to the twists and drops.

When Strider initiated an unexpected dive, Tallen felt his stomach rise and almost empty. Strider folded one wing and suddenly plummeted, snatching a bird in flight. The horse/hippogriff grasped the fowl using the talons of his right front foot and began to ingest it as he flew to rejoin the others.

Tallen was embarrassed by his unmanly yell at Strider's sudden move. It made his companions laugh. He secretly took satisfaction when their mounts periodically did the same.

That is, except for Hunter. Hunter seemed to maintain an even keel as he flew. When he changed his position in the formation, he did so without the jarring movements of the others. He would fly above the rest then, once far enough ahead, return to the same level as the others, positioning himself in front of them. Tallen wondered if Kit was the reason Hunter was so well behaved.

The sun was low on the horizon to their right when he waved to Zeal to come closer. Tallen shouted so his voice carried, "We should set camp before it gets dark."

"Good idea!" Zeal yelled back. "I don't know what or where would be an easy place for a hippogriff to go back to the ground. Do you think they hover? Or do they need to run prior to stopping, once they touch down?"

"I don't know." Tallen saw Kit was tense, claws extended as she gripped the pad in front of her. "What is wrong with Kit? Is she well?"

"She will be fine once we are on the ground. She is not happy up here. To be honest, she is a little fearful." Zeal rubbed Kit's back.

The sky casts no shadow. My kind does not belong up here, Kit admitted to them all.

"Hunter is looking after you. He hasn't done any of the fancy flying that the others have," Zeal reminded Kit. "There is nothing shameful in having something that gives you a scare. We'll get you down soon."

They both surveyed the land below. Tallen spotted a likely location. "Look up ahead to the left. There is a large opening in the forest. It even has a stream flowing over on the right."

"That looks good. We'll attempt to land there."

Within a few heartbeats, Tallen felt Strider change direction and begin his descent. Glancing at Kit, he decided she had communicated with the hippogriffs. He waved and shouted to get Mehrle's and Tulip's attention, gesturing toward the clearing.

The four winged steeds flew groundward together. They initially circled the open area then, one by one, broke away and landed, using a rapid flapping of their wings. Like the others, Strider took a few steps after his talons touched the ground, but, unlike the others, he stumbled.

Tallen cringed but became relieved when, moments later, Strider recovered, uninjured. If Strider had broken a leg when he'd missed his footing, would he have to be put down?

The hippogriffs furled their wings and held them close to their bodies. Strider's wings strangely felt comforting, warm against Tallen's legs.

Kit, no longer covered in shadows, leaped from Hunter's back and began to groom herself in the remaining sunlight.

Tulip untied her flight straps. "We should dismount and walk to the stream. Templar and the rest have done well for their first flight. Let's not have them suffer an injury trying to carry us on the ground. I don't know how capable their current form is at land travel."

Tallen appreciated Tulip's wisdom. He, Mehrle, and Zeal followed suit, and together they headed to the water. They had landed on a large, grass-covered knoll that was higher at its center, and the grass was short, as if it had been grazed.

The round clearing was a hill bordered by a large grove of trees. The slope rose twice Tallen's height from tree edge to top. He thought half of Havensharth would fit in the space.

They let the hippogriffs drink from the stream that ran along the west edge of the grove. The trees seemed to guard the knoll, and none seemed younger than many hundreds of seasons.

Several of the trees had healed scars on their bark, old ones. When Tallen placed his hand on the bark of an elder red asdic tree, he found a large area of cambial growth, indicating a past injury. He knew from experience that something had cut or torn into this spot, causing the damage, when the tree was much younger. The pattern made on the bark at the growth's center morphed and molded itself as he watched, making a stylized "D." The letter stayed for several heartbeats before the bark returned to its natural appearance. To Tallen, the tree now seemed content and slept in peace.

Tallen had continued to keep his affinity for trees to himself. Doing so had kept alive the memories of being alone with his mother in the woods. Only Kit knew about his past. She'd told him the talent would make him a better hunter. *You will let the others know when you are ready,* she'd once reassured him.

"Tallen, are you all right?" Mehrle asked.

"I'm fine. This would be a good place to camp. The area feels protected in some fashion. It won't be a good idea to hunt in this area, though. Only gather dead wood that is on the ground. Don't break any branches off the trees. I think it best that we start our fire by the stream and keep it small."

"What makes you leery about scavenging the area?" asked Mehrle.

Before he could think of an answer, Kit mindspoke to them, *Never stalk prey before you know you have the advantage.*

"Thank you, Kit. What you say is true." He looked briefly toward Tulip and Zeal.

"Is there some danger here you are aware of, Tallen, that you aren't sharing?" Mehrle studied their surroundings.

"Unlike your city of Arlanda, this forest is alive in many ways. I was taught to tread lightly in the wood and leave no mark of my passage. One should always respect the land. It may sound silly, but we need to be careful in this place."

Zeal interrupted the discussion. "Let's do as Tallen suggests. Kit and I trust his instincts."

"As do I," Tulip added.

Mehrle nodded. "Now, what do we do with our mounts?"

Remove everything. I will release the conjure.

Tallen lead Strider to an area that would safely entertain a fire. "We set up camp here. The fire should go there. Gather stones to make a ring."

He then proceeded to remove gear, saddle, and tack from Strider, taking care not to damage the feathers on his wings. He snuck a glance at the others as he worked. Each of them was touching, examining, smelling, and exploring their hippogriffs, too.

Strider's odor reminded Tallen of the scent of dust in the air when you harvested grain, sweet yet earthy. What he'd thought was hair on Strider's body was actually tough, fine feathers growing over a softer under-layer. The top coat was resilient to the rubbing of the tack and saddle. The feathers that comprised his tail, mane, wings, and that extended from the lower half of the legs were typical of a raptor's.

He had been so overwhelmed by their creation and the need to hurry far away from Havensharth that he hadn't before taken the time to marvel about the creature. "You've done well, Strider. You make a fine beast in any form."

His beaked head turned and looked Tallen in the eyes. After a brief perusal, Strider nodded in agreement then walked away to join his brethren, who stood waiting. Once together, they were encased in an opaque-green sphere and their shadowed forms altered.

Tallen searched for Kit but did not see what he expected. She lay next to Zeal, grooming herself, without any rod in her possession. She would occasionally look up and monitor the process as the shells darkened, cracked, and fell away, dissipating into mist.

They are horse. Her part completed, Kit curled into a ball and closed her eyes.

* * *

As Mehrle brought a second load of wood to the camp, she glanced at Kit, who appeared to be sleeping, but the subtle movement of one ear let her know that the Shadow Cat was on guard.

The horses looked no worse for wear from their transformations and travel. Tulip led them through the process of hoof inspection and care for their mounts, mainly for Tallen's and Zeal's benefit, since Mehrle already had the training. She shuddered when she guiltily considered the idea of having to clean clawed feet instead of hooves. She knew the difference shouldn't have bothered her, but it did.

The others were yet to return, so she decided to start the fire. It was easy to find stones from along the stream's bank and use them to make a ringed pit. Hanging moss and dropped cones made good tinder. She was finishing her preparations when her companions returned with more wood.

With flint and steel in hand, she heard Zeal announce, "There is no need for that." She hadn't heard him approach.

"Excuse me. I thought we wanted a fire?"

"We do." Zeal pointed at the ring she'd made, where flames were already dancing, briefly forming into an M before settling for a good burn.

"I forgot! I forgot about you. I just don't know what to expect. I never had a chance to ask, though—how does it feel to be connected to fire?

"It is hard to describe how it feels. Hold a moment."

Tallen and Tulip placed their wood on the pile and sat down next to the fire. Kit had turned her ears toward him.

"Will you help me show them?" Zeal asked her.

The answer came to Mehrle in the form of warmth. Suddenly, she felt as if she was floating in a hot pool that caressed her from the inside out. Flaming motes drifted around her, with one glowing brighter and wafting higher than the rest. A subtle, unidentifiable scent enveloped her; she found it relaxing, welcoming.

And then there was the *song*! Music crackled, popped, hissed, and snapped. Similar to water, it engulfed her, filling her empty spaces with a soothing balm. The melody spoke of the life and joy of being fire. When the sharing was over, she became cold again. Tears flowed down her face. She felt alone, saddened to be separated from the fiery whole.

"I knew not how it felt." Tallen's eyes were closed and he held his head in his hands.

Zeal was surprised by their response to the experience. "It never occurred to me to share in this fashion with anyone besides Kit."

Mehrle followed Tulip's example and wrapped her arms around Zeal. The closeness felt right, needed. Tallen joined them, and the four held each other. Not to be left out, Kit jumped onto Zeal's shoulders.

"Thank you both for that," Tulip said softly, her voice husky with emotion. "Don't you ever do that to me again, though, unless you can make them stay. Zeal, I now know why you keep collecting flames."

Mehrle asked, "How is Firemyst doing?"

"Not too well," Zeal sadly admitted. "If it wasn't for the crystal fire, he would be no longer."

"Tell him we all said to hold on," Mehrle insisted. "Don't let him give up."

Kit leapt off Zeal's shoulder and alighted on all four paws next to the black satchel. *Eat soon?*

"Good idea, Kit. Let's see if there is anything left in Qwen's gift." Mehrle gave Zeal a final squeeze before leaving the group hug.

They gathered next to the fire. Zeal opened the satchel, and the aroma of rich roast beast wafted from inside. He set out the large blue cloth, which was somehow as clean as it had been earlier in the morn. Roast beast already sliced, root vegetables sautéed and seasoned with herbs, and fresh greens covered with a berry vinaigrette were soon enjoyed by all. Of course, there was scraud for Kit on a fish-shaped platter similar to hers home, and bread pudding with spiced mead sauce to complete the meal.

They washed their eating ware in the stream and put it back into the satchel.

"I am going to have a long talk with Qwen when I get home," Mehrle burped loudly, offering a compliment to the meal. "I want my own satchel. What food supplies do we have to eat when the satchel is empty?"

"I thought we'd hunt and forage," Zeal answered. "It shouldn't be that hard for us. We all have some herb and plant lore, and I have learned to cook since we were last together."

Mehrle chuckled at Zeal's enthusiasm, remembering his sorry attempts in the kitchen when they were younger. She was troubled about the hunting and forage part, though. Other than Kit, none of them, including herself, had the appearance of a hunter. "So, how did you become such a good cook?"

Zeal grinned with pride. "I had lessons from Qwen then further instruction from Master Greyhook."

Mehrle turned to Tulip. "Is there hope for his cooking?"

She placed a hand on her sword hilt as she rose to her feet. "Yes, there is hope. He really has taken to the task quite handily. His food is passable now."

"Passable! It is more than passable," Zeal grumbled, mostly to himself.

Mehrle's eye was drawn to the crystal on Tulip's hilt. The usually cloudy crystal was clear. A sudden sneeze gripped her, causing her to blink involuntarily. When she looked back, the crystal had lost its clarity and was clouded over once again.

It must have been the light, she thought to herself.

* * *

The mound's guardian sensed something was different. The living had come to desecrate, rob, disrespect.

They will learn there is still a protector. Darkness comes soon. Their deaths will ensure peace and security.

CHAPTER TWENTY-EIGHT

ONCE THE SUN'S light faded, night swept forth to rapidly recapture all that the light had once embraced. Coolness accompanied the night, sucking the moisture into the air and creating a fog around them. The nearby trees were the only recognizable shapes distinguishable in the thickening mist.

Tulip finished seeing to the horses and then found a place beside Tallen. He put aside his journal and fed more wood to the fire. Mehrle tended to the saddles, checking their ties and straps critical to maintaining the safety of the riders when they were in the air. Zeal held Firemyst while Kit recharged the crystal fire. They had already created globes of light that floated over their campsite and provided illumination. The flame at the camp's center contributed a comforting, joyful warmth for them all.

* * *

It had a name once, lost now to itself, having been unused for an unknown number of seasons. Drawn, much as the vapor it resembled, it rose from the ground. Off-white, without substance, and moved by wind that didn't exist, it left the comfort of the mound.

With some effort, the wisp gathered pieces of fog to furnish itself form, flowing into the shape of a crude caricature of a man with long, clawed fingers and hollowed eyes that glowed a sick yellow in the darkness. The thing drifted down to the stream, where the life that needed ending drew breath.

Young, foolish, ignorant, they were unappreciative of their existence, the being thought. It moved outside the limits of the light that surrounded the living. Horses... many beats of the hearts of the living passed before the creatures—horses—were remembered. They did not pose a threat to those being protected.

Yes, that was its purpose now. The form appraising the interlopers was drawn to the two who were... one? Condensing more substance from the mist, it floated, listened, and evaluated. The boy was conversing with his pet. The pet was somehow communicating back.

Curious, the entity had never before been able to read the thoughts of the living. It would start with these.

* * *

Zeal placed the encapsulated Firemyst in his pack, sipped from his cup of beryl tea, and discovered it had cooled. With his inner flame, he re-heated the tea till he saw steam rise from the surface. Another sip confirmed it had reached an ideal warmth. He increased the temperature of his companions' drinks, as well.

The fog soaked up all the sounds they made. Strange, he thought, how the mist hadn't drifted into camp. Did the light from the globes ward the murk away?

Music cascaded into the night and became a beacon that chased away the gloom. Tallen was playing his pipes while Tulip sang in accompaniment. Melody and voice joined together with greater richness than either possessed alone.

They were working on the saga they planned to present during the celebration for new journeymen. It was based on the song Tulip and Tallen had first sung together for Greyhook.

Zeal stroked Kit's back as he listened. Her tail was twitchy. "You seem tense. Are you still bothered by our recent flight?"

No, not that. I sense the presence of another predator. Her vibrissae subtly moved as Kit stiffened. The hair on her back stood up, and her tail bristled. She grew to hunting size and her gaze fixed on something behind Zeal.

He looked back and was surprised to see a figure without flesh or substance, comprised entirely of mist, floating in the air. Its skeletal right hand extended within kissing distance of his lips. All he had to do was lean forward to complete contact.

The creature's own mouth was agape, displaying a pained grimace and the broken stubs of its remaining teeth. It had a hole where there should have been a nose and eyes that glowed yellow. Wisps of fog were simultaneously drawn to it and torn away, as it continually reformed itself.

* * *

Behind Zeal, the fog bulged forth into the light and slowly shifted closer to him. There was no scuff of boot on stone, rustle of clothing, or scent of body to give warning. A skeletal hand reached out to grasp the neck of its victim. The sweet essence of life would be snatched, consumed, put to a better use.

Music arose from within the camp and demanded its attention. Its eyes lifted from its intended target to locate the source of this distracting noise. Two of the encroachers were the source. It was not the girl's voice that gave it pause, although it had been a very long time since it had heard something that touched it in a tender fashion. No, it was the words she sang that caused it… consternation.

"Mendor, Mendor, why do you weep? The return of your fathers and sons do you seek. They left to protect their wives, families, and keep. None returned to tell you they are all buried deep."

"Please, stop what you are doing!" strongly exclaimed its intended target. "You are scaring Kit. How can I help you?" Distracted, it had missed his quarry.

Kit took a step back. *I do not fear! This is the stalker.*

I feel your fear and love you all the same, Zeal told her. *We will face our terrors together. Have Tallen and Tulip continue their play. Tell them not to stop.*

I have done so. Mother said to step away from what will kill you. What is dead yet still lives.

This Zeal creature did not seem surprised about it or even dread it. In fact, the target seemed to accept it. Not the emotions it had expected. Plus, these two seemed unaware it was able to listen in on their discussion. It wondered why it could it do so.

Perhaps the bond between them made them different, it surmised. The two-who-were-one had addressed it, which had startled it into lowering its hand.

It now attempted to do something it had not done in many a season: produce sound. At first, it was only a rumbled moan followed by a screech that settled into an overly loud, raspy whisper. "You... you... wish to help... me?"

It floated off the ground, distracted from its duty by the feeling expressed by the girl, who'd begun to dance.

"You cannot help me. I am beyond your aid and only seek to do my duty."

Zeal scooted back a little from the apparition. "What is it, your duty? Your appearance is disrupted. Can you pull yourself together more?"

"It is to protect those who rest here and kill all who yearn to desecrate them," it informed the Zeal.

"There are no robbers here. And we seek no ill will to you or from you." The boy gestured to include his companions. "My name is Zeal. What defiler would attempt to sit, visit, and hold a conversation with you?"

"May hap one daffy and light in the head, although that is not how you appear." It felt itself changing. The tune, the pipes, the voice, and pantomime joined to steal his anger. They snatched away the façade he used to interact with the living and left behind only the spirit he protected from them. It was left in the open for anyone to see.

"I like this look you have much better. You should wear it over the other. Are those your friends?" Zeal pointed toward the mound.

It saw his image reflected in the pupils of the large animal in front of him. A man standing in his armor, axe in hand, with no evidence of his mortal wounds.

It became he, and as he felt his feet touch the ground, he was no longer floating. He gained substance; tendrils of black hair stirred around his face. His head rotated rearward while his body remained unmoved. He saw the Host, both standards flying, standing rank and file behind him, watching and listening to their history as it was enacted before them. The girl's ballad told of their folly yet paid homage to their purpose. They had not been forgotten.

"How long…? How long has it been?" His head finished its circular rotation, returning again to face Zeal, unaware he had spoken his thoughts aloud.

"I don't understand your question," said Zeal, who was watching the large number of non-living.

"Zeal, what are you doing?" Mehrle's voice sounded concerned. "Who is it you are talking to?"

This quiet member of the camp approached him. She moved cautiously, the seed of fear planted in her being.

Zeal held up a hand. "Stay back, Mehrle. I don't know who this is, but I think we may be trespassing on a gravesite." Addressing him, Zeal asked, "Who are you?"

He contemplated Zeal's question while reaching for a name from the past. "I was known as Vole, commander of the army of Mendor."

"So, those are the forces of Mendor?" Zeal indicated the legion around the two banners.

"Of Mendor and Dearney both. All reside here, long forgotten," Vole said with regret.

"My companions and I had no intention to disturb your rest. Nor do we seek to rob you of your possessions. We planned to leave in the morn but will go now, if that is your desire," Zeal said.

"No. Stay. Never before have all assembled, drawn forth from their sleep as they have by the influence created by those two members of your troupe. We ask that they entertain us this night. If they do so, no harm will come to you." Vole watched Zeal for any sign of deceit.

Zeal glanced over at his companions. "Give me leave to talk to them. I will forward your request and return. I am sure they will be happy to conduct a performance for all of you."

"So be it. Return soonest with your decision." Vole listened to the conversation conducted between the encroachers, further judging them. The quiet one stood, arms folded, next to the performers, who had stopped their play. Strange, though they bore looks that questioned, none radiated fear.

"Tallen, Tulip, Mehrle, it appears we have stumbled not only on the site of the battle between Mendor and Dearney, but also the place where they are buried," Zeal said excitedly.

"Aren't those the two groups Tulip and Tallen were singing about moments ago?" Mehrle asked. She surveyed the mist surrounding their camp. "I still don't see anything there."

"Yes, they are the ones." Tallen stared into the mist, too. "You say it happened here? I think the tree was trying to tell me of this. It influenced my choice of what I played tonight."

"Tallen, the fact is the non-living buried here have awakened in response to your music and Tulip's song. They have requested the two of you to play for them. Specifically, the saga you created regarding their story. I have spoken to the guardian of some kind, Commander Vole. He states he was the leader of Mendor's forces." Zeal pointed toward the shifting vapor. "You'll have to take mine and Kit's word that the spirit armies of Mendor and Dearney are arrayed in the mist beneath their standards at this very moment."

Tulip bowed in the direction of the mound. "Zeal, you've told me before that those who have left life behind have not always left the living. I would agree to sing for them if it will give them peace. You will play, Tallen?"

"Yes, Tulip, I will. We should enact the whole saga from beginning to end. Mayhap they will agree to offer to share histories, so that we can correctly tell their story. It would be nice to get firsthand information. Zeal, will you ask for me? I am beginning to see value in your ability to communicate with the non-living."

Kit stayed close to Zeal's side. *I, as well. My claws and teeth are useless against such prey.*

"Thank you. I sense anger from them at the moment. I don't know what would happen if we just tried to leave." Zeal glanced back at the host. "I have never seen so many who have passed on in one place and are willing to remain, plus are capable of interacting with the living. I will let you know if they agree to your request. If so, I will act as interpreter between them and you. Mehrle, you look as if you have something to say."

"All these seasons, I never really believed you when you said you talked with the Guardian Spirits in the mausoleum at the Temple. Meeting Iris was strange enough, when you and Tulip first introduced me to her. But she isn't a spirit, although she does protect the Temple and those who live there. I just wanted to say I am sorry for doubting you. But please, don't share with me how it feels to talk to the dead. I am not curious about it, as I was with you and your fire."

"Thank you all the same. I am happy you are here, Mehrle, for whatever the need Master Slag has seen. Tallen, Tulip, how soon before you're ready to begin?"

"Tulip needs to sip a bit of tea to warm her throat," Tallen replied. "Once done, we can proceed. Let yonder presence know."

Vole stood silent as Zeal approached, satisfied no threat to those he warded existed from these living beings. "Zeal, we agree to share our history with you and your companions. It is right that our tale be rendered truthfully."

Tallen began to play, starting with a gentle melody that led into the introduction of the saga. Tulip joined him, her voice accenting the pipes, which complimented her in turn.

Zeal stayed awake, quietly conversing with the spirits, who relived a portion of their life through the song. Kit relaxed enough to return to hiding size and slept fitfully in his lap.

Tulip and Tallen repeated the saga more than a handful of times. Interspersed between each replay, Tallen presented songs and music that spanned the seasons. They didn't stop until late into the night, when voice and wind grew tired.

Mehrle watched everything, standing as a quiet sentinel until she, too, lost her battle with sleep. Distracted, Zeal forgot he was supposed to contact Deena to reassure her that all was well.

The host returned to the mound prior to dawn. Only then did Zeal rest alongside his companions.

* * *

MENDORIAN SAGA
(BATTLE OF THE LOST SONS)

Mendor, Mendor, why do you weep? The return of your fathers and sons do you seek? They left to protect their wives, families, and keep. None returned to tell you they are all buried deep.

Invaders from Dearney came to take all they dared. The two armies against each other were paired.

The sun rose on the misty morn of battle. Many would soon spew forth a death rattle.

The arrows that flew past each other in the air were thick. The ground on both sides was soon red and slick.

Mendor, Mendor, why do you weep? The return of your fathers and sons do you seek? They left to protect their wives, families and keep. None returned to tell you they are all buried deep.

Their footsteps caused the dust to rise. No fear did they let show forth from their eyes.

The sound the armies made when they met was louder than a thundering horn. Spear, sword, and axe against shield cried out in the morn.

Who had the right, who was in the wrong? It mattered not to the many that joined Death's song.

Mendor, Mendor, why do you weep? The return of your fathers and sons do you seek? They left to protect their wives, families and keep. None returned to tell you they are all buried deep.

A lone Champion was left to fight for each side. A promise was made before they engaged, a simultaneous blow was struck, and together they died.

Two Standards stood alone on the rise. Windblown markers of the two armies' demise.

The trees bore witness, the animals too. With time they buried the bodies, what more could they do?

Mendor, Mendor, why do you weep? The return of your fathers and sons do you seek? They left to protect their wives, families, and keep. None returned to tell you they are all buried deep.

One would think at some point the location lost would be found. Yet those who've left seeking have never come back around.

Dearney and Mendor had to join to survive. The wisdom of the women alone made sure all who remained stayed alive.

The death of so many was due to nothing but PRIDE.

Mendor, Mendor, why do you weep? The return of your fathers and sons do you seek? They left to protect their wives, families and keep. None returned to tell you they are all buried deep.

CHAPTER TWENTY-NINE

TULIP STRETCHED, trying to remove the kinks from her body. She had been awakened that morn by the horses calling to each other. Her throat felt scratchy from its overlong use. Six full marks of singing, chanting, and voice accompaniment to Tallen's portrayal of the chronicles from past to present had left her sounding husky.

She was tired of hot beryl tea, certain she must have drunk a mini-keg of it last eve. The cold water from the creek nearby would doubtless be more soothing. Her body reminded her she also needed to take a moment to water a tree before getting back into the saddle for the day's ride.

When she sat up, she felt something surprising under her left hand. The object was an ivory-colored long dagger. It was made of bone with a keen edge and a carved skull on its pommel. There was also something on her left wrist: a bracelet, braided from hair in an intricate, knotted pattern that was threaded through five rune-carved knucklebones from the little fingers of five different hands.

Zeal knelt beside her. "What is that you're holding, Tulip?"

"When I awakened, I found this weapon beside me. I am sure it wasn't here when I went to sleep." She showed him the circlet and handed him the blade.

"Neither was this." Tallen, too, held up an object.

"What is that? What is it made from?" She shuddered at the sight of Tallen's possession. She also noticed he wore an identical wristlet, but not Zeal.

"This is a flute and it appears to be created from the bone of a person's thigh."

"Are you really going to play that? Blow on a person's leg?" Tulip would never put such a thing in her mouth.

"I actually would love to hear how it sounds," Zeal returned the long dagger to her.

She shouldn't have been surprised by Zeal's reaction, but she was. Tallen's response made her feel less anxious.

"I don't think I want to try playing this instrument right now." He rose to his feet. "It might be best if I showed it to Masters Greyhook and Gennis and get their counsel first." Tallen then discovered a second object upon the edge of his blanket: an ivory case, also made of bone.

Mehrle stepped out of the trees, still wearing her mask. "What's all the fuss about?"

"If I'm not mistaken, Tallen and Tulip had an appreciative audience who left them gifts." Zeal pointed to his friends' new items. "Did you receive anything in the night, Mehrle?"

"Yes. I'd planned on asking you about it." She slid up her left sleeve, revealing her own hair-and-bone bracelet.

"Did we all receive one?" Tallen asked."

"I didn't," Zeal admitted, "but Kit did. She has hidden it from view using conjure. Commander Vole told me to tell you we are welcome to return. The hosts have provided these bracelets as a means for you to communicate with them. Obviously, I already have the ability. Before you ask, no, I don't know how to remove them."

Mehrle looked around the camp. "Where is Kit?"

"She is arranging our transportation," Zeal gestured to the horses down by the stream. "She fed earlier. I found a platter of uncooked beast steaks in the satchel for her."

The animals were already encapsulated in their opaque spheres. Kit stared at them intently, the rod and feather on the ground beside her. The color of the shells seemed a little richer than on the morn before and more iridescent. Tulip wondered why.

"Anything left in your satchel for the morning meal?" Tallen placed the flute in the case then the case in his pack.

Tulip felt her stomach growl, grateful Tallen had changed the subject. As Zeal removed pot, bowls, and spoons from the satchel, Tulip wondered about the mists she had seen last evening and how they had formed into hundreds of vaporous warriors from the two nations, all of them enraptured by her and Tallen's composition.

Initially, she had been too nervous to sing for the dead. Tallen had been so merry, however, clearly impressed that no other bard but he could claim that the dead had risen to see him perform. Eventually, her dread had been softened by the warm appreciation of their audience.

The satchel provided hot breakfast porridge with nuts, honey, and berries, and mugs of cold milk that soothed her throat when she drank it.

Mehrle ate in silence, her mask hanging free. It was the first time her features had been fully visible since she'd been introduced by Lady Phyllis in Havensharth. She looked like their friend Mehrle still, albeit older, yet in some ways not the same. The seasons had made changes, but Tulip would still have recognized her had they met by accident in Arlanda's Market Square.

"Why do you always have your face covered?" Tallen asked between spoonsful of porridge. "You no longer need to wear the mask. We all know who you are."

"Tallen, I am required by an oath, when on a mission as a member of the Set, that my identity be kept hidden, so no one will recognize me. I will return the mask to its place when I am done eating. It is possible I won't lower it again until my return to Arlanda. As you can see, I have not removed it, just pulled it aside. The mask is still worn." Mehrle resumed her meal.

"I gather I need to keep what you have told me to myself?" Tallen grumbled.

"Tulip," Mehrle said, "isn't it nice to see a male who has some intelligence?"

Tulip returned her smile. "Yes, it is. Kit and I have been training both Tallen and Zeal. Sometimes it shows."

Some cubs learn faster than others, Kit mindspoke to the group.

They all laughed at Kit's comment.

Tulip hoped Deena would be able to shed some light on the items left them in the night. Till then, she would leave hers be. She wrapped the bone dagger in cloth and placed it in her pack, but, like the others, she hadn't found a way to remove her bracelet, so she'd tucked it up under her leather bracer, hidden from view. It fit comfortably there and did not bind with movement.

"Zeal, should we mention Commander Vole and this place when we get back to Havensharth?" Tallen took his bowl to the stream and washed it in water. "I don't think it's a good idea."

"I agree with you, Tallen." Zeal squatted next to him and began to scrub his and Kit's dishes. "However, a report does need to be made. If it had not been for both of your interest in the Mendor and Dearney histories, our visit would have been very different. Your abilities prevented us from losing our lives in this place. Another traveler may not be so lucky."

"I don't think it was me and Tallen alone who changed the course of events," Tulip added. "Zeal, your talent played a large part."

Mehrle scrapped the last bit from her bowl. "Tulip is right. So, we tell no one?"

"I think Masters Greyhook, Ice, and Ladies Deena and Mirada can be trusted with the knowledge and to help decide what others should know," Zeal said.

The hippogriffs stood patiently, heads bowed, communicating silently with Kit. "Let's finish cleaning, pack up, and get ready to ride."

* * *

It was long past midday. The warm sun shone brightly in the clear sky off to Kit's right. She sat in her gathered shadows, the claws of her right forepaw impaled into the pad of the flight saddle. Except for her and the hippogriffs, everyone else slept. The mounts flew over a wide river that flowed toward their destination, according to Greyhook's map. A new range of mountains rose up to meet them in the distance.

Kit hadn't successfully hidden her dislike—yes, that's what it was—dislike of flying from Zeal, but she tolerated it for his and Firemyst's sake. Firemyst was quieter each cycle. She was concerned about him and had let Zeal know.

A large shadow momentarily shaded her before flowing ahead of them on the land below. Wait! The sky cast no shadow! Kit reached out for thoughts and detected other minds. She twisted, let go of the pad, looked into the sky behind them, and saw creatures diving to attack them. She recognized them: *griffins*, a natural enemy of hippogriffs.

Awake! Danger! Ware, Templar! She gave her companions the image of the creatures hunting them. Although hippogriffs were normally fierce fighters, Kit knew they wouldn't be able to defend themselves encumbered with riders and gear.

Templar dipped and furled his wings, attempting to avoid the strike. The shadow maker swooped into view. It had the body of a large feline, the head, legs, and feet of a raptor, and golden wings. It was a little more than half again the size of Kit's hippogriffs.

The talon of one foot tore into Templar where his right wing joined his body. Another talon scored Tulip, who had been asleep, leaning forward on Templar's back. Templar's screech of pain was met by Tulip's outcry as they fell groundward in uncontrolled flight. Their assailant winged skyward and circled for another attack.

Zeal become fully awake and focused his attention on Tulip and Templar. Mehrle and Tallen threw off the bonds of sleep.

Kit, ask Hunter to fly to Tulip and Templar, Zeal sent her.

Hunter canted his wings and drew them close to his body, dropping rapidly toward his comrade. As Hunter closed, strands of fire flowed from the fingers of Zeal's left hand, braiding together to create a flaming rope that wrapped around Templar's torso before looping back into itself to form a lasso.

Yes, Kit thought. Zeal using his fire.

A second griffin's shadow momentarily covered them, and Kit stepped into it. When she leaped out of the shadow, no longer hiding size but hunting size, she discovered she was higher in the sky than she had been on Hunter. She twisted in the air to bring all four paws to bear on the griffin, her claws extended.

Before she could use them to slash and rend the creature, something raked her across her right shoulder. Her intended prey banked sharply away from her before her claws found purchase. Much too soon, her upward momentum depleted, and, with her source of shadow flown off, she began to fall.

Kit sought Zeal through their bond. He was completing a conjure to lighten Templar's weight, so Hunter could support the two of them with his wings.

Kit's panic suddenly surged into Zeal, almost causing him to lose his focus. When he saw her falling from the sky, she felt him wrap mental arms around her.

I am here with you, Kit. You are not alone. You have no need to be alarmed.

The sky casts no shadow. Kit held firmly to Zeal's intense presence.

True. But even though you are Shadow Cat, you are more, much more. He placed a simple conjure into her mind and helped her cast.

Kit fell, windblown, fur streaming upward, tail twitching in the slipstream of her body. Screeching, she spat the final element and soared upward.

She had chosen well. Yes, she was Shadow Cat, but she was also a Practitioner of the Arts. Putting on a grin, she caressed Zeal with her thoughts, thanking him.

Mehrle and Tallen had been forgotten momentarily, so now Kit looked to her companions. Strider and Striker had flanked Hunter, protecting both him and Templar from further attack, while the hippogriffs headed for the protection of the trees below. The branches would prevent the griffins from attacking again from above.

Mehrle sat astride Striker, metal claws in hand, searching the sky for prey. Kit appreciated her now as a fellow hunter. Tallen let loose an arrow that struck a diving griffin, causing it to veer away and fly back to its kin. The three griffins joined together for another attack.

Zeal's right arm drew back and he shouted, "I have had enough of you. *Leave us alone!"* He released a sling stone-sized glowing red ball that flew toward the diving griffins. Just as the glowing object reaching the griffins, he snapped his fingers and the projectile exploded, forming a large fireball that engulfed them.

The concussive force of the blast caused the creatures to pinwheel uncontrolled, separating from one another. Two of the creatures recovered, instantly fleeing from their intended prey. The third, however, continued to fall till the ground ended its existence.

Kit fought the impulse to follow and kill the retreating griffins. But members of her Pride were injured and needed her protection. She remained flying, guarding her Pride, and searched for additional sources of life while Zeal guided them to a small opening in the trees below.

* * *

Mehrle resisted the impulse to constantly look skyward for further danger. After safely landing, they'd moved under the forest canopy, which provided them protection from an aerial attack. Kit had assured them the griffins had left the area and promised to keep mental watch in case they returned.

The dry ground below the branches was cushioned by many seasons' worth of decomposing needles and leaves. Heavily shadowed light filtered down, giving everything a mottled appearance. Mehrle liked the earthy odors released into air.

"Put your knife away, Tallen," she ordered. "Untie those straps, don't slash them. Quickly now, help me get Tulip out of the saddle."

Together, they placed Tulip on her sleep sack.

Zeal floated in the air, no longer astride Hunter, and somehow held Templar off the ground with his flaming rope. The blow to Tulip's back seemed only to have knocked the wind out of her, but Mehrle found a lump behind Tulips right ear, where she'd suffered a head injury.

Tallen anxiously knelt next to Tulip. "The claw went through her leathers, but where's the blood? I see a lot of it on her right leg, but I think all of it belongs to Templar."

Mehrle discovered Tulip was wearing her workshirt, so the spider silk had prevented her from a cutting or piercing injury, but not protected her so well from a crushing blow. Still, she was lucky to have been wearing it. Otherwise, the claw would have ripped into her back, flayed it open, and pierced her lung.

"Tulip was protected, but her injures could still be serious. She will kill us, if we destroy her leathers any further, so don't cut them off her. Try to be as gentle as you can, and help me remove her jerkin." They eased Tulip's leathers from her body.

"How is she?" Zeal lowered Templar to the ground a short distance from his mistress, the fiery rope crackling out of existence. Templar began to breathe heavy, painful breaths, and Zeal stroked Templar's neck to soothe him.

Mehrle knew that Zeal felt responsible for their group, as she had when they were growing up in Arlanda. "She received a blow to the head, and I don't know yet about her back and shoulder. She is breathing well, but I can't tell anymore about her condition."

I am with her. She still hunts. I am with Templar, too. He is concerned for Tulip.

"Let them both know we are helping them," Zeal turned to Kit. "Tell Templar I am going to place him on his uninjured side once we have the gear off him."

Templar knows we are helping him, Kit mindspoke a few moments later.

"Go ahead and help Zeal remove the tack and kit from Templar please Tallen," Mehrle pointed to the injured mount. "I will take care of Tulip. Templar needs our aid as well." Tallen gave Tulip one last, long, lingering look before turning away to do her bidding.

Mehrle ignored the boys and continued to appraise Tulip's injuries. She lifted Tulip's workshirt and discovered bruising that extended from her right shoulder blade to her neck. Mehrle gently probed the area and was sickened when she felt the bone under the bruising grind and move beneath her fingers. As she had feared, Tulip's shoulder blade was shattered. She moaned from the pain of Mehrle's inspection.

Mehrle was concerned that, if they didn't get Tulip back to Havensharth for help, she might not regain full use of her arm. As it was, they were probably going to have to put Templar down. She finished removing the workshirt but left Tulip's breasts covered by her binder.

Tallen told Zeal, "There. All the gear is off and out of the way. Go ahead and roll him."

Zeal gently settled Templar onto his left side, his wing out of the way, so his weight was not on it. Kit settled next to Templar, nose to beak. The wound was still bleeding, his ribs exposed in the torn flesh. The wing joint was clearly dislocated and broken.

"We have to turn back and get aid for Tulip," Mehrle announced. "One of us will need to put Templar out of his misery. If we leave now and fly through the night plus all the next day, we could get back in the next two sun cycles. I am sorry about Firemyst, but Tulip comes first."

Zeal looked at her like she had grown another head. Tallen stepped back, distancing himself from her until Zeal responded.

Kit spoke up first. ***Templar is Pride. The Pride must care for him.***

"Don't worry, Kit," Zeal assured her. "We are not going to kill Templar. If Tulip still needs more help once she is healed, she'll be returned to Havensharth." He reached inside his vest and removed something from one of the inner pockets then placed a vial in Mehrle's hand.

The small metal vial was embossed with the symbol of the Temple of the Ladies of life, the image of the sun with an iris bloom in its center. "You carry an *effusion*!" She gently rolled Tulip onto her uninjured side. Tallen brushed Zeal aside and pillowed Tulip's head in his lap.

Zeal knelt, taking Tulip's hand in his. "Good thing she's unconscious, because this is going to really hurt."

Healing this way was not without cost: the more severe the injury, the greater the pain. Mehrle held Tulip's head so she wouldn't choke and slowly administered the iridescent contents of the vial. "Hope you have access to more of these," she said. "This quest has not been without its hazards."

"Ne, all in a day." Tallen's light note made Mehrle smile.

The effect of the *effusion* could be seen immediately. Under Tulip's skin, pieces of her shoulder blade began to crawl toward one another and reunite. The bones ground loudly until the skin finally flattened and skin ceased moving; the swelling and bruising faded.

Although unconscious, Tulip still tried to heave and twist in response to the healing. Her breathing, which had become ragged from the agony of her repair, finally gentled, and she settled into a deep sleep. The swollen knot on her head was no longer there.

"Either of you have a suggestion on how to give an *effusion* to Templar?" Zeal held up a second vial. "I hope it works as well on him as it does on our kind. Unfortunately, Tulip would most likely know, but she is in no shape to tell us."

"Will he take it from you?" Tallen eyed the wounded hippogriff. "I sure wouldn't want to have that beak clamp down on my hand and arm."

He will drink. Kit's tone was firm.

"I don't know if it would be better to change him back into a horse first or give him the *effusion* as he is now," Zeal wondered aloud.

Hippogriff is hurt, Kit replied. *Not horse.*

She remained nose-to-beak with Templar, while the other three hippogriffs stood in a semicircle around them, heads bowed. When Zeal knelt next to Templar, he simply opened his beak and stuck out his narrow black tongue to receive the vial's contents. Zeal emptied the contents down the back of Templar's tongue; he swallowed then swallowed again. Zeal stroked Templar's neck and talked to him with a soothing tone.

"Easy now. We are all here for you. That's it, share the hurt with us. It won't be long now."

The hippogriff's wing joint moved and returned to its proper place with a loud pop. His muscles crawled as if they were worms and knitted into position, while his hide melded together until it was smooth and unblemished.

Templar repositioned himself with effort after holding himself, unmoving, through the healing. The other hippogriffs swayed side to side, vocalizing a soothing call to him until, finally comfortable, he went to sleep.

"They are both going to need to rest. I think at least through the next cycle." Zeal gave Templar one last gentle touch to his head. "Tallen, why don't you and I clean Tulip's leathers, while Mehrle gives Tulip a bath and places her in her sleep sack to rest? We can wake Tulip later to eat."

"Give me a few moments, then I'll do it." Tallen walked to a nearby tree and leaned his head against it.

"The *effusion* worked," Mehrle said softly. "I thought it would be a waste. What did you do? Templar seems so peaceful."

"It was Kit's idea," Zeal explained. "She thought of a way to have Templar's pain shared by his kin, as well as by me and Kit. I felt a dull ache in my arm and chest but nowhere near as intense, divided that way. I would like to try divvying the pain of healing if one of us is hurt again—not that I desire us any further injuries, mind you."

"Zeal, you have grown a lot since we were together as children."

He smiled slightly before he spoke. "I will be considered grown when Mother Essmee says so. Until then, no matter what, I remain a cub."

"A cub—I don't understand. Who is Mother Essmee?"

She is my mother.

Mehrle helped gather Tulip's gear to be cleaned, wondering why it mattered to Zeal what Kit's mother thought of him.

As she rubbed dirt and blood off the pommel of Tulip's sword, she exposed part of the clear crystal on the pommel's head. It absorbed the remaining blood on it before clouding over.

CHAPTER THIRTY

THE WOOD WHERE THEY sheltered was mostly a stand of white oaken, old growth that had never seen an axe or saw. Tallen felt comforted and welcomed by the trees and he touched them frequently as he walked around camp. Their leaves absorbed the sunlight, shading the ground beneath and allowing little else to grow. He could somehow sense the roots gripping the earth like anchors.

As he traveled along a game trail he had discovered on the edge of camp, he knelt beside a spoor that was several days old. He could not identify the beast that had left it in its passage.

He didn't want the others to know how much Tulip's injury had upset him but decided he had better get used to it. In her profession, it wouldn't be the last hurt she received.

The hippogriffs were back to being horses. Kit had let Templar rest for several marks before initiating the change. As Tallen meandered back into camp, he noticed Kit walking her own circle around the site, repeatedly stopping to pee as she went. He knew he should apologize to her.

Mehrle approached and began to walk alongside him. "What is Kit doing?" she asked.

"She is marking her territory, letting any other beast know to hunt somewhere else. You could ask her yourself, Mehrle," he chided, wondering what she really wanted to talk about. "She would give you an answer."

"How long have you known Zeal and Tulip?" Her eyes studied him through the openings in her mask.

Not seeing her face other than her eyes unnerved him a little. "We met when they first came to Havensharth."

"You were in Havensharth when they arrived?"

"No, we met on the road that goes between the landing on the river where the boats dock and Havensharth. Kit's mother rescued me, with Master Ice and Lady Mirada's help." Suddenly, he felt the stress of the day catch up to him. "I am sorry," he said. "I would rather not talk about it." He was about to turn back to the comfort of the wood when Zeal called out.

"Tallen! Would you come over for a moment?"

"Be right there." To Mehrle, he said, "Be at ease. I thought I could talk about my past, but it still hurts to do so." Then he walked away. "How can I help you?" he asked Zeal, who was sitting next to a sleeping Tulip. She had yet to waken from her healing, and while he and Mehrle seemed unfazed by the fact, Tallen was still worried.

"Sit with me." He reached for his pack. "If you haven't guessed, I planned to gift you and Tulip at your Advancements. I think it would be more useful to us all if I gave you your gift now, instead of waiting."

Tallen sat silent while Zeal pulled a long, cloth-covered item from his pack. The gift was far too big to have come out of there, he thought. The Apprentices' packs from the Temple in Arlanda never ceased to surprise him.

The bundle felt familiar, but when he'd freed it from its wrapping, he was surprised to discover Zeal had given him a bow. Tallen immediately fell in love with its rich red-brown, fine-grained wood hand-carved with runes. He wondered what purpose the runes served, as well as the large, white crystal in the grip. The string was silver-gray and braided from Anrotean Spider silk. "It is finely crafted. What is its name?"

Zeal handed Tallen a quiver containing three black arrows before answering. "The bow doesn't have one yet. You get to give it a name. Here is what you must remember. Only use two of the three arrows at a time. If one is left in the quiver overnight, then any used will replenish. Let me have a finger."

Tallen held out his right hand. Zeal removed his Fang, then painlessly pricked Tallen's index finger. Blood welled.

"Rub the blood on the crystal," Zeal commanded as he cleaned the blade with a cloth.

After doing as Zeal requested, Tallen sucked the remaining blood from his digit. Zeal grasped the hand Tallen held the bow with and began to speak in a language Tallen didn't recognize. He felt warmth flow into the bow from Zeal's hand through his. The crystal turned from white to red.

"The weapon is attuned to you. Whenever you hold it, it will be ready for use, strung. Not so for anyone else. When you desire, you can have a black-arrow flame. When it strikes your intended target, it will explode, creating a fireball similar to the one I made today, although not as large or forceful. You have three charges before the bow needs to replenish itself. However, remember not to use all three arrows. Always leave one in the quiver."

"This is too fine a gift. I can't accept it." Tallen tried to give the bow back to Zeal, who refused to take it from him.

"What is it?" Zeal asked earnestly. "Tell me. Something troubles you."

Tallen closed his eyes. Before he could answer, Mehrle settled quietly across from them. "I thought I had killed Kit. I shot an arrow at one of the griffins but then, before it struck, Kit appeared in front of it. When she jerked and started to fall, I thought I'd struck her instead."

Zeal leaned forward and placed a hand on Tallen's shoulder. "You had no idea she was going to step out of shadow and attack your intended target."

The fault was mine.

Kit joined him and Zeal and Mehrle inside his head.

This is our way. We hunt together from now on.

When he opened his eyes, he saw Kit lying across Zeal's shoulders, staring at him. "You are right, and I accept this gift."

"Where is mine?"

It was Tulip, awake but still groggy. Her eyes were heavy, but her mouth gaped wide in a yawn.

"I was sleeping and dreamed we were getting gifts. When I woke up, Tallen had his..." Her head dropped down and her lids drew together.

Zeal chuckled. "Go back to sleep, Tulip. Yours is not ready yet."

She soon began to softly snore.

Relieved that Tulip was recovering, Tallen thought of an answer to one his earlier questions. "You each have your Fang. This bow I will call my... Thorn."

* * *

Night arrived. The canopy overhead prevented Zeal from seeing the sky and stars as he sat next to the campfire, repacking the satchel. It was an amazing creation, and he wondered how much more food it contained.

The satchel had provided them a meal that night of stewed beast shank with root vegetables, grain muffins, and fresh greens. Kit ate two raw breasts of a fowl he could not identify, but it was huge in comparison to the breast from a diddle duck. She'd changed to hunting size to eat them. One breast alone would have fed the rest of them.

Why are you troubled because of Mother Deena? Kit asked him as he worked.

"I forgot to contact Deena last eve. So much has happened in such a short time. I am worried she will be upset with me."

Mothers are supposed to be upset with their cubs.

Zeal was not completely clear on Kit's meaning. "You may be right. Will you stay with me while I talk to Deena?"

I am here, always. She claimed his lap.

Zeal turned the blue crystal of the ring on his right middle finger toward his palm. As he rubbed the crystal with his thumb, he thought of Deena and felt her mind touch his.

Hello, my loves. I'd hoped you would find time to reach me this eve. We have all been worried. I expected a call sooner. How are all of you?

Zeal realized that Deena felt both him and Kit in their communication. *Everyone is resting at the moment.*

What aren't you telling me?

It was as if Deena were sitting in front of him. He could almost see her brow rise. *I don't know where to start. I am not intentionally keeping anything from you, but I also don't want to upset you.* Now he felt even less able to hide anything from Deena.

Start with how you have traveled such a distance in so short a time. I placed a locater on our rings, and my chart indicates you have traveled a greater span than riding horses alone would allow.

He wasn't happy to learn that their whereabouts were traceable but would trust Deena to keep the information to herself. *We have been flying. I used the rod of transfiguration.*

You gave the horses wings? Deena's thoughts were flavored with surprise and concern.

I made them hippogriff!

Thank you, Kit, for explaining. I did not fully take into account all of your unique contributions to this quest and will try to do so in the future. Did you bring enough rope to safely tie yourselves on your mounts?

We are not using rope. We're using flight saddles. Mehrle was sent here with them from Master Slag. Kit shared an image of the saddle with Deena.

You mean the Mehrle, whom Ice and Mirada met at the Temple? That Mehrle?

Yes. Somehow Master Slag knew we would need Mehrle's help and the special tack, as well. I would have talked to you last night, but we had guests in camp, and then while traveling earlier today, we were attacked by griffins. Tulip and Templar were hurt during the encounter but are healed now. They each used an effusion.

Deena was silent for several heartbeats. *Zeal, tell me truly, Tulip and Templar are fine? Don't make me ask Kit.*

I would not hide my tracks from you, Mother Deena.

Yes, they are. There is no need for you to worry, Zeal said openly.

Who is Templar? Another combat Apprentice?

No, Templar is Tulip's horse.

Deena's thoughts brightened. *I guess it is a good thing Templar was a hippogriff at the time of the attack. Griffins prefer to snack on horses that are unable to fight them back. Is your camp protected from attack from the sky?*

Yes, we are under cover of trees. Zeal asked Kit to share an image of their camp.

What of the visitors you spoke of?

Zeal gave Deena a short summary of their encounter with the companies of Dearney and Mendor. *Master Greyhook has access to Dearney's and Mendor's history. If you talk with him, please ask him not to discuss things with anyone other than you, Lady Mirada, and Master Ice.*

Deena gave him a mental nod. *I will do so. What are your plans for the morn?*

I'm thinking Tulip and Templar should be given another day to recover, and then we will set out the next sunrise.

I agree, but do be careful and stay in touch as often as you can. I will share our discussion with Ice, Greyhook, and Mirada. Pass on our love to Tulip and Tallen. Give Mehrle a hug from me.

Kit joined him in sending Deena their affection before the contact ended.

He went to check the status of his companions. Mehrle was sleeping. Tallen was making a slight alteration in the shaft below the nock on each of his arrows. "How are you, Tallen?" he asked.

"I'm well. Marking these, so I will be able to distinguish the black arrows by touch. You should get some rest." He slid an altered arrow into the new quiver.

"I'll retire soon."

Zeal went to finish his packing. They'd divided the night into watches. He was second, Tallen first, while Mehrle had chosen to be last. Kit would do what Kit wanted, and they'd decided Tulip should be allowed to sleep and not take a watch.

CHAPTER THIRTY-ONE

SUNLIGHT FILTERED through the leaves, creating small rays that illuminated patches of the ground. Traces of humidity kept the odors of tree and soil from dissipating in the still air. An occasional breeze did weakly ruffle the leaves and cool uncovered skin.

Tulip enjoyed a midday meal and rested with her companions. She was thankful that the night and next morn had been uneventful. The individual meat-and-vegetable pies provided by the satchel aptly matched their individual appetites.

Kit stepped away for a meal of griffin, refusing to let the remains of the one that fell from the sky go to waste. No one else expressed any interest in joining in her repast, though she'd offered to share. They agreed food from the satchel was more than adequate. Upon her return, Kit settled down to sun herself and clean the blood from her face.

The process of rapid healing had taken its toll on Tulip. As her body recovered and rebuilt itself, she felt the need for a nap but forced herself to stay awake a while longer. Making eye contact with Mehrle, she gave a subtle jerk of her head and stood. Mehrle followed quietly, and they left camp together.

"How are you?" Mehrle looked around the area while Tulip relieved herself. "I want a truthful answer."

"Other than being tired, I am well. I think Templar feels the same way. He was sleeping while the other horses guarded him when last I checked." She sniffed. "I could really use a good soaking right now."

Mehrle sighed. "I am starting to itch! And it has only been a few suns since we started our journey. Maybe our next camp can be near a source of water deep enough to bathe. Can I ask you a serious question Tulip?"

"Of course, Mehrle," she said, pulling up her pants. "I am done, so my turn to play look out."

"Thanks." Mehrle found her own spot in the bushes. "Does Zeal really know what he's about? I still remember him as a little boy I needed to mother. I'm not used to this person he has become."

"Back in Arlanda, you were the oldest by two seasons and our designated leader. Although you tried, we refused to allow you to mother us. Instead, we chose to take care of each other. Yes, Zeal was the smallest, but he was the deepest well of all of us." She held Mehrle's gaze. "You're beginning to fathom what I have always known. Zeal is capable of more than either of us can imagine. I'm not saying he has everything figured out. But don't forget he has help from you, me, Tallen, and Kit."

"That is a strong appraisal. I need to consider all you have said. Tell more about Tallen and Kit." Mehrle set her clothes back to right.

Feeling tired, Tulip leaned against a tree. "What exactly are you asking? I won't divulge their secrets. Talk to them, and let them tell you what they want you to know."

Mehrle held up her open palms in a placating way. "I tried to talk with Tallen yesterday, and he was too saddened by something in his past to discuss it. It had to do with meeting you and Zeal for the first time. And he mentioned Kit's mother played a part. I'm just curious."

"I can tell you a little," Tulip divulged Tallen's history and ended with giving Mehrle a warning. "Always remember, Tallen cares deeply and shares carefully but not very readily."

"No wonder he still has strong feelings and emotions around your meeting. What of Kit? What can you tell me about her?"

"Kit is as much a person as you or I. Don't think of her as a pet. I only pretend she is around strangers, as an advantage against them. She can be one of your best friends or worse enemies. Get used to the idea that she and Zeal are both Practitioners. I am honored to have her consider me part of her Pride,"

Mehrle momentarily pondered Tulip's answer. "What does it mean that Zeal is Kit's?"

"You should talk to the two of them about that. They are bonded. I am still learning what it means." Tulip pushed away from the tree and straightened. "Shall we head back to camp?"

"Thanks for answering my questions." Mehrle gestured for Tulip to take the lead. "I do have one more for you. How come the boys never venture to look out for us? They usually insist we all stay in view of one another and not wander."

Tulip couldn't help laughing at Mehrle's question. "You already know the answer to that. It's because we're never left unguarded." She saw Mehrle's face brighten with understanding. "Because we have Kit watching over all of us, and we in turn all look out for her."

"You have the right of it, Tulip. Kit is hard to spot sometimes, even when I know she is nearby. I'll catch a hint of movement, a bit of tail, or blink of an eye in the shadow. I think Kit allows me to see her."

"I've a thought, Mehrle. We should examine Greyhook's map and see how far we've come. With everything that has happened, we haven't had a chance to see what it has to offer. It might give us an idea if traveling by hippogriff has shortened the time it takes to reach our destination."

After returning to camp, Tulip retrieved Greyhook's map from her pack. "Tallen! Kit! Zeal! Come join Mehrle and me. Let's locate our present position and see how far we've traveled." Tulip weighted the map's corners down with small stones.

Zeal moved close to Tulip but left room for Kit, who slid between them. "I talked with Deena last night, and she indicated we were farther from Havensharth than expected. I told her it was because of travel by hippogriff."

Tallen asked, "How did you talk with Lady Deena? You never left us last eve." He leaned toward Kit. "Was it somehow *your* doing?"

Zeal held up his left hand and showed them the simple silver ring he wore, with its small blue crystal. "Deena has the mate to this ring, and with it we can communicate over long distances. She did say to tell you all that everyone sends their love and to give Mehrle a hug."

"You mean we are not in trouble for leaving?" Tulip asked, excited. "Our mentors aren't angry with us?"

"I didn't even approach that subject," Zeal replied sheepishly. "But it is nice to know they care about us."

"Well, pay up." Mehrle poked Zeal's arm.

"Excuse me? Pay up?"

Tulip hid her smile.

"Yes." Mehrle crossed her arms in front of her chest. "Didn't Lady Deena entrust you to deliver a hug to me, where is it?"

Tallen winked at Tulip while Zeal delivered a stiff, quick hug, as promised. He did soften when Mehrle gave him a more heartfelt embrace of her own.

"Thank you, Zeal. Now that you have completed Lady Deena's assigned task, we can all take a look at the map." Tulip placed her finger on the vellum. "Show my location."

Tallen looked more closely. "That can't be correct, can it? We have flown the length of Alkan, over the Turin Haa, and along the edge of the Western Eye Mountains. By this account, we were guests of Mendor and Dearney in the Lurin Moss Wood and attacked by griffins over the gorge created by the Del River."

A blinking, yellow spot between the green of Havensharth and the red for the Blood of Sartus was labeled *The Place*. Tulip hadn't asked the map to show her *The Place* and briefly wondered about it. "We've covered three weeks of land travel in a short period. This proves that flying is faster. Zeal, this is good news. I don't resent having spent the day in recovery, for we should arrive at the Blood's location much sooner than expected." She pointed to the glowing red spot on the map.

"I agree, but I think we need to get there as soon as we can. In the morn, I have decided to use a second rod. Firemyst has not been as active today, which worries me." Zeal drew an imaginary line between their current location and the Blood of Sartus. "We have to span the length of Saytos and most of Telgar to reach our destination in the Beast's Tail Mountains."

Tallen glanced momentarily toward Strider. "The second rod, what does it do?"

"It should quicken our hippogriffs and allow them to travel faster."

"Is it safe?" Tulip asked. "It won't hurt them, will it? I would hate to see something bad happen to Templar and the others."

"To be honest," Zeal said, "I don't really know. That is one of the reasons I wanted Templar healed before using the rod on him. I didn't think the rod of transfiguration would cause them harm, and so I will trust the conjure used to quicken them won't, either."

* * *

Tulip was allowed to sleep through the night again and not take a share of the watch. She was rested and well fed by the time the sun rose above the trees.

Zeal's black satchel, by way of Master Qwen, provided a breakfast of diddle duck omelets with shallots, mushrooms, and a sharp, smoked cheese, accompanied by fresh honey scones and hot beryl tea. While she and the others packed up camp, Kit transformed the horses into hippogriffs.

Their green shells had streaks of gold Tulip hadn't seen before. She wondered if the color difference was a result of the light.

Tallen made sure the fire was dead and would not flare after their departure. He turned to Tulip. "Are you back to normal? I'm sure we can convince Zeal to allow you to rest another sun."

A marlet settled in a nearby tree. and appeared to study them. Strange, Tulip thought. Marlets were typically skittish and didn't normally come near people. "I am ready to travel," she assured him. "You don't need to worry. Zeal is really concerned about Firemyst, so I don't want him to regret allowing Templar and me a chance to heal. By the way, I have one request."

"What is it? I will try to fulfill it, if possible."

Tulip forced herself not to smile. "Actually, it is Mehrle and I who ask this favor of you. We would like to have water at our next camp—a place with a pool or deep stream, if you can find such."

"I'll do my best," Tallen said and took his leave.

Out of the corner of her eye, Tulip saw a sudden movement. Kit held the now-dead marlet in her mouth. She did not eat it but presented it to Hunter, which made Tulip feel a little sad for the bird.

There was something wrong with it.

"What do you mean, Kit??"

It not had marlet thoughts.

Tulip was a little frustrated by Kit's answer, but no longer felt bad for the creature. Maybe Zeal could make more sense out of Kit's revelation.

Zeal was involved with the hippogriffs, gesturing with a blue rod encircling by silver bands and a whirling symbol, different than the green one Kit used. He spoke too softly for her to hear his conjure.

But the feathers on the hippogriff's wings and hocks stirred. Zeal tucked the rod away into his vest and announced, "I'm done. Once we are flying, please stay close together at first, so I can monitor the result of the conjure."

Tulip chuckled to herself because she hadn't been all that able to control Templar so far. She approached Zeal and confided, "Earlier, Kit killed a marlet that was acting unusual. It was perched near Tallen and me. I would have sworn it was spying on us, and Kit said the bird didn't have marlet thoughts."

After communicating with Kit, he said, "She believes the marlet carried another person's thoughts. She thinks she might be able to determine if any other creature we meet is doing the same. Kit didn't recognize what was happening at first, because she's never experienced such a thing before." He appeared worried.

* * *

The hippogriffs were walked to an opening in the trees before they were mounted and their safety straps cinched. Kit found a comfortable spot on Hunter's saddle and gathered shadow layers around her. Her eyes adjusted to the brightness of the light unfiltered by the canopy. The sky was clear, and, other than a hawk circling overhead, she detected no other animal life outside the members of her Pride.

She used her claws to adhere to her seat but did not dig them in too deeply. Even though she was still uneasy, she was a cat who could fly. She had stored the conjure for air travel inside the gem of her hiding chain, for ease of release. *Deena does make nice things for a cat to wear*, she thought, wondering if her mother might be convinced to consider wearing a useful crystal.

"Your thoughts are more at ease." Zeal stroked her back.

The love she felt from Zeal caused her to feel content. *The sky is not for my kind. But is now a new hunting ground… for me.*

"I had hoped you would learn to enjoy the experience of flight. You so love adventure—it is your nature." He leaned forward in the saddle and kissed the top of her head.

She noted his discomfort. *Your tail is busy. Why?*

"I worry because I don't know what effect the quickening I conjured will have on our mounts. I should have thought to ask Deena how it affects a person or creature it is cast on."

She gave him a knowing look. *Eat it, and see how it tastes.*

Zeal nodded. "I see your point. We should just get on with it."

Zeal advised the others to check their harness and prepare to travel. Once everyone acknowledged they were ready, Kit directed the hippogriffs to take flight.

Zeal laid a hand on Kit's back. "Ask them to slowly increase their speed, please, Kit. By the speed of passage of the land below and the wind's increase in strength, they are already moving faster than previously."

She ducked her head. *Hunter and the others understand.* The air stung her eyes, causing them to tear when she looked forward. Her fur was flattened by the press of the flow.

"I think we need a shield of some kind, to protect us and direct the force of the air away," Zeal turned his head, his eyes partially open.

Her companions were also being windblown. Tulip's and Tallen's hair streamed back snapping in the breeze. Mehrle had her hood tied forward and her mask protecting her face.

Kit remembered a conjure she had learned and offered it to Zeal. *Conjure a Weather Shell.*

"I think that can work," Zeal said loudly over the wind. "It should be centered in front of Hunter and extended outward, to protect the others, then shaped so it does not cause our mounts to work harder or fly into it. If maintaining it causes me to tire, we can land, and I can take a break."

I am here, she said, reminding Zeal they should use Marhdah and that he was not the lone Practitioner present. She directed Templar, Strider, and Striker to gather closer but stay safely distanced, so as not to interfere with one another's flight. She was not yet ready to fly again on her own.

Kit waited till Zeal began his conjure. "Ventai Clypen." Then she joined her intent to his. Marhdah and bond combined to ease and strengthen the conjure. Whenever she and Zeal joined together in this manner, conjure felt effortless. The energies taken from a Practitioner to complete a casting were greatly reduced by the sharing.

The wind suddenly cut off, no longer blowing at them, but instead around them.

They shaped the shell. The upper edge angled a few hands above the arc of the wingrise and lower edge below the wingdrop of Hunter's flight. They then extended the protection so it screened the other hippogriffs and their riders, who could finally sit at ease, no longer having to lean into the wind.

"Tell the hippogriffs they are free to fly as fast as they wish," Zeal said in a normal tone.

Kit felt Zeal's pleasure at how well the screen functioned. There was no sensation of increase in movement other than the escalation of wing beats and the boost in the air's noise as it flowed past the edges of the shell. When she looked down, the land below was moving ever faster.

Kit joined the Pride to her and Zeal, allowing talk between them.

This is what I call battle mind, Zeal said for Mehrle's benefit. *Whenever a situation dictates a need for us to share thoughts, coordinate actions, or communicate needs, this is how we'll do it. Let's practice, so we all get used to conversing this way.* He glanced over at them all. *If you have any questions, ask now.*

CHAPTER THIRTY-TWO

IT WAS A LITTLE past midday when Kit informed everyone the hippogriffs were hungry. Apparently, quickened hippogriffs needed to feed more often than before, so the party set down in a small valley surrounded by mountains with snow-covered peaks that had a misty lake in the center. A group of white-colored beasts, apparently disturbed by their arrival, departed up the slope to the west.

"This is a lovely place," Mehrle jumped down and loosened the girth on Strider's saddle, checking for any spots where the tack might have rubbed. "What are we going to feed our hungry hippogriffs?"

Meat. Kit, who'd located a warm, sunny spot in which to recline, stood and stretched from nose to tail in one sensuous movement. She then disappeared into the shadow cast by Hunter.

Tulip led Templar to the water and allowed him to drink. They were soon joined by Strider, Hunter, and Striker. "Zeal, how are you? The shell—is that what you called it? Is it hard for you to maintain?"

"I am a little tired, but less than I expected, so I should be able to continue. If I become fatigued, though, once we resume our travel, we'll stop." He knelt and sampled the water from the pool. "I didn't expect the water to be so cold, but it sure tastes good."

"Well, sit down and rest you then," Tallen removing his pipes from their case on his thigh and began to play.

"Oh my, would you look up there!" Mehrle pointed to the beasts they'd seen earlier, which were now frantically climbing higher up the escarpment and dispersing. First one then two and finally three disappeared completely from sight in rapid fashion. "What is going on up there?"

"That is easy, Mehrle," Tallen explained. "*Kit* is happening up there."

Soon thereafter, Kit, in hunting size, backed out of a shadow dragging three carcasses, one at a time. Each was a third her size with curved horns, sharp hooves, and thick, tightly curled white fur that looked moisture-repellant. The Shadow Cat dragged one of the animals to a sunny spot and began to eat it.

"I think these are a kind of mountain goat. How does it taste?" Tallen asked, putting away his pipes before drawing his knife to butcher one of the two remaining creatures. "We'll divide them up for the hippogriffs, but I want to try a few choice bits, if Zeal will help to roast them."

You would like the taste. Come take a few choice bits from this one.

"Kit did say she would feed you, Tallen." Zeal removed his own knife from his boot. "You are part of her Pride! Back strap and chops good enough for everyone?"

The meat cut from Kit's kill was tender, juicy, and flavorful. Zeal cooked it over a ball of fire after seasoning it with salt and spices from his pack. The satchel yielded warm, freshly baked bread and fruit for their meal, washed down with crisp, cold water from the pool.

The hippogriffs and Kit fed till only a few bones were left, and Zeal burned those to ash, to feed the soil. When the flame was no longer needed, he absorbed the ball into his hand then girths were tightened and harnesses checked. The hippogriffs were mounted and the journey resumed.

* * *

Camp was completed before the sun set. Kit monitored her Pride as they went about their various activities. In hiding size, she cleaned the blood from her claws after hunting a boar large enough to feed everyone, including the hippogriffs.

"Once we're finished eating," Tulip said, "I for one could use a good scrub. Hot water would be appreciated." She gave Zeal and Kit a wink with her entreaty. "After all, we do have two fine Practitioners with us."

Kit, having a useful tongue to clean with, didn't feel the girls' urgency. But they had camped near a waterfall with a bowl chest-deep, which should satisfy their request.

Zeal smiled. "I can heat water for folks to bathe in. In fact, if I create a small version of the shell I used today, it should work as a tub. We can all wash and rinse under the falls and then have a good hot soak in the shell after."

Tallen sniffed under his arms and frowned. "That would be a pleasure."

Mehrle laughed. "My small cloths could use a good washing, as well. I have used what I brought with me."

"Well, Mehrle," Tulip concurred, "we should all take the opportunity to do laundry, too. Maybe Zeal can dry the clothes for us."

Kit figured it was the right moment to finish marking the area as theirs for the limited period they would stay here. It was best to let other creatures know that a more dangerous predator was in the area and that her Pride was not prey. Upon returning from her circuit, she discovered Tallen and Zeal cleaning their skin covers downstream from Tulip and Mehrle, who were washing their own. The horses were resting, with Hunter on guard.

The moon had risen above the top of the trees, full and bright, by the time everyone was fed and settled. Though absent of warmth, the moon still lightened the soul. Tallen was smoking meat from the remains of the boar while Tulip and Mehrle attended to the horses. Kit joined Zeal, using Marhdah, and assisted his conjure of a fresh coating of crystal fire around Firemyst's egg. They attempted to intensify the amount of heat the crystal fire provided to the egg.

Firemyst is with us still.

"But he rarely responds when I try to communicate with him," Zeal said sadly. "His thoughts, when I hear him, are as if he is far away. I worry he may not have long."

I look forward to hunting with him. You must, as well.

"I understand. Don't give up hope. Well, let's see what distance we traveled today." He turned to Tulip. "Could we all get a look at your map?"

"Sure! Let me get it out." She gave Templar a pat on his nose, walked over to her bedroll, and opened her pack.

Tulip, accompanied by Tallen and Mehrle, brought over the map while Kit placed a paw on one corner, to keep the parchment from rolling closed. Zeal illuminated it by shifting a globe of light closer.

A yellow spot glowed brightly; it showed the party's current location. They had indeed journeyed far today. Alkan was now far behind. They had flown the length of Saytos and entered upper Telgar.

Finally, Tallen said, "If what I see is correct, I think we will arrive at our destination in time for a midday meal tomorrow."

Mehrle had been cleaning her teeth with a twig. She pointed at the blinking, yellow glow. "Are you certain what the map shows is correct? I find it hard to believe we traversed such a span in one day."

"Well, Mehrle," Zeal replied, pointing at the map, "most folk are unable to travel via quickened hippogriff. I do see a location that appeared yesterday, and it's in the same spot. The Place it's called. Do any of you know of it? It's strange, because the map hasn't added new information on itself at any other time during our travels."

The hunger of a beast on the hunt touched Kit's mind. The creature had taken an interest in the blood scent of the killed boar that flowed from their camp. She decided to inform the others.

Something comes.

Tallen, Tulip and Mehrle readied weapons while Zeal prepared a conjure. Kit made the horses aware of the danger, which was approaching downwind of them.

I claim this hunt, Kit informed her Pride, then she stood silent, waiting for the hunter to arrive. Her companions put away the map and readied themselves, too.

She finally located the predator standing on a thick branch up in a white oaken, just outside the boundary of the camp's light.

MINE! Kit's shouted her mental challenge throughout the wood.

"There is the beast." Mehrle pointed with one of her throwing knives. "In that tree." Golden light reflected from the eyes of the mottled green-and-brown feline. "It looks to be a little over half Kit's hunting size and weight.

Zeal shifted a light orb closer to the creature. "Tallen, can you tell what it is?"

"A male tree cat, I think. They are deadly killers and usually travel in pairs." Tallen raised his bow, which already had an arrow nocked on the string.

Zeal caught his bow arm. "Kit claimed this hunt. She will let us know if she needs any help. Look at her. Kit is still in her hiding size. Think what that means."

A shrill, howling wail, pitched to raise fear in any living creature, echoed around camp. Kit stood, fangs bared, fur on end, and back arched, after releasing the warning cry of a Shadow Cat protecting its own.

The Tree cat yowled a challenge back, unimpressed by Kit's current appearance.

Kit stepped into shadow. She emerged out of the darkness in hunting size behind the male, knocked it off its perch to the ground below, stepped back to the edge of camp, and let out another piercing hunting cry.

The tree cat rose slowly to his feet with a surprised look on his face. Wide-eyed and with his tail hanging between his legs, he backed away from the hunter now twice his size then quickly turned and ran into the night.

Kit resumed her place near the fire and graciously accepted accolades from the members of her Pride. She continued to monitor the tree cat as he fled further into the forest.

Zeal sat next to her. "He never had a chance. I almost felt sorry for the poor thing." He scratched Kit in her favorite place. "It was kind of you to let him live."

I was not hungry. Content, Kit closed her eyes and enjoyed the attention.

Everyone was up early the next morn and rapidly broke camp. Horses became hippogriffs and were quickened before being loaded and mounted. There was a sense of urgency shared by all as they traveled. As they flew toward the distant mountains, the only eventful occurrence was the appearance of a large flying reptile. The hippogriffs rapidly left it behind. Outdistanced by their speed of travel, the creature's intent remained unknown.

The sun was overhead as the hippogriffs began to spiral above a symmetric, snowcapped peak that had a lush forest growing up to its base. They slowed as they flew lower, and Tallen shouted, pointing at a grove of trees that towered above the rest.

They formed a triangle, pointing toward the side of the mountain. The party had arrived.

CHAPTER THIRTY-THREE

ANXIOUS TO HELP Firemyst, Zeal dismounted onto barren, black ground that sloped steeply upward. "I hadn't planned on scaling a mountain," he said, loosening the cinch of Hunter's saddle.

"I know you're in a hurry, Zeal," Tulip said, "but we need to tend to the hippogriffs before anything else is done."

Tamping down his frustration, he replied, "We could change them back to horses and let them graze."

Hippogriff is hunter, horse is prey, Kit reminded them.

"Understood. Let's feed and water them from our supplies since there does not appear to be a nearby source of water." Zeal hurriedly removed Hunter's tack and saddle and stashed them inside the trees. The others followed suit.

"We really should eat and drink ourselves before heading out since we don't know what we're going to encounter ahead." Tallen began unloading Strider.

After attending to the mounts, Zeal fed everyone from the satchel but barely touched his meal, staring quietly at the mountain, instead.

Kit butted him with her head. *Eat. Hunger does not make one a better stalker.*

Tallen asked between chews, "What is the problem, Zeal?"

"I don't see an entrance, and I have a feeling we should go inside the mountain." Half-heartedly, he took a few bites.

"Maybe there is a way in further up the slope," Mehrle

suggested.

"I didn't see any openings when we circled the area earlier," Tulip nudged him. "Zeal, I think you are missing the obvious."

Kit leaned against his thigh. "Tulip, I don't understand your meaning."

Tulip drank from her skin. "Get done eating and clean up. I will show you."

Frustrated but choosing not to show it, Zeal quickly finished his meal, helped hide the hippogriffs under the forest canopy, and then followed Tulip along with the others.

The soil beyond the grove turned into an expanse of empty, flowing black stone that extended to the mountainside. Zeal counted the hundred and forty strides to cross the smooth, sometimes twisted surface to a wall formed of the same material.

"Wait here a moment. I need to check something." Tulip abruptly moved away from the others.

She used her hands to feel along the wall's surface, sliding first to her right before probing the opposite direction. When she turned back to them, she smiled and blew them a kiss. Then, with a single step, she disappeared from sight.

Zeal, Tallen, and Mehrle raced to the spot where she'd vanished, but Kit got there before any of them. Feeling along the wall, Zeal discovered an overlay of stone that gave the illusion the surface was continuous. In reality, two walls overlapped with a gap between them wide enough for a person to slip through. As he was about to follow Tulip, she stepped back out.

"It gets dark shortly as you go in," Tulip informed them. "We will need a light source. Zeal, would you provide one?"

"If this is her idea of the obvious," Mehrle said with a laugh, "I would hate to see the alternative."

"Tulip, how did you know this was here?" Zeal conjured, "Laevin." A globe of light appeared in each of his hands. He released one above Tulip, the other above him, and told the globes, "Follow."

"I didn't know," Tulip replied as she moved forward into the passage. "However, I noticed, when we circled prior to landing and the rays of the sun struck this portion of the slope, for a brief moment there was a linear streak of darkness. At first, I thought I'd imagined it. We lucked out with the timing of our arrival. Otherwise, I would have missed seeing it."

Marching order established itself of its own accord. Mehrle followed Tallen, who walked behind Tulip, with Zeal and Kit in the rear. As Mehrle passed by him, Zeal noticed Mehrle loosen two of her throwing knives in their sheaths on her bandolier, readying them for use.

There was only enough space between the two walls to allow them to proceed sideways and not rub against their abrasive surfaces. They carried their packs in hand by their sides. If they were attacked by something or someone, they would be at a disadvantage.

Mehrle said just loudly enough for all to hear, "I appreciate light sources, but having them will announce our presence to anyone, or thing, that can see it. Sound will travel farther than you think. Anyone or thing could await us. Perhaps Kit should scout ahead?"

Zeal shook his head. "Her advantages will serve whether she is with us or not. I think we should stay together." Decision made, they proceeded, but he asked Kit, *Join all of us in battle mind please.*

Will do.

The narrow passage gradually opened into a tubular tunnel with a ceiling three hands above Tallen's head. He could extend his hands out at shoulder height and barely touch the walls on either side. They still would need to travel in single file, but Zeal didn't feel as closed in. Small sparkles in the stone, the size of a pinhead, reflected the illumination of their globes. They proceeded forward cautiously. The passage's gradient began to slope downward.

What are you doing, Tulip? Tallen seemed puzzled by her behavior. *We could advance faster if you weren't stopping so often.*

Leave her alone, Tallen, Mehrle scolded. *She knows what she is about. A false floor or trap in the walls or ceiling would catch the unwary, severely injuring or killing them.* Tulip continued the use of her Trade training without being prompted.

Why would anyone do such a thing? Tallen wondered, curious.

To protect something they valued, Zeal answered.

The underground passage continued to slope downward. They traveled for a little over two marks before entering a widened area where they could stand three abreast. Further progress was blocked by a heavy, lattice grille comprised of stone sculpted with forms of animals, plants, and flowers.

The passage on the other side of the barrier was filled with a thin, yellow mist that swirled as if stirred by an unseen ladle. In the vapors, they could see a skeleton lying on the ground, the metallic remains of its possessions intermixed with its bones.

That doesn't bode well, Zeal commented to the others.

Mehrle looked away from the remains and studied the lattice's patterns. *It is beautiful to look at, but how do we get past it?*

Good question, Mehrle. Tulip began her own inspection of the lattice. *Perhaps we could use Kit's services to transport us over?*

We would definitely avoid having to figure out how to open this, Tallen replied. *And allow us to get to the Blood sooner.*

Zeal knelt next to Kit and whispered, "What do you think about the idea of providing transport?"

"Well, I think it is a terrible idea, my lovelies," said a soft voice. "That is unless you would like to join me."

They all looked around, trying to locate the speaker. Mehrle held her throwing knife while Tulip grasped her sword and Tallen nocked an arrow. Kit became a tense ball of fur, and Zeal prepared a conjure.

I do not detect prey or hunter near us.

"Whoever said that, you should show yourself," Zeal demanded.

"Oh, dear! Did you all hear me? Now that is unusual. Make an appearance… That's amusing."

A movement caught Zeal's eye. Vapor joined with dust and sparkling pieces of stone, then the mixture rose upward through the remains on the ground, forming into a semitransparent female. The woman was dressed in tan leathers and a green cloak, and she had dark hair down to her shoulders.

"I see her." Mehrle took a step back. "Zeal, I see her *and* I heard her speak. But she is dead."

Zeal tried to gauge the spirit's demeanor. "Interesting. I'm thinking everyone can see and hear her." He sensed Kit's discomfort about this non-living, since she had yet to figure out how to hurt them, which bothered her.

"But I... Uh, *we're* not like you. How is this possible?" Tulip gawked at the figure before them.

"I think it is related to the gift you all received." Zeal directed his attention at the unknown female non-living. "I'm Zeal and happy to make your acquaintance. Thank you for the warning, but could you please explain the danger?"

"Call me Nadinae. That was what I used to go by. I did what you all planned to do and transported myself to the other side of the barrier before you. But the mist is poisonous. It doesn't need to be breathed in for it to affect you. My life was gone before I took three strides, and here I have been ever since."

"Sorry for your demise. How do you suggest we get by this hindrance?" Zeal asked.

"Well, my little dollies, you should open the grille," Nadinae suggested

"Why didn't you open it?" Mehrle asked.

"Because, sweetness, it is locked and I didn't have the key."

Zeal, Tulip, and Mehrle began to closely examine the intricate design on the grille. There seemed to be no keyhole, but then Tulip cried out, "I found it! In the eye of this beast."

"There is one here, as well." Mehrle pointed it out to the others.

After a few heartbeats, Mehrle asked, "Zeal, why are you still looking?"

"Think a moment. There are three members of the Trade on this quest. You were sent specifically because you are needed. If there were only two locks, Tulip and I could open them. I surmise there are three locks present. Ah, and here it is. In the bowl of this tree." The third hole was centered below the upper edge of the grille.

Mehrle said, "It's likely all three locks require opening simultaneously."

"What you say seems plausible." Zeal turned to the spirit.

"Nadinae, would you excuse us for a bit while we look into this possibility? I don't want you to feel we are ignoring you." He gave her a slight bow.

"By all means, press on. I must say this is quite entertaining, and I can't wait to see what you all do next." She drifted a little closer to the barrier.

Mehrle waited with Tulip and Tallen as Zeal studied the keyholes they pointed out to him. "I am surprised you all are acting so nonchalant, now that you have the ability to associate with those who have passed on." Zeal directed Kit to engage them in battle mind while he studied the grillwork. *Always remember, the dead may have their own agenda, just as they did while living. Don't allow yourself to be deceived by them. Some are good and others not so good. Unless you have a reason, don't touch their remains or former possessions, for they are usually jealously guarded.*

Can't kill dead prey.

Kit is wrong. There are ways of destroying what is left behind. I have learned that our Fangs can harm them. Once we get this open, keep an eye on Nadinae, and watch for other spirits. I find it curious she has not crossed to our side of the passage, with the way closed. Zeal continued out loud. "I don't see any other disguised keyholes. I agree with Mehrle. The locks should be opened together."

Zeal turned to Tallen. "The ditty children sing when they jump rope—would you please play that while we say our words, to help us synchronize our work? We'll let you know when to start." *Tulip, Mehrle, we need to coordinate this carefully. Mistakes can be made even with Kit linking us.*

"Yes, I find that little melody quite catchy." Tallen took his pipes from their pouch.

Mehrle removed her lock picks from a pocket hidden in her belt. "It is going to be a close fit for the three of us to work in this space."

"Here, let me get out of the way of you both." Zeal conjured, "Suvolo." He rose into the air till he was positioned in front of the uppermost lock. From there, he was able to view everyone and still keep an eye on Nadinae. "You two should have lots of room now."

Mehrle and Tulip set to work preparing their apertures. Zeal used a small metal mirror to reflect light in and around his opening before inspecting the surface by feel. The material was coarse to touch with minute, superficial pitting and small imperfections. He applied a small amount of oil in the hole and spread a thin coating outside it to loosen the internal components and ease their movement.

As he continued his inspection of the artwork, Mehrle exclaimed, "Hey! This pock is unlike the others. It is a borehole, a trap. Come see! Where there is one danger, there may be another."

After Tulip had a look, Zeal floated down and inspected Mehrle's find. "Remember the needle trap Master Slag had us disarm? We might have the same thing here."

Tallen peered over Zeal's shoulder. "What harm would a needle present?"

"Small, pokey things are usually coated with substances that are meant to kill the recipient," Tulip informed him.

Zeal floated back to his lock and began to extend his search. A quarter-mark later, he realized his lock had a trap, too.

Just then, Tulip announced, "I found you." As everyone including Kit crowded around to have a look, she pointed out two mesh openings hidden in the design around the lock. "I think this is meant to spray some kind of liquid."

"It could be for expelling a gas, too," Zeal suggested.

"What did you find?" Mehrle asked him, standing on her toes to get a better view.

"Here, here, and here," he replied, "this vine pattern actually forms three separate runes. I have never seen their like, but I sense that they are linked to fire in some way. If so, I should be able to mitigate the effects. I am concerned, however, about the traps on our locks. I doubt they were placed as a deterrent but to cause death." Privately, he added to Kit, *Will you please help protect Tulip and Mehrle, in case they trigger their traps? I might be a little busy dealing with my own.*

They are Pride.

"Well, let's get to it then." Zeal rose, positioning himself in front of his lock, and then carefully inserted his spring pick. He closed his eyes and used the pick to visualize the inside of the device by touch. "I have four pins. Anyone have more or less?"

A few moments later, Tulip and Mehrle confirmed they had four pins in their locks, as well.

"Okay, we need to practice our timing. Tallen, you can start playing."

Mehrle began to tap her right foot to the beat, as did Tulip, while Zeal moved his foot in the air. Kit joined their thoughts together, and they began to chant.

Zeal applied pressure using his tension wrench, and then, with his spring pick, felt the pins inside the lock. After putting the pins into a neutral position, he eased three of the pins upward until he felt them seat.

"I am ready," he announced then waited till both Mehrle and Tulip declared they were, as well. "This time. Let's do it."

Tallen played his pipes, and they began to sing. The music made Zeal feel more confident and centered.

Mistress Talley had a clock.

On its front, it had a lock

The face was large so she could see

To open it up she turned the key

The three of them acted as one. Zeal moved the fourth pin, and as it set into place, his tension wrench turned. The lock opened with a soft click. Flame formed above him, which he quickly gathered together to prevent the searing gasses from expanding. For a moment, he was frightened he wouldn't be able to control the discharge before it enveloped the others. Once the eruption culminated, he breathed a sigh of relief.

Then he heard a loud tap below him, near Mehrle, followed by the sizzling odor of a metal pot burning on the stove. A glowing ember the size of a sewing needle fell to the ground beside the toe of

PRACTIONER OF THE ARTS

her left boot.

Tulip yelped and tumbled away from the lattice. Kit conjured, drawing on him to support the casting. "Conlat." Spray flew out from the mesh and collected into a sphere, thanks to Kit.

The pipes' voices silenced. Tallen placed them behind his back to shield them from danger. "I'm guessing we weren't entirely correct in our assumptions."

Mehrle took a couple of steps away from the grille. Zeal remained where he was, sitting above her. The large ball of fire beside him swiftly shrank in size until he could grasped it in his right hand.

Five paces away, Tulip pointed at a head-sized globe of off-white liquid suspended in the air above where she had been standing, picking her lock. "Anyone have an idea what that is? Zeal, do I thank you for keeping whatever it is off me?"

No, not Zeal. Kit moved closer to the globe and sniffed it cautiously. *Bad acid,* was her pronouncement.

"You were lucky, Mehrle, your trap didn't trigger." Tallen put his pipes away and moved a little closer to the lattice.

Mehrle studied Kit's scary cat grin and bowed her head to Kit. "Oh, but it did, Tallen. Thank you, Kit, for protecting me. That hot needle was meant to burn itself into the brain of whoever stood in front of the opening."

"I asked Kit to put a shield in front of Mehrle's trap and capture any liquid or gas expelled through the meshes on Tulip's," Zeal explained. "I handled what I'd hoped was a fire trap. Our technique was perfect. Why were the traps triggered?"

"Because, my dollies, they were to be opened in order with minimal delay, not all together," Nadinae informed them.

"Nadinae, why didn't you say something earlier?" Zeal spun the fist-sized ball of flame in his right hand.

Mehrle grimaced at Nadinae's comment. *Hope you are you thinking of putting that fire to use.*

Nadinae's ghostly form shrugged. "Why, dearest, you didn't ask!"

"Do you intend to bar our passage?" Zeal asked

"Of course not. I am no guardian of the gate." Nadinae slowly drifted closer to barrier.

"Why do you even believe her?" Mehrle asked.

Zeal replied thoughtfully, "Nadinae has no reason to lie. Unless you have another suggestion, it does make sense."

I think I have it, Tallen shared proudly. *The order should be Mehrle, Tulip, and then Zeal. It was one hole, two mesh, and three vines.*

Zeal mentally chuckled. *Well, even if that isn't the correct method, it will sound good when you recite the ballad of our quest. But I do believe you have the right of it. Let's take a moment to compose ourselves, and then we can try again. Firemyst is depending on us. No more setting off traps.*

Tulip pointed to the floating sphere of liquid. "Move it, please." Kit shifted the liquid aside, and she resumed her place.

Zeal and Mehrle also settled in front of their locks. Zeal caused the fiery ball to rest, floating above and behind his left shoulder. Tallen took out his pipes and began to play. Together, they chanted:

> *Mistress Talley had a clock*
>
> *On the front, it had a lock*
>
> *The face was large so she could see*
>
> *To open it up, she turned the key*

Mehrle's lock opened first. Two heartbeats later, Tulip sprung hers. Zeal counted three beats before allowing his tension trench to turn. He removed his picks as the grille sunk slowly into the floor with loud grating noise, and the yellow mist began to thin and dissipate.

Kit's screeched as Nadinae swiftly floated to Tulip and begin to enter her body.

"NO!" Zeal reached toward Nadinae.

A bright glow appeared in the center of Tulip's armor, over her breastbone. At the same instant, the bracelet on Tulip's left wrist shrouded her in blackness.

Nadinae was rebuked. With a yelp of frustration, she retreated to float over her remains. "You weren't supposed to do that, dolly!"

You seek a member of my Pride, Kit hissed, spittle flying toward Nadinae.

"Just to live again. My former life ended so tragically. I have waited long for someone worthy to come along and open the barrier. Either one of the ladies will do. I would rather not be male or an animal."

Zeal placed himself between Nadinae and the others, his Fang in hand. Tallen stepped up beside him, holding his pipes. Mehrle pulled Tulip back.

The globe of acid moved as if on its own and momentarily hovered before it dropped, splashing over Nadinae's remains. Rapidly, it ate through the bones and remaining pieces of her belongings. Zeal's ball dropped. It rolled along the ground to the acid sludge. Nadinae released one long, loud wail as her form melted and the remnants of her body were consumed by the flames till nothing but a thin coating of ash was left behind. When the smoke cleared, the passage beyond them was empty of the yellow vapor, and Nadinae was no longer.

Saddened, Zeal turned to his companions. He always found it hard to take a life, even one that had once already lived. He'd liked Nadinae and concluded she had probably, in death, not changed from how she had been in life.

He searched the area for the presence of any other spirits but detected none. Kit felt no other live ones, either. Tulip, Mehrle, and Tallen appeared satisfied, while Kit wore her Kit grin.

"I see what you mean by the dead having their agenda," Mehrle said. "Could she really have possessed Tulip or me against our will?"

"It is possible," Zeal replied. "But if your will is strong enough, you can resist." He wondered if Tulip knew the amulet from Lady Iris had helped to defend her. "I think you each wear protection against such an attack. Tulip, are you okay?"

She rubbed the center of her chest as she studied her bracelet. "Nadinae touched me. I felt coldness here in my chest and a chill on my wrist. I could also smell iris blooms all around me right before she was cast away. Now I feel all warm inside. I'm fine."

Zeal felt relieved. "I'm so sorry. Nadinae acted too quickly for me to stop her."

All four moved into a warm hug, with Kit draped over his shoulders, a paw placed on Tulip's neck.

When Zeal broke away, he asked, "Shall we continue? I want to get Firemyst to the Blood of Sartus. We should use stealth and battle mind. Kit, please keep us together."

Cautiously, they began moving down the open passage, Tulip again in the lead.

* * *

They traveled less than a quarter mark before the tunnel opened into a large empty cavern with a dull, red glow on its far side.

Zeal stepped up beside Mehrle. *This cave is almost as large as the Casting Quad in Havensharth.*

The cavern floor was smooth like polished glass and solid under foot. As they entered, a platform rose up out of the floor made of the same dark substance as the rest of the cavern.

Spooky, Mehrle thought to the rest. She glanced around nervously, keeping a cautious eye the platform, which had an inverted chalice carved into its top.

Tallen reached toward it but then pulled back before touching it. *It's an altar. Look at the blood channel that drains toward the cup and those brown stains. Someone or something has been sacrificed in the past.*

Eager to accomplish their task, Zeal separated from the group and migrated beyond the altar in the direction of the red glow. The light globe followed him overhead, so he could see that the glow's source was partially obscured by a semitransparent, faintly blue barrier that separated them from the distal quarter of the cave.

On the other side of the barrier was a red pool, filled by flow from an opening in the far-left wall, which left out of an opening on the far right. Wisps of smoke and waves of heat rose from the bubbling surface; the hot liquid was the source of the dim, red glow. Beyond the barrier, there was a narrow ledge of black glass on the edge of the pool, similar to a beach along a lakeshore.

They had reached the Blood of Sartus.

Zeal studied the boundary for several heartbeats before suddenly reaching out his hand. It passed through the barrier unimpeded. After pulling it back, he walked to the right, alongside the semitransparent divider but still staying on their side, till he reached the cavern wall. There, he knelt, set his pack down, removed Firemyst from within, and gestured to them all to join him.

You sure that was wise of you, to stick your hand in there? What if it had been another trap? Tulip asked as they approached.

Zeal ignored her. *I am going to place Firemyst in the pool of Blood. I needed to test the barrier sooner or later. It apparently functions as a safeguard to keep the environment on the other side separate from this one. You all wait here.* He carried Firemyst's egg, cradled in his arms, along the semitransparent wall to the ledge on the opposite side.

Mehrle hoped they were not too late to help the firebird chick. Zeal released his conjure, dispelling the crystal fire.

Just then, from the opening to the tunnel, two large red slug shapes flew in toward Zeal. The creatures' bodies were as thick as Mehrle's upper thigh. They had blunt tails, flat, spade-shaped heads, yellow eyes with catlike pupils, and a mouth full of pointed, crystalline teeth, but no appendages. They undulated in the air, crossed the cavern, and wrapped their bodies around Zeal, who clutched Firemyst close to protect him. Caught unawares, Zeal was easily lifted off his feet, and both he and Firemyst were carried across the barrier and into the pool of Blood.

Suddenly, Zeal left their battle mind, and his light globe blinked out of existence. Everyone was gripped in shock, momentarily unable to act. Even Kit stood frozen, mind silent.

Zeal's disappearance was soon followed by an explosion of

laughter that erupted from a female figure who had entered and slowly crossed the cavern. She wore a red leather tunic and yellow leather skirt with an oversized pocket. Her heeled boots had been dyed red to match the jacket and added to her height. She ceased her advance once she'd reached the altar and stood facing them. A light floated above her that revealed her face for all to see. Her attractive, almond-shaped, black eyes, straight nose, and pert mouth were transformed into a maniacal look, a hideous mask.

Tulip and Tallen released her name into everyone's thoughts. Mehrle was instantly bathed in hate.

Who was this *LISTINA*?

CHAPTER THIRTY-FOUR

LISTINA REVELED in the success of her ambush. Zeal was dead—how joyful! There was no way he could have survived his forced plunge into the so-called Blood of Sartus. He and his miserable cat had carried an unpaid debt owed to her and almost ruined her life. Zeal's death was a partial payment.

She looked at her Rod of Control, which she had discovered amongst the possessions of the mentor her father hired to complete her training, after her unfair dismissal from Havensharth. Her mentor died on the very same evening he'd awarded her with her Master's Certification. She'd used the same conjure on him that had failed to end Zeal's life and his pet's, several seasons ago, but with the desired outcome. Now, she owned all that had been her teacher's.

Listina's servants rose out of the bubbling red pool, answering the rod's summons. When they crossed the semitransparent blue barrier, shimmering waves of heat radiated from their bodies and they smelled of rotten diddle duck egg.

She pointed at Zeal's surprised companions. "Destroy them."

The creatures surged forward, their conical teeth gnashing as they prepared to latch onto their quarry. But they crumpled against an unseen shield that hissed and crackled at their touch. The shell, where struck, fractured like poorly fired clay, evident by lines of light, but the protection held and then reformed, once the attack ended. Listina's creatures undulated away then circled back for another attempt at their prey.

Her smile melted. "How unfair! I try to give you a relatively quick and painful end, and you resist. Tallen, Tulip, I was not aware you had another Practitioner with you. Her mask adds an interesting touch. I might adopt the look myself."

Regally, Listina approached the barrier between her and the Blood of Sartus but stopped short of touching it. She maintained her distance from the Apprentices. *Interesting*, she thought to herself. The boundary kept anything on the other side from mixing with hers. Not even the sound of the flowing liquid passed through—likely why she had not had the pleasure of hearing Zeal's last screams.

The pool's surface was hardening and turning black like the stone cavern around them. Listina had seen this before: when water visibly froze after a rapid drop in temperature, the ice formed would sheet across the water's surface. She dismissed the phenomena as irrelevant despite having no idea why it was occurring.

Listina exerted her will and retrieved a palm-sized disc from the pocket of her skirt. Voicing the command "Devorae," she threw the disc at her adversaries' shield. It struck and partially embedded into the shell. Black tendrils spread slowly from the buried edge, weakening the barrier and clouding it gray.

Steam rose wherever her creatures made contact against the shell, as the heat of the creature's bodies caused moisture in the air to boil. Fractures spread further and over a wider area. But instead of failing and disappearing, the safeguard held and visibly healed. Even Listina's disc was pushed out, dropping to the floor as a deformed piece of metal.

Her puppets resumed circling in preparation for another assault.

"I've yet to meet a Practitioner as strong as you," Listina said. "But tire you will, and when you do, I will be waiting to put you out of your miserable existence. I'll cherish the possessions you deemed important enough to bring with you, since you won't have need of them any longer. Will you stay silent while your flesh cooks from the embrace of my minions?"

* * *

Tulip had more experience being linked with Zeal and Kit than the others. She was able tell when Kit excluded Zeal from sharing in a communication meant for her and Kit alone. But she'd always somehow felt Zeal in the background. Now, he was gone completely.

Why hadn't Kit detected Listina and warned them? How had Listina found them? Tulip would seek answers later.

Kit continued to maintain battle mind but kept herself closed off from the others, concealing her emotions and not sharing. Tulip barely fought back tears and her heavy heart ached despite all of Mirada's teaching about how hard it would be to fight on when a close comrade had been lost in battle beside you. Tulip knew they all had to push through the pain and turn it into a weapon against Listina.

Why does she think I am a Practitioner? Mehrle asked.

Only a select few are aware of Kit's ability to conjure, Tulip explained. *Listina is not one of them. Since she knows Tallen and I lack the talent, that leaves you as the likely Practitioner.*

Tell me of Listina, Mehrle demanded, her two daggers sheened with moisture, likely poisons.

Listina attempted to kill Zeal and Kit once before, Tallen rattled off, holding his bow with a black arrow knocked on the string. *She is a former Apprentice at Havensharth.*

Tulip tried to connect with Kit's thoughts and received... nothing.

Zeal, Mehrle asked gently. *Is he truly gone?*

He's no longer with us. Tallen glanced toward Kit. *I have never seen Kit so humbled.*

Tulip knelt and gathered Kit into her arms. *Make sure your arrow doesn't produce a ball of fire large enough to toast us along with Listina.* The fierce Shadow Cat's tail drooped; her body was flaccid with her ears lying flat to her skull, eyes closed, and her chest heaved as she panted and labored to breath. *Stay with us. We are here for you. You are ours, and we are your Pride. I promise to avenge him.*

Clearly, Tallen and Mehrle were determined to exact retribution, as well.

The shield that domed around them crackled and sparkled as Listina commanded yet another attack by the beasts.

Our protection gives us a moment to plan. Tulip stood with Kit cradled lovingly in her arms. *I'm more mad than scared, and I am not going to let Listina defeat me.*

Tallen shifted his aim slightly. *We can take her, all of us together. Perhaps her creatures will cease to attack if she is not alive to command them.*

Tulip saw movement near the cavern's entrance. *Somehow, Tallen, I don't think it will be that easy.*

Listina smiled at the party of five armed men who entered the cavern wearing travel cloaks. "Your arrival is fortuitous. The meat of this nut has yet to be picked, and the shell is tougher to crack than expected. Position yourselves. Have care, the masked one is a Practitioner. Be sure to deal with her first."

All but one of the men were unhooded. The hooded one, his face hidden in the head covering's depths, positioned himself protectively beside Listina while the four others arrayed themselves on the far side of the altar. They pointed their loaded crossbows at Mehrle. The short distance their bolts had to travel would put an end to her life before she had a chance to act.

Tulip gently laid the listless Kit on the ground next to her pack, and prepared to stuff the Shadow Cat inside, if need be. Then she reached for her sword... but the weapon and its sheath no longer hung at her side! Astonished, she searched the ground around her.

"Are you missing something?" Listina cackled gleefully.

When Tulip looked up, she saw her naked blade in Listina's hands, and its sheath was clutched by the man beside her.

Merrily, Listina kissed the flat of the blade. "Don't you wonder how we were able to find you? I've been tracking you with this since you left Havensharth. I should have been privy to your thoughts, Tulip, but for some reason you were almost always shrouded. But there were a few moments when I was able to reach through. One instance, I had to hide from one of you—I think it was your caster. I have, of course, since taken steps to conceal my thoughts from detection."

Mehrle shared, *The crystal on your weapon would at times clear but then return to being cloudy. Once, it even absorbed Templar's blood when it stained it. I always meant to ask you about the crystal, but somehow never remembered to do so.*

I don't know what you mean. The crystal on the pommel never changed its appearance! Tulip insisted. *The weapon was gifted to me by a friend.*

Tallen kept his eyes fixed on the hooded man. *No. You have it wrong. I was there, Tulip. You refused to accept his gift. Addis loaned you the sword.*

Listina interrupted. "You had the nerve to destroy my pets. You defeated the Argguile I sent—the poor thing was not allowed to serve its purpose. I meant for it to punish the inhabitants of Havensharth for what they'd done to me, but you prevented me from obtaining my revenge. When I used a bird to spy on you, that beast killed it."

Listina kept the sword's tip pointed at Kit during her rant. Tulip studied the silent, hooded figure next to Listina. There was something familiar about him.

The two sinuous beasts pressed their bodies against the protective barrier, but, even though the shield sizzled and the fractures deepened, it continued to hold. However, the fissures now spread further and took longer to heal.

Mehrle shifted position and attempted to stay loose. *Tallen may be right. Have Kit attack Listina and provide a distraction, while we each target one of the others. If we drop Listina, maybe the two creatures of hers will stop their attack. I know how to kill people, but not those things.* Although Mehrle's mask hid any expression, in the link, she could not hide emotion. She felt clearly stymied by their predicament.

Mehrle, Tulip replied, *I fear, if Kit were to leave us, the protection around us would, as well. Then we would be exposed to our opposition's crossbows and Listina's conjure. They would know we were up to something the moment we moved to bring our weapons to bear on them. Even if we were prepared to act before they do, they would still have a chance to counter.*

Tulip glanced toward Kit. *Kit isn't responding to me, anyway. I don't know what she is capable of doing right now or if she is even paying attention. Who knows what happens to a Shadow Cat when her bond is broken? We might have to wait for the shell to fail to be able to act.*

"Must I continue to carry this conversation on my own?" Listina snapped. "Why do you all stand mute? All you have done is stare at me and my armsmen, then at each other and the cat. Don't you have anything to say for yourselves? If you pleaded well enough, I might consider letting one of you live to serve me. On your knees! Entertain me. Or, better yet, let's hurry this along."

Listina reached into her pocket and retrieved another disc. She said softly, "Devorae," and flung it at the weakening shield, timing its arrival to coincide with her creatures' next attack. The disc completely embedded and was not extruded this time. It released threads of blackness that made tiny fractures in the shell and prevented them from closing. "I will soon have my satisfaction," she said. The smell of rotten eggs intensified as she prepared to conjure.

* * *

The relentless darkness and cold overcame his resistance. He had no fight left. Kit and Zeal's thoughts were comforting, but it took too much effort to communicate. Memory of them was fading.

Then the prison that encased him softened. Even through the closed membranes that covered his eyes, the unfailing darkness began to brighten. Was this the light he'd been told he would, one cycle, see? The shell around him disintegrated. Blessed warmth enveloped him. The Blood of Sartus bathed his desiccated and withered form. A band of supportive coolness held him, persisting in its presence.

He labored to channel and direct his metamorphosis, ignoring the pain that was not his own but that grew with every heartbeat. *The Blood must be filtered, siphoned at a rate that allows survival, not destruction.* During that fractured thought, his bones rapidly elongated, filled with the Blood, which formed into marrow before coursing outward through many pathways before coalescing in the chambers of... *TWO HEARTS*. Organs filled and enlarged. Muscles grew, their attached tendons lengthening. His skin stretched, expelling growths from its surface.

The pain worsened. The part of him that was not him would soon die, even though he continued to mitigate the effects of the Blood through himself. *He must leave.*

Talons grew, the extremities extended, more protuberances erupted. He rose toward the surface and encountered resistance. A barrier still existed that prevented his birth.

Diving down, he drove his wings through the Blood. He gathered speed and positioned himself, talons extended, to attack the impediment. Immediately before impact, he felt a sudden surge of strength coming from without yet within.

The extended self was dying. Ridden by need, he exploded through the casing, finally hatched. Firemyst was born, and he was hungry.

CHAPTER THIRTY-FIVE

CLEARLY, TULIP DIDN'T approve of their current situation. Well, neither did Mehrle.

She shared with the others, *We can't ignore Listina's armsmen. Something must be done about them. Tallen, that is your job. Tulip, you assist him and help reduce the numbers against us. I don't care if you both have a history with this gutter wench and want a piece of her. I will deal with Listina and keep her busy till you have the opportunity to aid me or take over, if needed.*

What of her flying friends? Tulip asked, her Fang in her off hand and her long knife in her right. *What do we do about them?*

Mehrle watched the beasts in question undulate away after again attacking the weakening shell.

Well, if Kit is still with us, I guess they are hers to play with. If she isn't, then you better be quick on your feet. Ready yourselves! I think our shell is dropping.

She knelt to one knee and spoke to Listina, intent on using Listina's assumption against her. "I will yield to you if you let me live. What I possess will be yours to have. Even the crystal I used to cast the barrier around us will be yours. I vow to not conjure against you. You have my word as a Practitioner. Will you accept my service?"

There was an audible pop as the barrier between them ceased to exist. Mehrle immediately tumbled forward and launched her second-best throwing knife at Listina. Crossbow bolts skipped off the cavern floor where she had knelt; all but one missed. A sharp pain in her left hip let her know one bolt had flown true. But then, immediately, the pain eased, drawn away as it was redirected between all of them. Mehrle's blade bounced off Listina's own unseen protective shell and fell to the ground.

Because of battle mind, Mehrle was not only aware that Tallen had released the black arrow, but, through him, viewed the arrow's passage. To Tallen, the arrow was an extension of himself. He could count the turns the fletching made as the arrow flew. He waited until the arrow was centered behind the armsmen before using his intent to release its energy.

A flaming ball formed and engulfed the cavern in blazing, concussive force, but the arrow's travel had taken it far enough away so Tallen and his cohort did not suffer the effects of the discharge. The four men and two flying attackers, however, were caught within the fiery burst and driven to the ground; unfortunately, Listina and her guardian were out of the affected area.

As the blast dissipated, Tulip advanced on the nearest advisory, who was struggling to his feet. He reacted by swinging his crossbow at her, which she deflected past her head with her Fang then buried her long knife in his throat. She twisted the blade before directing it forward. Its passage severed the airway, major vessels, and anterior muscles on both sides of his neck, leaving the spine alone to hold his head attached to his shoulders. His blood sprayed onto the altar. She moved to her next target before his body hit the floor. Her new adversary stood waiting, sword in hand, ready to receive her.

Tallen's next arrow flew through the haze left by the fireball and struck the third armsman, who'd stepped forward to engage Tulip. The arrow buried deep into the man's shoulder. The force of the arrow caused him to lose his balance. He tripped on his own feet and fell, hitting the ground with enough force to lose his grip on his weapon. This left Tulip facing a lone opponent.

The fourth crossbow man had immediately run to attack Tallen. Once up close, the man took away Tallen's ability to use his bow. Armed with an axe, he swung, intent on splitting Tallen like a piece of wood. With regret, Tallen used his bow to parry the blow—it was either have it severely damaged or himself.

Doubting that Listina's protection had suddenly taken leave, Mehrle flung her best throwing knife at Tallen's attacker. It pierced the man's left eye and lodged in the armsman's braincase. His body abruptly dropped at Tallen's feet. Mehrle received Tallen's appreciative thought.

Tulip's opponent thrust his weapon forward. She crossed her blades in front of her face, enabling her to grab his sword between them. She directed his weapon up and away from her and then drove her foot forcefully between his legs. He let out a howl of anguish which she quickly silenced. Flicking the blood off her long knife, she knelt and ended the life of the man who had been impaled by Tallen's arrow.

Listina shouted, "*Enough of this farce!*" She handed her sword to the figure at her side. "You admire her so much, take this, and go deal with her. Your Tulip has butted into my affairs for the last time. Take care of her before I do." She motioned with her rod at the two creatures before pointing first at Mehrle and then at Tallen. "Destroy them!"

The creatures moved to do her bidding.

"I have something special for you, little puss." A guttural phrase rolled from the back of Listina's throat, "Arcess Canàe." Gray mist appeared in front of her as she conjured. The vapor bellowed outward, thickened, and solidified into a Dread Hound. Listina directed the hound at Kit. "Eat it. Now!"

Mehrle returned to her feet with difficulty, supporting most of her weight on her uninjured right leg. Listina's hound had coarse, gray fur and red eyes that showed a malevolent intelligence. The beast seemed to assess the field of battle then nodded at Listina and began its advance. Long yellow canines erupted from black gums in its blocky muzzle. It looked to weigh thirty stone.

Pay attention, Kit! Mehrle urged. *You need to get up.* She took heart when Kit began to stir in reaction to her call, but the Shadow Cat still seemed lethargic and slow to respond to the danger padding her way.

Drool dripped from the hound's open jaws as it approached.

Mehrle became convinced all hope for Kit was lost, certain she was about to view her companion's end

You threaten me with a mere dog!

Suddenly, inconceivably, a hiding sized Kit reached out with a hunting sized paw, its sharp claws extended, and struck the hound in the muzzle. Then she slipped into the shadow cast over her by the beast. Mehrle smiled, seeing Kit respond had provided her with a surge of hope and energy. She turned to face the fiery creature sent by Listina, readied her Fang, and prepared to defend herself.

The creature stopped in front of her, hissing its contempt. She felt heat radiate from its body before it opened its maw and lunged forward, intent on sinking its crystalline teeth into her masked face. But it suddenly stopped short of reaching her. Its tail had been grasped by the hooked beak of a humped-back, two-headed monster.

Her attacker was jerked away and messily eaten, swallowed whole, like a bird eating a worm. A drop of ichor landed on her hand. It burned worse than hot oil and shocked Mehrle out of her surprise.

Her savior was comparable in size to one of their horses in height. It had two legs, was twice as thick in the body, and was covered by a dark glass-like substance that flaked off as it moved. Its second head extended from the hump on its back.

As the hump's eyes swiveled toward Listina, Mehrle suddenly felt a familiar—and unfamiliar—presence join their battle mind.

Be ready to help the others, Zeal told her explicitly.

The monster—no! A fused Zeal and Firemyst turned to face Listina and her remaining familiar, still by her side.

It's a Salamander! Zeal exclaimed, identifying the creature.

Then, in a raspy voice, Zeal addressed it by vocalizing sounds like flames in a crackling hearth. The salamander answered by backing away from Listina to hover on the Blood side of the translucent barrier.

The hound had recovered from being momentarily stunned by Kit's slap. Not able to find Kit, it took the opportunity to advance on Tallen, who stood distracted by the appearance of the Zeal-Firemyst amalgam.

The hound bit into Tallen's left arm and shoulder then began to shake its head side to side. Tallen's bow dropped from his hand and Mehrle's arm ached as the pain from Tallen's wound was shared.

Tallen grabbed an arrow from his quiver and stabbed back over his left shoulder, hitting a tender part of the hound. It yelped and released him. Tallen rolled away before turning to face his attacker. The hound took one last step forward before it abruptly stopped.

Mine!

Tallen knew without looking that Kit was behind him. A hunting sized Kit padded between him and the hound, her claws and teeth encased in a blue nimbus. Without warning, the two adversaries sprang into the air toward each other. Kit shrunk to hiding size, stepped into the hound's shadow, and reappeared behind Listina. She immediately clawed Listina in the back with her right forepaw, circumventing the protective shell in front of Listina. The attack interrupted Listina's conjure.

Kit emerged in the air above the confused hound and pounced onto his back, sinking her teeth into the hound's neck and raked it with all four claws. She stripped the flesh from its sides as her claws scraped the ribs below the skin and muscle, then she bit down till the spine crushed with a satisfying crunch. The hound dropped to the floor dead beneath her.

Listina screamed, the pain from Kit's assault burning with each breath. She was not prepared for Kit's abilities, and clearly no one had informed her Kit was more than Zeal's pet. How was this cat able to wound her through her imbued clothing? She cringed as the two-headed monster came closer and stopped in front of the protective barrier she had cast. The smaller head spoke, voice deep and cold.

"I let it be known once before, Listina, that if you ever tried to harm me or mine, you would burn." Zeal's voice was utterly unfeeling.

"Impossible, impossible, impossible," fell repeatedly from Listina's lips. "Zeal, what have you become?"

Listina threw her rod at the Zeal chimera. It passed through her shell, bounced harmlessly off the chest of the monstrosity, and rolled a short distance away. "I don't know how you made my salamander stop following my commands. You shouldn't even be alive. The so-called Blood of Sartus has turned you into an abomination. Everyone will thank me for exterminating you."

The smaller of the two heads only smiled back at her pronouncement. Listina began to conjure. The area of the floor under her feet began to glow. Engrossed in her conjure and protected by her imbued shoes, she was unaware of her peril. Then the glass surface liquefied, and she dropped knee-deep into the molten pool beneath her. Intense pain ratcheted through her. Unable to concentrate, Listina's mouth opened impossibly wide, and the protective shell in front of her evaporated. As she was about to let out a primordial bellow, it was interrupted: Firemyst had bitten off her head.

Zeal sighed. *Firemyst, don't eat that. It may be bad for you.*

Firemyst hacked and retched. He regurgitated Listina's head, which hit the ground with a moist thump. Her face was scorched and blistered while her once-lush hair had been burnt away. Instructed by Zeal, Firemyst pulled Listina's torso out of the red pool. Only bare bones, coated black, remained of her lower legs. The liquid surface gelled as it cooled and returned to its glassy state just before Firemyst dropped the body.

The hooded armsman stopped his advance toward Tulip and retreated to Listina's corpse. Wordlessly, he retrieved her head and tenderly placed it next to the body then began to gently stroke her face.

Tulip, though surprised, realized she knew this man. "Addis! What are you doing here? Why are you with Listina? I thought you were my friend."

Addis lowered his hood. His face was the picture of sorrow and loss. "Listina is my sister. I came with her because, in our family, we always defended one another. I have failed her. But I won't fail her completely. I will leave here and take her home."

"Your sister! How come no one seemed to know?" Zeal asked.

"Listina wanted it that way, for our relation to be a secret. She wanted us to stand on our own in Havensharth, judged by our individual worth. Why did Zeal have to lie about her?"

"Zeal never lied," Tulip replied. "Listina truly made her own troubles."

The pain in Mehrle's hip had become an annoyance. She knew she couldn't stand much longer, plus her left arm and shoulder had a dull ache. Kit lay watching everyone present, including the cavern opening, and ate from the dead hound's haunch. Tallen cradled his left arm close to his chest with his right while Tulip kept her distance from Addis, still puzzled and on the defensive.

Zeal, still fused to the creature Firemyst, said to them, *Addis can't be allowed to take Listina away.*

Why not let him have her? Tallen asked. *Listina won't be harming anyone else.*

I wouldn't be so quick to believe that, Tallen. All of you, look closely. What do you see?

A ghostly form stood over the headless body. It was Listina! *She is still here!* Mehrle exclaimed. *She is like Nadinae.*

I think there is more to this. Zeal addressed Addis when he knelt to gather his sister. "I am sorry, but I can't allow you to take Listina's remains. She told you to do so, didn't she?"

Addis rose, sword in hand. "It was a demand she made me promise to fulfill. Who are you to deny me the right?"

"Did she say she had a way to return to life? I think she did," Zeal kept his tone conversational and conjured a barrier over Listina's body.

"What is it to you, the reason?" Addis's feet suddenly slid, pushed back by the barrier. "I am sorry, Tulip. I cared for you like you were my little sister, but Listina is kin. I will kill every one of you, if I have to."

"You'll have to start with me," Tulip said, then informed her team, *I claim this hunt. If Addis is to die, I feel I should be the one to end the life of a former friend.*

The crystal on Addis's sword turned black and the edge of its blade assumed a purple hue. Addis began his approach, circling and stalking her as he appraised her defense. "We have fought each other every sun for seasons. We have both been trained by Master Cowlin. This is going to be the contest we should have had from the moment we first met."

Tulip matched Addis's movement, Fang and her long knife held defensively. As the distance between them shortened, she felt the pains in her hip and shoulder wane, the sharing with her friends cut off. "You are bigger, stronger, and have a longer reach. Obviously, you are better armed. There is nothing I have learned from Master Cowlin that you have not mastered before me. There is, however, one minor fact you have over looked."

"What, pray tell, have I missed? I doubt whatever it is will save you." Addis brought the pommel of the weapon to his mouth and whispered a phrase too soft to be heard by the others. Suddenly, the sword morphed in his hand, and the blade became twice as long. "This is more to my liking."

"I may be an apprentice of Master Cowlin, but I am also an apprentice of Lady Mirada. What teachings I have acquired from her I have never shown you."

There was no loud roar of challenge. No flashy blade twirl to distract their opponent. Between one heartbeat and the next, weapons clashed. Tulip used her blades to deflect Addis's series of attacks while she looked for an opening in his defense. Addis tried to end the encounter quickly, holding nothing back as he repeatedly stormed her with his blade. His used his sword's length to keep her at a distance and prevented her from touching him with her shorter weapons.

They settled into an intricate dance. Money would have changed hands many times if the match had been in a different venue. Addis slashed. Unable to deflect the attack with her long knife, Tulip used it to block the blows instead. Then her knife was shattered by Addis's imbued blade, and a metallic shard sliced her cheek as it flew by.

Addis continued his assault. "First blood is mine."

Tulip took a left-hand stance. She could feel fatigue starting to set in. Armed with only her Fang, she needed to stop fighting defensively. She threw the stub of her long knife at Addis, interrupting his lunge and causing him to twist away. Then she tumbled inside his guard and rose up in front of him, cutting upward with her Fang.

Caught off balance he was unable to retreat. Sparks flew from their weapons as he parried her thrusts with his sword, interposing it between him and her Fang. She rapidly jabbed him twice in the face with the fist of her free hand. Pressing her attack, she stabbed him in the forearm that held the sword, causing him to drop his weapon.

Addis bellowed with rage. He violently twisted his injured arm away from the Fang, but the blade had passed between the long bones and poked out the other side of his forearm. Caught by the long bones, the Fang was snagged from Tulip's grip. He backhanded Tulip with his other hand and knocked her away from him.

Tulip took several steps rearward before tripping over the dead body of one of the armsmen. She landed hard. Her head struck the floor leaving her momentarily stunned.

Addis wrenched the Fang free. He ignored the blood running from the wound that dripped from the fingers of his injured arm and advanced.

Mehrle reached for a throwing knife to stop Addis. Linked in battle mind, she spoke to the others. *We need to do something.*

Kit turned to them. **No! Not your hunt!**

Tallen had an arrow drawn but reluctantly relaxed the string's tension. *I can't promise to stand aside when I can save one of you. Though I respect you, Kit, I am not a Shadow Cat, and you can't expect me to always follow your ideals.*

Zeal gently interrupted. *Tallen, I understand both of you. I, too, want to jump in and help, but I honor both Tulip and her request. Please do not interfere.*

Where was your honor when Firemyst killed Listina? Mehrle demanded. *Wasn't Listina your hunt to claim?*

Firemyst is a babe and knows nothing of our ways. I will teach him. You, however, know better.

I know one thing, Tallen said.* I will not place honor above love!* He released his arrow at Addis. As he did, there was a rattling noise from Tulip's open pack. Kit leaped into the air and grasped the arrow in her jaws, breaking it into three pieces.

Everyone's pain hit Tulip full-force, awakening her to alertness. Her nose was broken and it hurt! Then, all at once, her discomforts and her fatigue washed away. Tulip opened her eyes just as Addis straddled her.

He raised her Fang in his good hand and stabbed down toward her heart. She stopped it, grasping his forearm in both hands. Addis used his injured arm and body to apply leverage. The Fang drew closer. Tulip used all her strength to push up and, after a moment, to lock her elbows and keep Addis at bay.

She released her hold with her right arm and frantically felt around for anything to use as a weapon. Not able to find one, she yelled in frustration, *"Damn you, Fate! Throw me a bone here!"* To her surprise, she was holding an actual bone.

Flying out of Tulip's pack and into her hand was the knife made from bone, gifted to her by the armies of Mendor and Dearney. Tulip plunged the blade into Addis's chest and pierced him through the heart.

CHAPTER THIRTY-SIX

TULIP PUSHED ADDIS off to the side. She retrieved her Fang from his grasp, cleaned the blade on his cloak, and sheathed it. Her hand shook slightly when she did the same to the bone blade. She placed it in her long knife's empty scabbard.

"I guess you have a name now, don't you, Fate?" she said quietly to the knife. Tulip realized she would have to learn more about the bone blade once she'd returned to Havensharth.

When she turned to face her companions, Kit winked at her. Then Tulip was flooded with all her aches again plus a portion of everyone else's.

Tallen engulfed her one-armed when she limped over to them. *I thought I had lost you.*

I thought I had lost me, as well. How are the rest of you faring? Are we all still here? she asked, assessing their injuries.

Mehrle broke the shaft of the arrow imbedded near her hip, leaving four fingers' length protruding from the wound. *That's better. The hip pain we all feel is due to my injury,* she explained. *The shoulder is Tallen's. The face is obviously yours. Kit is uninjured, and I don't know what to say about Zeal and Firemyst.*

Tulip disengaged herself from Tallen's embrace. *Zeal, what has happened to you and Firemyst? Is this a permanent change?* They were still in battle mind, because Zeal was having difficulty speaking in his new form.

We need to deal with your injuries and Listina before I tell tales. Zeal's mentioning Listina made them all return their attention to her spirit, which hovered over her remains, glaring at them. Even the eyes of her dismembered head appeared to stare their way.

Tulip shuddered. Disturbed by the sight, she wanted to turn away, but forced herself to keep an eye on Listina. Disembodied head or not, one does not ignore an enemy. *Zeal, I think you should burn the bodies like you did Nadinae's.*

I am of similar mind, Tulip. That will prevent Listina from returning. I refuse to give her the opportunity to haunt me in this life or any other. Zeal sounded angry. *Gather the corpses and I will deal with them.*

Wait! Mehrle said from behind her mask. *You all are forgetting one of the tenets of the Trade. Master Slag insists one should not squander an opportunity to take advantage of what an enemy or mark has to offer.*

You are right, Mehrle. Master Slag always gave wise advice. We should search the bodies and see what they carry, Tulip said, but she was determined to let someone other than herself examine Addis.

Kit, let's take a look at Listina's body. The Zeal-Firemyst construct took a position between Listina and the others. *Due to her recent demise, her spirit is likely not as strong as Nadinae's, but still, everyone be careful near Listina.*

The Zeal-Firemyst entity was coated in congealed Blood of Sartus. Small fragments flaked off as it moved, and Tulip wasn't sure she wanted to see what was hidden underneath.

With Kit's assistance, the party conducted a thorough search of Listina's corpse. They discovered and removed a necklace, two rings, and a broach. The large pocket on Listina's skirt contained a small, round, metallic disc, a black book, and several mundane items.

The jewelry, disc, Listina's clothing, and rod are imbued, Zeal informed them. *I'm impressed by the effort and expense it took for Listina to dress in such a fashion. I doubt she did the workings herself.*

Tulip thought the book looked familiar. *Zeal, we've seen this book before.* She opened the cover. *This is the copy of Master

Feneas's treatise on necromancy that Master Ice brought to Havensharth and presented to Master Namrin. Listina must have stolen it.*

You have the right of it, Zeal said. *I'm sure Listina learned the necromantic conjure she used on Kit and me from this book. I bet, somewhere in the volume, she found a way to conjure herself back to life. Master Namrin will be happy to have this brought back to him. Kit, do you see anything we may have missed in our inspection?*

No, but the necklace tried to hide me from you when I held it.

I see. So, it was the necklace that kept Listina from being detected by you. But our bond prevented it from doing the same with us. Tallen, Tulip, would you please check the other bodies? Oh, and Tulip, he asked gently, *what should be done with Addis's weapon?*

Mehrle scooted over to the body nearest her. *I can still help.*

Listina said her family could trace it and that she used it to spy on me. Tulip didn't hesitate. *Destroy the thing. We shouldn't take it nor just leave it behind. I don't know who might start to look for Listina or Addis, once they are discovered missing. We shouldn't give them any cause to look our direction, even though no one was supposed to know we were here.*

I'll throw into the pool of Blood, Zeal declared. *The Blood will liquefy and reclaim the sword.*

Nothing much was on the other bodies, just serviceable gear, well maintained. Kit didn't point out any other imbued objects. Mehrle held up five clay pieces she and Tallen had discovered. *Except these oversized clay coins.*

Let me see one of those please. Zeal closely examined the fist-sized, round object embossed with the rune used to symbolize flowing water. *What you are holding is a recall wafer. It is a means of returning to wherever they came from. You have to intend to break it. Very hard to do accidentally. And then you are transported to the designated destination chosen at the time of the wafer's making. Unless one of you desires to make a side trip to, probably, Listina's lair, I think they should go into the pool along with Addis's sword and the rest of Listina's stuff. I for one have no desire to see where the wafer will take me.*

Mehrle placed the wafers, along with Listina's imbued possessions, except for her clothes, next to Zeal's pack. *I think we'll all pass. You hold on to the wafers until you are ready to have the pool deal with them.*

That can be a handy way to travel. Is it safe? Tallen asked the Practitioners.

Well, Tallen, from what I have learned it is. I have only begun to study the conjures involved. Zeal directed his gaze toward his Shadow Cat. *Believe it or not, Kit's the one who got me interested in journey by conjure.*

Every hunter needs to be able to return to the den on their own.

Tulip stood with her hand on the pommel of her bone knife. *Zeal, can we get this over with? Doesn't anyone else feel uncomfortable having Listina glare at us?*

The Zeal-Firemyst amalgam used a foot to shove Addis's corpse next to his sister's. *Pile the others together by the altar.*

Once the bodies were arranged, Tulip, Tallen, Mehrle, and Kit gathered behind Zeal-Firemyst.

"Addis." Zeal's voice sounded raspy when he spoke. "You were doing what you thought was right and good. To you and the others, I hope you find peace. Listina, you can take your curses with you. May you obtain penance when you meet again those you have wronged."

The remains glowed white with no heat, smoke, or smell and were instantly incinerated, leaving no ash or stain behind on the floor. Listina was no more, her ghostly form gone.

I think now is the right moment for me to do something about my condition. In my current state, I'm not much use. The Zeal-Firemyst amalgam moved to the far side of the cavern. Once there, Zeal closed his eyes and concentrated. *Be ready, Firemyst. You might have to help me. Everyone, keep back!*

A warmth enveloped Tulip's mind. Nothing happened at first, and then there was a sudden, loud report, similar to a staff shattering during a fight, followed by several muffled crackles. Firemyst's hump fissured at its base, fractures streaked up and around it. Small shards broke off, followed by larger pieces. The fragments were absorbed when they touched the floor.

Kit conjured, *Clypen.* The black substance suddenly exploded off the amalgam, momentarily obscuring Zeal-Firemyst from view.

Incased by Kit's shield, the material swirled, partially obscuring its occupants from sight as it settled. Then there was a moist sucking sound, followed by a much louder crash like mounds of shattering glass. Tulip smiled. Zeal and Firemyst were incased in what looked like an oversized snow globe filled with black snow. When the particles settled, Zeal was astride Firemyst, wearing only his workshirt, which reached down to just above his knees, and his remarkable vest. His lower legs were covered by Firemyst's wings.

Firemyst was an impressive raptor the size of a horse. His eyes were black facets that did not reflect back the light. His feathers were the colors of flames: reds, oranges, and yellows that flowed together. His tail and flight feathers, hooked beak, and feet were black. Firemyst was equipped with long, sharp talons made of the crystalline cavern substance.

Through battle mind, all could feel how proud Zeal was of Firemyst. And Firemyst was beautiful. Stunning, yet scary. Tulip yearned to touch the firebird.

Firemyst carefully moved toward Zeal's pack. Using his wings to keep Zeal from falling off his back, he settled to his belly. Tulip rushed over and helped Zeal dismount while Kit, now hunting size, appeared instantly alongside Zeal. He held in one hand a long, black shard, twice the length of his arm, which he kept from touching the floor, the only remaining fragment of the congealed Blood that had once coated him and Firemyst.

My head aches. In fact, I hurt everywhere. Zeal leaned heavily on Kit. Assisted by Tulip, he slowly shuffled over to his gear and settled next to it.

Kit stayed close but continued to eye the cavern entrance. Tulip sat beside Zeal and helped him access his pack. *Tallen, Mehrle, would you come over here please?* Firemyst kept his distance, intently studying them all.

Tulip retrieved a mirror from her pack and handed it to Zeal.

Either I have gotten weaker or you have somehow gained weight and grown taller. Stop a moment. Take a look at yourself.

Zeal's eyes went wide with amazement. His skin was sun-touched. His hair had lengthened and was streaked with red. He was four hands taller than before his exposure to the effects of the Blood, and the weight he'd gained was all muscle mass. "How..?" he asked. His voice had lost its youthfulness. It was deeper, more mature.

"How indeed?" Tallen asked.

"I don't know. Somehow, aiding Firemyst to survive his birth caused my own metamorphosis. You know the empty space inside where I keep my fires? It filled and nearly overflowed. If it had, I would have ruptured like a bubble. It was Firemyst who saved me and kept me from popping." He smiled at the firebird.

Tulip put away the mirror. "What do you need, besides a new pair of trousers?"

"Let me eat something first. I am starving." Zeal placed the shard spear inside his vest, pulled three *effusions* from an inner pocket, and handed one vial each to Tallen, Tulip, and Mehrle. "Drink these. I can see and feel you are all injured."

Tulip set the black satchel next to Zeal. To her surprise, it opened of its own accord. From inside rose a glass bottle filled with green liquid. It was covered in condensation and had a note attached. It hovered in the air in front of her and Zeal. Tulip read the fine script.

Zeal, drink this.

Qwen

Zeal grabbed the bottle, which opened upon his touch, and slowly took four large gulps. He closed his eyes, took a deep breath, and held it for several heart beats then gradually allowed the air to escape his lungs. When he raised his lids, his eyes were more alert, and he looked energized. He sat straighter. "Why haven't you used your *effusions*?"

"We don't want to miss what happens. The *effusion* will put us into a healing sleep," Tulip reminded him.

"For some reason, I forgot about that." Zeal studied the bottle, which still held three remaining swallows. "This is some kind of restorative. Drink your *effusions*. I think the contents of this bottle will stave off the sleep effect long enough for us to finish our business and find a safe place to rest. Now drink, but not at the same time, so we'll suffer the effects of the healing spaced apart, not all together. The pain, even shared amongst us all, might still be overwhelming."

Tallen sat before downing his vial. He leaned forward and supported his weight using his uninjured arm. His broken collarbone grew together, the torn muscles knit, and his wounds closed. Zeal slid over and gave him a swallow of Qwen's liquid.

The discomfort in Tulip's arm and shoulder intensified but was, for the most part, tolerable before it faded. There was something to say about sharing with others the discomfort of healing by *effusion*.

Mehrle drank as soon as the shoulder ache subsided. Pain shot down her leg and into her groin as her body extruded the broadhead and her wound closed. It didn't take long for the *effusion* to restore her to health. Zeal gave her the restorative even before her torment had faded.

Tulip didn't hesitate to quaff her vial's contents. She didn't realize she'd drifted to sleep until she was awakened by Zeal and Tallen offering her the restorative. The sweat on her body was the only reminder of the rigors of her healing. Qwen's elixir was cool and refreshing, washing away her fatigue and need for sleep.

Mehrle had food ready for them from the satchel—sliced meats, boiled diddle duck eggs, fruit, cheese, and warm flatbread.

"We all need to eat," Zeal said. "I don't know how long the effects of the Qwen's bottle will last. Plus, you need to replace the fuel your body consumed in the healing." He picked up the arrowhead next to Mehrle and held it for a few moments. "Mehrle, this bolt that struck you was imbued. That is why it penetrated your armor and workshirt."

Tulip took a bite of flatbread wrapped around meat and cheese and discovered she was ravenous with hunger. She lost herself in the pleasure of eating till there wasn't room for another morsel. She looked up and saw everyone, including Kit and Firemyst, looking at her.

Mehrle laughed. "We enjoyed watching you inhale your food. You should have seen Zeal. He ate nonstop and three times as much as you and Tallen."

Kit and Firemyst lay consuming the hound between them. The salamander still maintained its distance, remaining on the other side of the barrier, where it had gone after its discussion with Zeal.

Tulip looked for the rod that controlled it, but it was not on the floor where Listina had tossed it. She suddenly released a loud burp.

You can have a portion of hound if you still hunger, Tulip.

"Thank you, Kit," she said. "You and Firemyst can finish my share of hound."

Kit nodded then resumed her watch on the cavern entrance. *The Pride must be fed.*

"Why are Kit and Firemyst so fixated with the entryway?" Tallen asked.

Zeal explained, "Kit didn't appreciate Listina wearing an item that masked her presence. The two of them are keeping an eye on the entrance, in case we have more visitors with the same capability."

CHAPTER THIRTY-SEVEN

ZEAL FELT TULIP'S LINGERING pain through their battle mind. She'd cared for Addis as a friend and bore witness for his death in place of his family. Zeal sensed she didn't care one whit for the other recently departed, especially Listina, but had been moved by his sensitive comments.

The ever-pragmatic Mehrle broke the silence within the cavern. "Can we go now?"

"Before we leave here," Zeal said, standing as he stretched his unfamiliar form, "there is something I want to do. I'll not pass this way again anytime soon, so I'd like to take advantage of having come here. I've been thinking about how to get Firemyst to the surface. He'll never fit through the passage beyond the lattice, so Kit will need to help him with that part. I also want to make sure the lattice is returned to its upright position. There has to be a reason why this place is protected." He took a quick walk around the party. "I am going to have to get used to this body."

He grabbed his pack, placed it on the altar, and removed a pony cask plus his largest piece of star metal. Before leaving Havensharth, he'd hoped the Blood would prove to be a heat source hot enough to enable him to work the metal. He now knew, due to the changes the Blood had made in him, he was more than capable of managing the task alone and wanted to incorporate the Blood's characteristics into his creation.

"You brought the star metal with you?" Tallen asked "Why?"

"I thought the Blood of Sartus might allow me to make something out of it." He took the black shard from inside his vest and handed it to Tulip. "Please, hold this and keep it away from any cavern surface." He placed the cask next to the altar. "Firemyst, may I please have one of your feathers?"

Firemyst took one of his primary flight feathers within his beak and jerked it out for Zeal then preened the feathers in the spot. As they watched, a replacement grew in.

At the altar, Zeal laid the feather on the cask, tucked the fallen star under his arm, and picked up both Addis's sword and Listina's jewelry. He conjured a casting he'd learned from *The Book of Flames* to protect him from the harmful vapors and temperature he was going to encounter then crossed through the semitransparent barrier and approached the salamander.

Setting everything on the ground beside him, he removed Listina's rod from his vest and handed it to the beast, who took it with its teeth. Zeal's voice crackled and rasped as he spoke using fire tongue. "This rod bound you to another. I give it to you. Destroy it and free yourself.

He placed a palm on the beast's face when the creature abased itself in front of him. Then the salamander jerked his head and threw the rod into the flowing red liquid. The crust that had formed during Firemyst's birth had reliquified. The rod settled lightly, floating on the Blood's surface, before bursting into flames and sinking from view.

Tulip, Tallen, and Mehrle moved closer to the barrier to watch Zeal, while Kit and Firemyst stayed in place, guarding the entrance to the cavern.

Zeal cast Addis's sword into the pool. It pierced the surface blade-first and disappeared with barely a splash, just an ever-widening ripple left. He retrieved the wafers and skipped them along the surface until they each settled and sank. So that nothing could be traced back to him or his companions, he disposed of Listina's imbued objects in the pool.

Then he knelt at the edge of the liquid, grasped the star metal in his right hand, and plunged it into the Blood. When he felt the metal begin to soften, he removed it and returned to the altar with the semi-molten sphere.

"I don't know if this altar has been used for good or ill." He placed the metal on the altar. "For now, it will serve a creative purpose." Waves of heat rose from the sphere's surface. He conjured in rapid succession, "Arumm Malleol, Arumm Malleol... Arumm Malleol."

Pounded by unseen waves of force, the semi-molten metal flowed and elongated. With a gesture, he caused half of the material to break off and float to his waiting hand, cooling it as it went. Its color dimmed from yellow to red and finally turned black as it spun in the air. Zeal placed the separated portion inside a pocket of his vest and continued to work on the balance of material left on the altar.

"Hand me the shard, please, Tulip."

He visually measured and snapped off a portion of the black crystalline material to match the length of the elongated metal, which he then placed in the center of the forming sword. The remainder was returned to his vest. As Zeal flowed the shard into the blade, the blade darkened and turned a dull shade of gray.

The weapon was shaped further by the unseen hammers he conjured. A pommel, grip, cross guard, and rain guard were extruded. The sword, cast as it was in one piece with no tang, now had added strength.

Zeal picked up Firemyst's feather from the top of the cask. The container's lid popped off and its contents rose into the air, forming into a narrow column of fluid. Iris petals floated in the clear liquid, and the noise from the invisible hammers ceased. The newly forged tool lifted from the altar and stood, pommel downward, parallel to the fluid column.

Zeal wrapped Firemyst's feather in a spiral on the grip then drew his Fang from its sheath. "Let me have your hand, please, Tulip. I am going to make a shallow cut on your palm, and then I want you to take the sword. Plunge it and your hand into the liquid to temper the weapon. I won't let its heat harm you. The weapon will become your tool to use from now on."

There was trust in Tulip's eyes as she gave him her hand. Zeal made a quick, precise cut. The Fang's edge was so sharp, Tulip didn't even react to its kiss. She fearlessly gripped the glowing weapon and quickly submerged it and her hand in the liquid. The fragrance of the iris blooms enveloped them.

Through the link, Zeal felt his heart partner with Tulip's and the beat of both their hearts increased. Tulip's pulse throbbed down her arm and flowed through her fist into the sword. Steam bloomed, momentarily obscuring her hand, then the vapor dissipated.

Zeal smiled shyly. "That is the gift I promised you would have, in celebration of leaving your apprenticeship behind and becoming a journeyman."

Tulip inspected her new sword. It was double edged, its surface subtly patterned with etched iris blooms. The fuller was black, identical in color to the material that comprised the cavern. The grip was shaped to her hand, but she couldn't see where Firemyst's feather had been wrapped on the pommel. "It is beautiful," she said, her eyes welling with emotion.

"Looks bigger than the weapon you usually carry," Tallen said. Isn't it a little long for you, Tulip?"

Tulip shook her head. "It is a bastard sword. See how the pommel is longer, so I can use it one- or two-handed with ease? I'll have more reach and therefore greater defense. And I can still wield a knife offhand, if I choose." As she swung the blade through a few practice forms, she squealed with delight.

Zeal's smile broadened. He was happy she was pleased with her gift. "The sword should be lighter, given the metal it is made of."

"You are right, Zeal. It has the weight of a long sword and is well within my comfort zone. Somehow, you've gotten the balance perfect." She tested the edge on the back of her nail. "And the thing's already sharpened!"

The long claw will make you a better hunter, Tulip.

Mehrle quipped, "You know, Zeal, I like presents, too."

Zeal answered shyly, "Mehrle, let me think on what I can create special for you."

"I don't have a sheath for this, so I'll place it in my pack. My arm would eventually tire from carrying it around."

"What are you going to call the weapon? A sword that fine deserves to have a name." Tallen glanced knowingly at his bow.

"I think I am going to call her Firestar." Tulip looked at the palm of her hand and then showed it to the others. "Zeal, the cut you made, it's healed."

"That is one of the characteristics of the sword, thanks to Firemyst's feather. The weapon can heal minor wounds you take, or at least stop you from bleeding out from a more serious one. You will have to discover, through use, its limitations. It will also burst into flame, which will not harm you, when you direct it to do so. And it will never dull."

Tulip gave Zeal a long hug and whispered her thanks into his ear. "I will use Firestar proudly and will always think of you, Kit, and Firemyst whenever I wield her."

"Zeal, did I tell you I really like presents?" Mehrle interjected.

Zeal laughed. "Yes, Mehrle. I can take a hint. Once we've returned to Havensharth, we can discuss what gift would best fit your needs. I'm ready to leave now. Gather your gear."

Mehrle picked up her pack. "What of the salamander?"

Zeal stood silent before answering, "For now, the salamander comes with us. I can't leave it to starve, and it's Listina's fault the creature is here and attacked us. We no longer have anything to fear from it, and I think it will pay heed to my guidance."

Tallen was perplexed. "I hope you don't mean to take it home. What will it do if it gets loose? You saw how dangerous it is."

"Look, everyone, I have an obligation to it. It is a creature of fire. I made a vow to help such and offer it my aid, as I did for Firemyst."

"Take the 'Save all of Sartus' expression off your face," Tulip said with a grin. "Just make sure it behaves. And the salamander had better not try to take a bite out of Templar, or I will show the creature how functional your gift really is!"

Tulip silently led them back the way they came, followed by Mehrle then Tallen, who had Firemyst lumbering behind him. Kit padded beside Zeal while the salamander undulated in the air at the rear.

* * *

As the last of the light faded from the chamber, none of them heard the words rumbled in a deep voice from the red pool on the other side of the semitransparent barrier.

"Your gifts and sacrifices are accepted. You may leave with my blessing."

* * *

Zeal waited until everyone, including Firemyst and the salamander, had crossed the boundary created by the lattice. The grille rose silently behind him, lodging into place with the sound of one large rock striking another. He then heard the three locks click, one by one, as they reset.

Pleased that the entrance to the Blood of Sartus had been left secured, he said to them all, *I think this is as far as Firemyst can go. Just ahead, the passage starts to narrow too much for him. The salamander will be fine, though, and able to travel through to the exit. I suspect this is how it and Listina entered the mountain.*

How do you propose to get Firemyst out of here? Mehrle asked.

I will take Firemyst though shadow.

It will be easier for Kit to accomplish this without the light of our globes diluting the darkness. Zeal gave Kit a hug and stroked Firemyst's neck. *We'll see you both outside. Tulip, lead on, please.*

When he looked back, the blackness rapidly engulfed the Firebird and Shadow Cat. Everyone remained linked together in battle mode as they separated, but the humans seemed uneasy.

I'm disappointed, Tallen shared.

Why is that, Tallen? Zeal asked, though he thought he knew the answer.

I wanted to witness the first meeting between the hippogriffs and Firemyst. I will now have to guess what took place.

Zeal nodded. *There may be a way Kit can help you view her

memory of the meeting, if you ask her.*

The bard didn't comment further, but he, Mehrle, and Tulip began to flag as they left the mountain. The small amount of restorative they'd ingested was losing effectiveness.

Kit and Firemyst, along with their mounts, who were in horse form, met them at the entrance, and they all rode bareback to the camp. It was a few marks before sunrise when they arrived. Zeal realized that they'd been inside the mountain much longer than he'd thought.

Once back at camp, he assessed his companions as they slid, exhausted, from their horses. Everyone was dust-covered. Tulip and Tallen's battered leathers and torn clothing were evidence of their recent conflicts. Mehrle looked relatively unscathed.

"We should eat before you rest," Zeal was surprised when the satchel opened for him of its own accord. "Get out your bed rolls while I prepare something for us."

They ate a hearty stew of chunky root vegetables and tender, succulent meat, black bread sweetened with honey and clotted cream, and hot beryl tea with berry tarts.

Their full stomachs lulled Tulip, Tallen, and Mehrle to sleep, while Kit's hunting provided for her and Firemyst. The salamander ate dead branches off nearby trees before it settled, keeping Zeal between it and the rest of the party. Zeal fed the horses grain brought from Havensharth and remained on alert.

He had consumed a larger amount of restorative and had not needed healing, so, with Kit's help, he kept watch and allowed the others to sleep and recover. Kit, in hiding size, curled next to him while Firemyst roosted on the ground on Zeal's right, warming the air around them.

At their current elevation, the air temperature was cool. Sparse clouds drifted lazily in the sky above while intermittent puffs of wind stirred the leaves. The night was quiet, but not unnaturally so.

He removed a pair of small clothes from his pack. When he put them on, he didn't feel as breezy under his workshirt any longer. Taking out *The Book of Flames*, he reviewed its information on salamanders, sharing aloud with Kit and Firemyst.

"You can come closer," he said to the salamander. "No one here is going to hurt you."

The salamander stayed put.

"The book states you are from the Terrene of Fire. You require a heat source to remain comfortable, and if one is not available, you have to feed continuously to fuel yourself. You consume minerals and any combustibles." He glanced at Firemyst. "Firemyst, you looked puzzled. Combustible means basically anything that burns. Apparently, there are male and females of your species. The females have a forked tongue."

The salamander leaned forward slightly and opened its mouth, cautiously sliding out its tongue.

"Your tongue is forked! You are a girl salamander. Do you have a name?" Zeal asked quietly.

When the salamander spoke, her words crackled, popped, and snapped like the sounds of damp wood burning. "I was taken when young, along with the one who became my mate. Once enslaved by the rod's maker, we lost all choice. We served. I have no name. Now what is to become of me?"

"If it pleases you, do you mind if I give you a name?"

The salamander gave what Zeal interpreted as a shrug.

"Shalie. Would Shalie be an acceptable name for you to take?"

The salamander nodded once in acceptance, her eyes welling with moisture. When one tear dropped to the ground, the dry vegetation and soil smoked and blackened at its touch.

Shalie's head slumped down. "Why should I believe you? The eater of my mate may well desire to feast on me."

Zeal looked over to Firemyst, who answered, "I will not eat you."

Zeal placed his hand on Firemyst. "Firemyst is not at fault. You and your mate were attacking us. Firemyst acted as he did to prevent my companion's death. I was informed by Kit after the combat ended that you were compelled to follow Listina's orders, by the Rod of Control she wielded."

"Because of you, the rod is destroyed," Shalie admitted. "I am free to do as I will and go where I wish."

"I am Zeal, and this is Kit. You know Firemyst's name. The sleeping ones, who are of my kind, are Mehrle, Tulip, and Tallen. The four other creatures here are Hunter, Strider, Striker, and Templar. You are safe with us and will not be forced to do anyone else's bidding."

Hunter, Strider, Templar, and Striker know not to fear Firemyst and Shalie.

The horses still kept a cautious eye on Shalie and Firemyst whenever one of them came close. "Firemyst, how was your journey through shadow?"

"Not like," the Firebird replied. "Too akin to life inside egg before birth."

Zeal quickly gathered dead wood that Shalie hadn't consumed and used a mote of inner flame to ignite it. "This will help ward off a little of the evening chill. It will be warmer if you come nearer."

Shalie cautiously undulated closer to the fire. "I know not what to do. I don't belong here and don't know where I belong."

Zeal desired to reach out and touch Shalie, to comfort her, but he held back. "What do you wish? I don't know how, but I will try to help you. If I can, I will endeavor to return you to your Terrene."

Shalie stared intently at Zeal for several long moments. "I will stay with you for now. Your words carry heat."

Kit huffed. **Has the Pride grown then?**

"Yes, I guess it has. Firemyst, do you need anything? *The Book of Flames* doesn't tell me how to care for a Firebird chick. But you should be a lot smaller, according to the information given. You are already the size of an adult, and you were just born. The Blood of Sartus must have caused you to mature physically, but I doubt you were given a life's worth of experience."

Shalie leaned closer. "It is true that Firemyst is newly from the egg?"

Firemyst fluffed his feathers. "Yes, I am. I have much to learn about myself and the Terrene we are in. Zeal and Kit have vowed to teach, protect, and help me grow. If not for them, I would have died in the egg, unborn."

"Kit and I only did what was right."

Firemyst shifted closer, and their bodies touched.

Zeal continued to read the book out loud. "Apparently, a mature firebird can morph into a flame form. I wonder if that would allow you to pass through places you normally wouldn't be able to. Would you like to try to turn into flame? It might make it easier for you to fly."

Firemyst shook his head. "I am not ready. I will know when the moment is right."

Zeal nodded. "A Firebird can regenerate, which you already demonstrated, and is capable of healing from all but a fatal injury. You can heal others, if you wish, even those not of your kind. If you meet death, you are capable of being born again and will retain all prior knowledge."

Firemyst seemed to shrug: his head dipped, his neck drew inward, and his wings rose slightly above his shoulders. "This is my first birth, as you call it. I have no other—how you put it?—prior knowledge to use."

"Both you and Shalie need to learn how to live amongst my kind. Well, Kit, I guess we are all going back to Havensharth. Now what do I do?"

Ask one called Deena.

Zeal's ring of communication was still on his finger despite all he'd been through in the Blood. He must have unknowingly protected it, so he turned the stone palmward and concentrated.

Deena? He waited several heartbeats and repeated the call. *Deena?*

Zeal! How are my two dear ones and the rest of your companions doing? I had hoped to hear from you both. I was sleeping and thought I'd dreamed you were talking me!

Along with Kit, Zeal felt Deena's love for them pulse through the ring. *We are all well. Tallen, Tulip, and Mehrle are sleeping.*

We had our tails twisted, but they are all straight now.

Zeal started to explain but was interrupted by Deena.

I understood Kit. You had some difficulty and now are fine. Take your time, and give me the short version. What has happened with Firemyst?

With Kit's help, Zeal, recounted the events of the past sun but

JAMES D. MACON

did not elaborate on his own change.

Deena was silent for several moments. *I am saddened by the loss of life. Listina was a troubled child and forged her own shackles. Addis will be missed. He had worth. What is done was needed. Don't chain them to you. Let them go. Their Mentors are responsible for the events that have transpired. You are not at fault.*

Deena's words released the last guilt Zeal carried and lifted the burden off his shoulders.

Zeal, what are your plans?

I'll see how the others are doing when they awaken, and we will start home as soon as we can. He looked forward to returning to Havensharth.

You don't need to make a long trip home. Kit, haven't you seen a Threshold Circle conjured?

Yes. I understand what you wish but have not done.

She and Deena explained the conjure to Zeal. He was excited by this new knowledge. *The circle will enable us to return much sooner than I expected.*

Why don't you all rest where you are, and we can attempt the conjure two marks after sunset. I'll contact you beforehand and help you and Kit complete the casting. The Casting Quad is a good target. Ice, Mirada, Greyhook, Namrin, and I will meet you there. We'll shroud the Quad so your return is kept private. I'll prepare a means to manage Firemyst's and Shalie's introduction to Havensharth. From what you both have told me and the images I received from Kit, I think it would be best to hide what they are in plain sight, as we have done with her. Deena sent them her love.

Thank you, Deena. Zeal felt Deena's absence as their connection through the Rings of Communication ended.

CHAPTER THIRTY-EIGHT

THE SUN HAD BEEN up for several marks before the sleeping trio began to awaken. They'd rested soundly and recovered from their healings. Zeal had already attended to himself and the horses, while Kit had acquired a meal for her and Firemyst. Birds called to each other in the trees but stayed hidden from view. Shalie foraged for fuel to consume.

During their rest, Shalie had drawn warmth and sustenance through physical contact with Zeal, so she hadn't felt the need to constantly feed. His seemingly infinite inner source of flame replenished itself as long as part of his exposed skin was in contact with the ground. The bit of his fiery reserves Shalie absorbed felt insignificant to him.

Zeal spent several marks during the night contemplating this new insight and wondering about his limitations. The effects of the restorative were wearing off, and he was beginning to tire. He would need to rest before long.

Tulip was the first to rouse. Zeal handed her a cup of tea and bread from the satchel. "Here. Have something to eat and drink. How are you this morn?"

"Not as exhausted as I would have expected. I need to find out what Qwen puts in his restorative." She tucked into the food. "You look tired. I bet you stayed up and kept watch."

"You would win that bet. I wasn't sleepy, and the three of you really needed the rest."

Shalie was curled around the fire, absorbing heat, while Firemyst and Kit were communing with the horses. Firemyst appeared keenly interested in a pair of marlets that were flying around the camp.

"You have any more of that food?" Tallen sat up and rubbed the sleep from his eyes.

Mehrle grumbled, "I might as well get up, too. My bladder won't let me sleep, and you all are too noisy."

Tulip gave her a hand up. "Let's go for a short walk. Zeal will have food ready when we return." They strolled away into the trees.

Zeal prepared breakfast for Tallen. "Here you go, my friend."

Tallen chewed as he spoke. "Before you ask, other than needing more sleep, I'm fine."

When Tulip and Mehrle returned, everyone ate and drank their fill. Then Zeal said, "Folks, I want to you introduce you to Shalie. I've decided she is definitely accompanying us to Havensharth."

Shalie raised her head and watched the party closely.

Tallen choked on a piece of the meat. Mehrle pounded on his back as he blurted out, "Are you serious? If I remember correctly, Shalie tried to chew off my arm. Can it— I mean, can she be trusted?"

"She can. If you won't take my word alone, ask Kit."

Shalie is now Pride.

Tallen shook his head. "Okay, fine. But I plan to keep an eye on our salamander the whole way back to Havensharth."

Mehrle nodded agreement. "How do you know Shalie is a she? I like her name, by the way."

Tulip laughed. "I know the answer to your question. Zeal read it in a book."

He smiled. "I did indeed. Shalie, Firemyst, Kit, and I had a lengthy discussion while you three were sleeping. Since Shalie is no longer dominated by Listina's rod, she is her own salamander, so to speak." He explained to Shalie why they were all talking about her and added more wood to the flames for her comfort. She'd coiled her body more tightly in the coals of their fire. "Kit, would you please help me include Shalie and Firemyst in our discussion?"

I will. But she and Firemyst continued their private meeting with the horses.

Mehrle was gripped by a vicious yawn then said, "So, we hold here the remainder of this sun and head out the next sunrise? I admit, I am not looking forward to the long flight to Havensharth."

"Perhaps we should use the rod that enables Templar and the others to travel faster to get us back quickly," Tulip suggested. "We've discovered safe places to stop on the way."

Zeal tried to sound nonchalant. "Or, we rest for now and arrive in Havensharth two marks after darkfall." The grin on his face finally erupted fully. "I talked with Deena while you all slept. She and Kit know a conjure that will take us all home."

Tallen was not the only one with surprise on his face. "You mean without several suns of travel?"

"Yes. It is a different way to step from one place to another," Zeal explained.

Mehrle looked thoughtful. "Why didn't we travel here in the same manner you intend to take us to Havensharth?"

One must know the place you go to before you conjure.

"Thanks, Kit. Since neither she nor I had ever been here physically, we couldn't conjure to this location. And think of all the fun we would have missed, not to mention the story Tallen wouldn't have to tell!"

Tulip quietly chuckled. "I could have missed the painful parts, thank you very much. Mehrle, why don't you and Tallen get more rest. Zeal and Kit should, as well. I'll keep watch, since I'm not tired, and I'll awaken you well before nightfall. Sooner, if needed."

Zeal built up the fire for Shalie before crawling into his sleep sack, where Kit soon joined him. Tallen and Mehrle had already drifted off.

Exhausted emotionally and physically, Zeal closed his eyes and soon dreamed.

* * *

It was a still-tired Zeal who was later awakened by Tulip. "How long did you let me sleep?" he asked.

Tulip handed him a cup of hot tea. "For six marks. We will lose light in a mark. The sun has already dropped below the treetops. I think we should wake the others, tidy up camp, and eat before we travel."

Zeal pulled the satchel from his pack. "Good planning. You wake the others, and I'll see what the satchel has planned for us."

Tulip chuckled. "You make it sound as if it has a life of its own."

"It just might."

"You want me to wake up Kit?" Tulip asked more seriously.

"No. Let her keep her eyes closed. She is not sleeping. She is fast a cat and only pretending to be asleep."

Kit opened one eye and stuck her tongue out at them both before closing her eye and tucking her nose under her tail.

Inside the satchel were two trenchers of scraud, one piled high with raw filets. The other had steaming pieces that had been battered and fried in light oil. There was also a sweet-and-sour dipping sauce and a fresh, mixed-green salad tossed with a beryl-berry vinaigrette dressing. Dessert was bread pudding covered with a spiced mead sauce. There was even a bag full of mixed coal and coke, for Shalie. How did Qwen know about Shalie? Zeal wondered.

After the meal was consumed, they packed camp rapidly, and then Tallen walked around the site, replacing any stones they had disturbed, and picking up pieces of trash, disposing of them in the fire. Tallen believed strongly that, when you abandoned a location, no one should be able to tell you had stayed there.

It was Tulip who broached the inevitable subject of what folks planned to do after they all returned to Havensharth.

Mehrle was the first to answer, saying, "Well, I should report to Lady Phyllis. It might not be a bad idea for you two to do the same." She gestured to Zeal and Tulip. "Then, I go back to Arlanda and enlighten Master Slag. I am sure Qwen will want to know what occurred on our journey, as well."

Tulip nodded. "I, for one, wouldn't mind if you stayed in Havensharth for a bit. Do you continue to plan on joining Master

Turk's Set? Or have you decided to do something else?"

Zeal was fully aware that he and Tulip both had enjoyed Mehrle's company.

"Yes, I will. Our recent adventure has let me know I am not ready to fly on my own, so to speak. I need more experience and training. What say you, Tallen?"

"I'll compose a ballad of our journey. Some things will need leaving out or changed. Of course, I plan to give a full report to Master Greyhook. I am sure he'll want to know of Addis, Listina, and the burial mound. Then I will resume my studies and hope I'm elevated to journeyman."

Zeal placed a hand on Tallen's shoulder. "Tallen, you need not worry. From what you have demonstrated on this quest, you more than qualify to leave apprenticeship behind. You'll see."

Tulip socked Tallen in the shoulder. "Mehrle and I both agree with Zeal. If not, Masters Greyhook and Gennis will receive a piece of my mind."

Mehrle asked her, "What do you plan to do?"

"Same as Tallen. Resume my training, even though, every sun I train, I will be reminded of Addis. It pains me I can't ever tell Master Cowlin what became of his favorite student." Tears began to roll down her face.

One by one, they embraced her while she quietly wept. Kit joined them together in battle mind. No one was allowed to feel alone. Together, they had experienced physical and emotional trauma, the highs and lows of battle, the support of friendship, and death.

Zeal relayed what Deena had earlier impressed upon him regarding where the true fault lay with Addis's death. Tulip took heart from his words and even laughed when Templar trotted over, nuzzled her hair, and offered his share of comfort.

After Tulip recovered, all eyes turned toward Zeal, so he could tell them his plans. "I was hoping we would have this discussion after we were back in Havensharth and I'd had a chance to manage the disagreeableness I expect to encounter on our return. First off, Shalie and Firemyst need coaching on how to coexist with our kind.

Next, I have a door to open."

"True," Tallen said with a grin. "They will stand out like a lightning-struck tree in an orchard after a stormy night."

Zeal joined everyone in a laugh. "It is as you say, Tallen. But Deena is working on a solution. Likely, we will hide their nature in plain sight, as we have Kit's."

"You know we'll all be there to help," Tallen said. "You won't be alone."

Mehrle laid her hand on Zeal's arm. "If you need me, I can get to you from Arlanda pretty quickly."

Zeal turned away so no one could see his face as he reined in his emotions. "I know I can count on all of you. I am fortunate that Kit and I have you as part of our Pride."

"What do you mean you have a door to open?" Mehrle asked.

"Yes, what is so important about this door?" Tallen added. "Might we have more adventure coming our way?"

"I don't recall you mentioning a door when you first showed me Firemyst's egg," Tulip said.

"I was so focused on Firemyst, I didn't even think of telling you about the door back then. When Kit and I found Firemyst's egg, it was on the floor in front of a tapestry hanging on the wall. The door was hidden behind the tapestry. From the moment I discovered it, I've had a strong need to open it. Helping Firemyst was Kit's and my priority, so the door has remained uninvestigated."

Mehrle asked, "Speaking of you, Kit, what do you plan?"

Hunt the knowledge of healing conjure. My Pride seems to frequently step on thorns. Zeal, I sense a need to go see Mother. She has a worry.

Zeal knew he and Kit were due for a visit to Arlanda. Perhaps they could provide transport for Mehrle and return to Arlanda with her. It would be so nice to see Mother Essmee, Iris, Lady Izlan, and the rest of Trade Apprentices. He sent to Kit, *I will go with you to see about Mother Essmee's worry, if you wish.*

I would like it if you do, she said to him alone.

They all chatted in kind with one another while they finished gathering their belongings and packing the horses. "Kit and I are in contact with Deena," Zeal announced. "We are leaving soon."

Everyone grew quiet while Zeal, with Deena and Kit's help, conjured, "Resig Limenn Cincul Casting Quad."

He used flame, of course, and created a Threshold Circle made of fire in the air. It resembled an enlarged flaming hoop that acrobats jump through on a dare. Two of the horses, ridden by their riders, could pass through the Circle side by side. It floated in the air, half a hand above the ground, with the Casting Quad seen through the opening.

Waiting for them there were Masters Ice, Greyhook, and Namrin, along with Ladies Deena, Mirada, and Phyllis.

Kit sent the horses through first and then, in hiding size, followed them. Under her direction, the animals didn't hesitate. Firemyst walked through behind her. Once on the other side, Firemyst turned back to Zeal and the others.

"I will go last," Zeal said, sweeping his arm forward to usher Tulip and Merle through. They linked arms with Tallen and the three stepped through together. Then Zeal took one last look around and entered the Casting Quad with Shalie undulating through the air beside him. Other than feeling a warm, tingling sensation on his skin, his crossing the threshold seemed just like moving through an open doorway.

Zeal was excited to return home yet anxious. What would be the consequence of his actions?

He released his conjure, and the Threshold Circle disappeared as if it had never existed.

CHAPTER THIRTY-NINE

DEENA WAITED, hand-in-hand with Ice, for the young ones to return. She, Ice, and the other Mentors were gathered in the Casting Quad, which had been shrouded and locked down to prevent anyone else from stumbling in on the reunion. Deena had given Zeal and Kit specific instructions for how to open a Threshold Circle under the Quad's current conditions.

She and Ice had been surprised when Lady Phyllis knocked on their door while they supped. She had sat down to eat, as if invited, and informed them she would accompany them to meet with the travelers, when they arrived. When asked how she knew of their plans, her only reply was she had received a missive from Slag.

Deena wished Lady Phyllis had contacted her sooner; she would have worried a bit less about Zeal's, Kit's, and the others' safe return.

When the Circle opened, Ice whispered to Deena, "You can stop trying to squeeze my hand off, love."

She mouthed, "Sorry," and gave Kit a mental hug when the Shadow Cat entered the Quad. The large, striking raptor alongside her could only be Firemyst. Deena was immediately curious and desired to touch him, yet resisted the impulse. She was sure his wingspan would be impressive—a handsome firebird he was, indeed. How excellent that Zeal had aided Firemyst and ensured his birth.

The beat of Deena's heart sped when Tallen, Tulip, and Mehrle crossed through the Circle. She was sure her heart skipped when

Zeal stepped into the Quad, accompanied by what could only be Shalie.

Clearly, Zeal had undergone a mystical change: he hadn't been away long enough for his body to have matured to this degree. Gone was her little boy; a barefoot young man missing his pants had somehow replaced him. He was easily as tall as Ice, and maybe a little bit more. And Zeal had muscles: he had the body of a warrior Apprentice and the carriage of an acrobat. Also, his skin was sun-touched.

Her eyes were drawn to Shalie as the Circle closed. She had never before seen a salamander. The red, serpentine creature undulated in the air alongside Zeal had the appearance of an incredibly large slug without eyestalks. Shalie's gaze darted over the people and surroundings, and she sensed the area with her tongue. Her vocalizations to Zeal reminded Deena of the crackle of logs in the hearth.

She wasn't sure who made the first move, but suddenly she had her arms wrapped around both her lost lambs. Tulip was simultaneously embraced by Mirada, Mehrle by Phyllis, and Tallen by Greyhook, who proceeded to pull Tallen into a shared hug with Tulip and Mirada. Ice tried to wrap his arms around Zeal, Kit, and her all at once. Soon, Firemyst, Shalie, and the horses had joined themselves together to form a protective circle around them all.

Sounds of welcome were exchanged, some more privately then others. "I am so happy to see you both," Zeal whispered to her and Ice.

"Ice and I missed you and Kit, as well." Deena felt Ice's arms tighten around her and Zeal. "We are grateful you are all home safe."

"Deena updated me on your progress after every communication you had with her," Ice added. "We shared your reports with Mirada, Greyhook, and Namrin. We've agreed to let Tallen and Greyhook decide what to share with Master Gennis."

"I am sorry I worried you both," Zeal said contritely. "We confirmed, if we had waited, it would have been too late to save Firemyst. I will take whatever punishment you elect to give me.

Blame me, not Tallen or Tulip."

Deena gently cupped Zeal's face in her hands. "Ice and I have discussed this with Mirada and Greyhook. We understood the importance of your actions on behalf of Firemyst. You did the right thing. Now I have to do something about Shalie and Firemyst."

She let go of her charges and conjured, "Adjo Par Adprehin." When next she spoke, both Shalie and Firemyst understood her words. She then addressed everyone present.

"Size does matter, as we learned with Kit. Firemyst and Shalie need to appear less menacing. I shall make them both appear smaller than they are." She pulled two chains from a pouch belted at her waist. They were comprised of metals in a mixture of dark hues braided together, similar to a child's hair. One had a small blue crystal encased in a mounting and attached by a bezel.

She held this chain up for Shalie to see. "Worn, this will enable you to shrink to the size of a bracer. It will shroud you from sight when you desire. I know you have been mistreated, Shalie. No one here will tolerate such abuse to you or any other entity." Deena held the second chain for Firemyst to examine. "A raptor that is comparable to Kit in her hiding size is still an impressive creature. I would not insult you by making you as small as songbird. Zeal wants you both to learn more about our kind, but to do so, you'll need to be able to interact with us and see us for what we really are."

Firemyst nodded and extended his head forward. Deena fastened his chain around his neck, with Shalie closely observing Deena's every move.

"Use your intent and you will become much smaller," Deena instructed.

The Firebird shrunk in stages till he matched Kit's size. She approached and stood nose-to-beak with him. They appeared to be intently discussing some concern.

Zeal knelt and lifted Firemyst from the ground. Firemyst suddenly burst into flame, the ends of his feathers rippling with light. Zeal flung him upward. Launched into the air, Firemyst's wings beat strongly and he flew four times around the Quad, awing everyone present, before landing on Zeal's extended arm.

"Firemyst, even in this reduced state, you still weigh almost a stone!" Zeal exclaimed. Firemyst changed from his flaming to his feathered form. "You are quite handsome, fiery or not. How was your first flight?"

"I will fly more, and Kit insists on teaching me to hunt." Firemyst adjusted a flight feather with his beak.

Lady Phyllis stepped forward to get a closer look at the firebird. "What was that all about?"

Firemyst wanting to fly. Kit gave Phyllis a toothy grin.

Phyllis stepped back with a wary eye focused on Kit. "I always suspected there was something different about you, due to Zeal's and your relationship. We need to have a long talk."

You need to have a listen, Kit replied.

Deena almost missed Zeal's slight nod to Lady Phyllis in acknowledgment of the subtle order. "Firemyst, because of his size, inexperience, and the lack of space where we were in the wood, has never attempted to use his wings. Kit felt, since we were in the Quad, that now was the right moment for him to try. Firemyst has studied birds in flight and discussed the subject with our mounts. Heat rises. I thought, if he was in flame form, it would be easier for him to take to the air. It worked." Zeal grinned.

"I am happy for your success." Deena turned from Firemyst to Shalie., "The person who places this on you will still be able see you." She handed the chain to Zeal.

Zeal placed Firemyst on his shoulder and called the quest members to gather close. "Then, with Shalie's permission, we will put the chain on her together. I'll keep her natural hotness from hurting anyone."

Shalie backed away, her eyes open wide with fear. "Why should I let you ensnare me again?"

Zeal bowed and knelt before her. "You have my promise this is no trap. I held the rod in my hand and gave it to you. Do my words still carry heat?"

Shalie slowly moved forward and put her head against Zeal's. "Yes. Place it while I can allow you to do so."

Mehrle, Tallen, Tulip, and Deena gathered close to Zeal so they could simultaneously touch the chain. Firemyst, on Zeal's shoulder, grabbed a link with his beak. Kit conjured, "Suvolo," levitated into the air, and hooked a claw in a loop.

Deena appreciated the courage Shalie demonstrated. The salamander trembled when Zeal fastened the chain around her neck. To everyone else in the room, Shalie disappeared from view. Encouraged by Zeal, she shrank to the size of a bracer and wrapped herself around his wrist.

"I feel no compulsion," Shalie said surprised.

"Not all my kind are like Listina or the one who bound you with the Rod of Control. We sincerely wish to help you." Deena placed her monocle on her eye, so she could see the salamander. "Ice, you and Greyhook take the horses to the stable while the rest of us go to our place. I'll start feeding everyone. I promise you won't miss anything. Discussion can wait till we are all together."

Deena's man jumped to do her biding for once without pause and led the horses to the Quad's entrance. She gestured and softly spoke the words that dropped the Casting Quad's shroud and protections. Finally feeling at peace, she gathered Kit in one arm and took Zeal by the hand.

* * *

Zeal sat on the floor at Deena's feet. Kit was in Deena's lap, happily enjoying the attention. Deena hadn't let either of them stray very far, and Zeal desired to be close to her and Ice.

It is good to be home, Kit mindspoke to Zeal alone.

Yes, it is, Zeal sent back.

He allowed Tallen, Tulip, and Mehrle to tell the tale of their adventure, starting with their first night's stay and their meeting with the forces of Mendor and Dearney. Then Tallen and Tulip enacted the Mendorian Saga for everyone.

Greyhook's eyes danced. "You should perform the Saga as part of the Ceremonies of Advancement. They are in two days. I am happy you arrived in time to participate."

"Tallen and Tulip will still become journeymen?" Zeal quietly asked.

"But of course. If there was any question of their competence, they have proved through your travels they are qualified." Greyhook looked to the other Mentors, who nodded in agreement.

Zeal closed his eyes and sighed with relief. Apparently, he had not ruined his friends' chance for success.

"We will have a word with Masters Gennis and Cowlin in the morn." Greyhook added. "But I really don't see a problem."

Zeal, Mehrle, Tallen, and Tulip smiled broadly at each other. Kit joined them in battle mind.

Told you everything would be fine. Tulip winked at Zeal.

Zeal always found a way to worm us out of trouble when we were younger. Nice to see some things never change, Mehrle added, amused.

Oh! Tallen exclaimed. *I forgot. We haven't gotten to the part about the gifts we received. I need to show Master Greyhook the bone flute.* He relayed everything about their discovery of the items on the morning after their encounter with the forces of Dearney and Mendor, and then he retrieved the flute from the bone case in his pack and held it for Greyhook to examine.

Greyhook visually inspected the flute. "It is made from a thigh bone. Have you played it yet?"

Tallen shook his head. "I haven't and I am not sure I want to. I thought it best to consult with you all first."

"May I?" Deena put on the gloves she wore when she worked with imbued objects. Tallen placed the flute in her waiting hands.

Ice and Namrin gathered around her. Deena used her monocle to inspect the object while Namrin placed his gazers on his nose. Ice conjured, "Praesen Adspectis," and leaned in for a closer look. They huddled over the flute, conjured intermittently in whispers, and held a quiet discussion for almost half a mark before Deena handed the instrument back to Tallen.

Kit used her keen hearing in an attempt to learn the elements of the conjures used by the three Master Practitioners, to Zeal's amusement. Her tail and ears twitched as she placed the gestures needed to conjure the castings into her memory.

We could just ask Deena to teach us, you know, Zeal reminded her.

We should. We will. Until then, a hunter always observes and learns the ways of another predator.

Deena handed the case to Ice and Namrin, for them to evaluate. "Tallen, the flute is imbued and not cursed. However, it can only be played by one musician, and that musician is you. Anyone else who attempts to play it may be injured. The flute somehow determines who gets hurt and by how much."

"You mean, if a child who didn't know any better tried to use the flute, she would remain unharmed, but someone with intent to steal or misuse the instrument would be punished?" Mirada asked.

"We don't know. It may be as you suggest. There is more, but neither, Ice, Namrin, nor I could pierce the item's remaining secrets. Tallen, you'll have to learn the secrets for yourself."

Zeal had a sudden thought. "I know where he should play the flute."

"Where is that?" Tallen asked.

"The crypt in the Repository. Play for the Masters resting there."

Greyhook spoke up quickly. "Hold on. I offer no disrespect. But Zeal, you want Tallen to give a concert using an imbued instrument given to him by the spirits of the dead, at the burial site of some of the most powerful Practitioners ever known, without foreknowledge of what will happen? Anyone else see a potential problem with this suggestion?"

Deena laughed. "Zeal was right about Firemyst. Don't say no for now, and we will think more on his idea." She caught Zeal's eye.

"Okay," Zeal agreed. "I promise Kit and I will not sneak Tallen in to play music in the crypt behind your backs."

Why not play the flute someplace safe, such as out in the woods or in the Casting Quad? Kit mindspoke to everyone.

"Good idea, Kit." Greyhook lightly touched the flute Tallen held in his hands. "I want to be in attendance when you first use the flute, and I am sure Master Gennis will, as well."

Namrin cleared his throat. "I'm sure *everyone* present desires to hear Tallen play his flute."

"Why isn't Master Gennis here with us now?" Phyllis enquired. "He was notably absent from the Casting Quad to greet Tallen on his return."

Zeal spoke up. "Master Gennis doesn't know about Kit."

Deena gave Lady Phyllis a discerning look. "Not only Kit. You see, Ice and I suggested to Greyhook and Namrin that the fewer who knew the details regarding Shalie and Firemyst, the better. I am aware that acquisition of information is part of your trade, but you were already an active participant, having aided in the quest to help Firemyst."

Phyllis nodded acceptance. "Thanks for the clarification."

Ice set the bone case next to Tallen's pack. "The case is imbued and is, for the most, part impervious to damage. It will keep safe anything put inside it, including the flute. Show us the other items you all received."

Tallen, Tulip, and Mehrle showed the adults their bracelets.

Zeal spoke up, "Kit wears one as well. They're unable to take them off."

"What do you mean you can't take them off?" Mirada held Tulips arm to the light for a closer inspection.

Deena conjured over Mehrle's wrist, "Esser Gomet Tius Piscondi." "Removing them will destroy the imbued properties encased in these items. I believe the conjures placed on the bracelets are not intended to endanger but rather to aid the wearer. Each one is linked to an individual recipient."

"We were indeed helped by having them," Tallen confirmed. "I don't want mine removed." His fellow travelers all agreed they wanted to keep their gift.

Tulip passed around the bone long dagger, Fate, so it could be perused. No new abilities were identified for it or the bracelets.

Tallen finished presenting the events of their travel, showing how he had truly developed his bardic skills. Zeal found he could close his eyes and relive their journey through the storytelling, including the risks and costs.

"Zeal," Deena said gently, "tell us what happened during Firemyst's birth. We have heard from Tulip, Mehrle, Tallen, but not from you and Kit."

"I was caught in the middle, linked with Kit in Marhdah, so I helped sustain the shield Kit formed to protect her, Tulip, Tallen, and Mehrle. Kit assisted me as I struggled to support Firemyst, and she and Firemyst joined together to keep me from being consumed by the Blood of Sartus. The Blood made changes in me, as it did to Firemyst. Then, when he escaped the pool, the Blood solidified over us, and I turned my attention to the battle with Listina. I placed a shroud over Firemyst and myself. He lent Kit and me his strength through the connection between us, and then he and I joined the fight."

Deena bowed to the Firebird. "Thank you for helping bring back our loved ones. I am in your debt." Deena's voice was husky with emotion. To the salamander, she said, "I am sorry you had to lose someone close to you, Shalie."

Zeal looked around for her. The salamander was in her reduced form, basking in the flames of the hearth, at a comfortable vantage point to study all the beings around her.

Mirada wrapped her arms around Tulip's neck and shoulders. "Yes, we are all thankful."

Namrin said solemnly, "You all have been touched by the actions you were forced to take. Ending a person's life, no matter the reason, marks you. I take full responsibility for the deaths due to my inability to see Listina for who she really was. My office is always open, if any of you feel the need to talk."

Kit jumped back to her spot in Deena's lap and rubbed her face against Deena's hand. *We are hunters who seek prey together. The Pride will be fed.*

"Kit, I understand you feel you will always be successful in your adventures and return home safe. But mothers will always worry for their cubs, no matter if they are grown up or not. Now, finish your tale." Deena blew her nose on a cloth Ice handed her then tucked it up her sleeve.

Firemyst bobbed his head, speaking with his crackle. "We were saved by helping each other. That is a lesson I learned from Kit and Zeal."

Tallen finished his recitation with their stepping through the Circle into the Casting Quad. Greyhook disappeared into Deena's kitchen. He placed a mixing bowl and flour canister on the counter. "Namrin and I will handle any enquiries regarding Listina and Addis. They are no longer your concern."

Tulip handed Firestar to Mirada. "Zeal, would you come over here?"

Zeal did so without saying anything.

"This is a remarkable weapon, Zeal," Mirada remarked. "Who taught you to forge metal?"

"I learned from Master Brost. The sword, for the most part, made itself. All I did was help it along and let it know what Tulip needed. Fortunately, I had everything at hand to accomplish the task." He stood shyly as Mirada examined the weapon and Tulip described Firestar's qualities.

Mirada handed Firestar back to Tulip. "Do you plan to create anything else in the near future? I would like to observe, if you don't mind."

Tulip laughed quietly. "Yes, he does! He promised to make something for Mehrle."

Zeal took a deep breath and let it out slowly. He had promised, hadn't he? Just then, the door opened and Charese entered, breathless. She must have run clear across Havensharth.

"Come quick!" Charese said with a huff. "It's the horses."

"The horses? What is wrong with the horses?" Greyhook asked calmly, while adding butter to the bowl. "They were fine when Ice and I put them away."

"One of the stable boys must have heard you and decided to investigate. He found the horses returned and ran to our place to inform Papa, who decided to take a look for himself. I followed Papa to the stable, because I also wanted to know if you'd returned. When we got there, the horses were awake, agitated, and kicking their stalls. I knew something was wrong." While still animated, her breathing began to settle as she spoke.

"What did you see?" Mehrle asked.

"Papa went straight to Hunter's stall. When he opened the gate, what came out was not a horse. It was a creature with wings!"

Zeal smiled and looked at Kit, who sat regally in Deena's lap, her ear tufts erect. "Kit, what did you do?"

Only what they requested of me. Hunter and the others are Pride and enjoy flying. I added Permanence and Control when I conjured them to hippogriff.

"That is why we were met by horses outside the mountain instead of hippogriffs!" Tulip exclaimed. "I wondered about that. I thought maybe you had changed them back while you were waiting for us."

Deena laughed and gave Kit a kiss. "So now Hunter and the others can choose to go between hippogriff and horse form whenever they desire? Poor Cowlin. I doubt he will want to ride a hippogriff."

"Papa didn't know I was there. He was quite upset, and by the language I heard him use, I have to agree with your assessment," Charese informed them.

Deena gave Kit one last squeeze before setting her on her paws. "Well done, dear one. Ice, Namrin, Greyhook, shall we go take care of this problem before Cowlin does something he will regret?"

Charese led the way to the stables.

I agree with Deena, Zeal told Kit. *Nice.*

Horses did ask.

Zeal felt Kit smile to him in return.

EPILOGUE

BROST FINISHED CLEANING the clinker from his forge. Attending the celebration for the newly made Journeymen and Masters had put him behind in his work.

He'd loved the performances given by the bards. The young man who'd played both pipes and a flute, seen only by his shadow cast on the curtain, had left the whole of Havensharth stunned. The journeyman bard had stepped from behind the curtain, bowed, and walked off the stage before Brost and the audience had realized the performance was completed. The lad had talent.

Brost's father had been a butcher. Brost thought the flute's shape, cast on the curtain, resembled a bone of some kind. Maybe he should take an apprentice, he was thinking to himself, when there was a soft knock on the door. Moments after, it was quietly opened.

"Master Brost, I have someone I would like you to meet. We would like to make use of your forge."

It was the lad, Zeal. He had his pet with him and was accompanied by the Ladies Mirada and Deena.

Brost's interest was piqued. "Of course. I know who you bring with you. Welcome. Now what can I help you with tonight?"

"Zeal needs to make a weapon, and we've come to help," Deena answered.

Mirada chuckled. "No, *you've* come to help. I just want to observe."

Brost recognized the metal Zeal pulled from inside his vest.

Studying the lad, he noted how Zeal had changed physically, matured, and put on muscle. It was almost as if he had spent a few seasons working at a forge. What had happened to him during his journey with his mates?

"Zeal, you know I can't work star metal."

Mirada smiled. "But Zeal can."

Coming Soon
Book 3 in *The Phosfire Journeys* series:
Opener of Doors

PLEASE ENJOY THIS SNEAK PREVIEW OF *OPENER OF DOORS*

THE STREETS OF ARLANDA had mostly emptied with the coming of night. Darkness was held at bay by lanterns at the entrances to buildings that illuminated portions of the roads and walkways. Arlanda didn't feel as familiar as it had when, as a Trade apprentice, Zeal had claimed the city as his own.

He repositioned Kit, in her hiding size, across his shoulders and waited while she distributed her weight evenly and made herself comfortable. He smiled when she rubbed her face against his before giving him a playful nip on his ear. She was just trying to lift his spirits. Not being able to come up with a plan to help Master Feneas and Kit's mother, Essmee, had left him frustrated.

I am hungry.

"We'll find food after our meeting with Master Slag. I think you can wait that long."

Tulip reached up and scratched Kit under the chin. "I have a little smoked diddle duck in my pouch. You can have it, if Zeal is neglecting you."

"Don't encourage her. Kit hunted this morn before we left Havensharth. I'm thinking she has a desire for scraud."

One who loved me would feed me scraud.

Kit's first taste of the delectable fish had been her reward from the captain of the *White Swan,* after she had rid the ship of its vermin. "I'll take you to the wharf," he said, "and buy the biggest fish they have before we go back to Havensharth. Now what do you have to say?"

As you should.

"She has told you, Mouse. If I recall correctly, if we take this alley and cross over the next three streets, we should be able to get to the meeting quicker. I don't want to be late."

"Good idea. It wouldn't be wise to keep the Trade Master waiting."

They were well into the alley when Zeal became aware that Kit had the three of them joined together in what he referred to as battle mind.

Someone thinks we are prey.

Walking towards them up the alley, he saw three figures approaching. *Is that all of them?* He was grateful that Shadow Cats were capable of detecting nearby life forms and recognizing if they posed any threat.

Two track us. One more above in shadow.

Zeal concluded there was someone on the roof of the building on the darker side of the alley and that two more people were coming up behind them. *Let's wait here and see what they want.*

Tulip positioned herself with her back towards his, facing the way they had come. *The two behind us are blocking the alley.*

He knelt, set Kit on her feet so she was between him and Tulip, thereby making Kit difficult to be seen.

Three people—two male, the middle one a female—stopped ten paces away. The woman said, "Set your possessions on the ground and walk away. No one needs to get hurt."

The man on her right pointed at Kit. "Leave the animal. We haven't eaten yet. I likes me the taste of cat."

ACKNOWLEDGMENTS

I WISH TO THANK Dr. Janice Lovelace for her unwavering support and for caring about the characters as much as I do. The journey began with you.

Thanks to the readers of manuscript drafts, Sharon Castillo, William Rutherford, Charles McGovern, Jake Rainwater, and Dr. Janice Lovelace.

A special heartfelt thanks to the members of my writing group, Karen MacLeod, Kay Morison, Dr. Lisa Murphy, and Cindy Wyckoff. You continue to inspire and guide me.

To my editor, Kathryn F. Galan, I offer my sincere thanks and I apologize for the headaches I caused.

Thank you, Liza Brown, for your wonderful artistic ability.

You all have helped me to continue to share my stories and I am in your debt.

ABOUT THE AUTHOR

James D. Macon is a physician who lives and works in Washington State with his family. Although he spends most of his time caring for others, he also has a strong desire to share his stories.

His first novel was Book 1 in *The Phosfire Journeys* series, *Purveyors and Acquirers*. The third book in the series is *Opener of Doors*.

Visit the author's web page at:
www.JDMacon.com.

91608010R00222

Made in the USA
Middletown, DE
01 October 2018